VOID

INCLUDES *HEX, SHADOWS, GHOSTS*

RHIANNON LASSITER

SIMON PULSE
New York London Toronto Sydney New Delhi

ᗰᗰ

SIMON PULSE
An imprint of Simon & Schuster Children's Publishing Division
1230 Avenue of the Americas, New York, NY 10020
This Simon Pulse paperback edition November 2011
Hex copyright © 1998 by Rhiannon Lassiter
Shadows copyright © 1999 by Rhiannon Lassiter
Ghosts copyright © 2000 by Rhiannon Lassiter
Published by arrangement with Macmillan Children's Books,
a division of Macmillan Publishers, Ltd.
Originally published in Great Britain in 1998
by Macmillan Children's Books, a division of
Macmillan Publishers, Ltd.
All rights reserved, including the right of reproduction
in whole or in part in any form.
SIMON PULSE and colophon are registered trademarks
of Simon & Schuster, Inc.
For information about special discounts for bulk purchases,
please contact Simon & Schuster Special Sales at 1-866-506-1949
or business@simonandschuster.com.
The Simon & Schuster Speakers Bureau can bring authors
to your live event. For more information or to book an
event contact the Simon & Schuster Speakers Bureau at
1-866-248-3049 or visit our website at www.simonspeakers.com.
Designed by Mike Rosamilia
The text of this book was set in Minion.
Manufactured in the United States of America
4 6 8 10 9 7 5 3
Library of Congress Control Number 2011932811
ISBN 978-1-4424-2929-1
These titles were previously published individually.

Dedicated with love
to the crew of the SS *RHI*

CONTENTS

HEX

1

HOVER THROUGH THE FOG

It was the middle of the night in London but two miles above the ground the city was wide awake. Lights shone in the windows of the city towers and glared in the headlights of vehicles speeding along the network of arched bridges that linked the gleaming heights. Winter was drawing in and the thick fog that wrapped itself around the towers made visibility poor. Wraith piloted his flitter between the skyscrapers with care, still unfamiliar with the complex controls, but other flitters whipped past in an instant, their occupants in search of the city's nightlife. Wraith ignored them; he was on a more serious search and had much further to travel. As he guided the flitter lower down, a holoscreen ad sprang to life ahead of the craft, and Wraith blinked with annoyance as he shot through the center of a phantom image. Slogans glared from other 2D screens, flashing suddenly out of the murky darkness, advertising some of the delights the city had to offer; signs flashed everywhere, blurring into the distance as far as he could see. This was obviously the center of clubland, the signs advertising casinos, cinemas, and clubs, all exclusive and expensive—a playground for the rich. The flitter was still descending slowly and Wraith was forced to concentrate harder on the controls as the network of bridges became denser, with fewer spaces for the aerial craft to pass through.

Wraith was beginning to wonder if he should have hired a skimmer. Traveling across the bridges was beginning to seem safer than flying between them, wreathed as they were in fog. Another flitter banked and wheeled around directly in front of him, and Wraith had to pull back hard on the controls to prevent himself crashing into the support struts of one of the bridges. He halted the flitter centimeters away from the thick metal bar and let it hover while he caught his breath.

As the flitter hovered, the display screen on its control panel sprang into life and the fizzing gray pixels swirled before resolving themselves into an image. Raven grinned out of the screen at him as her voice came out of a speaker instead of through the transceiver surgically inserted in his right ear:

"Taking a rest, brother?"

"Raven." Wraith frowned at the screen. "How are you doing that? This isn't a vidcom." The flitter was an old model and as far as he knew the screen was only capable of showing views from the cameras positioned on the four sides of the vehicle.

"Ways and means," Raven said enigmatically, and her screen

image winked. Leaning forward to look at it, Wraith realized that it didn't have the resolution of a vidcom image or the accuracy. Raven's representation of herself was schematic. Her dark eyes stared out of the screen, framed by a mass of tangled black elf locks. But the image was basic and two-dimensional. He shrugged, used to Raven's secrecy about her Hex abilities, understandable since any of them was enough to get her killed. His expression grew grimmer at the thought but he smiled as Raven raised an eyebrow to ask:

"Want me to drive?"

"Can you do that from where you are?" Wraith asked in surprise.

"Of course," Raven told him and lights glowed on the control panel as the flitter began cruising again. *"Keep your hands on the controls,"* she warned him, *"otherwise people might wonder how come you're not crashing into things."*

"OK." He nodded. "But it would be easier if you detached yourself from the circuitry and piloted this thing for real."

"I'm investigating," she said sharply. *"To do that I need to be in the net."*

"Have you found anything yet?" Wraith asked, his voice softer. The screen image shook her head.

"Nothing," she told him. *"You'll have to try a physical search. The records we're looking for don't seem to be on the main net."*

"What about a secured system?"

"I can get into those, it just takes a little longer," Raven told him. *"But I don't think this is going to be a computer job. It'll take a flesh-and-blood search for us to find Rachel."*

"Don't worry," he assured her. "We'll find her."

"*Yeah.*" The image nodded. "*I have to go, Wraith. There's a lot of documentation we're going to need while we're in this city. It'll take me some time to change the records.*"

"OK," Wraith told the screen as Raven's image fizzed and was replaced with the normal camera view.

"*Stay ice,*" her voice said with a faint laugh. "*You can try to drive now.*"

Wraith took hold of the controls again with reluctance but found that it was becoming easier to pilot the craft. The towers and bridges were still well lit and it took a moment for him to realize that he was seeing fewer street signs and fewer vehicles were speeding along the bridges or passing him in the air. This district seemed to be more residential. The bridges widened out into plazas at intervals and it took Wraith longer and longer to find gaps to pass through to lower levels. He could almost believe that he was gliding over the ground as he glimpsed tree-lined avenues and stretches of grass beneath him. But his destination lay further on and further down. Eventually the buildings began to look less well-kept, the street lighting grew dimmer and the plazas disappeared.

The flitter sank deeper into the darkness, passing deserted levels of buildings and damaged bridges. Wraith resisted the inclination to turn up the headlights, knowing that this darkness would be home to the urban parasites that haunted every city. He had no intention of falling prey to London's criminal element, although it was among them that he hoped to find what he sought. But the darkness did not continue for long. Below the flitter the greasy lights of gangland were appearing.

As London had grown up into the sky, it had left its slums behind on the ground. Now far below the gleaming heights of the skyscrapers lay the urban jungle of gangland. The high-rises were where they had their corporations, hospitals, schools, and homes. But outside the protective inner circle were the wastelands of the abandoned suburbs where the gangers thrived. These levels were rarely policed, the security services only venturing in when a politician ordered a preelection cleanup. The people who lived in these slums didn't have an official identity; they couldn't get jobs or medical treatment, no children would ever see the inside of a school. The only way to survive was to join a gang or try to make a living outside the law. Prostitution, black-market trading, illegal drug-dealing—vices old and new found a home in every city in the twenty-third century. Wraith had no doubt that London was exactly the same.

It was the first time he had visited this city but he worked according to a well-proven method, navigating the flitter slowly past the walkways until he found what he wanted. The first person to approach the craft was a boy, who quickened his approach as its window slid down. Wraith placed his age at about thirteen years old but his hazel eyes held the jaded cynicism of an old man. His clothes were torn and his skin was grimy, but his bronze hair was clean and glimmered under the dim streetlights.

"You looking for something, friend?" the boy asked. "Drink, women, drugs? For twenty creds I can tell you where to go."

"I'm looking for a guide," Wraith replied, considering the small figure. "I need someone who knows the city, who can tell me who owns the turf. Would that be you?"

"I can tell you what you want to know," the boy declared emphatically. "Thirty creds."

"Get in," Wraith told him, releasing the door control so that it hissed open.

"Creds first," the boy said, extending a slender grasping hand.

"Here." Wraith dug out a handful of coins from his jacket pocket, more than the boy had asked for, but he didn't hand them over at once. "Get in," he said again, and after a moment's hesitation, the boy obeyed. He was reaching for the coins almost before the door had hissed shut, but Wraith waited until the flitter was back in motion before giving them to him. They disappeared immediately into an inside pocket of the boy's battered denim jacket. Wraith smiled grimly as his passenger became immediately less wary, apparently satisfied with the transaction.

"So why are you looking for gangers?" the boy asked in an indifferent tone of voice.

"I'm not," Wraith told him, and saw the wary look spring back into the child's experienced eyes.

"Hey, friend, you better not be thinking of nothing skitzo," his passenger cautioned, his muscles tensing and a hand reaching for the door release.

"Don't try that," Wraith told him, speeding up the flitter as an extra emphasis. "I want information. If you can't give it to me, I'll let you out. If you can, I'll make it worth your while. OK?"

"What sort of information?" The boy had stopped looking ready to run but he was still tense and suspicious.

"I want to find someone who knows how to work the ganglands, who can put me in touch with the right people for a deal. Information retrieval, you scan?"

"I scan." The boy nodded. "You're looking for a fixer. But I can't get you an intro, I don't know anyone personal. I can only tell you a place, right?"

"A place is fine," Wraith agreed. "I'll make my own way after that. But make sure it's someone competent."

"The Countess is electric," the boy told him. "But she'll cost you."

"That's not a problem," Wraith replied briefly. "Where's the place?"

"Creds first. You agreed." The hand was extended again.

"Right." This time Wraith handed over a fifty-credit piece. "But she had better be worth it."

"Sure thing, friend," the boy replied. "Turn off here, you need to go down a couple more levels."

Despite a few misgivings, due to the fact that this method had not been universally successful, Wraith found that he had chosen his guide well. Kez had been working the streets long enough to know the names of the major players in gangland and, when a few more coins had changed hands, became loquacious enough to fill Wraith in on the gangs who claimed the territory they were passing through. These areas overlapped, naturally, and like anywhere else gang-feuds were continually in motion. A few times Wraith picked up speed when he saw another craft, not waiting to find out if it displayed gang colors. Kez evidently approved of his caution and the boy was quick to assert that he had no ties to any gang.

"Staying neutral's the only way to do business." He shrugged.

"I pay tolls to the enforcers like everybody. Try anything else and you'll get flatlined. But I don't wear colors and I don't hang with the gangers, except for business."

"I scan." Wraith nodded. It was the same in any city. But the facts that had become clichés for him long ago left a bitter taste in his mouth when personified in a child who would be lucky to make it through adolescence.

It wasn't long before they reached their destination. Wraith let the flitter coast down gradually to rest on a wide walkway which passed the building Kez had indicated. He reached back for the pack that contained his possessions and released the flitter's doors. Kez got out slowly, watching as Wraith coded the doors shut. It wouldn't deter a thief intent on stealing the vehicle, but he didn't imagine that much would.

"Thanks for the directions," he told Kez. "Catch you around."

"I could wait for you while you do business," the boy suggested, and Wraith gave him a sharp look. He didn't delude himself that Kez had become attached to him after a ten-minute conversation. After the rate he had been handing out credits it was no surprise that the boy was unwilling to see the source of supply dry up. Usually he would have made it clear straight off that their association was terminated. But here, in a city he didn't know, he didn't make any objections.

"You can wait here if you want." He shrugged. "But I'll be some time. You can watch the flitter for me."

"Sure thing," Kez agreed, leaning back against the small craft as Wraith began to walk away.

The only obvious approach to the building Kez had identified as belonging to the Countess's operation was along a narrow spur of walkway which still seemed in relatively good repair. But as Wraith headed toward it a figure detached itself from the shadows and stepped in front of him to bar the way. It was a big man, dressed in combat gear and holding a heavy assault rifle menacingly. Muscle, Wraith realized, hired to guard the building.

"You lost, friend?" the man asked, tightening his grip on the rifle.

"I'm looking to do some business," Wraith told him, his own stance carefully nonthreatening. He had weapons if he chose to use them, but this was a formality, not a genuine confrontation.

"The Countess know you're coming?" the guard asked.

"Not yet, I'm from out of town."

"A ganger?"

"Not anymore."

"OK, go on in," the guard said eventually. "But no trouble."

"Thank you," Wraith acknowledged and stepped out onto the walkway. It was only a short distance to the main door of the building, which stood open. The windows were metal-shielded all the way up to the next level, giving the building the appearance of a fortress. Apparently the Countess was good enough to maintain considerable security precautions and Wraith was favorably impressed.

The inside of the building was dark and when he stepped inside the door he stood still for a moment, blinking to adjust to the dim lighting. He was standing in a wide empty hall, obviously designed as the foyer of a corporation building or hotel. There were about eight doors leading off in various directions but all except one were shielded and blocked up with rubble. The only empty door was protected by two guards, a man and a woman, both dressed similarly to the man outside. They stood at ease as Wraith approached, but they held their weapons with a cool confidence.

"State your name and business into the vidcom," the woman told him, stepping aside to reveal a screen set into the wall. "The Countess will decide whether to see you." The screen was dark, not revealing the person on the other end, either the Countess herself or someone working for her. The unit itself was a recent design, probably programmed to scan as well as transmit.

"Wraith," he said levelly. "I need to find some people for a deal." There was a pause before a dry voice spoke out of the vidcom.

"What kind of deal?"

"An investigation," he said into the unit. "I can't say any more here."

"All right," the voice said, after waiting for a few moments. "You can come up, but leave your weapons behind." Wraith hesitated. But from the look on the guards' faces this issue was not open for discussion. Reaching into his jacket he brought out his laser pistol, then he removed the blade from the sheath on his back and handed both weapons to the female guard.

"What's in the bag?" the woman asked.

"Clothes, computer disks," Wraith told her, and the woman nodded in confirmation after glancing at a readout beside the screen. Obviously he had been right about the vidcom scanning him.

"OK, you can go now," the male guard told him, and Wraith nodded. Their system was not infallible; it had failed to scan the extra knife he had not given up, but there were probably more guards further up.

The main hall had been dilapidated and dark but as Wraith walked past the two guards everything changed. He found himself at the foot of a wide staircase, the floor, walls, and ceiling covered in a brilliantly reflective shielding. He couldn't see the light source but the stairway was brightly lit. He could see his own figure reflected disorientingly into infinity and found it difficult to balance with any sureness. That was undoubtedly intentional, he thought as he made his way up the stairs. They curved gradually and he couldn't be sure in what direction he was heading. However, he must have climbed up at least two floors by the time the stairs came to an end and he found himself standing on a narrow landing, staring at his own reflection in a blank, mirrored wall. His face gleamed eerily from the metal surface like a ghost: gray eyes set in a narrow, chalk-white face, framed by wild white hair.

Part of the wall slid away silently to reveal the Countess's center of operations. Terminals and screens covered the walls, connecting her to her information network. Cases of equipment were stacked around the room, all flawlessly new. In the center of the room stood the woman he had come to see. She was thin and above-average height, dressed plainly in black. Her dark hair had been cropped close to her head and the effect was one of unconcern with her appearance. She wore multiple armbands, ten on each arm, set with mini-screens and remote control buttons for the different kinds of terminals around the room. Sharp, brown eyes regarded him from a fierce, birdlike face.

"Come in," she ordered. "Tell me what you want."

"Are you the Countess?" Wraith asked.

"I am."

"I need your help."

"So you said." The Countess frowned impatiently. "What is it you want?"

"I'm trying to find someone in the city," Wraith said quickly. "A girl, about eleven years old. She hasn't shown up on any of the computer nets yet."

"How do you know?" the fixer asked sharply, her eyes sweeping over him appraisingly. "You're no hacker."

"I'm here with my sister," Wraith admitted. "She's the hacker."

"A physical search will take time," the Countess told him. "But I can use some contacts if you can give me some more info on the girl." She crossed to one of her terminals.

"Her name's Rachel," Wraith told her. "She's my younger sister. I haven't seen her for two years. Rachel was living with adoptive parents when they took off with her. They haven't contacted us since but I heard news they were in London."

"Are you planning a retrieval operation?" the Countess asked. "To get the girl back?"

"No." Wraith shook his head. "I just want to know if she's OK."

"All right." The fixer nodded. "I'll need all the information you have on her and on the couple who adopted her. Names, pictures, bio details, the works."

"Right." Wraith pulled out an unmarked computer disk from his bag and passed it to the fixer. She slotted it into the machine and Wraith watched as a blur of details flickered across the screen. When the transfer of information had been completed the fixer tapped a few keys to bring up Rachel's image.

"I'll have this sent out to some contacts," she told him. "That way we should find out something. But it's strange that the girl doesn't appear on the net. There should at least be school records."

"Yeah," Wraith agreed. His gaze was fixed on the picture. Rachel looked like any other kid: brown hair in a neat bob, big shining brown eyes, and a crooked grin. But Wraith knew it was crucial that he find her, and not just because she was his sister.

"When I've had some initial reports in we can decide whether or not to hire some people to search more actively," the Countess told him. "That should be in a few days. But I'll need a basic fee now."

"How much?"

"Five hundred," the fixer told him and Wraith nodded. The price might be a little high, but he needed the Countess's support more than he needed to haggle over money.

"OK," he agreed and reached for a cred card.

It had taken Kez two minutes to get into the flitter. He hadn't been able to catch sight of the owner's code but the flitter was an old model and it was easy to force the hatch open. It was done before the guard further down the walkway had noticed anything untoward—and there was nothing suspicious about Kez getting into the flitter when he had arrived in it. Once inside the boy cast a practiced eye over the controls. The white-haired guy had operated it clumsily but Kez had driven this kind of craft many times before. He powered up the main drive and watched with satisfaction as the control panel lit up. Then he frowned. The console's view screen was fizzing strangely although it had been working normally on the way to the fixer's building. He punched a few buttons to get an image but nothing worked. Shrugging, he decided to take the flitter up without the screen; the front window showed enough without it. He reached for the controls and froze as a voice rang out of the speakers.

"If you're serious about stealing this flitter, prepare for the ride of your life."

"What?" Kez looked around quickly but there was no room for anyone to hide in the tiny craft. "Who is that?"

"Wouldn't you like to know?" the voice came back at him. It was a girl's voice and she was laughing. Kez sneered.

"Whoever you are, you ain't gonna do nothing on the other side of a com channel," he told it and grabbed the controls. The flitter lifted off the bridge smoothly and then Kez was thrown back in his seat as it leaped forward into the air. He was no longer holding the controls but the flitter swept easily past the buildings, faster than he'd ever seen one move before. Laughter was ringing in his ears and the voice spoke through it.

"But I'm not on the other side of a com channel," it said and the flitter went into a wild spin. Kez clung to the sides of his seat, clutching for the safety harness as he was whipped around by the gyrations of the craft. Once he had the clasps snapped in place he grabbed the controls again, but the entire panel was dead. He let go, recognizing

the futility of the attempt, as the flitter came out of its spin and streaked upward through the city's levels. It was the fastest ride Kez had ever taken and to his surprise he found himself enjoying it. He whooped in delight as he sped past the hazards of the metropolis.

Then a siren went off, and, looking back, Kez saw two flitters start in pursuit.

"Seccies," he warned automatically.

"*I see them,*" the voice told him and the flitter dived. The screen sprang into life to display the back view from the craft and Kez watched as within seconds the Security Services vehicles were left behind. As soon as they were out of sight the flitter assumed a more usual speed as it coasted through the city.

"That was wild." The boy grinned. "I ain't never seen driving like that."

"*Thank you,*" his companion replied, and suddenly a girl's face appeared on the screen. She was older than him, about fifteen, with a fierce grin. She bent her head in a mocking bow as Kez stared.

"You really are something," Kez said, impressed.

"*Of course,*" she replied.

"But if you're controlling this hunk of junk, where are you?" he asked suspiciously. "It's impossible. No one can do that. It's like magic." Then he tensed. "You're not some kind of freak, are you?" The screen fizzed and the image disappeared abruptly. The flitter touched down on one of the walkways and the driver's door hissed open, obviously a sign for him to leave.

Kez realized he had made a mistake. He looked out into the night. He wasn't far from his usual patch and it wouldn't take him long to get back there. But something about the mysterious ghost-like stranger and now this other ghost in the machine had caught his imagination. He stayed firmly in his seat.

"Hey, calm down," he told the fizzing screen, hoping no one would pass and see him talking to a flitter. "I didn't mean to offend you, but I never met a Hex before."

"Are you intending to broadcast the information to the entire neighborhood?" the girl's voice asked coldly, her words a confirmation of his suspicions.

"You opened the door, not me," Kez reminded her. The door stayed open and he looked hopefully at the screen. "Why don't we start this whole thing again?" he offered. "I'm Kez," he said leaning toward the screen hopefully. The door slid shut and after a moment the screen came to life again.

"I'm Raven," the girl told him, as the flitter took off. *"The guy you were about to steal this flitter from is my brother, Wraith."*

"I wouldn't have got much for it." Kez shrugged. "It's a real old model."

"Wraith won't be too pleased about you trying to steal it at all," Raven said. *"Especially after he gave you nearly a hundred credits."*

"Could you maybe not tell him?" the boy suggested.

"Maybe." Raven grinned. *"Since you survived the ride."* She winked at him. *"But don't try to cheat him again, OK?"*

"Sure thing," Kez agreed as the flitter touched down in the same spot it had occupied before. "Hey, Raven, when do I get to meet you in person?"

"Tonight, if you can find Wraith a safe place to stay," she told him as the door opened again. Kez got ready to get out, but Raven's voice called him back. *"And, Kez, don't tell him anything about this. That I spoke to you, or that you know what I am, OK?"*

"I scan." Kez saluted the screen and Raven winked again before her image dissolved. Kez sat grinning back at the screen until he realized he had better get out of the flitter before Wraith got back.

When Wraith returned, Kez was leaning against the side of the flitter in the same position as when he had left, watching him with intent hazel eyes.

"Business OK?" he asked as Wraith approached.

"Yeah, I think so," Wraith replied. "Anyone try to steal the flitter?"

"Not with me here," Kez told him but felt an unusual pang of guilt as he caught the cred coin he was tossed. "Hey, friend," he said, as Wraith keyed open the flitter doors, "you got someplace to stay tonight?"

"Not yet." Wraith looked at the boy in some surprise as he got back into the car, but decided he was hoping for more money.

"I'll show you a place," Kez offered, "if I can hang with you a while."

"You will?" Wraith got into the flitter and watched as Kez swung quickly into the passenger seat. He didn't want any additional burdens on this trip and he opened his mouth to refuse when a voice buzzed from his transceiver, too low for Kez to hear.

"Accept the offer, brother. The sooner you find a place, the sooner I can meet you."

"OK," Wraith said, in response to both his sister and Kez. "Where to?"

The place Kez directed him to was a shabby flophouse deep within the slum district but not part of gangland. It was a dismal area, most of the buildings derelict. The room Wraith and Kez were given was probably better than most. It possessed three beds, made up with grubby sheets, a rickety table and chairs, and a computer unit with a vidscreen. Its only window was boarded up and a second door led to a small bathroom. Wraith dumped his bag by one of the beds and Kez seated himself on another.

"How come you asked for three beds?" he asked, and Wraith looked at him sharply.

"I'm meeting my sister," he said shortly.

"You going to call her and tell her where you are?" Kez asked, and Wraith shook his head quickly.

"No need. I have a tracking device so she can find me." He pulled out a cred card from his jacket and held it out to Kez. "Why don't you go get something for us to eat?" he suggested, hoping to be able to avoid the boy's questions for a while. "Get enough for three."

"OK." Kez took the card. "What do you want?"

"Anything." Wraith shrugged. "No, wait a minute." He thought for a second. "My sister likes Chinese food."

"Sure thing." Kez grinned and was gone. Wraith wondered for

a moment if he had been wise to give the boy the card, which had about eight hundred credits on it. But since Kez seemed so eager to hang around with him, he was unlikely to do a flit. He lay back on his bed to wait.

Twenty minutes later there was a knock at the door, and without waiting for an answer, someone swung it open. Wraith sat up and then leaped to his feet as he saw his sister. She was carrying a duffel bag and dressed in black combat gear and a fringed suede jacket. Her black hair was wet and straggled into her dark eyes but she was grinning as she hugged him. Wraith hadn't seen her since they had arrived in England three days ago. They had separated then, nominally in order to attract less attention but in actuality because Raven was used to independence.

Wraith, Raven, and Rachel had been placed in an asylum blockhouse when their parents died. Wraith had been fifteen, Raven nine, and Rachel five. Blockhouses were safe but dreary and unpleasant, and those children unfortunate enough to end up in one dedicated all their energies to escaping. Wraith had achieved this by joining a gang, the Kali, as an enforcer. Shortly afterward Raven had also escaped. Her determination to do so had become a necessity when Raven had discovered that she was a Hex. Mutants who possessed the Hex gene were no more welcome in Denver than anywhere else in the world. Regular sweeps were made of the asylums to detect anyone who showed signs of mutant abilities. If Raven had been discovered she would have been turned over to the government for extermination. At the first opportunity Raven had made herself scarce and entered the ganglands, working as a highly efficient computer hacker.

But neither of them was able to take care of Rachel. According to Raven she had never shown any signs of being a Hex and was therefore safe enough in the asylum for the time being. Later Wraith was relieved when a couple had requested to adopt her. He hadn't imagined that they would abscond with Rachel. Their disappearance had impelled Wraith to take action to find them. If Rachel did turn out to be a Hex she would be in danger and he considered himself responsible for her safety. But it was not until she had been gone for two years that Wraith had had any leads about her whereabouts.

Raven had been uninterested in his search. The fact that her life had been in danger since she was a child had affected her personality. Wraith saw her very rarely as she had become increasingly difficult to communicate with. Her moods ranged from paranoid depression to reckless hyperactivity. It had been so long since they had been close that Wraith could not be sure why Raven had agreed to accompany him to London. But he appreciated her presence. Not only was it useful to have a Hex with him, he also had a deep affection for his sister. The fact that Raven rarely appeared to reciprocate his affection worried and angered him.

Now Raven pulled back from the hug awkwardly and ruffled her hair to cover up her reaction.

"It's raining really heavily out there," she told him.

"Here," Wraith offered, throwing her a blanket from his bed. "Use this."

"Thanks." Raven wrinkled her nose. "It's not very clean, is it?" She glanced round at the room dismissively.

"The Hilton was booked up," Wraith replied wryly as Raven started to rough-towel her hair.

"So I see," she said, her voice muffled by the blanket. "What happened to your friend?"

"I sent him to get something to eat—he was asking too many questions."

"Oh." Raven's head re-emerged and she began to comb her hair absently with her fingers.

"We should get rid of him," Wraith urged. "He's the most mercenary child I've ever met and completely amoral. He'd sell his own soul for a few credits."

"He's a streetrat, Wraith," his sister said flatly. "Money's all that stands between them and the abyss. You're mercenary too, you've just become inured to it." Finishing with her hair she walked over to the wall terminal and started punching buttons. "This is really ancient," she protested.

"It's operative," Wraith said shortly, not allowing her to change the subject. "What about the kid?"

"We'll discuss it later," Raven replied. Then she smiled and pulled out a flat package from her jacket. "Here, this is for you. Your new identity."

"Thank you." Wraith took the package and opened it. Inside was a neat stack of cards. Three bank cred cards and an ID card. The ID card had the name Ryan Donahue printed neatly under an image of Wraith; the same was on the three certified cred cards.

Wraith examined the ID card carefully. "What else is coded into this?"

"You're an American freelance holovid producer," Raven told him. "Media people always look like gangers."

"What about you?" Wraith asked.

"I'm Elizabeth Black, a researcher for a fictional US vidchannel," she told him. "We can use the IDs together or separately."

"Clever," Wraith commented.

"I'm glad you approve," Raven was saying when they heard footsteps outside the door and a knock.

"Come in," Wraith called and Kez entered.

It was obviously still raining outside as Kez was soaking wet, but he was carrying two large paper bags, which he held out triumphantly as he came in. Raven swooped on them before Kez had even shut the door. He watched as she unpacked the plastic cartons of Chinese food quickly. She looked older than her computer image and less approachable. But she had the same mocking smile and her black hair fanned out in a silky cloud around her face. She and Wraith were like the positive and negative versions of the same photograph; their features were almost identical but the colors were reversed.

Raven made no mention of their earlier meeting, introducing herself only as Wraith's sister. Wraith seemed unwilling to discuss anything with Kez but Kez's questioning eventually elicited the information from Raven that they were trying to hunt down their younger sister.

"But I'm going to make some contacts while I'm here," she

added, chasing a grain of rice with her chopsticks. "I might come with you the next time you visit the Countess, Wraith."

"I told her you were a hacker," Wraith said diffidently. "She might offer you work."

"That's not a problem." Raven shrugged. "I could use the credits."

"Are you going to log on again now?" Wraith asked as Raven got up from the table.

"Later," she told him. "I've got to get some rest first." She unlaced her large black army boots and lay down on the bed fully dressed. She was asleep in under a minute and Kez looked at Wraith in surprise.

"She's a heavy sleeper," he explained. "Don't worry, you won't wake her." He got up and headed toward the bathroom. "I'm going to take a shower—don't steal anything."

"Hey!" Kez began, but Wraith had already left. He grimaced at the closed door. Wraith had obviously decided that he wasn't to be trusted without even knowing about his attempt to make off with the flitter and despite the fact that Kez had returned the cred card. Sullenly he pulled a chair in front of the computer unit and idly punched buttons to operate the vidscreen. He could get only a few channels and he flipped through them several times before switching the unit off again. Raven was still out of it and Kez decided to follow her example. He didn't bother to take off his boots, crawling under the covers and wrapping himself tightly in the thin blankets. By the time Wraith returned from the bathroom Kez was already half asleep.

2

PROPHETIC GREETING

Raven had slept dreamlessly for two hours when the sound of an alarm going off somewhere outside jerked her awake. Kez and Wraith were still fast asleep, the boy wrapped in a cocoon of blankets, Wraith tossing uneasily on top of his bed. Raven got out of bed and crossed to the computer unit. The alarm had already ceased its wail but since she was awake she might as well take the opportunity to hack in privately. She wasn't solitary by nature, although she knew that was what her brother believed, but she was wary about being observed in the symbiotic connection she had with computers. No one could mistake Raven for an ordinary hacker when she was working for real. She could, if she chose, act like an ordinary user, her fingers flying soundlessly across the keypad to perform the necessary operations. But she found it a tedious and distasteful method. Now she let her hands rest lightly on the keypad and closed her eyes as her consciousness entered the computer.

This was where Raven was now, speeding down data pathways in a microsecond. No system was closed to her and she extended tendrils of her consciousness in all directions, searching always for a mention of Rachel. Her perception of the net was not something she could describe, the way the circuitry resolved itself in her mind into shapes and colors, tastes, textures, sounds, and smells. Every sense was wrapped up in the experience so that she could not explain how she knew something, only that she knew it. That was how she realized something was different when she ran into something new at the end of a data pathway.

Instantly all her tendrils of consciousness were concentrated in one place, wrapping around the strangeness to identify it. Incredibly there was resistance and Raven knew suddenly with a flash of insight that this was more than a program. It was another personality in the net. An amateur undoubtedly. The other was suffused with fear and in its disorientation betrayed its inexperience.

> **relax** < Raven commanded, whether in words or thoughts she didn't know, holding the stranger firmly in place. > **who/what are you?** < She was aware of another struggle to be free and added impatiently: > **i am not part of the security services or the cps. if i were, could i do/ feel/be this?** <

> **let me go!** < the other pleaded, fluttering tendrils of itself in all directions.

> **your name?** < Raven ordered, clamping down. The other

could resist no more than the locked programs that swung open at Raven's approach.

> **ali** < responded the other and Raven was almost overwhelmed with a flood of images that the name had set free. A sixteen-year-old schoolgirl from somewhere far above in the shielded security complexes of the rich. This was her second foray into the net and she was terrified to have been caught. Raven laughed. The girl was a novice. In a few microseconds she had disgorged enough information for Raven to trace her identity and current location while Raven herself had revealed nothing. The stranger could do virtually nothing in the net, but however inept her bunglings, she would not be caught while within the circuitry. It was more likely that she would betray herself in the real world. In a flash Raven transmitted that information to the girl, still giving away nothing about her own identity. Disengaging, Raven prepared to let herself be swept back into the net.

> **wait!** < Ali pleaded. Her immediate panic was dulled by the information Raven had communicated while its substance deeply frightened her. > **you must wait—please wait—don't leave me!** <

> **why?** < Raven demanded, already bored by the exchange and considering she had done enough for the unknown Hex.

> **you have to stay/help me/stop the cps catching me.** <

> **(?)** < Raven was annoyed now, her responses becoming more basic.

> **because you're like me. we (you/me) are the same.** <

> **each of us is on our own** < Raven replied. > **this conversation is terminated.** < And she was gone, leaving nothing of her

essence behind with which the stranger could trace her. But now she knew indisputably where to find the girl, should she want to do so. Ali's signature would be imprinted on her eidetic computerized memory until she chose to expunge it.

Raven shot through a thousand data pathways in search of records. Names, dates, ages swam in and out of her awareness. School records, vidcom registrations, bank accounts, mailing lists. Nowhere could she find any sign of Rachel. But a thousand data-bases was a fraction of the city's computer network. She wouldn't complete the search tonight. Releasing her hold on the information that whirled round her, obeying her commands, she fell back through the net to her originating node. Releasing herself slowly from the circuitry she re-entered her body.

For a while she blinked, trying to assimilate the impressions of her senses, so different from what she had been experiencing in the net. Slowly she reacquainted herself with reality. The dark room, the breathing sounds of the two sleepers, the flat keypad under her hands and the lingering smell of Chinese take-out food when she breathed in deeply. She stood and stretched, moving awkwardly like an underwater swimmer, her body slow to respond. She walked carefully toward her bed, lying down with a deliberate precision and was asleep before her head hit the pillow.

Ali slammed back into her body and realized she was shaking. The encounter with the stranger in the network had terrified her. At first she had thought it was the end, that the CPS had found her. The discovery that the stranger was also a Hex had been almost as alarming. The feel of that other presence had been cold and alien. The stranger had been chillingly confident of his or her own abilities and openly contemptuous of Ali's. She remembered the feeling of that flood of information sweeping over her, the knowledge that the stranger knew everything about her. But worst of all had been the stranger's refusal to help her before disappearing without a trace. Intellectually she knew that the last person to betray her would be another Hex but up until now no one else had ever known her secret.

Getting up from the computer terminal, Ali walked to the window and looked out into the night. Somewhere out there was the person she had met in the computer network. Standing alone in the apartment, Ali didn't know whether she hoped for or feared a repetition of that meeting.

The lounge was a large room, furnished in zinc-white and ice-blue. Hi-tech appliances were built into three of the four walls. The fourth held a giant window of polarized glass with a serene view of the residential district. The Belgravia apartment complex was located in one of the most expensive, exclusive areas of the city. It was named after an equally exclusive region of Old London, long since lost under the developing city. Now when Ali looked at the apartment she couldn't help thinking that this was what she stood to lose if her secret was ever discovered. She tugged anxiously at a strand of her ash-blonde hair, reminding herself that no one except for the stranger in the network knew the truth.

None of her friends could possibly imagine that she could be a Hex. She was pretty, popular, and rich. And she was a member of the largest clique in school because her father was a well-known media magnate and could afford an apartment in the Belgravia Complex where the rest of the clique lived. Bob Tarrell owned five newsfeeds and seven holovision channels. He had a reputation for working and playing hard, which was why he was hardly ever at home. Tonight Ali had no idea if he was working late at the Tarrell Corporation or out with one of the null-brained starlets he liked to date. But even though her father was often away he was a generous parent. Ali had unlimited money to spend on holovid parties, shopping excursions, and visits to Arkade, the district's recreational complex.

Now that there was less and less open land available, places like Arkade held parks, zoos, swimming pools, and skating rinks: every activity was catered for. The parkland that had survived for centuries within the heart of London was now swallowed up by the industrial buildings that hugged the ground while the city soared into the sky. The ancient river was forced to flow underground to make room for the bases of the skyscrapers. With the land disappeared, the old buildings, even the medieval Tower of London, survivor of historic sieges, had fallen before the inexorable march of progress. Older people complained that the city had swallowed up its own history. But Ali, like all her friends, was only interested in the future and she intended to be part of that future.

Her chief ambition was to become a holovid director, a career for which she considered herself eminently suited. She had her future planned out and liked to fantasize about the fame and fortune she would have some day if everything worked out. Turning back, Ali turned off the computer terminal with a decisive snap. From now on she intended to use it only for homework assignments like any other kid. If she didn't act like a Hex maybe those abilities which were so burdensome to her would just go away. Ali shook her hair out with a smile. Her reflections had restored her confidence. She had no intention of letting the CPS take her away, whatever the anonymous stranger might think.

As Raven and Ali withdrew from the net, information continued to fly between computer systems. The data pathways, invisible to anyone but a Hex, spun a complex web across the city, linking it to other cities, other countries, other continents. From the most basic public terminals to the vast computer systems of world governments, almost everywhere was linked to the net. Its tendrils stretched out to encompass facilities in the most far-flung areas, but here and there were blank spots, places the net circled but did not touch.

In a blank, white room without a computer interface, or any other furniture except a plain hospital bed, a boy stared up at the ceiling. Unaware of Raven's existence, he was praying for her success, for the success of any other Hex. To the men in scientists' coats who were watching him, he seemed oblivious of everything, including their presence. But as they readied their instruments, Luciel was hating them. The straps that held him to the bed couldn't influence his thoughts, and all his thoughts just then were focused on the hope that somewhere, somehow a Hex could survive.

The long needle entered Luciel's arm. There was no anesthetic and the serum it held would keep him delirious for hours. In the time that remained to him before he lost consciousness he concentrated on the pain as the last real thing he would know. Somewhere in the distance, beyond the swirling in his head, he recognized the object of his hatred and filled his stare with all the bitterness inside him, as poisonous as the drug that raced through his veins. But the white-haired scientist was not looking at him. Finishing the notations on his clipboard he glanced at his companions to say:

"Time for the next subject."

Kez woke the next morning to the sound of an argument in full flow. Wraith's voice was harsh and tense and Raven's cold and sarcastic but they were keeping their voices low in order not to wake him. He fought his way out of the bedclothes in time to hear Wraith saying:

"The whole point of staying here is to keep out of sight, safely anonymous. I can't believe that you would want to change that."

"Wraith, I have no intention of living in a slum when we can afford something better. What are you afraid of? Our new identities are established—why should anyone question our moving higher up?"

"I'm not afraid," Wraith replied, his voice rising. "What you are failing to take into account is that our identities are fictional, our cred cards are fictional, everything about us is fictional. We only exist because you've fooled the computer network into believing that we do."

"If the network says we exist, we exist," Raven insisted, throwing herself down on her bed in frustration. As she did so she met Kez's eyes and turned to frown at her brother. "Now you've woken Kez!"

"So what?" Wraith asked and walked out of the room, slamming the door behind him.

Kez looked anxiously across at Raven who shook her head in exasperation.

"Don't worry about him," she said. "He'll come around."

"What were you arguing about?" Kez asked sleepily.

"Wraith doesn't want to move up into the heights of the city," Raven said, from where she was lying flat on her back. "He thinks we'll draw unnecessary attention to ourselves."

"But you don't?" Kez frowned.

"There are advantages to having a respectable official identity," Raven told him. Smiling, she added: "And I've always wanted to live in a really expensive apartment."

"Can you afford that kind of place?"

"If I tell the computer I can." Raven smiled.

"Can every hacker do that, or is it because you're a . . ." Kez's voice trailed off as Wraith reopened the door.

In retrospect it had been unwise of Kez to assume that Wraith would not be back for a while. In a neighborhood he didn't know there wasn't anywhere for him to go. He had returned to the room to attempt a calm, reasoned discussion with Raven. But the words he heard as he entered the room erased that intention.

"You didn't tell him?" he exclaimed in disbelief. "After I told you not to trust him?"

"Since when do you run my life, Wraith?" His sister sat up on the bed and glared at him antagonistically.

"You have to be crazy!" Wraith strode across the room and grabbed Raven's wrists. "This isn't about us! This could cost you your life!" He turned aside to shoot a hostile glance at Kez. "How could you be so careless?"

"Let me go." Raven wrenched out of Wraith's grip, white marks left by the pressure of his fingers. But before she could continue Kez got to his feet with clenched fists.

"Hey, man," he addressed Wraith. "I'm not gonna tell nobody."

"Oh yeah?" Wraith asked coldly. "You sell anything on the streets for enough money and you expect me to believe you wouldn't sell us as well?" He shook his head. "Raven, we've got to get rid of this kid."

"No!" Kez's freckled skin turned several degrees lighter and he took a step backward instinctively. "Oh no."

"Cool it, Wraith, and you, Kez." Raven crossed to the boy's side and put a reassuring arm around his shoulders. She grinned at Kez. "He thinks he's really something, but he's a nice guy. He wouldn't flatline a thirteen-year-old kid, even if he doesn't like you."

"I'm not talking about killing him," Wraith snarled. "Let's just leave him here and find another place to stay and another fixer." He was already grabbing his bag but Raven shook her head.

"Don't be ridiculous," she said. "If you're worried about Kez, we'll just watch him until you stop worrying. But you're right about getting out of here. I can't stay in this skanky room for another hour."

"This is serious." Wraith scowled at his sister. "We've spent years keeping out of the government's notice. How can you totally disregard the danger of being found out now?"

"Because I know what I can do," Raven told him with exaggerated patience. "And there is no longer any possibility of the CPS or anyone else catching me."

"You're overconfident," Wraith said coldly. "And you're endangering both of us, as well as Rachel, if we ever find her."

"No I'm not." Raven turned her back on him and began to make her bed, obviously preparing to leave. "Believe it or not, Wraith, we'll be much safer out of the ganglands. This is the first place the Seccies would look for a Hex. Up in the heights we'll be right under their noses and they won't so much as blink. They'll actually be protecting us themselves in our characters of ordinary citizens and we'll be much safer than if we continue to hide from them down here."

"This discussion isn't over," Wraith warned, but neither he nor Raven made any attempt to continue it and after a silence of a few minutes Kez left them to take a shower. He was beginning to feel that he was in over his head and wondering if it was worth staying with the strangers any longer, Raven's charm notwithstanding. At thirteen he was already tired of living on the edge.

Ali was sitting by the apartment window, drinking orange juice while she waited for her ride to school, when her father emerged from his room. Bob Tarrell was a big man, with rugged good looks and a powerful wrestler's stance. He needed very little sleep, and even after the excesses of last night, he looked relaxed and alert.

"Hi, sweetheart," he said, tousling Ali's hair. "Could you get me a glass of that?"

"Sure," Ali replied, walking over to the Nutromac unit that served the functions of a kitchen, providing meals for people too busy to cook the old-fashioned way. "Did you have a date last night?"

"I went out with Carla," her father said. "But I was working late as well." He took the glass she offered him, gratefully, and drank most of its contents in a single gulp. "Thanks, honey. Carla wasn't too happy about that, but ratings are way down again. I'm probably going to have to change the entire format of at least one of the channels. Maybe try something controversial to grab people's interest."

"Really?" Ali assumed an expression of interest. Most of the time her father's discussion of his work bored her. But as long as he thought she was interested he continued to get her invites to the celebrity glitzfests that added to her social standing in the eyes of her friends and, she hoped, would some day gain her important contacts in the entertainment industry.

Bob was still musing over his difficulties, tapping the side of his glass with his fingers.

"Tell you what, sweetheart," he suggested. "Why don't you talk to your friends for me, see if they have any ideas for the channel?"

"Sure, Dad," Ali agreed. "I'll talk to them today."

"You do that." Her father was still frowning. "I've got to get some kind of hook before the party this weekend. Something to announce to people. It is a working event, Ali. They're not all coming here just for fun, you know."

"I know," Ali replied consolingly, thinking silently that for her the party would be anything but work. She intended to have a totally ultra time, playing the hostess to her father's celebrity guests.

Ali didn't have to listen to her father's work problems for long. A few minutes later a skimmer drew up in front of the apartment. She said good-bye to her father and headed outside, passing through three sets of security shielded doors to reach the outside. It was a bright, cold morning and far above her Ali caught a glimpse of the sun in a pale blue, cloudless sky. To compensate for any shadow from the towers and bridges above, the streetlighting was set to simulate daylight. As she crossed over to the car, a sleek, streamlined vehicle, one of its back doors hissed open and she climbed inside to join Caitlin and Zircarda. The door hissed shut behind her as they exchanged casual greetings.

"So, Ali," Zircarda began, leaning back against the cream seat cushions. "Tell us more about the party. The whole gang's coming, right?"

"Definitely." Ali smiled, completely in her element. "But not Carol, she's way too freaky."

"She couldn't come anyway," Caitlin informed her, shaking out her luxuriant chestnut curls. "Didn't Mira call you last night?"

"Carol's dad got dumped by his company," Zircarda interrupted. "They're moving out of Belgravia. So she won't be in the clique anymore."

"And you can't invite anyone who's not one of us," Caitlin chimed in automatically.

"God, no." Ali shuddered and it was not entirely fake. The conversation served to remind her that she could not afford to fall out of favor. It hardly took any effort for her to laugh. "So Carol's out of it, is she? Thank heaven for that." As the skimmer sped across the bridges, Ali was careful not to look out of the windows, unwilling to catch even a glimpse of the darkness far down below.

Kez sat awkwardly beside Raven, his hair still damp from his shower. She was hacking into the network, her fingers flying over the keypad faster than he would have thought possible as information scrolled up the screen. She was in a good mood, willing to explain some of what she was doing and to let Kez watch her. But his enjoyment was frustrated by the presence of Wraith behind him. He had said nothing for the last hour, and was only a disapproving presence as he checked and rechecked his laser pistol as if preparing for battle. It was a comment on Raven's decision to move higher up in the city and Kez was not entirely sure that Wraith was wrong.

He might have ambitions to live in the heights but the reality of such a move scared him. At best all he could hope for was embarrassing himself, at worst the Seccies would be completely sanguine about arresting him if he didn't fit in. The fact that Raven was a Hex made him estimate his chances of being allowed to go free if he were caught worse than those of a snowflake in hell. He also secretly admitted that in allowing him to discover that she was a Hex, Raven had hardly been playing it safe. Whatever he might think of Wraith's opinion of him, letting a streetkid know something that could get them flatlined was a disastrous move by anyone's standards. But Kez was swiftly realizing that caution wasn't one of Raven's priorities. She had a kind of reckless confidence in her own abilities that led her to openly ignore Wraith's warnings. But Kez had no idea of the true extent of those abilities and he suspected Wraith didn't either, which was why he sat uncomfortably on the edge of his chair, wondering if at any moment he would hear the sirens of Seccies coming to get them.

Raven was creating a new ID for Kez. It was in fact the first real ID he had ever had, never having made it onto any official census records. He was amazed at the ease with which Raven hacked into the government files. Despite the fact that he had never known a hacker before, the street price for fake IDs was high enough for him to gather that this kind of operation could only be attempted by the most electric of experts. But Raven wasn't even concentrating properly, turning her head to talk to him as her fingers lightly touched the keypad.

"How would you like to be my cousin, Kez?" she asked.

"A what?" he wrinkled his nose in puzzlement.

"My ID claims I'm a researcher for a US vidchannel named AdAstra. It would be convenient for you to be related to me." She grinned. "I would tell the computer you're my brother but we don't look enough alike."

"You don't look much like Wraith," Kez pointed out.

"That's because he looks like a freak," she replied, raising her voice a little so her brother would be certain to hear her. "Rachel and I were perfect little asylum orphans but everyone looked askance at Wraith. It's ironic that he's never shown the slightest sign of being a Hex, despite the fact that he looks about as freaky as you can get."

"Wraith looks like a ganger," Kez said, trying to smooth things over. "It's not really freaky, just scary." He bit his lip, thinking of the gangers he had been unfortunate enough to know, but Raven just laughed.

"That's ironic as well. I'm much more frightening than Wraith," she told him, then glanced back at the computer before he could attempt a reply. "OK, I'm done here. Would you like to know your new name?"

"It's not anything weird, is it?" Kez asked, mistrusting Raven's sense of humor.

"Would I do that?" Raven asked facetiously. "No, it's as close to your real name as I could make it. You are now Kester Chirac, a Canadian national. You flew over from San Francisco last week, traveling executive class, seat 14C. Your cousin, Elizabeth Black, had seat 14B. AdAstra's research department paid for both fares—media people are expected to scam their company for their family's benefit."

"Is that really all in the records?" Kez asked in astonishment.

"And a lot more." Raven leaned back in her chair with a self-satisfied expression. "Do you want to know about the flitter that took you from the airport to London, or the hotel you stayed in last week?" She leaned forward again, sweeping her hands across the keypad. "There's your hotel bill at the Regent."

Kez stared at the screen in fascination and was aware that Wraith had come up behind them and was looking as well.

"It's a large bill for just a week," he commented.

"Kez charged a lot to room service," Raven said dryly and Kez realized with relief that they were reconciled again.

"When did I check out?" he asked, studying the lines of type.

"Tomorrow," Raven told him. "When we move into our apartment."

"And where is this apartment?" Wraith asked, his voice impassive.

"The Belgravia Complex." Raven shrugged. "It's full of media people, null-brainers, and phoneys. But I guess we can stand it for a while."

"Electric!" Kez said under his breath. He had decided that, whatever the risk, he wasn't about to get separated from his new-found companions just yet.

3
STRANGE MATTERS

Raven and Kez moved into the Belgravia Complex the next
afternoon in style. Wraith had gone to find the Countess, unwilling
to participate in arranging for an apartment, an action he hadn't
condoned, so they went ahead without him. The apartment Raven
had rented at an astronomical price was luxurious in the extreme,
and the furnishings that arrived in a huge transit a few minutes
after their flitter pulled up outside the complex were equally so.
According to Raven, the apartment had originally been fitted out
in pale pastels but, unbeknownst to Wraith, she had ordered deco-
rators to refit it according to her specifications.

As the people from the furnishing company moved their new
possessions into the apartment, Kez began to get quite a comprehensive idea of what Raven's preferences were. Apparently she
favored dark colors, particularly deep crimson and russet-brown.

She also liked loud music. Technicians were rewiring the apartment's music system to accommodate the industrial-strength megawatt speakers Raven had requested, and the first thing she did when the furnishings were moved in was to call up a music company and order what sounded like half their listings. Kez hadn't heard of any of it, but when the lasdisks began to stack up in the lounge, he privately decided it was ganger-style music. Some was relatively recent, jetrock and acidtechno, but there were reissues from way back in the late twentieth century with the most dismal and depressing lyrics he had ever heard.

"It's *fin de siècle* music," Raven told him, when he protested. "It's got realism. Those musicians saw the deluge coming and they weren't afraid to say so, when the politicians were too scared to admit it."

"What are you talking about?" Kez asked, straining to be heard over the crashing backbeats of the sound system.

"The technological age," Raven replied, turning the music down a fraction in consideration for his ringing ears. "The loss of history in the march of progress. How do you think the genetics experiments came about? Throughout the whole of the twenty-first century, scientists tried to improve people to bring them into line with the new technology. Science took over the world—that's how come London shot three kilometers into the sky." She laughed, as she flipped through the assortment of disks. "The only reason it isn't even higher was that the cities slowed down a bit after the crash of New York; and they'd reached five kilometers before the supports gave way."

"Could that happen here?" Kez asked, alarmed for the first time in his life about the city's stability.

"No chance." Raven grinned at his expression. "New alloys, new building techniques. Terrorists tried to blow up LA in 2314 and couldn't do any more than smash a few bridges. The skyrises are here to stay."

Raven wasn't really in a mood for conversation and Kez could only stand so much of the thumping music. Leaving her to play with the system, he went out to explore the complex, armed with the fake IDs that had arrived by registered courier as they moved in. With an account balance of 800 credits Kez was ready to sample some of Belgravia's much vaunted facilities.

The experience left him bewildered. He had flagged down a skimmer to take him to the rec complex and it blew his mind. He had never seen so much space devoted to recreation. Arkade had areas he hadn't even heard of. He had no idea how to ice skate and he stared at the glittering expanse of frozen water in incomprehension. And he was even puzzled by the museum. Kez couldn't imagine why anyone would want to look at carved rocks and pictures of dead people they didn't even know. But it was full of old people, looking at the stuff with evident fascination. In the end he followed a group of kids, a couple of years older than him, who had just got out of school. He tailed them around for about half an hour as they checked out music and clothes stores; eventually buying some vid-disks he thought Raven might like because he couldn't think what else to get and was worried about being stopped by a store cop. He was looking at a synthleather jacket, wondering if he should get rid of his old denim one, when he noticed one of the girls in the group he had been following standing next to him.

She flashed him a brilliant smile as he turned to look at her and held out a smooth hand. He took it, more out of surprise than anything else, as she introduced herself.

"I'm Zircarda Anthony—my parents run the Anthony Corporation," she told him. "You must be new to Belgravia, right?"

"I'm Kez, Kester Chirac," he added. "I just moved in today."

"Are you going to go to Gateshall?" Zircarda asked. "We all do." She waved airily at the rest of her group of friends.

"That's a school, isn't it?" Kez said, alarmed at the possibility and wondering why this girl was asking him so many questions. "No, I don't think so." The girl looked surprised and he lied quickly, his instincts taking over. "I go to school back in the States. I've come over with my cousin—she's a researcher for a vidchannel."

"What channel?" a girl with ash-blonde hair asked authoritatively.

"AdAstra," Kez replied, desperately trying to remember the cover story Raven had primed him with.

"I haven't heard of it," the second girl said superciliously and a third, this one with curly brown hair, informed him:

"Ali's father owns seven vidchannels."

"Really?" Kez's heart sank and he wondered how he was going to get out of this one. The answer came to him just as he was getting desperate. "AdAstra's kind of alternative. It's into twentieth-century music, kind of *fin de siècle*." He was pretty sure that he had

46

pronounced the last phrase wrong, but it looked as if the girls had accepted it.

"I knew you would be into alternative music as soon as I saw you," Zircarda pronounced triumphantly. "You know your jacket makes you look just like a ganger."

"Yeah," Kez replied, too astonished to think what else to say. But the group of kids talked enough for it not to matter. Zircarda introduced them all, with brief explanations attached.

"This is Ali, Bob Terrell's daughter, and Caitlin, her father's an MP, and Mira, her mother is Martia West the actress . . ." The list went on and on as Kez was presented to each and every member of a group of kids who apparently thought of themselves as a kind of exclusive gang for the children of the very rich.

Within minutes Zircarda had extracted from him the location of the apartment Raven had rented and his "cousin's" name, and had quizzed him in detail about *fin de siècle* rock. He was completely terrified at what Wraith might say when he found out about this and worried that any minute he would get tangled up in his own lies. Eventually he got away, claiming his cousin was expecting him back, and flagged down a fast flitter outside Arkade to take him back to the apartment.

As it happened, Kez had no chance to explain what had gone on at the rec complex. He arrived back at the apartment only seconds after Wraith, who was as excited as the boy had ever seen him. Raven had actually turned off the screeching music in order to listen to what he was saying.

"The Countess has found Rachel's adoptive parents," he announced as Kez walked in the door. "One of her contacts recognized their pictures, some ganger who works the area. They've changed their names, which was why we couldn't find them."

"What about Rachel?" Raven asked.

"Nothing." Wraith's face clouded over a little. "The person who recognized them didn't remember having seen her. But he said they had two kids."

"That's great!" Kez said enthusiastically, inwardly wondering if Raven and Wraith would dump him as soon as they found their sister. "Are you going to find them now?"

"Let me check them out in the nets instead," Raven suggested. Kez was surprised at this uncharacteristic display of caution but Wraith's reaction was one he couldn't have anticipated.

"Instead?" He stared piercingly at Raven. "Don't you want to see Rachel?"

"I came to London with you, didn't I?" Raven bristled, taking umbrage at her brother's tone. "I'm just not as obsessed with this thing as you are, OK?"

"This isn't obsession." Wraith shook his head. "You just have no idea, do you, Raven? You can't relate to other people at all, just machinery." His gray eyes were as hard as ice and Raven stared back at him, white with rage. She was too angry even to speak. Swinging around, she headed for one of the bedrooms, slamming the door behind her with a crash.

Kez stared after her in alarm, then turned to look at Wraith, utterly astonished.

"It sounded like you hate her," he said in amazement.

"I don't know Raven very well anymore," Wraith said stiffly. "When she stops sulking, tell her I've gone to find Rachel." Kez only hesitated for a moment.

"I'm coming with you," he told Wraith.

"I don't recall inviting you," Wraith said coldly.

"Oh no." Kez shook his head. "You're not leaving me behind now. You got her into this mood—I don't want to be here until she gets out of it."

"Come on then," Wraith said shortly and headed for the door. Kez followed him as quickly as he could. But they had barely reached the flitter when they heard the music starting up behind them, even louder than before.

As he strapped himself into the passenger seat of the flitter Kez wondered if he should have told Raven about his encounter with the Gateshall clique in the mall. But the thudding noise he could hear even with the flitter's doors shut warned him against returning to the apartment. As Wraith took off, Kez settled himself more comfortably in his seat, hoping that in subjecting herself to that atonal din Raven would work herself back into a reasonable mood.

When the group left Arkade, Zircarda and Caitlin went back with Ali to her apartment. By the time they had stretched out in the lounge in front of the vidscreen, Ali and Caitlin were bored by the thought of Elizabeth Black and Kester Chirac. However, Zircarda had decided Kez was an original: dressing like a ganger but too young to be a genuine threat. A new addition to Belgravia was always an event since the complex attracted some of the richest and most influential people in the city. Knowing the new arrivals before anyone else would add to Zircarda's social standing and, through Kez, she would be bound to be one of the first to meet Elizabeth. If anyone else had gone on in this way Ali and Caitlin would have absented themselves. After all, Zircarda had only met a weird kid at least three years younger than them. But Zircarda was the undisputed leader of their clique and they listened patiently, agreeing whenever Zircarda paused for breath.

She had finally wound to a standstill in the middle of UltraX's chart show, which Ali and Caitlin had been watching with half an eye as they listened to her, when Bob Tarrell came in the front door of the apartment.

"Dad, what are you doing home?" Ali asked in surprise.

"I need to work on the arrangements for the party, honey," he replied, already heading for his study. "Try and keep it down in here, kids, OK?"

"Sure, Dad," Ali said and turned back to see Zircarda regarding her with an expression she had come to recognize. The brilliant smile, coupled with the calculating look in her eyes, could only mean that her friend wanted something.

"Hey, Ali," Zircarda began, with a casual air. "What do you think of inviting Kez and his cousin to your party?"

"I don't know if my Dad would be keen on me inviting any more of my friends," Ali replied uneasily. "He keeps saying that it's supposed to be for work." Zircarda's expression began to change and Caitlin leaped in quickly before things could get uncomfortable:

"Ali, didn't you tell us yesterday that your Dad wants to change the format of one of his channels, and that he needs ideas?"

"Yes, I did," Ali replied slowly.

"Well, Kez's cousin works for an alternative rock channel—maybe she would have some ideas," Caitlin suggested, glancing at Zircarda for approval. She got it.

"And if your father invites Kez's cousin, we can introduce her to everybody!" she proclaimed triumphantly. Ali knew when she was beaten.

"I'll ask him when he next stops for a break," she said. "He'll just be mad if I disturb him now."

"OK," Zircarda agreed, allowing the minor point now that she had got her own way again. "This party's going to be the most!"

The flitter pulled up on a tree-lined bridge in a quiet residential district. It was not as luxurious as the Belgravia Complex, but Kez thought it looked nice, attractive and peaceful. As they got out of the flitter he felt out of place in a way he hadn't in Belgravia. Wraith looked forbidding enough in his black leathers, and Kez felt as if anyone could tell at a glance that he was just a streetrat. When Wraith locked up the flitter he didn't move from its side.

"What's the matter?" Wraith asked.

"I shouldn't be here," Kez said gruffly. "I don't fit in."

"Snap out of it," Wraith told him. Then, when Kez didn't move, he rested a hand lightly on his shoulder. "Come on, kid," he said quietly. "No one here knows anything about you."

"I'm not one of them," Kez hissed. "I want to stay in the flitter."

"I'm not going to leave you here," Wraith informed him and Kez clenched his fists.

"I'm not going to steal it, Wraith." He glared furiously. Then he deflated. "But I almost did, when you first picked me up. Raven wouldn't let me. You were right about me, weren't you? You can't trust anyone who lives on the streets!" He turned away, not wanting Wraith to look at him.

"Kez." Wraith slung an arm on his shoulders. "Calm down."

"Why don't you just get rid of me now?" Kez replied bitterly. "You'll do it anyway, just as soon as you find your sister."

"No I won't," Wraith replied seriously. He turned Kez to face him. "You really don't know anything about me, Kez," he said. "And you definitely don't know anything about Raven." He shook his head. "She attached you on a whim, Kez, and she could just as easily dump you again, probably without thinking twice about it." He frowned. "But you needn't worry about what'll happen when we leave. I'll make sure you won't have to go back to the streets." He sighed. "I might not trust you, Kez, and I know you don't like me very much. But I was a ganger for a long time, and the Kali always took care of their own." He took Kez's arm firmly, forcing him to walk off down the bridge with him. "Now, come on. I don't want to waste any time."

Kez fell into step with him obediently, wondering if he had misjudged Wraith. It was a few minutes before he could trust himself to speak.

"Do you still run with them, your gang?"

"No." Wraith shook his head. "We parted company about a

year ago. I was tired of being on the wrong side of the law at the time."

"But Raven wasn't?"

"Raven's existence puts her on the wrong side of the law to start off with," Wraith said. "She's never cared very much for conventional morality." He didn't look at Kez as he added: "We haven't been close for a long time, but I've heard a lot about her from friends of mine. She's not really normal, Kez. In more ways than one."

"Oh." Kez was silent again. Not really knowing what to say, he decided to ask a question that had been bugging him since he first met them. "Are those your real names?" he asked. "Wraith and Raven."

"No." Wraith smiled, for the first time since Kez had met him. "Raven probably wouldn't be too pleased if I told you her real name. I think I'm the only one who remembers it. She's expunged all records of her original identity from the net. But mine is, was, Rhys. The Kali called me Wraith because of my hair."

"And your skin, and your eyes," Kez added, beginning to regain his confidence.

"As you say." Wraith nodded. "Raven chose her own name. She has quite a reputation back in Denver."

"Not a good one, huh?" Kez asked.

"No," Wraith said grimly. Then he came to a halt outside one of the towers. "This is it. Three floors up."

"I hope you find your sister," Kez said, as they entered the building. "You must really miss her."

"I'm responsible for her," Wraith replied, a little sternly. Then he added: "But yes, I miss her as well."

The apartment they wanted was numbered thirty-seven, and when Wraith touched the call signal beside the door it opened almost immediately. The woman who opened it was middle-aged and dressed conservatively. She regarded Wraith and Kez a little dubiously but seemed reassured by Wraith's polite tone of voice.

"Mrs. Hollis?" he asked.

"Yes?" she replied.

"I wonder if I could speak to you for a moment?" Wraith said. "It's quite important."

"Well, all right." The woman opened the door just wide enough for them to enter and Kez followed Wraith into a plainly decorated room. Two little girls with blonde hair tied up in ribbons, aged about six, were seated in front of the vidscreen, watching an animation.

"Camilla, Tamara, go and play in your room," the woman told them. "Don't argue," she added sharply, "you can watch the screen any time." Kez watched as the little girls got up and left. He remembered Wraith saying that Rachel's adoptive parents were known to have only two children, and he wondered if the Countess had made a mistake. If these were the kids, where was Rachel?

Wraith was looking grim again, his eyes troubled. But he thanked the woman politely as she invited him to sit down.

"Mrs. Hollis," he said, once she had seated herself facing them. "Am I correct in believing that you and your husband adopted a child six years ago in Denver, under the names Vanessa and Carl Michaelson?"

"Oh my god," Mrs. Hollis whispered, the color draining from her face. "What do you want?"

"I'm not here to cause any trouble," Wraith said quietly. "But the child you adopted was my sister, Rachel. I just want to know that she's all right." Kez knew the answer before Mrs. Hollis spoke—nothing good could come out of fear like that.

"I'm sorry," she said, standing up. "Please leave. I can't tell you anything."

"Mrs. Hollis." Wraith stood up as well and faced her. He was several inches taller and she seemed to shrink before him. "I'm afraid I can't leave until you give me some answers. Rachel obviously isn't here. What happened to her? Is she even still alive?"

"I don't know," the woman said hoarsely. "I swear to you, I don't know. They came and took her. She's not here anymore."

"Who, who took her?" Wraith demanded.

"The CPS," Mrs. Hollis told him, leaning back against her chair. "Over a year ago. They said a mutation had shown up in her medical examination." Her eyes were clouded with unshed tears. "I'm sorry," she said. "I can't have children of my own. Rachel was just like my own daughter. Please don't tell anyone I told you all this. The CPS operatives said we shouldn't mention it to anyone. If the Security Services find out I've spoken to you they could take the twins away. I don't know what I'd do if I lost them."

"I said I wasn't here to cause you any trouble," Wraith replied. "Thank you for telling me the truth." He turned to leave. "Come on, Kez, let's go. There's nothing more for us to do here." Wraith keyed the door open and Kez followed him out. As they left, Mrs. Hollis watched them go, a pathetic crumpled figure sitting on the arm of the chair.

Wraith didn't stop walking until they had left the building far behind. Then he came to a halt at the beginning of the bridge where they had left the flitter. He looked over, gazing down through the hundreds of levels of the city, saying nothing. Kez didn't know what to say. Everyone knew that the CPS coming for someone was a death sentence. Wraith had just heard evidence that his sister was dead, after searching for her for four years.

"I'm sorry," he said quietly.

"I know." Wraith stared down into the darkness of the depths far below. "Raven said Rachel wasn't a Hex," he said after a while. Kez was silent. A few minutes passed slowly before he wondered if Wraith wanted to be alone. He was about to back away when Wraith spoke:

"Just give me a minute," he said, glancing up. "I have to think."

"OK," Kez replied and leaned against the balustrade next to Wraith. He assumed that the ganger was coming to terms with his failure. Flitters passed overhead and skimmers moved behind them on the bridge, but neither of them spoke again for some time.

Bob Tarrell could hear the music pounding as he walked up to the apartment. He recognized the wail of an electric guitar somewhere in the cacophony but the rest of the music was as dissonant as anything he'd ever heard. However, he didn't allow that to faze him as he put his hand to the black metal plate by the door. When there was no answer he pressed it again. Eventually a voice came out of the wall speaker:

"Who is it?"

"I'm Bob Tarrell, of the Tarrell media corporation," he told it, looking up at the security camera. Its light was turned on even though no image had appeared on the screen facing him. "I live in the Complex." He waited a while and was about to speak again when the main door of the apartment slid smoothly open.

A girl was standing there. She was dressed in black, the color complementing her stark black hair and her black eyes, dark against her pale face. She was frowning as she looked at him.

"Have you come to complain about the music?" she asked, before he could speak.

"Definitely not," he assured her. Then he extended his hand. "You must be Elizabeth Black. My daughter knows your cousin."

"She does?" The girl raised her eyebrows, then abruptly smiled, taking his hand in a firm grasp. "I'm sorry, Mr. Tarrell. Please, come in."

Inside she took a moment to key the music down to a barely audible hum and offered him a drink. He accepted the offer of sake and the girl collected two cups from the Nutromac, handing one to him.

"I'm very pleased to meet you, Mr. Tarrell," she told him. "Your corporation pretty much dominates the British media, and maintains a presence in the European Federation in general, I believe."

"You flatter me, Miss Black." Bob smiled. "It will be a while yet before the Tarrell corporation makes a real name for itself in Europe."

"Elizabeth, please," she told him, and he nodded.

"Elizabeth, I hear that you're a researcher for a US vidchannel. My daughter's friends met your cousin this afternoon at Arkade."

"News travels quickly," the girl replied, flashing him a quick grin.

"It does in the Belgravia Complex." Bob smiled back. "And, seeing as we're in the same business, I was naturally interested. I'm afraid I haven't heard of AdAstra before though."

"It's still only a small channel," she replied smoothly. "But we hope to move on to bigger things. One of the reasons Kez and I are here is to investigate the possibility of a British connection. Do you think your corporation would be interested?"

"Perhaps," Bob replied cautiously. "I'd certainly be interested in discussing it with you. But I'm not quite sure how well your style would succeed in Britain."

"Ah, yes." The girl stretched like a cat and studied him with dark, unreadable eyes. "How much do you know about my channel, Mr. Tarrell?"

"Only that it's centered on alternative rock of the late twentieth century. My daughter couldn't tell me much more. But even that seems a pretty radical approach."

"In the present climate, the more radical a channel is, the better," she stated seriously. "And AdAstra's following, although small, is very devoted." She gestured at the stacks of lasdisks in the lounge. "This kind of music has a cult status. The mood of the late twentieth century was very dark and its music reflects that. A lot of people find it very addictive."

"You are obviously one of them," he said and Elizabeth inclined her head slightly in assent. "I think I'd like to know more about your channel," he told her. "And particularly about this music."

Bob Tarrell had intended to stay for only about fifteen minutes. He ended up staying for over an hour. During that time, Elizabeth had played him several tracks from her vast selection and given him a comprehensive induction into twentieth-century music. Of everything she told him it was the expression "cult" that had interested him the most. Alternative music with a cult status would be a new departure for him, but it was the kind of thing that might generate the interest he needed in his failing channel. By the time he finally left Elizabeth's apartment he had already decided how he would alter its format, with the help of AdAstra's young researcher. And he had invited both Elizabeth and her cousin to his get-together that weekend. He was almost certain that, by then, she would be his star guest.

Kez realized that something must have occurred to calm Raven down by the time he and Wraith got back to the apartment. The music was no longer painfully audible, and was playing at an acceptable level as they entered the door. Raven had been watching the vidscreen but she looked up as they came in. She looked as if she was gearing herself up to be angry again, but her expression changed as she saw Wraith's face.

"What happened?" she asked in surprise.

"The CPS took Rachel over a year ago," Wraith told her levelly. "It seems my search is over."

There was a silence in the room, broken only by the pulsating beat of the music, still playing in the background. With a quick flick of her wrist Raven turned it off.

"I want to know everything you've got on this adoptive family," she told Wraith.

"Why?" Kez asked. "It won't do any good now." Raven flickered a glance at him.

"Rachel never showed any signs of being a Hex when I knew her," she said. "I want to know what made the CPS find her out." She took the flat black disk Wraith was handing her and turned to the computer terminal. "And if she's dead, as you obviously think, I want to know exactly when and how she died."

"How could you find out?" Wraith asked coldly, sitting down on the dark red couch. "And why do you need to? Everyone knows Hexes are exterminated when they're discovered."

"I'm suspicious of things that everyone knows," Raven said shortly. "And, as to how I intend to find out, I'm going to hack into the CPS's own records." She smiled ferociously. "Believe me, Wraith. I'll find out the truth of what happened. Nothing can stop me now."

4

FATAL ENTRANCE

Raven sank into the computer like a swimmer into the sea, immersing herself in the electronic labyrinth. It was a maze to which only she had the key and she moved through it like a goddess, contemptuous of the pathetic attempts of human users to fathom its fascinating complexities. It was easy for her to be seduced by the glowing trails of information pathways, leading away from her in all directions, but she concentrated on the focus of her search—the name Rachel Hollis.

Raven did not move straight to the CPS's databases. Despite her confidence, she as yet had no idea how she would find those records. So her first action was to stream down the net toward the computer system of the British government. This was one of the most impressively shielded systems in the country, but no computer could hope to be secure from Raven. However, it put up an amusing resistance. As she entered the system an automatic watch-dog program intercepted her.

> **request authorization please?** < it demanded.

> **correct authorization submitted—doubleplus priority user** < Raven informed it, snowing it with information. She had penetrated this system many times before and the challenge was decreasing exponentially with each attempt.

> **authorization validated. pass user** < the watchdog replied and with that the system opened itself to her. Disgustingly easy, Raven reflected as she streaked through the access node; she could have designed a better security system in her sleep.

Deep inside the government system now, she paused a little and allowed fragments of her consciousness to snake out in all directions, searching according to the parameters she had already set. She relaxed, sinking into a semi-aware state, feeling her sphere of influence extending all around her. Suddenly there was a tweak at the end of one of her tendrils of thought. All the others raced to meet it. It was another access node, leading into a secondary system. Raven could not have explained how, but she knew that what she sought lay beyond that gate. Another watchdog approached. Raven didn't wait for it to question her. Instead she overwhelmed it with a stream of authorizations.

> **open sesame** < The gate swung open at her command.

The new system felt darker, there were more shielded data-bases, security hung over everything like a fog. But none of this impeded Raven. It took her microseconds to identify the system as that belonging to the Security Services. One more microsecond and it was completely under her command. She hadn't entered this system before and therefore took slightly longer to explore it. She was reassured to find no record of her existence in the database; Wraith was equally invisible to the Seccies. A flicker to the edge of her search parameters informed her that Kez had two convictions for theft. A thought erased the data; Kez became invisible to the system. Then she found it. The contents of a datafile filled her mind. A Security Services team, accompanied by three CPS operatives, took into custody a ten-year-old Hex named Rachel Hollis on the fifteenth of March 2366.

Raven imprinted the contents of the file on her eidetic memory, but did not erase the original from the system. Among the threads of data that accompanied the file was a string of numbers and characters designed to execute a lead away from the government system to an alternative address. Raven dived through the net, information whirling above and beneath her. The location of the system she was heading for was more impressively shielded than anything she'd seen before and her search took her on a roller-coaster ride through the net. Any other hacker would have been shaken off long ago but Raven found it as exhilarating as the flitter ride she had forced Kez to take. She felt the same way about speed as she did about loud music—the more of it the better. Finally she crashed through four secured nodes in a row before coming to rest at the main entrance to the central system of the CPS.

The gates into the system were firmly shut; no watchdog program waited for her outside. With a mental shrug Raven exerted a little pressure and the security sprang to life with the most advanced question and answer routine she had ever encountered.

> **?who** <

> **accepted user** < she told it.

> **?authorization** <

> **authorization provided** <

> **password** <

> **correct password.** < Raven was disappointed. It was easier to fool this system than she had anticipated. It was designed to catch out an illegal access attempt by requesting certain responses. But Raven, deep in the heart of the net, need only tell the circuitry that she had provided the correct answers for it to believe her. In another few microseconds she had gone through an elaborate sequence of security protocols none of which put up the slightest resistance at all. Finally the system delivered itself up to her just as absolutely as the government system had.

> **you may enter. database records/programs/operating specifications of this system are at your disposal.** < If Raven had been present in the flesh she would have laughed. The system of the main agency for exterminating Hexes had just thrown itself open to one of them without providing any resistance at all.

But entering the system did not automatically provide Raven with the answers she needed. It took her a while to find the entries for the date 15.03.2366. And more microseconds passed before she located the entry she wanted. It was three lines long.

> **at 1400 hours three cps operatives (names appended) collected suspected hex—rachel hollis—from her place of residence.**

at 1530 hours the hex was delivered to dr. kalden. background trace results in database. < Raven called up the database and discovered that the CPS had traced Rachel as far back as her adoption in 2361 by Carl and Vanessa Michaelson in Denver, Colorado, USA. They had even discovered the specific orphan asylum and it was at that point that Raven discovered the single most alarming line of data that had ever drawn her attention.

> **?siblings ?hexes. initial search = no results. ?indepth search** <

For a moment Raven considered erasing the whole entry, the whole database if necessary. She would have been prepared to crash the entire system to protect herself. But a moment's thought assured her that this was unnecessary. Instead she appended an addendum to the file.

> **indepth search completed. results negative. no siblings exist. results confirmed. no further investigation possible.** < Having achieved what she considered the most important point, concealing her own existence, Raven continued her investigation, centering in on Dr. Kalden.

She discovered something surprising. Raven had never bothered to think much about the CPS. Her priority had been to stay out of the sight of any official databases and out of the way of any security services. Gangers in Denver had considered that hiring Raven was worth the trouble of putting up with her difficult personality because she was so meticulous in keeping them out of the sight of the law. But now that Raven was actually inside the system of an agency devoted to exterminating Hexes, she found it was not exactly what she might have expected.

The European arm of the Center for Paranormal Studies was run by Governor Charles Alverstead, who was politically responsible only to the central parliament of the European Federation. But underneath him was a whole host of operatives who were responsible for the day-to-day running of the agency. From what Raven could discover they were apparently divided into three main categories. Two of these were what she might have expected. There were the administrators and investigators whose work was to track down suspected Hexes. Then there were the operatives who processed known Hexes to the death chambers where they were given lethal injections to exterminate them. All of this was what Raven had anticipated and she was unaffected by the cold-bloodedness of the operation. What had surprised her was the existence of a third area of the CPS where no other area should have existed. What else was there for an extermination agency to do?

References to this third area were obscure, mentioning only Dr. Kalden and results obtained by his department. Raven had to search through the files for over an hour of real time before she could piece together the fragments of information to get some kind of idea of the overall picture. Her conclusions were staggering.

When the CPS had been converted from a research department to an extermination agency, in the year 2098, it had retained a portion of its original facilities for surgical experimentation—principally a laboratory and hospital where the initial investigations of the Hex gene had taken place. That facility had remained largely disused until over two hundred years later, in 2320, when suddenly all references to it were classified as confidential. Raven deduced that the laboratory had started up again to continue the experiments. Nothing else could explain the information in the databases. The majority of Hexes were listed as collected by operatives and exterminated according to the due process of law. But one in eight had the same entry as Rachel's file, concerning the Hex's delivery to Dr. Kalden. Raven could draw only one conclusion.

Detaching herself from the system Raven raced back through the net, making each connection with the speed of thought. Reaching her own terminal she rejoined her body in an instant and turned round.

"Wraith," she said, "I think Rachel's still alive."

As the leader of a vast corporation Bob Tarrell was used to working fast. It had been Wednesday afternoon when he had his conversation with the Belgravia Complex's new resident. By Thursday morning he had informed the staff of the Mirage vidchannel that he would be changing its entire format. By midday the same day, six different program proposals lay on his desk and the wheels were in motion for announcing the launch of a radical new rock channel that weekend at his party.

Although prior commitments had prevented him from meeting Elizabeth Black at his offices, he had contacted her via her vidcom. The image on his screen had looked tired and overworked but when he told her of his plans for an alternative rock channel she had agreed to download all the information she had on rock music through the net. It had arrived within the hour. The speed had impressed the media magnate and he was seriously considering offering the young researcher a job. He had attempted to call the management of AdAstra as well but their line had been engaged consistently. However, one of his assistants had linked up with their computer database which, although small, had provided the information about channel ratings which he had wanted.

The board of directors had voted unanimously in favor of Bob's proposal to alter Mirage's format, and the shareholders, concerned about its consistently dropping ratings, had welcomed the chance to revive its fortunes. Already several well-known presenters had been wooed away from other music channels with the promise of larger salaries and the hope of achieving cult status. Mirage's logo had vanished from holoscreen billboards and the channel's main studios. Already artists had submitted graphic designs for the logo of CultRock.

Personally Bob Tarrell considered twentieth-century rock music to be the most horrific din, but the initial reactions from his company had confirmed his belief that there was money in it. Therefore he had let it be known that he had a great admiration for the genre. As interest in the new channel grew steadily, Bob Tarrell had visions of revitalizing the entire music scene.

While her father was pretending an interest in alternative rock music his daughter had made the decision to despise it. This considered judgment had been the result of sitting through three hours of it with Caitlin and Zircarda. All three would have been perfectly willing to hail it as the most exciting thing they had ever heard. But when the final track had eventually screeched to an end, Zircarda, lifting a cautious hand to her ringing ears, had said deliberately:

"I don't think it's really us, do you?"

Sighing with relief, Ali and Caitlin had concurred willingly. Although all three had congratulated Bob Tarrell on his wild idea and assured him that it would be the latest craze, within an hour the word had discreetly been spread to the rest of the clique that CultRock was not for them. Naturally this made no difference to the group's plans to come to Tarrell's glitzfest that weekend. Rubbing shoulders with celebrities was worth pretending an interest in alternative rock for an evening.

In any other situation Raven would have been ready and willing to help Bob Tarrell with the launch of his new channel. But ever since she had discovered the puzzle within the CPS's database she had been hacking through the net in the attempt to gain more information. She had only halted her search twice. Once to speak to Bob Tarrell over the vidcom and send him information on alternative rock music and once to set up a system for the nonexistent company AdAstra, complete with a faulty vidcom line. Interest in Raven's preferred musical genre had been snowballing and the only reason Wraith had not been warning her about unnecessary exposure was that he was so wrapped up in the possibility that Rachel was still alive.

The information she had found about the Hex laboratory was scarce. The only addition to the scraps of data she had already discovered was the issue of the lab's connection to Dr. Kalden. The date when all references to the disused lab became confidential was the same as the date given for Kalden, then twenty-three, leaving a highly lucrative research post. After that all references to him seemed to cease. He stopped publishing in the scientific and medical journals where he had once been an authority on experimental neural psychology. He broke all contact with the remaining members of his family and hadn't registered to vote in forty-seven years.

Raven found this suspicious enough to center her research on Kalden. But her probing of the net yielded nothing more concrete. The last picture of Kalden showed him as a young man whereas now he must be seventy years old. It showed an anonymous scientist, dressed plainly in white, the only distinguishing mark a pair of piercing blue eyes. In or out of the net Kalden was a shadow. Anyone but Raven might have believed him dead. But the datapaths only she could trace, the information hidden to any other eyes, and her own instinct convinced her he was still alive. As she stared at the scientist's unreadable eyes she was certain there would be some way to find out where he was.

Many miles away Luciel stared into the same pair of cold blue eyes. He was still weak from the ravages of the last drugs to pass through his body but he tried to keep upright as the scientists examined him. There was no way to conceal his weakness from them but he was scared to collapse in front of Kalden. The doctor rarely participated in the experimentation, although he devised most of it. The only reasons for him to attend a session were if a subject was yielding especially rewarding results or was providing particularly useless data. In the latter case his presence would mean Luciel was scheduled for extermination since no more use could be made of him.

Luciel couldn't believe Kalden could be there because the experiments had shown anything positive. Day after day he was pumped full of drugs and wired up to machinery he couldn't begin to understand. Scanners measured electrical impulses in his brain and the machinery but he couldn't imagine what the scientists could be learning from him. They went through the motions of the experiments with mechanical precision but they seemed uninterested in the findings. Luciel suspected he rarely provided them with any usable results. Half the experiments they performed seemed futile and some seemed to have no reason other than to break his spirit.

As well as the bruises from the injections, his skin was covered in faded scars and burns. His dreams when delirious were nightmares, but even through the clouds of hallucination he knew that some of what he remembered was true. The metal chair they strapped him in, the electric current that raced through his body a hundred times as fast as the flutters of his beating heart, and the smell of his own skin burning when the power was turned up too high. These were things he believed in and when Kalden fixed him with that considering stare Luciel felt as frightened as a laboratory rat with as little hope of saving himself.

Raven had been unable to prove her suppositions. Theoretically if a laboratory was performing secret experiments on Hexes, a computer database of their results should exist. But Raven could find no system that corresponded to that of the laboratory. She searched consistently for two whole days before finally detaching herself from the terminal and smashing her fist against the keypad with frustration.

"Nothing!" she seethed. "I swear, if there was anything there I'd have found it by now."

"Maybe your hypothesis was incorrect," Wraith said and Kez flashed him a warning look. But Raven seemed too angry with the terminal to care.

"I'm not wrong," she told him. "The laboratory exists. I could even make a guess as to where it is. But I can't find the computer system." She massaged the back of her neck, her movements heavy with exhaustion.

"Maybe you should get some sleep," Kez suggested cautiously.

"Not until I've worked this out," Raven replied firmly. Crossing over to the Nutromac she ordered tea and carried the cup over to the couch, sitting beside Wraith and stretching her legs out in front of her. Kez sat opposite, watching as she sank into the cushions.

"Perhaps the CPS hid the system so that it couldn't be found by a Hex," Kez said.

"That's what I would have thought," Raven replied. "But you haven't seen their main system. It was pitifully easy to hack into. Even a regular hacker could have cracked it in time."

There was a pause. Raven had closed her eyes and was beginning to drift off into sleep before Wraith suddenly spoke.

"Raven," he said, frowning.

"What?" She opened one eye, apparently wondering if it was worth her while to listen to him.

"Do the CPS know that you're more than just a regular hacker?" he asked.

"The CPS don't even know I exist," Raven replied. "And I intend to keep it that way."

"You're missing the point." Wraith shook his head. "What I meant was, do they know what any Hex can do?"

"Explain," Raven said, both eyes open now.

"I've never known another Hex apart from you," Wraith told her, "so I don't know if this is right. But all of your mutant abilities are connected to computers, are they not?"

"More or less." Raven sat up. "There are other aspects, but the basic bent is clearly technological."

"Does the CPS know that?"

"I don't know." Raven frowned. "At least, I'm not certain, because I haven't found the results of any recent experiments." Then she shook her head. "No, Wraith, you're wrong. They must know, that's how the Hex gene was created in the first place."

"How?" Kez asked. He hadn't really expected Raven to answer but she turned to look at him with a sudden interest.

"Kez, what do you know about Hexes?" she asked. "I mean, what did you know before you met me?"

"I figured it was like magic," he said slowly, a little embarrassed. "Or aliens, something like that. I had no idea it involved computers."

Raven nodded slowly, glancing at Wraith, who was watching her intently. Then she began to speak, thinking out loud.

"Most people don't know anything about Hexes, except that they're illegal," she said. "The genetics experiments and the extermination laws are ancient history now."

"That was when the Hex gene was created?" Wraith asked.

"Don't you know any history either?" Raven raised her eyebrows.

"Gangers generally have their minds on other things," Wraith pointed out dryly.

"OK." Raven shrugged. "There's not much to tell." She looked at Kez. "But it's connected to what I was telling you the other day about the rush to create more advanced technology during the twenty-first century. One of the areas that was affected was genetic research. A lot of mutated genes were grafted on to human DNA. They were designed to make the human race more efficient and adaptable. Most of the mutations didn't have much effect so in the end the experimentation was abandoned. But the Hex gene which was created was widely adopted until 2098 when Hexes were made illegal."

"Why was it widely adopted?" Wraith asked.

"It was designed to increase computer literacy," Raven told him. "They were trying to improve programming skills, things like that."

"So, why are Hexes exterminated?" Kez asked. "I would have thought that computer literacy was a good thing."

"Something must have gone wrong," Wraith mused.

"The extermination laws were passed in 2098," Raven said.

"And you don't know why?" Kez asked.

"The whole thing was shrouded in secrecy," Raven told him. "Sanctioning the murder of a whole sub-strain of mutated humans is a controversial thing to do."

"Do you think they found out about what you can do?" Kez asked.

"They must have guessed that a Hex could become the ultimate hacker," Raven said. "But I'm more than just a hacker—nothing I've found in the CPS's system indicates that they know about the way I enter the net."

"Raven, an intelligent hacker would be bad enough," Wraith said. "Computers are used all over the world. International government and finance depend on those systems being secure."

"So they started exterminating," Raven agreed. "Maybe before they had the chance to work out exactly how far the Hex abilities extend. That would explain why they reopened that lab—to investigate what we can actually do." Then she slammed a hand onto the arm of the couch. "But none of this is helping me find that system."

"If it exists, it's meant to be secret," Wraith pointed out. "Experimenting on humans is illegal, even Hexes."

"Raven, how would *you* set up a secret system?" Kez asked shyly. Raven grinned at his admiring tone of voice, then narrowed her eyes as she thought.

"I'd keep it independent of the net," she said slowly. "Accessible through only one terminal."

"Can that be done?" Wraith asked.

"Perhaps." Raven nodded. "But if that's what the laboratory is using we won't find out if Rachel is still alive without breaking into it."

Ali studied herself in the full-length mirror. The holodress shimmered when she moved, projecting images of a flurry of rainbow crystals circling her figure. She smiled at her reflection, while the mirror doubled the swirl of phantom crystals, then swayed out of the way to avoid being squashed by Caitlin. They were in Zircarda's parents' apartment. All Saturday afternoon people had been arriving at the Tarrell apartment to set up for the party, and all afternoon the three girls had been dressing up. Caitlin's glossy curls now betrayed a new hint of auburn, which contrasted vividly with her forest-green dress, made from individual leaves spun together and preserved by an artificial gelling agent. Zircarda was wearing red. Her fascination with ganger-style fashion had made her spend a huge amount of money on a genuine leather dress in a signal-flare crimson. Now she stepped in front of Caitlin to check her makeup. Ali sat back on the bed as Zircarda looked flirtatiously at her reflection through long eyelashes. Caitlin joined her and smiled conspiratorially.

"I can't wait to meet your Dad's guests," she whispered. "There was an item on the news today about the launch of CultRock."

"I know, I saw it," Ali grimaced. "I just hope they won't be playing that kind of music all evening."

"Maybe we should get a move on," Caitlin suggested. "It's nearly eight."

"What time were people supposed to arrive, Ali?" Zircarda asked casually.

"Start time's seven thirty," Ali told her.

"It's still a little early." Zircarda frowned.

"It doesn't really matter, though," Ali reminded her. "I'm almost the hostess, aren't I? So I can be as early as I want."

"OK, then." Zircarda reached for her coat. "I'll call a flitter."

"We could walk, and be there before the flitter arrives," Caitlin pointed out.

"I think we should take a flitter," Zircarda said firmly and the other two shrugged and agreed.

When they eventually got there, Ali hardly recognized her own apartment. Rock music pounded out of huge speakers and the four main rooms were packed solid with celebrities. Even Zircarda was a little intimidated. Instead of trying to approach someone like Yannis Kastell or Elohim, two of the most popular artists of the day, she clustered with the rest of the clique in the corner of the room sipping champagne and pointing out celebrities to each other.

Just as Ali wondered if she would be spending the entire evening as a wallflower, her father caught sight of her and waved. Smiling, Ali went to greet him, followed closely by Zircarda. Bob slung an arm around his daughter's shoulders and ruffled her hair.

"This is my daughter Ali," he said to the man he had been talking to. "Ali, this is Gideon Ash. He'll be hosting a program on the new channel."

"Pleased to meet you, Mr. Ash," Ali said politely, shaking hands with the presenter, before a movement beside her reminded her to introduce him to Zircarda. Listening to a somewhat desultory conversation about the new channel, the two girls were ideally positioned to catch the first glimpse of Bob Tarrell's star guest, as she entered the apartment.

"Elizabeth!" he called and, forging a path through the other guests, went to greet her, followed by Gideon Ash, Zircarda, and Ali. "I thought you were never coming!"

A glance sideways told Ali that Zircarda's face had the same frozen look she could feel on her own. She had an instinctive feeling that she wasn't going to like Elizabeth Black. The girl looked younger than she did but she had an utter possession that made Zircarda's self-confidence seem weak in comparison. She wore a skin-tight black catsuit that displayed to advantage a perfect figure, covered by a loose mesh tunic of platinum chain-links. A cloud of black hair framed her face and her black eyes were outlined in gold. It was several moments before Ali even noticed her two companions. Kez, dressed simply in dark red, and a tall man with perfect features, dead white skin, and starkly white hair, dressed entirely in black cycle leathers. Elizabeth stepped forward and took Bob Tarrell's outstretched hand, supremely unconscious that people were turning to look at her.

"How are you, Bob?" she smiled. "This is my cousin, Kez, and my friend, Ryan. Ryan's a holovid producer."

"I'm pleased to meet you," Bob told them both, shaking hands earnestly. "And, Elizabeth, you look incredible tonight.

Truly electric, as my daughter would say." He motioned Gideon forward. "This is Gideon Ash, one of my presenters." He paused to allow Ash to offer an admiring greeting. "Zircarda Anthony, one of my daughter's friends, and my daughter herself, Ali. Ali, this is Elizabeth."

"I'm fascinated to meet you, Ali," the black-haired girl told her, looking directly at her with the darkest eyes the girl had ever seen.

Ali froze. She couldn't have explained the fear that had consumed her. But as the young researcher's eyes had met hers the thought had leaped into the forefront of her mind. *She knows!* It was inescapable. Those obsidian eyes had looked straight through her, had seen her soul. Now Elizabeth was laughing in response to something Bob had said. In another few moments she had moved on to the dance floor, joined in seconds by Elohim who was wasting no time in introducing himself. It wasn't until Zircarda had been speaking for some time that Ali connected with reality again.

"Can you believe that outfit?" her friend was asking with a barely concealed jealousy.

"What about the way Elohim's all over her?" a voice chimed in from behind and Ali didn't need to look to know that it belonged to Caitlin. "She's younger than us, for God's sake!"

Ali wasn't listening. She was frantically studying Elizabeth's two companions. Kez was looking around him with a bemused fascination, but the white-haired man was leaning against the wall. His eyes, covered with dark shades, could be watching anyone. Ali shuddered. She was wondering wildly if they could possibly be from the CPS despite the fact that the logical part of her brain was telling her that the CPS would hardly bother to engage in such a pointless masquerade.

Raven was high on celebrity. For the first time since arriving in London she was actually enjoying herself. Wraith had been conducting his search for Rachel with a single-minded monotony that came close to driving her insane with boredom. But recent events, moving into the Belgravia Complex, the mystery of the secret laboratory, and the launch of CultRock were bringing Raven back to life. She felt the pounding music flood through her, echoing the beat of her heart, in the darkened room and grinned fiercely.

It had been a surprise to see Ali. She might have made the connection between Bob Tarrell and the stranger in the network earlier if she hadn't been sluggish with boredom. The moment of recognition hadn't actually come until Bob had introduced his daughter. The fear that had leaped into the girl's eyes as Raven had studied her had confirmed it. Raven was amused at the incongruity. If she hadn't known for a fact that the spoiled, shallow socialite was a Hex she would never have believed it.

If Wraith had known Ali's secret he would probably have demanded that Raven show her how to avert her danger. Raven dismissed the idea with contempt. The only sure way for a Hex to escape the eagle eyes of the CPS was to become invisible, to fade out of the world as she had done. The girl suppressed a laugh, thinking how successful her own fade had been, enough so that she could be standing in the middle of a room of celebrities, and yet, she might as well have not been there. Being here at all was a risk, but Raven enjoyed the danger. Ali didn't look as if she was enjoying it. A glance to the side of the room gave Raven a split-second glimpse of Ali's tense expression. This time she did laugh aloud. What use would it do for her to warn Ali to run? There was no way a spoiled little rich girl would survive out in the real world.

Bob Tarrell announced the launch of CultRock at midnight. His guests, high on vintage champagne, cheered enthusiastically. A generous man by nature, Bob gave full credit for the inspiration to Elizabeth Black, a researcher from AdAstra, and the girl returned his compliments politely. Everything was exactly as might have been expected. But Ali, separated from her celebrity-spotting friends, felt as if she had been turned to stone. She couldn't even lift her glass in the obligatory toast. When she finally lifted the champagne to her lips with a leaden hand, she might have been drinking stale water for all the enjoyment she got from it.

It was like the worst kind of nightmare. All her senses were screaming danger, and there was nothing she could do about it. Dark eyes regarded her from across the room, then flickered away as if the glance had only been accidental. Ali knew better. That casual smile was as treacherous as the grin of a crocodile.

It wasn't until the early hours of the morning, when the guests finally departed and Ali curled up in a ball under the white counterpane of her bed, that the fear finally began to recede. But her dreams that night were menacing and confused, running from something she couldn't see with legs that refused to bear her weight. The appearance of the girl had been a catalyst. She had brought to life all the anxiety that Ali had tried to suppress since the discovery of her own deadly secret. For the first time in her life, Ali Tarrell was possessed by terror.

5

LIGHT THICKENS

Three sets of architectural blueprints from different elevations were spread out on the floor of the lounge. Raven, back in her rumpled army castoffs, her hair once more a wild mass of tangles, sat cross-legged in front of them, holding a stylus. Wraith sat across from her, studying them equally intently, and Kez, kneeling on the couch, leaned over the back, looking down on them.

Raven's brows were drawn into a frown and Kez was not surprised when, throwing down the stylus, she shook her head.

"It's not going to work this way, Wraith."

"It's all we have to go on," Wraith replied, not looking up from the plans.

"Wraith," Raven said, waiting until she had got his full attention. When his eyes finally met hers she went on. "These are the design blueprints for the original laboratory—they were all I could pull out of the CPS database. By now that entire facility will have been remodeled." She stood up, and crossed to the couch. "These plans are about three hundred years old."

"Do you have any other suggestions?" Wraith asked.

"I will have."

"That's not good enough," he told her. "We've got to get into that lab as soon as possible."

"Well, why don't you ask Kez for an idea?" Raven suggested nastily. "I don't recall that he's been that much use so far."

"We didn't bring Kez to help us find Rachel," Wraith said with exasperation. "He's here because you brought him with us on a whim."

"And I can easily hit the road if you've changed your mind," Kez told her, angry and disenchanted with Raven.

Raven was smiling; she was bored and frustrated, and baiting Wraith and Kez was the only thing she could do to remove her apathy, other than turning on the sound system to its highest volume, or taking off in the flitter and hot-wiring the acceleration. But it didn't take Raven long to switch from boredom to anger and Kez's next comment provided the necessary spark.

"Maybe I do have an idea," he told her. "If you're so keen to get into that lab why don't you turn yourself over to the CPS?"

"What a sensational idea," she hissed at him. "Why don't you make the call and see what I do to you."

"Hey, Raven, stay chill," Kez said uneasily, and Wraith came to his rescue. Finally standing up and abandoning the plans, he walked round to stand behind Kez, resting a light hand on his shoulder.

"It's not actually a bad idea," he said calmly. "Why shouldn't we try it, Raven?"

"It would be me trying it, not you," she told him. "And there's no chance."

"If you can get in and out of the CPS's database as easily as you claim, surely you can get in and out of the laboratory?"

"They wouldn't take me to the laboratory," Raven said unequivocally. "I've been working out how they decide who to take to the lab." She locked eyes with Wraith, trying to convince him. "It wouldn't be me."

"Why not?" Kez asked, and Wraith added:

"I'm not sure I believe you, Raven."

"Sit down," Raven commanded, waiting until Wraith had complied, seating himself on the arm of the couch. He hadn't dropped his eyes and she smiled slightly at the intensity of his scrutiny.

"Go on, then," he said. "Convince me."

"Did I tell you the CPS take one in eight of the suspected Hexes they capture to the laboratory?" Raven asked. Wraith gave a brief nod and she continued: "There's a pattern to that. They always take the youngest and most inexperienced. The ones that are found through medical results or unusual behavior, not the convicted computer hackers, and never anyone older than about twenty. It's almost always children, as well."

"You're only fifteen, Raven," Wraith pointed out. "And for all your illegal ventures into the net, it's not as if you've ever been discovered. You fit into those categories."

"No I don't," she shook her head. "I may be barely an adult as

85

far as the CPS and you are concerned, but I've been active as a Hex for a long time. I don't think I've reached the height of my abilities, but they certainly extend far further than those of the novices the CPS like to experiment on. I'm much too dangerous to them. They'd work that out in five minutes; even they can't be that stupid. And then they'd exterminate me, without even waiting for an official authorization."

"I thought you always said there was no way the CPS could do that to you," Kez pointed out.

"That's because they would *never* get me as far as one of their facilities," she informed him coldly. "If the CPS did ever arrive to collect me, which I doubt would happen because I've taken precautions against it, they wouldn't get me more than ten meters. Their vehicles would shut down, their communicators wouldn't work, and either I'd escape or they'd kill me." She shrugged. "It's as simple as that. And it's not a risk I'd be willing to take for *anyone.*"

"I suppose I can't blame you," Wraith said slowly. "And, in this case, I do believe you."

"Thank you," Raven replied with exaggerated sarcasm.

"But we've still got to find a way into that facility," Wraith added. "Even if we can't use you as bait."

Ali was in her room when it happened. She was lying on her bed, feeling particularly bedraggled. Zircarda and Caitlin were still recovering from the excesses of the night before and Ali, even though she'd barely drunk anything, felt as if she had all the aftereffects. She lay on her stomach, staring across the room at the blank screen of her computer terminal. She hadn't used it in nearly a week.

The last time she had attempted to do so she had found herself slipping into the trance that had overtaken her once before while working at the terminal. Ali sighed. That first time had been almost wonderful, certainly the most exciting thing that had ever happened to her, and when she had realized what it had signified she had almost been pleased. Being a Hex seemed somehow special. It was not until the second time she had tried it that she had been scared. She shivered, remembering how it had felt to be caught and held against her will. Then the sudden outward flood of information that had overwhelmed her, the stranger's contempt coupled with the conviction that Ali would be caught and exterminated. That other essence had read her mind in a split second, but given nothing away itself.

The simple fact that someone existed who knew her secret had terrified Ali. Then, yesterday, she had met someone else who knew it, who had looked through her and with a glance turned her inside out. Ali buried her head in her arms, wishing with all her might that Elizabeth Black would go back to America, and even more fervently that the Hex gene had never even existed.

A faint noise, just on the edge of hearing, made her look up again, frowning. She listened intently, hearing nothing. But it had been a sound that she knew. Instinctively she glanced over at the terminal and suddenly knew what had caught her attention. It had been the sound of the computer powering up. She watched it with fixation, as if the sleek gray wall unit was a deadly snake. The screen was glowing, showing that it was on. But it was impossible for the terminal to switch itself on.

Then slowly, inexorably, letters began to march across the screen. Too far away for Ali to read them, but unmistakably letters. And yet no one had touched the keypad, none of this was possible. The letters came to a halt; a single sentence now glowed on the screen. The room suddenly seemed much colder and very dark. Ali crossed to the terminal, moving as if she was made of glass and a sudden movement might break her. The sentence faced her, starkly uncompromising.

> **come to apartment 103 immediately** <

It was almost innocent. A simple request. But it had appeared almost supernaturally on the screen. And it was not a request. It was a demand. One that Ali did not dare refuse.

She picked up her synthetic woolen jacket and put it on, then she walked toward the door, like someone approaching their execution. She didn't even notice the terminal switching itself off behind her. She left the apartment with leaden footsteps, the door swishing shut behind her. Slowly she walked along the covered security-shielded walkways that would take her to her destination. She reached it in less than fifteen minutes. The outer door was identical to her own. Reaching out a heavy hand she touched the wall-plate. Three seconds later the door slid open. Someone had been waiting for her. Ali took a deep breath and stepped inside. Behind her the door slid shut again.

Raven smiled icily as the teenager entered the apartment. She was not happy about the course of action she had chosen. She didn't like revealing herself in this way, but betraying some of her Hex abilities had been necessary to intimidate Ali. She might have managed to maintain her disguise for a short while at Tarrell's glitzfest, but she had no expectation of sustaining that image without an added lever. Looking at the slim blonde girl, facing her across the room, Raven was conscious of feeling annoyed. Ali was slightly taller than her.

Raven had never felt inferior to anyone. At nine years old she had forced people to respect her in order to survive. Her ability to do things far beyond the capabilities of other people meant that most of the time she considered herself superior to anyone else. As a person and as a Hex, Ali was beneath her contempt. But Ali was the spoiled daughter of a wealthy and influential man; Kez had told her all about the Gateshall clique before their visit to the Tarrell's apartment. For an instant, as Ali entered the room, Raven felt like a streetrat from the slums of Denver, and she had to force her hands not to curl into fists.

Ali's eyes were wide with apprehension as she looked at the younger girl. The sophisticated Elizabeth Black, whom Zircarda had been so jealous of, had melted away. In her place, dressed in black army gear, staring straight at her, was the stranger in the matrix. The veneer of deceptive artifice had cracked, revealing something rawer and much more dangerous. For the first time in her life Ali faced someone who had the power to destroy her and the will to do it. But strangely, she didn't shudder. She had passed beyond terror and her voice was level as she spoke.

"Who are you?"

Dark eyes flashed, something unpleasant glinting in their depths. But for once, their owner did not even consider dissembling.

"Call me Raven."

"What do you want?" Ali held herself perfectly still, awaiting the answer. Before Raven could reply, the door opened.

Wraith and Kez stopped dead as they saw Ali. Raven hadn't expected them to be back so quickly. Now she resigned herself to the inevitable, as Wraith placed the two heavy duffel bags he was carrying on the floor, and turned to confront her.

"Raven?" he asked.

"Come in, Wraith," she told him. "Both of you, you might as well hear this as well."

"Hear what?" Kez asked, studying Ali curiously.

"Sit down," Raven insisted, including Ali in the invitation, and seating herself where she could keep her eyes on the girl. "I think I might have found us a way into that lab."

Kez's eyes widened incredulously, but Wraith was quicker to comprehend. He looked seriously at Ali who was sitting uneasily on the edge of a chair, before looking back at Raven.

"Does she know?" he asked.

"Do I know what?" Ali demanded. Now that she didn't have to face Raven alone she was becoming bolder and Raven realized it. In a moment she had seized the initiative again.

"I was just about to explain it to her," she told Wraith. Then she fixed Ali with a level stare. "How long have you known you were a Hex?" she asked.

"Me?" Ali froze to her seat, but it was no more than she had expected, and she answered honestly, fixed in the headlight glare from Raven's eyes. "Only about a month." She hesitated. "Are you going to turn me in?"

"No," Wraith replied, unequivocally, earning himself a disapproving sideways glance from Raven.

"You're a Hex too, aren't you?" Ali said. "It was you I met in the network that time."

"Yes, it was me." Raven leaned back in her chair. "And I'm not going to turn you in, although everything I warned you about still holds true. I'm going to offer you a proposition. And you would be wise to accept it."

"What kind of proposition?" Ali asked suspiciously. Strangely enough, the dark-eyed girl was beginning to remind her of Zircarda; she had the same look in her eyes that the leader of the Gateshall clique got when she was determined to do something.

"Let me explain," Wraith intervened. "It's a long story."

"Go on." Ali waited.

"None of us are exactly what we seem to be," Wraith began and Ali raised her eyebrows expectantly, hardly surprised. He smiled wryly and continued: "Raven and I are brother and sister. We, and Kez," he glanced briefly at the boy, "have been searching for my other sister, Rachel. . . ."

As Wraith elaborated, Ali slowly began to relax. The story was one of the strangest she had ever heard, involving gangers, government organizations, secret laboratories, and covert plans. It was almost as implausible as a vidfilm, but somehow Ali believed it. The strangest part of all was Wraith's account of how they gained their information. Ali was fascinated by the idea of how Raven was able to control the network, but the younger girl volunteered no information and Ali was too intimidated by her stark stare to ask any questions. But Wraith's measured explanation, coupled with the fact that it didn't look as if she was going to be turned over to the CPS, was gradually calming her down. But when Wraith reached his conclusion her alarm returned.

"You want to use me as bait for the CPS?" she said in shock.

"It's our best chance of finding Rachel." Wraith began but Ali didn't let him finish.

"No chance," she told him, standing up to leave. "I'm not doing this." She shook her head. "I'm sorry, Wraith. But I doubt your sister's even alive. The CPS kill people, and I don't want to be one of them."

"Don't be so hasty," Raven snapped. "You might regret it."

"Are you threatening me?" Ali asked, and Raven smiled.

"No," Wraith said quietly. "If you're unwilling to help us, we won't force you. But please give it more consideration."

"I can't," Ali told him. "I'm sorry." With that she turned and left the apartment without looking back.

Wraith watched her go with troubled gray eyes, but he didn't try to stop her. As the door swished shut behind Ali, Raven hissed with annoyance.

"I could have made her do it," she told him.

"She's only a child, Raven," he said sternly. "I refuse to allow you to manipulate her. This is our problem, not hers." For a moment he looked as if he might say something more, but he changed his mind and left the room without adding anything.

Raven and Kez looked at each other: Outmaneuvered, Raven didn't seem to know what to say, and Kez didn't feel in a mood to say anything. Wraith had been scrupulously honest in telling his story to Ali—too honest, Kez felt. The ganger hadn't neglected to mention how Kez had joined their group and he hadn't missed the expression of contempt that crossed Ali's face.

"So much for your idea," he said eventually.

"It was your idea to start off with," Raven reminded him. "I simply provided an alternative Hex."

"Do you know anyone else we could use?" Kez asked.

"What do you think I am?" Raven frowned. "A detective agency? I only found her out by accident when she was fooling around in the net." She drummed her fingers on the side of her chair with irritation.

"You don't like her very much, huh?" Kez asked.

"She's almost as brainless as she looks," Raven said. Then she gave him a considering look. "Somehow I doubt you'll be seeing much more of that clique she belongs to."

"I don't want to," Kez said angrily. But he was angry with Wraith, rather than Raven. "Let's get out of here," he said impulsively. "Your cover's been blown now, anyway."

"You're right," Raven agreed. "I'm sick and tired of this whole business. If Wraith doesn't like my ideas that's his problem."

"Are you going to give up?" Kez asked.

"Why not?" Raven shrugged. "Anything's got to be more interesting than this."

Kez hesitated. He was angry with Wraith, and Raven's disenchantment with his way of operating was infectious. But he couldn't help remembering how Wraith had looked when he had thought Rachel was dead, and now that he had got involved with the ganger's search, Kez felt reluctant to abandon it so easily. Raven was waiting for him to reply and Kez wanted to be able to agree and just take off with her, despite the fact that he didn't trust her anymore. But he couldn't do it.

"I think we should stick with Wraith," he said reluctantly.

"Wraith can't be helped," Raven told him scornfully. "He's obsessed with ethics—it's like a disease."

"Do you think we could persuade Ali to agree to help us?"

"I could," she shrugged. "But it's no use if Wraith negates everything I say."

"Then we'll have to go around him," Kez told her.

"Oh?" Raven waited curiously, and taking a deep breath, Kez made his suggestion:

"Tell Ali the CPS are already after her," he said. "Then she'd have no reason not to join us. With her inside that lab, we could find Rachel and break them both out. Without us, she'd be stuck there forever."

"As long as she lived," Raven interjected. "We'd have to make sure she got sent to the lab. Otherwise she's no use to us."

"You seemed pretty sure she would be," Kez reminded her.

"I still am," Raven said. "But there's an element of chance in everything." She thought for a moment, then nodded decisively. "We'll do it. But not yet. I have to make the discovery accidentally."

"Why?" Kez looked suspicious and Raven sighed with annoyance.

"Because Wraith has to be the one to tell her," she informed him. "You saw the way she behaved. She trusts him, and she'll believe whatever he tells her."

"That means we've got to convince Wraith too," Kez said doubtfully. Raven shrugged.

"We'd have to do that anyway," she replied. "We couldn't tell Ali something like that without him finding out. But if we can make Wraith believe Ali's in danger and tell her so, she'll do as we say."

"If Wraith finds out we've tricked him . . . ," Kez began, but Raven interrupted him:

"If he does find out, it'll be too late to object," she declared. "Wraith wants into that lab more than either of us. This is the way to do it."

When Raven suggested that they move out of the Belgravia Complex, just in case Ali reported them to the Security Services, Wraith didn't make any objection. He had been against moving into the complex to start off with, and although he didn't think Ali would risk calling out the Seccies, he preferred to err on the side of caution. The next morning, after having been at the complex for less than a week, Elizabeth Black and Kester disappeared. As far as the housing corporation were concerned, they had notified them of their intention not to renew the lease on the apartment for another month, a removal company had been hired to sell the furniture and forward the proceeds to an American bank account, their flitter had been returned to the rental company, and Nimbus Airlines' database registered them as having traveled to San Francisco on the 9:00 a.m. flight, together with a Mr. Ryan Donahue.

In actual fact Wraith, Raven, and Kez had moved no further than the Stratos Hotel, signing in under different names and requesting a secluded suite. The hotel had been Raven's choice and she had brought her collection of disks with her, packed into three large crates in the customized skimmer that had replaced the flitter. Apart from that they had mostly traveled light, taking only what they could carry. But this had included the equipment Wraith and Kez had collected.

It was standard electronic equipment, obtainable perfectly legally from any store, but what Raven was using it for was completely unorthodox. Since she had agreed to go ahead with the decision to keep looking for Rachel, even without Ali's assistance, she was making elaborate preparations. Wraith allowed her to make adjustments to his laser pistol and didn't inquire what she intended to do with the rest of the equipment. He considered himself fortunate that she hadn't flown into a rage after he had stymied her attempts to use Ali as bait. But Kez, who had more or less resolved his difference with Raven, had the heap of electronic innards explained to him in detail during their first day at the hotel.

"Most of this is to do with getting into the lab's system," Raven had explained. "If I can find their central control room I'll be able to control it without physical intervention. But until I get there I'll have to trip circuits and fool security, all of it manually. For that I need tools."

"You're making them yourself?" Kez asked.

"I told you it wasn't just computers I had an affinity with," Raven reminded him. "Who do you think made Wraith's transceiver?" By then Kez had had that device explained to him in more detail than he felt able to cope with, but he knew why Raven had brought up that particular piece of equipment as an example. Among the spaghetti of cables and wires on the long dining table of the hotel suite was a more delicate piece of electronics. It was tiny, involving microcircuitry that the stores could not have provided. Raven had produced the miniature circuit-board and some specialized tools from the duffel bag that she had brought with her to gangland when Kez had first met her. From it she had created a transceiver device similar to Wraith's. But this one was not intended to be surgically implanted. It took the form of a plain white ear-stud, something that would hardly be noticed. Especially not when worn by a seventeen-year-old girl. Raven had even produced a matching stud for the other ear, although this one was without circuitry. But the first stud was a piece of equipment any electronics designer would have been proud of. Barely five millimeters in diameter, it contained a transmitter, receiver, location beacon, and private sensor. If Kez's plan worked and Ali went into the lab, Raven would be able to keep complete track of her, every second she was there.

Bob Tarrell was surprised by the sudden disappearance of his new acquaintances. But Elizabeth had left a message on his vidcom, apologizing and explaining that AdAstra had unexpectedly recalled her to the States, and after all there was no reason for him to be especially concerned. The media was full of the news of his new channel and the shareholders were predicting a roaring success.

His daughter was more alarmed. She watched the morning news with her father on Monday on Populix, one of his channels. The main story was the launch of CultRock, showing that her father had exploited his ownership of the news channel again. But she was not concentrating on the program. Her thoughts revolved round the gangers' departure and what it signified and she barely noticed the screen until a brief remark at the end of the item.

"While CultRock looks set to be a major success, the US channel that first encouraged this latest music sensation has gone into receivership. AdAstra is no longer online and its database has disappeared from the net." For a split second the reporter's expression wavered between annoyed and puzzled and finally settled on tolerant. *"The channel has refused Populix access to any footage of its programming and has recalled Elizabeth Black, an AdAstra researcher who assisted in the launch of CultRock."* The reporter adopted a more upbeat tone as the channel moved on to show pictures of celebrities arriving at the Tarrells' apartment for the launch of CultRock, and Ali subsided.

Despite the matter-of-fact way the story had appeared on the news, she was suspicious of the official explanation. She knew that Raven wasn't really "Elizabeth Black," and she also had doubts about AdAstra. It seemed a bit too convenient the way the channel had simply disappeared. Obviously the gangers had decided to cover their tracks when they departed. That suited Ali. She hadn't wanted to get involved with them in the first place and the further away they were, the better. She had no intention of reporting them to the Security Services though. Aside from the fact that she was nervous of being questioned about her involvement with them, she had nothing substantial to report. To go to the Seccies with the story she had been told, starring a white-haired ganger called Wraith and his sister, a dangerous and perhaps insane Hex named Raven, would be ludicrous. She kept her own counsel. But it had been difficult for her to cope with the questions of the rest of the clique that day at school.

Listening to the vapid conversation, Ali almost agreed with Raven's contempt for these people, even though it included her. Her encounter with the gangland Hex had affected her in more ways than she had realized at first, and one of them was the way it had distanced her from the rest of the Gateshall students and her clique in particular. Even though she was safely ensconced in the middle of the group she felt as isolated from them as if the CPS had found her out and were already driving her away. Raven's repeated assertion that she would be caught had sunk in. She was no longer able to convince herself that she was safe. Raven renting that apartment had been like gangers bypassing security and invading the heights of London. Nothing felt normal to Ali anymore.

Kez was feeling equally uncomfortable. He had suggested that they deceive Ali in order to help Wraith. He wanted to help the ganger find his sister and he hadn't forgotten that Wraith had promised to take care of him, while Raven had obviously never even considered it. But, despite wanting to help Wraith, he was beginning to feel that he had made a deal with the devil.

In order to take his mind off how miserable he was, Kez tried to make himself useful. Gradually he was beginning to learn some of the most basic concepts of electronic science, despite the fact that Raven was not the most patient of teachers. Her natural aptitude for anything technological, coupled with her years of experience, made him less than a novice compared to her. But at least he was doing something, and in reward for his persistence Raven didn't subject him to any sudden flares of anger when he made a mistake. He spent most of his time creating the frequency-activated explosive charges with which Raven intended to blast their way into the lab. They were basically simple devices, although Raven supervised the final installment of the charge that would activate the explosive. Wraith obtained more lethal equipment from the Countess and had opened negotiations with her to hire the services of some men to act as muscle backup when they broke into the facility. The whole operation was looking increasingly serious. Kez doubted that it would succeed the way Wraith envisaged it. But he hoped that, with the additional element that he and Raven were devising, the plan might yet work.

Kez's only worry was how Wraith would react if he discovered what he and Raven had decided to do. He had enough faith in the ganger's perception to suspect that sooner or later Wraith might well find out how Ali had been tricked and he hoped fervently that, if Wraith did find out, it would be too late for him to do anything about it. Otherwise his sense of honor would oblige him to warn her and the operation would be hopeless. Kez knew Raven wouldn't stick with a hopeless cause and he didn't think he could either.

6

UNNATURAL TROUBLES

To his surprise, Wraith was becoming interested in politics.
The extermination of Hexes, something he had never thought
about before in terms of its morality, was troubling him now that
Rachel might be one of those at risk. It hadn't affected him so much
with Raven. She had always seemed able to take care of herself, and
in the slums of Denver, morality was rarely an important consideration. But the Kali's code of honor, which had affected Wraith so
much, was making its presence felt.

The people with the Hex gene were the result of a perfectly
legal scientific advance. But for over two hundred and fifty years
they had been exterminated by their own governments because of
the potential threat they posed to the computerized society. Wraith
had worked out that even if the CPS only exterminated one person a day, the death count would be nearly a hundred thousand

people by now, and Raven estimated the numbers were far higher. It didn't seem to trouble her that much. Raven had never been particularly interested in other Hexes and was confident enough of her own safety for the massive death tolls to leave her unaffected. But Wraith was more disturbed by them, and especially by the laws that had made this wholesale slaughter legal.

If Hexes had been allowed to exist, Raven would not have had to fear for her life ever since she'd been a child; she might have been a different person without that burden, lacking the manic-depressive streak that made her hell to live with. Ali wouldn't be scared that she would die before she even reached her eighteenth birthday. Rachel wouldn't have been taken away for experimentation at ten years old and delivered to Dr. Kalden's research lab.

The more he considered the whole question of the illegality of Hexes, the more certain Wraith was that the extermination laws were a horrific crime against humanity. But he seemed to be unable to bring Raven and Kez to his way of thinking.

"There's no point in brooding over it," Raven told him, in a bored tone of voice. "I've had to live with this for most of my life. But there's nothing that can be done about it."

"Bad things happen," Kez shrugged. "I was living on the streets at the same age that Raven was fleeing for her life. Gangers have trashed the lower levels of London. People get flatlined every day for no other season than they were in the wrong place at the wrong time. Little kids get raped and murdered." He shook his head. "You can't *do* anything about it. It's just *there*."

"But it shouldn't be," Wraith insisted, taking hope from the fact that Kez's response had at least showed concern, unlike Raven, who had already turned back to her wires and fuses. "Those things are illegal. But the murder of Hexes is sanctioned by every government in the world. There's nowhere you can escape from the CPS."

"Unless you're good enough," Raven pointed out.

"And how many people are?" Wraith demanded. "You discovered your abilities young enough to be able to use them. Most people are only just working it out when they're hauled off to a death chamber."

"But the government figures that if they weren't, things would be even worse," Kez reminded him. "Raven goes through a computer system like a knife through butter. What if there were thousands of people doing that?"

"Then governments could design better computer systems," Wraith pointed out. "Raven, could you design a system that even you couldn't get into?"

"It's a difficult question," she said thoughtfully. "I would say that the kind of system Dr. Kalden's lab has is one of the best. But if I can physically penetrate the facility, the computers will be a walkover." She thought a while longer. "I might be able to design a system that most Hexes couldn't get into, though," she said eventually. "Maybe even one that it would take me a long time to crack."

"Then why don't the government use Hexes, instead of exterminating them?" Wraith frowned. It was Kez who provided the answer.

"Because it would make people like Raven incredibly powerful," he said. "She could do anything she wanted with the network."

"Most people choose not to act illegally," Wraith said seriously. "Why shouldn't Hexes be the same?"

"I don't think it would work," Kez replied and bent over his own bunch of wires. Wraith fell silent. He could guess what the boy was thinking. Someone like Raven, if there could be more than one of her, wouldn't agree to play by the rules any more than they could be forced to.

They had been at the hotel for two days by the time Raven entered the net again. She told Wraith that she was still unhappy with the scarcity of information on the laboratory and was going to make one last attempt at pulling more information out of the CPS database. Even though her professed intention seemed bland enough, Kez suddenly felt as tense as a spring. This was the moment. He watched Raven disappear into her room with apprehension—she still preferred to keep her ventures into the net private—before bending his head diligently over his work. Wraith asked him a question about how many explosive devices they would have in the end, and he replied mechanically with the figure Raven had determined upon. It seemed to take forever for the girl to finally emerge from her room, although in reality it was only about fifteen minutes.

When she eventually returned to the main room of the hotel suite her eyes were bright with excitement.

"They're after her," she said immediately.

"What?" Wraith looked up and Kez held his breath.

"The CPS," Raven explained. "They're after Ali. They've got a file on her as a suspected Hex."

"Can you remove it from the database?" Wraith asked quickly and mentally Kez kicked himself—he hadn't thought of that. But Raven had obviously anticipated the question.

"It would be counterproductive," she said. "There's certain to be some physical documentation as well. If her file disappeared from the database their suspicions would be confirmed and they'd schedule her for extermination for certain."

Wraith considered for a while, his eyes troubled and his brows furrowed in thought. Finally he came to a decision.

"We have to warn her," he said.

"And get her to help us," Kez put in—after all, Wraith would be surprised if it wasn't suggested. "She hasn't got any choice now."

"Kez is right," Raven agreed. "We're her only way out of the CPS's clutches, just as she's our best shot at getting Rachel out."

"I agree," Wraith nodded. "Can you contact her, Raven?"

"Me?" she grimaced. "Ali wouldn't trust me any further than she could throw me. She'll think I'm just pressuring her. It would be better if you told her, Wraith."

"OK," he agreed. "But we had better not meet Ali here or at the Belgravia Complex. Any suggestions as to a good place to see her?"

"We could pick her up in the skimmer," Raven said.

"But not from the apartment complex," Wraith added. "It's too dangerous."

"Why not from Arkade?" Kez suggested. "They have the most boring collection of junk you've ever seen. No one would notice us picking her up from there."

"The museum?" Raven arched an eyebrow. "Trust you to be original, Kez."

"OK, the museum will do," Wraith agreed. "Raven, send a message to Ali, saying we want to meet with her there this evening at eight."

The skimmer pulled up that evening outside the museum just under one of the glowing streetlamps. Night had fallen on the city, dusk coming early in winter, and all through the levels of London the lights were on. Down in gangland night was dangerous but Arkade had impressive security in order to keep the custom of the families from Belgravia.

Ali stood on the pavement of one of the bridges that enmeshed the recreation complex, waiting for them. Raven, in the driving seat of the skimmer, grimaced slightly as she brought the vehicle to a halt. She was dressed, as always, in black. But her thick silky hair was for once neatly tied back at the nape of her neck in a businesslike way. Kez was sitting in the passenger seat and Wraith waited in the back of the vehicle. As Ali approached, Raven released the security lock on the door, but Wraith had to slide it open himself. Ali got in, closing the door behind her, anxious not to be seen with them, and Raven sped the skimmer back into the flow of traffic as Wraith spoke.

"Thank you for agreeing to meet with us," he said.

"I haven't changed my mind, you know," Ali told him. "And you'd better not be planning anything weird." Raven wrinkled her nose and glanced back at the girl, still keeping the skimmer under perfect control. Looking through long lashes she said softly:

"How about a brief trip to gangland, Ali? Do you feel lucky tonight?"

Kez giggled but Wraith looked annoyed.

"Keep us on this level," he warned Raven sharply. "There's no need to play games."

The girl shrugged and turned back to the control console, exchanging an amused glance with Kez who was grinning at Ali's obvious discomfort. But Wraith ignored them.

"Ali," he said. "I'm afraid I have bad news."

"What's happened?" Ali looked alarmed. "Is it to do with your sister?"

"No." Wraith shook his head in reply. "This is about you. It seems the CPS already suspect you of being a Hex."

"Are you sure?" Ali asked, paling. "How do you know? Are they going to come after me . . . ?" Her voice trailed off as her eyes fixed desperately on Wraith, hoping against hope that it was all a mistake. Kez looked studiedly out of the window, unable to look at Wraith and Ali. But Raven's mouth curved in a slow smile.

"Having second thoughts?" she asked softly. Kez froze and Raven's dark eyes drifted slowly over him before she turned and glanced back at Ali. "About joining us, I mean," she qualified.

"We still won't force you," Wraith added. "But perhaps you should think again."

"It doesn't look like I have much choice, does it?" Ali asked, a little stiffly. But the fact that Wraith had not tried to threaten her made her want to trust him. Her brown eyes narrowed as they met Raven's. The younger girl was apparently taking no notice at all of the controls, but the skimmer sped on smoothly through the evening traffic. "But how do I know you won't just use me to find your sister and then dump me?"

"You don't," Raven replied expressionlessly. But Wraith contradicted her.

"You can trust *me*," he said. "I promise, if you help us, we'll save you from the CPS and help you start a new life somewhere."

If possible Ali turned even paler. Suddenly a new reality was coming home to her. If she was captured by the CPS, even if Wraith managed to rescue her, she could never return to her old life. Belgravia Complex would be the first place the Seccies would look for her, even if her father tried to shelter her from them. And Ali couldn't really believe that Bob Tarrell would give up his media empire, risking imprisonment and disgrace, to hide an illegal mutant from the Security Services, even if the mutant was his daughter. She would truly have nowhere to go without the gangers' help. Her mother was long dead, she had no other close relatives. As for her friends, if the situation had not been so desperate Ali would have laughed. Of all of them Caitlin was the best, but not even Caitlin would suffer the social stigma of even acknowledging a Hex as a friend. She wrapped her arms around herself to keep out the cold. But she didn't permit herself to give in to misery. Raven might have turned back to the skimmer's control panel but Ali could feel her silent gloating. Taking a deep breath the girl looked back at Wraith.

"All right," she said. "I'll join you."

• • •

With her father still absorbed in CultRock it was easy for Ali to take a day off school without him noticing. For the last few days he had been leaving early in the morning before Zircarda and Caitlin collected her and not returning until late at night. That Friday, the day after meeting the gangers at Arkade, Ali called Zircarda and told her she was too ill to go in to school. After cross-questioning her for ten minutes to make sure that Ali really was sick, Zircarda was apparently satisfied and got off the vidcom. The next call Ali placed was for a flitter to collect her from Belgravia.

In less than half an hour she was entering the suite the gangers had rented at the Stratos, Wraith apparently deciding that it was safe for her to know where they were staying now that she had agreed to help them. The gangers had just finished breakfast and Wraith was piling the remains on a side table to spread out several sheets of design blueprints in front of Ali while Raven finished a cup of black coffee.

As Ali joined them, Wraith reseated himself and glanced briefly at Raven and Kez, making sure he had their attention, before beginning to speak:

"These are the only plans we have of the laboratory where we believe Rachel is being held," he told her. "Hopefully they'll be good enough to get us into the facility, as most of that will involve just blasting our way in. But we don't have time to mount a long search through the lab, as most of this will be very different by now."

"That's where you come in," Kez said and flushed when she uneasily met his eyes. Wraith didn't appear to notice the tension or if he did, disregarded it.

"We believe that, as a young Hex and somewhat inexperienced, you will probably be automatically taken to this laboratory," he went on.

"I see." Ali had no trouble guessing who had provided that definition of her, but she declined to even look at Raven. "What if they just take me to an extermination facility instead?" she asked.

"The CPS has to get official permission for every extermination," Wraith told her. "You'd be taken to a holding area first, while they sorted out the paperwork. And if that happens we'll abort the plan and get you out straightaway."

"How?" Ali asked.

"We'd hijack the transport on the way from the holding area to the death chambers," Kez told her. "Raven can deal with that, no problem." He looked at the Hex, who was still silently drinking coffee, with an expression that made Ali blink with a sudden realization. She would have laughed. But suddenly Raven looked up and she didn't dare.

"It's most probable that you'll be taken to the laboratory," Wraith was saying. "And, once there, we hope you'll be able to find Rachel for us. I'll show you a holo so you'll know what she looks like."

"What if they keep me in restraints?" Ali asked.

"We hope you'll be mobile for at least part of the time," Wraith told her. "But if any thing untoward happens you'll be able to inform us." He looked expectantly at Raven who spoke for the first time.

"You'll be wearing this transceiver," she told Ali, holding out a small object on the palm of her hand. "It took a long time to build it, so don't screw with it, OK?" Her tone was antagonistic and Ali didn't dare do anything more than nod. "Wraith has a similar device surgically implanted," Raven went on. "I can contact him through it, in or out of the network."

"How?" Ali asked in amazement, her surprise getting past her fear of Raven.

"Does it matter?" Raven said sarcastically. "You couldn't do it."

"Are you certain about that?" Wraith asked. "It might be easier if Ali could contact us as well."

"Quite certain," Raven said. "I only gave you your transceiver when we left for Europe, remember? I couldn't have even made it a year before that let alone even used it. If Ali was capable of that kind of thing, she'd be headed straight for extermination now."

"But could she be?" Kez asked.

"Hypothetically?" Wraith added and Raven sighed.

"If all Hexes have the innate capacity to improve their skills, then yes," she agreed. "But if there are different levels of ability, it's highly probable that I just have more abilities than Ali." She ignored the older girl's annoyed expression and continued: "I'd like to see what kind of conclusions Dr. Kalden has reached about Hexes. That information should be easy to find when I get into the lab's main database."

"That's what we're planning to do," Wraith informed Ali. "When you've located Rachel, we'll blast our way in. Then Raven will find the lab's control room and enter their computer system.

That'll give us control of their security systems and we should be able to get out again without too much trouble."

"Do you want me to find the control room as well?" Ali asked, striving to be as businesslike as Wraith.

"You wouldn't be able to," Raven said briefly.

"There's no real need," Wraith said, less harshly. "The first terminal we find should be able to lead Raven right to it." He hesitated, then added: "And I think Raven's right. You'll be a prisoner there, Ali. I don't think they'll give you a chance to see the control room."

By the time Wraith had explained everything to his satisfaction Ali was feeling exhausted. But the fact that the ganger had turned out to be such a meticulous and conscientious organizer had given her a new confidence in his plan. She could even find herself believing for the first time that everything would be all right. She would find Rachel and then Wraith would come and break them out of the lab. The fact that what would happen after that was still unclear was something Ali didn't allow herself to dwell on.

To her surprise she found herself admiring the ghostlike ganger. Despite his strange white hair he was actually strikingly attractive and had a confidence that made him the accepted leader of the group. Ali tried to ignore the fact that the features that she admired in Wraith were doubled in Raven. She was just as attractive—she had proved that at Ali's father's party even if at the moment she was dressed like a mercenary soldier—and she was the most supremely self-confident person Ali had ever met.

Raven's arrogance was emphasized by the fact that she claimed the CPS had made a mistake in capturing Rachel and that the girl wasn't a Hex at all. Ali couldn't see how it mattered, seeing as Rachel *had* been captured, but Raven obviously took the suggestion that she might have made a mistake as a personal slight.

"I'm willing to bet over half the people they've slaughtered over the years haven't been Hexes either," she insisted. "Just people unlucky enough to be suspected, and then exterminated just in case the suspicions were correct."

"The government wouldn't allow that," Ali said firmly, having gradually gained enough confidence to contradict Raven. "The CPS has to have a warrant for every person they . . . dispose of."

"Dispose of?" Wraith asked. "That's a very callous way of describing it."

"It's legal," Ali said defensively. "You can't deny that."

"I guess you think the government is infallible," Kez interjected. "The Seccies are always happy enough to shoot first and ask questions later—why shouldn't the CPS be the same?"

"It's different in gangland," Ali said coldly. "The Security Services aren't like that up here."

"And you're all law-abiding citizens?" Kez said. "Give it a rest." Wraith looked as if he was about to warn the boy off, but Raven suddenly agreed:

"There isn't so much crime up here, at least not violent crime, but anyone can be guilty of being a Hex. A lot of people the CPS pick up come from families in the heights. Most of them, actually, probably because in gangland people have the sense to run."

"That's how they caught Rachel," Wraith added. "I should have never let that adoption go through."

"Come on, Wraith," Raven said. "You were hardly able to take care of a five-year-old kid. What were you going to do, blast your way through Denver with a little girl holding your hand?"

"You weren't running with a gang," Wraith said, a little harshly.

"I was just a kid myself, Wraith." Raven looked disgusted, too contemptuous of her brother's remark to be angry. "What was I supposed to do? I spent a year living in a cellar before I persuaded people to take me seriously as a hacker." Remembering what company she was in, she turned to look at Ali. "You can sneer at Kez, because you've never had to live on the streets. But if it wasn't for us, who grew up there, you'd have no way to escape the CPS."

"You were just lucky," Ali replied uneasily.

"It wasn't luck," Wraith said, "and Raven's right. But Ali shouldn't have to flee for her life," he added. "Sometimes I doubt I'll ever get this across to you."

"Wraith seems to want to form a solidarity group for Hexes," Raven said, not quite to Ali but in her general direction. "But the fact is that anyone good enough to escape the CPS isn't going to want to load themselves down with people who aren't."

"Then why are you trying to help Rachel?" Ali demanded, taking Raven's remark personally. "Do you care about her or is it just that you think the CPS got it wrong and you're curious to find out why they thought she was a Hex?"

Wraith and Kez exchanged glances—apparently Ali's thoughts

had mirrored theirs. But Raven seemed unaffected by their suspicion.

"I don't have to explain myself to you," she said coldly. "Why don't you just concentrate on the fact that I'm going to be saving your life?"

Kez was relieved when Ali finally left in the early afternoon. She had at least stopped looking at him as if he was a bug in her food. It seemed that some of Raven's comments about her privileged lifestyle had struck home. But he still felt uncomfortable with her, and that discomfort was compounded by the fact that it was he who had suggested Raven lie about the CPS being after her.

Ali and Wraith both believed in the lie completely, and Raven seemed utterly unconscious of guilt, now that she had got her own way. She had even given Ali the transceiver with relatively good humor, although she had insisted that the girl did not remove it at all. Ali was sufficiently scared of the CPS to obey Raven, despite her clear dislike of her. But Kez, knowing there was no real need for Ali to wear it just yet, and understanding a bit more about how the transceiver worked, suspected that Raven just wanted the chance to eavesdrop on Ali and make sure that she wasn't about to betray them.

When Wraith was engrossed in watching the news on the vidscreen, his conviction that the extermination laws were wrong fueling his interest in politics, Kez brought up a question that had been worrying him.

"Raven, how are we going to make sure the CPS take Ali to

that lab?" he whispered. "Why should they, when they don't even know she's a Hex?"

"I'll alter their files so they do suspect her," Raven said. "Or make an anonymous call. It'll have the same result either way. I'll do it sometime next week, it's too soon just now."

"It's a bit unfair, isn't it?" Kez said hesitantly. "It's going to wreck her whole life."

"Why should you care?" Raven shrugged. "She wouldn't care about wrecking yours."

"There isn't much she could do to make it worse," Kez said bitterly. "But she's got everything I could ever want, and we're going to take it away just like that."

"You are so strange, Kez." Raven was grinning. "Wraith thinks you're the most amoral person he's ever met but you're almost as worried about doing the right thing as he is."

"Maybe because I'm not on the streets anymore," Kez pointed out. "And that's because of Wraith."

"It is?" Raven looked annoyed. "Wraith wanted to get rid of you, as I recall. It was me who let you stay."

"But now I'm here, Wraith says he won't just dump me back on the streets, and you couldn't care less about me," Kez said, before he could help himself. The fact that Raven seemed utterly uninterested in him still rankled.

"I see," Raven said slowly, studying him. Kez went red under that intense scrutiny, but then Raven turned away abruptly, picking up one of her disks and heading toward the sound system. As she loaded it into the player, she said over her shoulder: "If it makes you feel better, the CPS would have caught Ali sooner or later; she's much too careless." And with that the conversation appeared to be over. Raven had been as unaffected by his criticism as she was by Ali's or Wraith's.

Kez woke up late the next morning, light streaming in through the huge window of the room he shared with Wraith. The ganger had already left the room, presumably to get something to eat or watch the morning news. After trying for a while to get back to sleep, Kez gave up the attempt and went to stand at the window. Up in the heights of the city it was possible to be woken up by the sun. Down in gangland the shadows of the upper levels perpetually blocked out the light. If the streetlighting broke down it wasn't safe to venture outside.

Kez basked in the cold winter sunshine, looking out at the city through the double thickness of glass, necessary in case of flitter accidents. Already the air was full of the silver streaks of metal as workers raced off to early appointments, trying to beat the traffic. The bridges were congested with skimmers, moving at a slow crawl, and Kez could even make out a few bikers weaving in and out of the traffic. No pedestrians; even up here that much hadn't changed. People only walked short distances—it took too long to navigate across the network of arches between the levels on foot.

Kez was drifting into a lazy dream, as he watched the city waking up, when suddenly a shout from the main room made him start.

"Raven, Kez! Wake up, quickly!"

"What is it?" Kez asked, as he ran out of the bedroom, ready to believe the Seccies were at the door. Wraith was staring fixedly at the vidscreen and he didn't take his gaze off it for a second as he explained:

"They've got Ali."

A reporter was babbling confusedly about a sudden shock for Bob Tarrell, owner of another news channel, and suddenly the screen filled with what was, he claimed, exclusive footage of events happening live that morning. It was the Belgravia Complex. The reporter was explaining that there had been a news team stationed there on the watch for celebrities when this extraordinary event had occurred. Behind him, Kez heard another door swish open and Raven emerged from her room, still heavy-eyed and wrapped in one of the blankets from her bed. As she saw the screen her eyes opened wide and she sat on the arm of the couch as she watched it.

Three vehicles had pulled up outside the Tarrells' apartment, including a flitter and a skimmer, both marked with the Seccies' logo. A second large unmarked flitter was with them, and a group of men clustered around them. The soundtrack was explaining that this was a team of Security Services men and CPS operatives, when the door of the apartment opened and two more Seccies appeared, holding between them a confused-looking Ali. She appeared to have had time to dress and wasn't struggling with her guards. Instead she looked vacant and passively allowed herself to be manhandled into the CPS flitter. Bob Tarrell was at the door angrily demanding explanations and the Seccies were handing over papers, obviously their warrant, as the CPS operatives locked up the back of their flitter and got into it. The camera panned over from the gesticulating media magnate to focus on the plain flitter. The CPS weren't waiting for Bob Tarrell to have everything explained to him. The vehicle took off, the camera staying on it, until it had disappeared behind one of the skyrises. The reporter returned, to attempt some discreet mudslinging and comment on the possible results of Bob Tarrell's daughter being revealed as a Hex, but Wraith muted the volume, turning to look at the others.

Kez was too astonished to think about what he was saying. Still wide-eyed with shock he exclaimed:

"How did the CPS find out she was a Hex?"

"What did you say?" Wraith demanded, taking him by the shoulders. Looking past the ganger Kez saw Raven roll her eyes, but it was too late for him to explain away his mistake.

"I . . . I . . . ," he began, and stammered to a halt, frightened by Wraith's sudden anger.

"You lied, didn't you?" Wraith said, releasing Kez and swinging around to face Raven. "Both of you."

"Yes," Raven replied, meeting Wraith's eyes unashamedly.

"Whose idea was this?" Wraith asked and Kez finally managed to find the courage to speak:

"It was mine," he admitted. "The plan couldn't work without Ali, and you wouldn't have let us force her."

Wraith looked as if he wouldn't mind wringing Kez's neck for his innovative idea. But Raven's voice called him back to himself.

"What the hell does it matter, Wraith?" she asked. "It looks like we told the truth without realizing it. The CPS *have* come for

Ali, without our intervention. We may have lied when we said they knew about Ali, but it turns out it was true."

"And what have they done with her?" Wraith asked, concentrating on the most important factor. "Do you know where she is?"

Raven closed her eyes, her expression becoming blank as she concentrated. This was different from entering the network through a computer. She let her consciousness rove through the living city, searching for a signal which she alone could recognize. Wraith's presence next to her was confusing, his own transceiver gave out the same signal, and it was difficult to search for another one. She concentrated, trying to distinguish the tracking device which would locate Ali from the multitude of electronic signals buzzing through the ether. A minute passed, slowly, then her eyes snapped open.

"They're heading out of London," she said. "Toward the north."

"Are they taking her to the lab?" Wraith demanded. "Or are they taking her for extermination?"

"I think the lab," Raven said. "There are extermination facilities in London."

"Check," said Wraith coldly. "We don't want to make a mistake."

"OK." Raven didn't argue. She walked over to the wall terminal, still wrapped in her blanket, and let her hands rest on the keypad. Wraith and Kez waited, for over five minutes this time, until Raven's eyes focused again and she looked up from the terminal. "It's the laboratory," she stated. "Those operatives are ordered to hand Ali over to Dr. Kalden, just as Rachel was."

"Can you speak to her?" Wraith asked. "Is the transceiver working?"

"It's working," Raven replied. "But I can't contact her—if the CPS pick up the transmission we'd be endangering ourselves as well as Ali."

"All right." Wraith nodded grimly. "I want you to keep in constant contact with Ali's transceiver. Tell me when you find out exactly where the lab is, but don't lose contact. I want you to know what's happening to her every minute."

"Wraith, stay chill . . . ," Raven began, but Wraith didn't let her finish.

"I don't want to hear it, Raven," he said coldly. "You were responsible for trying to get Ali caught by the CPS. Now she has been and you're to make sure that nothing worse happens to her." He looked at Kez. "And you can stay with her—try and be useful." Then he turned and headed for the main door to the suite. "I'm going to get something to eat."

"Well, that went down well," Raven said sarcastically as the door closed behind Wraith. "I think he's losing sight of the main issue here. Does he want to rescue Rachel, or not?" She shrugged one shoulder and turned back to the terminal as Kez miserably sat down to watch her.

The flitter coasted through the skies, over the sprawling suburbs, and out toward the north. It would have been difficult for Ali to tell where the city ended and the country began, as the congested freeway below them was bordered by industrial development. But the back of the flitter was shielded in any case, with no way for her to see where she was going.

She had been pushed onto a steel bench with restraints that fixed around her wrists holding her to it. Two CPS operatives, a man and a woman, sat facing her, as if unwilling to contaminate themselves with closer association. The inside of the flitter was stripped of all other equipment, and a thick shield separated the back of the vehicle from the control console in the front.

Ali was shaking, clutching the bench she was locked to. She kept her head down, unable to look at the CPS agents. But even more than terror, the emotion that overwhelmed her was shame. She had seen the camera crew filming her humiliation as she was dragged out of the door of her apartment and all she could think of was what Zircarda and Caitlin would say, watching the news together. But what hurt the most had been her father's reaction. When he had called her out of her room, she had thought at first he had found out about her visit to the Stratos the day before. But then she had seen the five uniformed men standing by the main door of the apartment and knew with a horrified realization that they had come for her. Her father had looked at her with a mixture of disappointment and fear. It was the fear that had made her start to shake. He had never looked at her with anything other than affection and tolerance. She wasn't really clever enough to earn his admiration—her school record had always been average at best— but he had always been fond of her without that. To have him be afraid of her was something Ali had never envisaged.

The Seccies had told her to get dressed quickly and one of

them, a woman, had stayed with her while she did so. Once she was dressed the woman took her back into the main room, where one of the other Seccies was examining the computer terminals. Another immediately sealed the door of her room and attached an SS classification to it. It was only then that Bob had begun to recover his composure.

"What is this?" he demanded. "What's going to happen to my daughter?"

"Your daughter is a suspected Hex, Mr. Tarrell," one of the officers said emotionlessly. "She will be taken for evaluation and when the mutation is confirmed, she will be disposed of." Ali felt a hysterical laugh building inside her as the man used the same term that Wraith had criticized her for using. She clamped down hard on it, holding her mouth tight shut.

"And what if she isn't a Hex?" her father was saying.

"If that is the case she will be returned to you before the end of the day," the man told him. "But it is rarely the case that a person is suspected incorrectly. Extermination is scheduled for this evening."

Her father had looked so stunned that Ali had wanted to tell him what Wraith and Raven had found out about the laboratory, that there was a good chance she would be taken there. But she knew that telling him that would mean she would be exterminated for certain and kept silent. She felt dazed as two Seccies took her out of the apartment, barely hearing her father's protests. The men had bundled her into the flitter, handing her over to two CPS operatives who had checked her for concealed weapons before

124

locking her into the restraints. Ali had felt horribly conscious of the transceiver ear-stud, which she hadn't removed the night before. But the CPS people didn't even seem to notice it. As the flitter took off, Ali prayed that Raven was tracking her. Despite the fact that it was Wraith she trusted and Wraith who was the leader of the group, it was Raven who held her life in her hands.

Ali thought of Raven with all her might as the flitter sped on. She remembered what the girl had told her in the hotel: "Concentrate on the fact that I'm going to be saving your life." She had meant it as a warning, Ali was certain, to prevent any more criticism of her motives. But now Ali recalled it as a promise. The CPS had no idea of how far Raven's powers extended. They didn't even know she existed. And for whatever reasons, whether to save Rachel or satisfy a morbid curiosity, Raven would be watching out for her. It was the only hope Ali had and she clung to it.

7

NATURE'S MISCHIEF

The room Ali had been left in was plain and windowless, and something like a private room at a hospital. There was a single bed and some equipment to monitor life-signs and brainwaves, standing near it. But it contained no computer equipment. There was also a small metal table and a single chair, both bolted to the floor. Apart from that the room was empty. Lying on the bed were the white coveralls Ali had been told to put on, made of a thin material. But somehow her own clothes seemed like her last link with home and she made no move to change, sitting hunched against the wall.

There was no lock on the door and it had a large pane of shatterproof glass set into it, as if to emphasize the complete lack of privacy. Under the circumstances Ali had made no move to close the door, which the CPS operatives had left open—it would have been a pointless exercise. So she was surprised when she heard a quiet knock, although she didn't move from her position against the wall. There was a pause, and then she heard the door swing further open as someone entered the room.

"Are you OK?" a voice asked.

Ali looked up then, if only to tell the speaker exactly what she thought of such an utterly stupid and pointless question. But she was arrested by the sight that awaited her. It was a boy, perhaps about her age, but she found it hard to tell for certain. He was painfully thin, almost emaciated, and his white coveralls hung off his scarecrow figure like rags. The sleeves of the coveralls were short enough for Ali to see the yellow bruises that covered his arms, like those of a drug user. He saw her looking and his mouth pulled into a travesty of a smile.

"My name's Luciel," he told her. "They're testing to see if drugs break my connection with electronics. I guess they haven't found the right formula yet."

"I'm Ali," she said, standing up awkwardly, and glancing at the open door. "Are we allowed to talk?"

"We pretty much do what we want to," the boy said. "Unless someone's door is guarded. That means they're doing experiments."

"Who exactly are *they*?" Ali asked, although she could already guess the answer.

"The scientists," Luciel replied uneasily.

"Is one of them called Dr. Kalden?"

"Shhh," Luciel warned, suddenly alarmed. "We don't talk about them, and especially not about *him*." He tried to smile again.

"I came to see you because I knew you'd be scared, everyone is. But it helps that we're allowed to talk to each other."

"Yes, it does," Ali admitted. She hesitated. "Can I ask you another question?"

"OK," Luciel replied slowly.

"Is there a girl called Rachel here?" Ali asked. "She's a . . . a friend of mine. About eleven years old, brown hair, brown eyes . . ."

"I'm sorry." Luciel shook his head. "I can't think of anyone like that." Ali's heart sank; everything felt cut from under her. But then Luciel added, "But there are a lot of people here and I don't know them all. Your friend could still be here."

Despite Luciel's claim that they were allowed to go anywhere they wanted, the boy seemed unwilling to venture out into the rest of the laboratory, although he did his best to make Ali feel resigned to her new situation. He was very different from Raven. Not only did he lack her magnetism and self-confidence, he was generally much more uncertain about himself and his own abilities. After the contempt Raven had shown toward Ali's two ventures into the net she had thought herself a novice. But, according to Luciel, no one in the facility had much more experience than that either.

However, Ali did not describe Raven to him as an example. She steered clear of the entire subject of the gangers. After all, she didn't know who could be trusted in this place and, even more, she was beginning to feel guilty about the whole situation. She had been thinking of her venture into the lab almost as a game, but people here were being experimented on, in ways that she could only guess at. Anything she imagined could only be guesswork, as Luciel was unwilling to tell her anything about the experimentation.

"It's better not to know," he said when she demanded he enlighten her further.

"How can I not know?" she asked. "They're going to be experimenting on me, aren't they?"

"But not for a while," Luciel replied uncomfortably. "First they run a whole lot of tests, to try to find out your capabilities, stuff like that. It's only when they've found out as much as they can that the scientists really start experimenting."

"Do they always do . . . what they've done to you?" Ali found it difficult to look at Luciel's bruised arms.

"No . . . ," he said reluctantly. "They do different things to different people. You'll see when you meet the others."

"OK, then." Ali made a motion as if to leave the room, but Luciel shook his head.

"You can't yet," he told her. "Not until they've examined you."

"Is that a rule?" Ali asked.

"No, it's . . . it's . . . it's just the way things are." Luciel shrugged his thin shoulders. "They'll probably be here soon," he said. "I'd better go. Good luck, Ali." He paused just before leaving the room. "You'd better put the coveralls on," he told her, "just so as not to annoy them."

Ali changed into the white coveralls. It wasn't so much Luciel's words that had affected her as the haunted look in his eyes. She wondered miserably what she had got herself into and, sitting slumped on the bed, felt bitterly angry with the gangers who had got her into all this.

"I wish I'd never met that *bitch*!" she said under her breath and gave a convulsive start when a voice in her ears answered:

"Do you mean me?"

"Raven!" Ali exclaimed. "You can hear me?"

"That is what this device is for," Raven reminded her, the Hex's voice reverberating in Ali's ears. *"According to the transmitter, you are alone and there are no monitoring devices in the room."*

"Did you hear my conversation with Luciel?" Ali asked.

"The transmitter can pick up any sounds within a ten-meter radius."

"Then you heard what he said about Rachel," Ali said, "that she might not be here."

"I'm not an idiot," Raven said caustically. *"I have always been aware of the possibility that Rachel is already dead. But you'll have to meet the other people being held to find out for sure."* There was a short silence, and Ali wondered if Raven had signed off before she heard the girl's voice again. *"Are you OK?"*

"I can't believe you'd be concerned," Ali told her. There was a longer silence. This time Ali knew Raven was still there and she waited for the reply, wondering what the girl would come out with this time. But Raven's answer, when it finally came, surprised her. *"I don't like the sound of that lab,"* she said. *"I wouldn't like to be in your place."*

"I'm afraid," Ali admitted, disarmed by Raven's unexpected empathy.

"I'll be in constant contact," Raven told her, adding ironically, *"I don't know if you'll find that a comfort."*

"If something happens . . . if they start experimenting on me," Ali asked quietly, "will you get me out of here?" She dreaded the answer, wondered if she had asked too much too soon. Raven didn't have her brother's moral code, and even if the loyalty of the group lay with him, she held the sum of the power. It was Raven's support she needed. She didn't expect the younger girl to react with sympathy—that would have been too much to ask. But Raven hadn't exaggerated when she said she didn't like the sound of the lab.

"I'll tell Wraith we should get into position," she said eventually. *"Just in case."*

Kez glanced up in surprise as Raven disengaged herself from the terminal. She had been speaking softly into its audio pickup, too quietly for him to overhear. But now she got up from her chair and stretched her aching muscles. She was still wearing the baggy gray sweater, sweatpants, and thick socks she had slept in; the blanket lay discarded on the floor beside the computer terminal. Kez had left his silent vigil to get dressed, but Raven had been glued to the terminal for the past three hours and had looked up only once to tell him that Ali had arrived at the lab.

Now she stretched her legs to get some feeling back into them, flexing her fingers experimentally.

"Is Wraith back yet?" she asked.

"He came back about an hour ago," Kez told her, easily able to believe that her intense concentration had blocked out her brother's presence. It wasn't as if Wraith had said anything to either of them. "But he went out again, almost right away."

"I see," Raven said and stretched again. "God, I really need a shower."

"Wraith didn't want you to leave the terminal," Kez cautioned her.

"I'm still in contact," Raven told him. "It's harder without the net to rely on, but it can be done." She rubbed her shoulders, wincing a little. "I feel awful," she complained, and glanced back at Kez, "and you look worse."

"Wraith's really angry," he said, looking down at the ground.

"He'll get over it—relax," Raven advised. "I've spoken to Ali," she added.

"Is she OK?" Kez asked guiltily.

"She seems to be." Raven wrinkled her nose. "But she wants to be sure that we can break her out if we need to. We'd better get moving. When Wraith gets back tell him to get ready to leave. I'll call the Countess and make sure our transport's ready."

"Why can't *you* tell Wraith?" Kez protested, wary of speaking to the ganger in his current mood.

"Because I'm going to take a shower," Raven said definitively and left the room.

The scientists came not long after Ali had spoken to Raven. The two Hexes hadn't had much to say to each other, their brief rapport had been too tenuous for that. But Ali did find it comforting to think that Raven was monitoring her over the transceiver link, even though that didn't help much when she was confronted with the reality of the scientists.

In actual fact the examination wasn't that different from the check-ups her doctor gave her, although it was a little more extensive. She was examined by a woman scientist in a spotless white lab coat wearing a face mask and thin transparent gloves over her hands, while another woman took down details on paper. Obviously the CPS weren't risking the chance of a Hex getting linked up to a computer. Two regular CPS operatives, without lab coats, stood guard outside the door while Ali was examined. It took over an hour for the scientists to get all the results they needed, linking Ali up to most of the scanners in the room to perform some of the more complex tests.

Finally the woman who had been running tests on Ali stepped back and went to look at her companion's clipboard.

"That's the lot, isn't it?" she said, in an undertone.

"Everything," the second scientist replied. "I'd better take these results to be processed. Once we have the confirmation of the genetic scan, we can send out the notification of death to the family."

"Fine." The first scientist nodded, then she looked back at Ali and addressed her as if she was an imbecile, enunciating every syllable: "We have finished examining you," she said. "Meals will be brought to you twice a day. You may interact with the other test subjects if you wish. There is a clearly signed washing room, for the use of the subjects on this corridor, three doors away from this room. We will return when it is time for your second series of tests.

If you are obedient and not obstructive you will be treated well."
Then both scientists left the room, taking Ali's discarded clothes
with them in a sealed plastic bag. Ali could hear the booted footsteps of the guards following them away down the corridor.

Once they had gone she reached up to touch the white ear-stud
in her right ear. It had been concealed by her hair for most of the
examination, but the few times when it must have been seen the
scientist had paid no attention. She had seemed reluctant even to
look at Ali, plainly considering her on a par with an unpleasant
micro-virus she had been ordered to test. It was a new experience for the spoiled rich kid from Belgravia, and one that Ali was
anxious to forget.

Walking to the door of the room, she looked out at the corridor. It was plain and white, stretching for quite a long way. No
one was visible in either direction and Ali left the room cautiously.
She could see doors set into the walls at regular intervals. One had
a sign on it marked *Washing Room.* At one end of the corridor was
an elevator; at the other end was a set of double doors with large
panes of shatterproof glass set into them. Ali walked toward the
end of the corridor with the doors in it, resisting the urge to look
into the rooms she passed on either side. When she reached the
doors, she pushed them open gingerly. There wasn't much to see.
Another corridor stretched out, again in two directions, double
doors at both ends. Halfway up this second corridor was another
washing room.

Ali felt any desire to explore further leeched out of her by the
featureless, institutionalized atmosphere of the facility. She won-

dered how she would ever find Rachel. But she supposed she had better try. Returning to her own corridor, she walked down to the elevator. There was an unmarked touchpad beside it. Ali didn't have the nerve to press it. Instead she began to methodically work her way down the corridor, looking in each of the rooms. They were all marked with a short code sequence, but the codes didn't seem to be arranged in any order.

At first Ali's curiosity was not indulged. The first three rooms were all empty and apparently unoccupied, not even containing the medical equipment she had found in her own. The fourth was also unoccupied, but the room was full of medical scanners; like the other equipment Ali had seen in the lab they had no computer interface. The bed was unmade and an untouched tray of food lay on the small table. The tray was plastic and divided up into sections; each of which held a puréed substance of different colors. The only utensil was a metal spoon. It was the most unappetizing meal Ali had ever seen; she wasn't surprised that it had been left uneaten. Moving on she looked through the window of the next room.

A child lay unconscious on the bed, linked up to the machines that surrounded it. Tubes were connected to his mouth and nose, and monitors were attached to his wrists and forehead. He didn't look more than six or seven years old. Going into the room to look at him more closely, Ali felt as if she was desecrating a tomb, one of the cemeteries that still existed in parts of Europe, unusable for farmland or industrial expansion. The boy was like the living dead, lying in the midst of a mass of machinery, like a fly in the web of a mechanical spider.

She heard footsteps behind her as someone else entered the room and she turned to see Luciel, meeting his shadowed eyes contritely.

"This is why I didn't want you to look around, just yet," he told her. "It's hard to take, at first."

"Are a lot of people like this?" Ali asked.

"Some," Luciel replied. "Not everyone's as bad as this, though." He bit his lips before adding: "A few are worse."

"What could be worse than this?" Ali asked in horror and realized almost instantaneously that she didn't want to know.

"We don't talk about it," Luciel said. Not looking at the boy on the bed, he headed out of the room. Ali followed him and waited as he closed the door behind them.

"What's his name?" she asked.

"I'm not sure." Luciel shrugged. "Does it matter? Jack or Jesse, something like that. He used to cry at night and he wet the bed. And he was always asking questions."

"Don't you care?" Ali asked incredulously, and she felt like Wraith.

"I don't know." Luciel met her eyes unashamedly. "Is it wrong to be glad it's not me?"

"I'm not sure." Ali thought for a while, leaning up against the corridor wall. "I think I'd feel the same way. But . . . I have a friend, a sort of friend, who said that the reason Hexes didn't help each other was that anyone clever enough to escape the CPS wouldn't care about someone who got caught. I was angry with her for thinking that way, because she only cares about herself."

"Was she a Hex?" Luciel asked softly, checking to see that they weren't being overheard.

"Yes," whispered Ali, wondering if Raven was listening, and what the girl would say later if she was.

"And she hasn't been caught?" Luciel asked, even more quietly if it was possible.

"No," Ali replied.

"Then maybe she was right to think that way," Luciel said. "I didn't and I was caught. If it would have changed anything I'd have been as selfish as I could."

Ali didn't say anything, but inwardly she resolved that she wouldn't be leaving the lab alone, even if she didn't manage to find Rachel. Now that she'd seen two other inmates, she felt guilty at the thought of leaving without them. She realized what Wraith had meant about the callousness of the experimentation; just a few hours in the lab had convinced her that he was right. But the thought of Rachel recalled her to the fact that she had a mission.

When Ali reminded Luciel that she wanted to find someone, he was perfectly willing to help.

"It's not as if there's anything else to do here," he pointed out. "There's nothing to read, and nothing to see. We don't get access to vidscreens, and God forbid that we should even *look* at a computer terminal."

"Do you know if there's a main computer control room?" Ali asked as casually as she could.

"I guess there must be," Luciel replied, puzzled. "But if there is, we'd never get the chance to see it."

"I guess not," Ali agreed. Looking down the long corridor, she felt apprehensive. "How many people are there here?"

"Hundreds, I think," Luciel said, adding: "But people keep dying, and they bring in new Hexes all the time. Mostly kids."

"Is everyone a Hex?" Ali asked, remembering Raven's insistence that the CPS had got it wrong. "Definitely a Hex?"

"I guess so," Luciel said. "No one who comes here is ever sent back home again, anyhow."

When Wraith returned to the hotel suite Kez was packing up the electronic equipment.

"What are you doing?" he asked immediately. "Where's Raven?"

"She's spoken to Ali," Kez said, trying to choose the response least likely to annoy Wraith. "She thinks it's time to get closer to the lab; Ali wants us to be ready to break in if she gets into any trouble."

"I can't believe that Raven would care about that," Wraith said sarcastically. "Or that you do, come to think of it."

"I don't want anything to happen to Ali," Kez said, carefully packing up the homemade explosives.

"You surprise me," Wraith said coldly and Kez felt a sudden flash of anger. He felt that Wraith was treating him unfairly, especially considering that he had lied for him, so he could find his sister.

"Why do I surprise you?" he asked, "You told Raven you'd never known anyone with fewer morals, so how can you be surprised that I lied to you?"

Wraith met Kez's eyes.

"Maybe because I wanted to trust you," he said. "I tend to automatically suspect Raven's advice because I don't understand her motivations. But I thought I did understand you."

"Because there isn't much to understand?" Kez asked.

"Because you're not so different from the gangers I knew in Denver," Wraith told him. He studied Kez for a while. "I can guess why you lied, Kez, and this time I'll forget it. But don't do it again. I have to be able to trust someone, and this group is so mismatched that it really has to be you."

"Does that mean you want the group to stay together?" Kez asked, considering how such an intention would affect him.

"Perhaps, if we're successful in breaking Rachel and Ali out of the lab."

"OK, then." Kez had made his decision. "You can trust me."

Wraith nodded, although he still wasn't sure if he could believe Kez's promise. He began crating up the rest of the gear they would need to take with them, deliberately ignoring Raven's heaps of lasdisks. Now that Ali was inside the lab the operation had become too serious for his sister's eccentricity.

Raven emerged from her room before he was finished, obviously ready to leave. She didn't look very different from when she had first arrived in the gangland slum district. But instead of her jacket she was carrying a long coat, one of her more recent acquisitions, which she began to load with some of the smaller and more complex pieces of electrical equipment.

"The Countess has transport and muscle backup waiting," she

told Wraith. "We'll need a combat weapon of some kind for Kez."

"Can you use a gun?" Wraith asked the boy and Kez shrugged. "I'm better with a knife."

"Too risky," Raven said, echoing Wraith's unspoken thoughts. "You won't get close enough to use it."

"I'll show you how to operate a laser pistol," Wraith said. "It sights automatically and it burns rather than blasts."

"Is that what you carry?" Kez asked the ganger and Raven grinned.

"It's generally regarded as a breach of etiquette to ask a ganger that question," she informed him.

"Since we're going in on this raid together, it's best to know what kind of firepower each of us has," Wraith pointed out. "I have been carrying a laser pistol but I think breaking into the lab will require something heavier. I'll get that from the Countess and you can use my pistol."

"What about Raven?" Kez asked curiously, eyeing the deep inner pockets of the girl's long coat, into which her tools had disappeared.

"Keep guessing," she told him, with a sideways glance at Wraith. Kez looked inquiringly at the ganger.

"I don't even know if she carries weapons," he said. "Is there anything you want from the Countess, Raven?"

"If there is, I'll deal with it myself," she said. "But don't worry about how I'll defend myself, Wraith. This isn't the first time I've been part of this kind of operation." She smiled slightly, but didn't say anything more, and neither Wraith nor Kez asked anything else.

They left the hotel suite half an hour after Wraith's return, once the skimmer was loaded with what they would need to attack the lab. Raven dealt with checking out of the Stratos, paying from one of the immense credit balances she had persuaded a bank to give her. She also arranged to have her disk collection packaged up and sent to Bob Tarrell, with the compliments of AdAstra. Wraith had refused to take it with them and Raven, now that she was no longer suffering from the monotony of the search, didn't really feel the need to surround herself with high-decibel rock music.

However, she did retain a few disks, so that as the skimmer wound its way down through the levels of the city, a pounding backbeat filled the vehicle. Raven drove fast, bringing back memories for Kez of the sickening trip she had sent the flitter on when he first encountered her. Wraith sat in a grim silence, mentally checking and rechecking his plans. He was very aware of the fact that Ali was in Kalden's laboratory and felt that it was his responsibility to get her out again. Too many people had died already for him to sacrifice Ali for a chance to save Rachel.

Ali had begun to dread finding Rachel. It had been made clear to her that anyone who'd been in the lab for over a year was unlikely to be found undamaged. And some of the experiments being performed in the lab were horrific. Luciel had actually been one of the luckier ones. The CPS scientists had used their imaginations to the utmost when devising experiments to test the capabilities of the child Hexes brought into the lab. On Ali's floor alone there seemed to be endless corridors of test subjects and she had no idea what might lie above or below. Luciel had informed her that the elevator was restricted to laboratory staff and had no more idea than her of the actual size of the facility.

Ali hadn't found Rachel among the children, and any kind of methodical search was proving difficult. She had first ventured out of her room when the others were having the first of the two meals of the day, served at midmorning. But before long the silent corridors were very different. The younger children seemed relentlessly hyperactive and antisocial, racing down the corridors and banging into anyone who got in their way. Then a lot of the older ones were unwilling even to speak to Luciel, let alone Ali, and there were many who were unable to speak. They were forced to progress slowly and Ali was grateful that Luciel had agreed to help her, since most of the other test subjects regarded her with suspicion. Her companion explained it as jealousy, that she hadn't been subjected to the methods of the scientists' endless quest for knowledge. His bruised arms and jerky, uncertain movements were almost a badge of honor in the facility and Ali discovered that he had been there longer than most people.

"Two and a half years," he told her with resignation. "I think my immune system is becoming resistant to the drugs they keep testing on me. A lot of the others died from the course of injections."

"If you've been here that long you must have seen Rachel brought in," Ali said and Luciel sighed.

"I don't notice everyone," he said. "It's only recently I've been trying to meet new inmates, and I don't always realize when they're bringing in someone new. Besides there could be other floors full of us. Believe me, Ali, if I knew anything about your friend I'd tell you."

"I know," Ali said, trusting him absolutely. Luciel was trying hard to help her find Rachel. Since their search of the corridors was proving impossible, he took her to meet other people who might know when the girl had been brought in and if she was still there.

The first person he took her to find was, he explained, difficult to deal with. But he had been at the lab nearly as long as Luciel and might know something about Rachel. Thomas's initial reaction to Ali's presence was not positive.

"What do you want?" he asked gruffly, when Luciel knocked at the open door of his room. He was a stocky teenager, at least as old as Ali, built like a wrestler. But he didn't stand up to greet them, watching suspiciously from where he sat on his bed. His thick, muscular frame was concealed by what appeared to be body armor strapped to his arms and legs. Smooth white metal enclosed his shins and ankles in a viselike grip, similar devices were attached to his forearms and wrists, two more ringed his torso and encircled his neck. He looked almost robotic, so thoroughly encased in metal. Thomas saw her looking and glared.

"What are you staring at?" he demanded and got to his feet. His movements were heavy and ponderous and there was a mechanical purr from the devices strapped to his legs.

"Calm down, Tom," Luciel said placatingly. "Ali's only just arrived. She's trying to find a friend of hers, a little girl." He spoke quickly, as if to avert sudden violence, and the ferocious expression on Thomas's face gradually smoothed out.

"Don't stare at me," he told Ali, who flushed, retreating a little behind Luciel.

"Sorry," she mumbled uncomfortably.

"Just wait till they start taking you apart," Thomas told her roughly. "You won't be looking so cool then." He clenched a fist, enclosed in a metal mesh, and electronics hummed audibly. "I *hate* that noise," he told her fiercely. "I try to lie still at night so I won't have to hear it. They've made it so I don't even want to move anymore, but when they come to check on me I have to. They take me up in the elevator and make me walk round a room while they watch me. Do you know what that feels like?"

"I'm sorry," Ali said again, but couldn't quell the flood of bitterness emanating from Tom.

"I used to play basketball at school," he told her. "I was gonna be a professional. Not much chance of that now, is there?"

"I was going to be a scientist," Luciel said quietly and Ali shivered.

"I wanted to be a holovid director," she said, realizing that, even if she did escape from the lab, that would never happen now.

They all stood still, looking at each other. Thomas was the first to break the silence.

"What was that you were saying earlier?" he asked Luciel.

"Oh." Luciel came back to earth abruptly. "Ali's looking for a friend, a girl named Rachel. She was captured by the CPS about a year and a half ago. We were hoping you might remember someone like that coming into the lab."

"What does she look like?" Tom asked and Ali tried to visualize the picture Wraith had shown her.

"Dark brown hair in a short bob, brown eyes, light brown skin, a big smile," she recited.

"If she was brought here she wouldn't be smiling long," Tom said and then shook his head. "No, I don't remember her. But wasn't it about then that they were doing memory experiments?" He looked at Luciel rather than at Ali and the other boy's eyes clouded.

"It might have been," he said. "I find it hard to keep track of time sometimes."

"What were the memory experiments?" Ali asked, with an ominous feeling.

"They only went on for a couple of months," Tom told her. "They were abandoned because almost everyone who was experimented on died." Ali blanched and Luciel shot a warning look at Thomas, taking up the narrative himself.

"They linked up a group of kids to a computer database," he said, "with electrodes so they couldn't disengage themselves, and ran it twenty-four hours a day." He thought for a second. "I think the idea was to find out how much information a Hex could hold in their head, since a lot of us have eidetic memories."

"What happened?" Ali managed to ask, finding her voice again.

"Most people did die, I'm afraid," Luciel admitted, more gently than his friend had. "But two or three are still around—one of them might be able to tell you if Rachel was on the project."

"You're kidding yourself," Tom told him, raising his voice a little to cover the drone of machinery as he moved back to his bed. "None of those flakes will be telling you anything."

"Why not?" Ali asked. Luciel wouldn't look at her and she turned back to Tom.

"They're complete null-brainers," he said callously. "Esther sits in her room dribbling and playing with her food, Mikhail's covered in more machinery than I am, and Revenge has to be strapped to her bed with restraints because otherwise she tries to claw your eyes out." He paused to see how his words had affected Ali and seemed satisfied with her expression because he continued: "None of them'll tell you anything because they won't tolerate anyone anywhere near 'em, and even if they were willing to, their brains are too fritzed to remember what happened yesterday, let alone the name of some girl who might not even have been sent here in the first place."

"I'm sorry, Ali," Luciel said softly. "Tom's right. If Rachel was part of those experiments, she's lucky to be dead."

8

HELL IS MURKY

Kez had a feeling of déjà vu as the skimmer coasted along the last bridge and came to rest near the spur of walkway that led to the Countess's center of operations, where she traded information and abilities. Kez moved to unfasten his seat belt but Wraith forestalled him.

"Wait," he said. "Someone should stay and guard the skimmer. We need this stuff."

"OK," Kez said, trying hard not to remember what had been the outcome of his last attempt at watching a vehicle for Wraith. "But what can I do if someone does try to steal it?"

"Don't confront them," Raven said. "They won't be able to unlock the doors anyway." She got out of the driver's seat and Wraith followed her example. Sitting in the front of the vehicle, Kez felt a little abandoned as they set off toward the building together. But, before they were completely out of sight, Raven turned and waved. Wraith, in what appeared to be a demonstration of trust, didn't look back at all.

This time Wraith wasn't challenged as he approached the building. When he entered, it looked like it hadn't changed at all since his last visit. However, only one of the two guards from last time, the woman, stood in front of the door which led upstairs.

"Names and business," she demanded, although her eyes showed recognition as she glanced at Wraith.

"Wraith and Raven," the ganger said, addressing the vidcom screen on the wall beside the guard. "The Countess knows my business already."

"You may come up," the voice spoke out of the wall unit. "Leave your weapons behind."

"OK," Wraith agreed, obediently handing over his laser pistol and one of his knives. The guard accepted them and turned expectantly to Raven.

"No," Raven told her and the guard shifted her grip on the combat rifle she carried.

"Do you have some reason for objecting?" the Countess asked from the vidcom, although the screen was still blacked out.

"Just caution," Raven told her, with a shrug. "If I have to disarm, I'd rather stay down here."

"In some cases I am willing to make exceptions," the Countess said dryly, "and I am willing to make one for you. But any trouble and you won't know what hit you."

"I scan," Raven said, slipping into the gangland argot that seemed to overtake her in the slums.

"Go ahead," the guard said, with a sour look at Raven, stepping aside for them to pass by.

Wraith was curious to see how his sister would react to the disorienting stairway with its mirror shielding, and noticed her expression of distaste as she ascended beside him. She walked as slowly and carefully as he did, disliking the loss of balance that the multiple reflections engendered.

"Effective, isn't it?" he said, and she gave him a sideways glance.

"Narcissistic," she said. "But I'd like to know what's behind it. Shielding like this could conceal anything, motion sensors, monitors, transmitters, maybe a few explosives just in case." Her cold smile was multiplied in every direction. "It seems as if you've found a good contact, though."

"I hope so," Wraith replied as they reached the top of the stairs and the mirrored wall slid away.

The Countess was waiting for them, watching with interest as they entered. Raven's dark eyes flickered over the screens and terminals that filled the room before coming to rest on the woman herself with the intensity that often alarmed people. The Countess returned her gaze speculatively.

"You must be a technician as well as a hacker, if you could guess all that about my shielding," she said. "Is that why you wouldn't give up your weapons?"

"Good guess," Raven replied, with a grin. "I'm not biting."

"I don't like customized weaponry," the Countess told her

matter-of-factly. "Always lets you down when you really need it. Makes me think it's a bad idea to tinker with it."

"I don't tinker," Raven said in annoyance, stung into a rejoinder. The Countess's expression brightened and Raven narrowed her eyes in response, disliking the way she was being manipulated.

"Your transport's ready, Wraith," the Countess continued. "I'll have it brought into the building. I've got muscle for you as well but the main question is where you want to take them. You originally contacted me to locate your sister's adoptive parents and you claimed then you weren't planning a retrieval. Since I ascertained the whereabouts of the Hollis family, you have bought some heavy artillery and now you want muscle as well. I doubt that you are intending to break into the Hollises' apartment with quite that much firepower."

"Rachel wasn't at the apartment," Wraith admitted cautiously, keeping an eye on Raven. "I want to retrieve her from the place she is now."

"Which is?" The Countess waited, her stance making it clear that no further business could be done without an answer.

"A laboratory run by the CPS," Raven said suddenly.

"Then she's a Hex," the Countess stated definitively.

"It would appear so," Raven agreed, not entirely willing to concede the point.

"And what about you?" the Countess asked. "Your brother told me on our first meeting that you were a hacker. Are you a Hex as well?"

"If I was I would hardly admit it," Raven pointed out.

"I imagine not," the Countess agreed. "And it would be bad for business if my clients lost faith in my discretion." She waited for Raven's nod of assent before continuing. "However, this development does entail that your backup is equally discreet. That means a higher fee and I can't guarantee they'll agree to this kind of work. Not all of my contacts would be sanguine about breaking into a CPS facility to rescue a Hex."

Ali was lying on the hard hospital bed trying to think. Ever since she had parted from Luciel she had been trying to work out what to do and how Rachel's death would affect the group. But her mind had been a confusion of impressions and ideas, and thinking was difficult in the abattoir-like laboratory. She felt almost able to see the mutilated children behind the walls in the rooms on her corridor, the other corridors on that floor, and all the others who had ever occupied the laboratory, no matter how briefly.

On the small table lay the remains of the food tray that had been brought to her late that afternoon. Two uniformed operatives had wheeled trolleys down the hallway, ordering children out of their rooms to collect their trays. A scientist, following behind, had adjusted the intravenous feeding-tubes of those confined to their beds. Ali had accepted her tray obediently, but hadn't been able to stomach more than a few mouthfuls of the tasteless substances that passed for food.

With a sigh, Ali sat up. She was getting nowhere trying to work this out on her own. Cautiously, almost furtively she moved to the door of her room on silent bare feet. There was no one outside.

She shut the door, wishing there was some way to cover the see-through opening, and returned to the bed. This time she lay on her stomach so no one looking in would be able to see her face. Then, hoping that this would work, she whispered:

"Raven?"

There was no answer. Ali felt like crying. Digging her nails hard into the palms of her hands, using the pain to block out her despair, she tried again. It was almost like praying, she thought hysterically, as she whispered Raven's name into the silence of her room. Trying to contact someone who might not be listening.

"Raven, can you hear me?" Ali was losing hope. "Raven, if you're there, please answer me . . . please . . ."

"I can hear you. What's happening?" a cool voice answered and Ali felt almost numb with relief.

"I need to talk to you," she said quickly. "A lot's happened."

"I'm here," Raven told her, *"and there's nothing that requires my immediate attention elsewhere. So, why do you feel this sudden need for conversation?"*

"It's horrible here," Ali said, but strangely, the sound of Raven's voice, unchanged and slightly sarcastic, was comforting. It reassured her that there was a world outside the laboratory and that she was still in contact with it.

"What do you mean by 'horrible'?" Raven asked slowly.

"The scientists have been performing the most gruesome experiments on people," Ali said. "There's a boy who's had all his nerves destroyed. He can only move by sending electrical impulses to the machinery they've strapped around his body, and Luciel gets injected with drugs all the time, to try to block the parts of his brain that make him a Hex, and. . ."

"Cool it, Ali," Raven said suddenly. *"You sound hysterical. Get it together."*

"Don't tell me that," Ali gasped. "You're not the one who's stuck here. How can I be calm? They could be coming to get me any time!"

"They haven't even processed your test results yet," Raven said firmly.

"How do you know that?" Ali demanded. "I thought you couldn't even contact the computer system here."

"I still can't," Raven said. *"But I listened in while you were examined this morning, and the scientists said that when your results had been processed a death certificate would be sent to your father. Well, he hasn't been notified yet—I've checked his terminal— and even when he has been you have at least one more set of tests to go."* She waited for a while for Ali to regain control of herself. *"Now, are you calm?"* she asked.

"I'm calm," Ali replied, with a little irritation. "Now will you listen to me?"

"I'm listening," Raven said with exaggerated patience and Ali launched into an account of the day's events.

Raven listened in silence for a while—at least Ali presumed she was still listening—but when it came to the reference to memory experiments she interrupted, insisting that Ali recount the conversation in more detail. Unwillingly, Ali told her everything that Tom had said about the only survivors of the experiments. When she had finished there was a long silence.

"Are you still there?" she asked, somewhat dubiously.

"Yes, I'm still here," Raven replied. *"Shut up and let me think."*

"OK, OK," Ali told her and waited.

"What were their names?" Raven said eventually.

"The kids in the memory experiments?" Ali asked. "I told you that."

"Tell me again," Raven insisted. *"Their names."*

"I think Tom said they were called Mikhail, Esther, and Revenge," Ali said. "I can check with him, though."

"No, there's no need," Raven said. *"But I want you to try and see them."*

"It won't do any good," Ali protested. "Luciel agreed with Tom—they wouldn't remember anything about Rachel."

"Ali, go and see them," Raven ordered.

"Why?" Ali objected.

"Because I have a . . . a hunch," Raven said, almost uncertainly. *"Look, Ali, just do it, OK?"*

"What's your hunch?" Ali asked, but Raven was obdurate.

"I can't tell you, not yet," she insisted. *"But see them as soon as you can. I'll be listening in."*

Wraith and Kez were in the gigantic foyer of the Countess's building, attempting to load the customized flitter that the Countess had provided them with. It was large enough to hold six people as well as the equipment they would need. But the loading was proving difficult as they were forced to work around Raven, who had already seated herself in the back of the vehicle and alternated between staring into space and suddenly turning to glare at them when they inadvertently interrupted her. Wraith was also trying to keep a look out for the backup the Countess had arranged for them. She had agreed to provide them with three of her own guards, although the price had been high, but had only said that they would be available shortly.

Wraith was keen to get moving. He wanted to break into the laboratory as soon as possible, ending the anxiety he felt for Ali as well as Rachel. But Raven, despite her suggestion that they get into position, had refused to provide him with any progress reports on her connection with Ali. He loaded the last case of munitions into the back of the flitter, stacking it carefully so it wouldn't come loose when they took off. Raven was drumming her fingers impatiently on another case, no longer locked into her transceiver link. When he had finished checking the gear, he crossed to sit opposite her.

"How's it going?" he asked.

"It's difficult to keep the link without access to the net," she told him. "Where's Kez?"

"Just outside," he replied. "Do you need him?"

"Not yet." Raven was frowning. "But he'll have to pilot the flitter, unless one of the people you've hired can. If there's an emergency I might not be able to and you certainly can't."

Wraith ignored the aspersion.

"What has Ali said?" he asked. "Has she found Rachel?"

"Not yet." Raven gave him an odd look. "Don't ask me anything more, Wraith. I'm trying to think."

Wraith gave up the attempt to get anything out of Raven and

left the flitter. Kez was outside, looking almost ready to run. In front of him stood three men, all in blue and gold gang colors, looking at him rather contemptuously. As Wraith appeared, the tallest turned to look at him.

"You're Wraith?" he asked belligerently.

"Yes," Wraith said coolly, adopting a confident stance; he could sense that this was going to be difficult.

"Melek," the ganger told him, then gestured to his two companions. "They're Finn and Jeeva." Finn only jerked his head at Wraith, but Jeeva took his hand in a firm grip. Wraith took a moment to consider his new companions. They were dressed much as the Countess's other guards, but gang motifs glared from their militaristic clothing and all three had braided hair dyed a dark blue and strung with metallic beads.

"This should be a simple retrieval operation," Wraith said, watching the gangers closely for any negative reaction. "But the place we're going up against will probably have some heavy security."

"The Countess said you're breaking into a government lab," Melek said. "No matter what kind of weaponry you're packing, four of us won't be enough people for that kind of op. The security will be too heavy." He paused for a moment before adding: "But I can bring some more people in . . ."

"No." Wraith cut him off and saw Melek's immediate glare echoed by his companions. He couldn't back down; the last thing he wanted was to have his operation taken over by gangers, but he didn't want to antagonize the people he would have to work with either. While he was considering his next move, Kez provided a distraction.

"What about me?" he demanded. "I'll be there too."

"Keep out of this, kid," Melek drawled dismissively, but Finn was more vocal.

"Stick to what you know," he sneered, looking Kez over deliberately. "*You* couldn't use our kind of weaponry." He grinned and Kez flushed angrily, his fists clenching.

"Leave it, Kez," Wraith warned, not wanting to get into a confrontation on this subject. In all honesty, he had his own doubts about Kez's presence. He trusted the boy, but Kez had no experience at this kind of operation, and he couldn't blame the gangers for considering him a liability.

Unfortunately, Kez looked angry enough to press the issue and Wraith tried to change tack by switching back to the original discussion.

"Bringing more people in would be a mistake," he said swiftly. "I don't plan to launch a full-scale attack on the place. It'd take an army to succeed that way. I want to make a low-level run, compromising the outer perimeter of security. Once we're in we'll hack into the security system to nullify any additional threat."

"You're taking a risk," Melek said dubiously. "It'd take an *electric* hacker to break into a strange system and screw with it before we're burned by security."

"Raven can do it," Wraith assured them, but Finn was already shaking his head.

"No way we should run with this, till we've seen what he's

got, Mel," he said brusquely. "I'm not getting flatlined because his hacker screwed up, and we couldn't pull out in time."

"I'll go with that," the other ganger added and Melek turned to Wraith with a mocking smile.

"You heard my brothers," he challenged. "We want to see what your hacker's got before we go with you."

"That wasn't the deal," Wraith objected.

"It is now," Melek told him, and waited.

The sound of raised voices distracted Raven; it was a niggling itch in the back of her head that disrupted her already fragile connection with Ali's transceiver. Annoyed at the reminder that her abilities were not as far-ranging as she might wish, she abandoned the link and got to her feet, emerging from the flitter just in time to hear Melek declare the change in plans.

She noticed with satisfaction that Kez blanched as she jumped down from the vehicle to join the group. She was in a sufficiently bad mood to welcome an argument and it seemed that one was in the cards. Ignoring the presence of the strangers she spoke directly to Wraith.

"How long are we going to hang about here?" she demanded. "I want us to be in position by 1900 this evening. Let's get going."

"We may have a problem here, Raven . . . ," Wraith began slowly but was interrupted.

"This is your hacker?" Melek demanded incredulously, turning to look Raven over carefully. Raven returned the look, stare for stare, and registered at the back of her mind that both Wraith and

Kez took a step backward as the tension built. She was always ready for a confrontation. Wary of the fact that she had no reputation in England, she had prepared herself for this. The black-eyed stare that Ali had found so disconcerting was not an untried tactic, and it was one with a high success rate. Raven didn't just look at the ganger, she looked *through* him. And as her gaze washed over him like ice-cold water she filled it with everything she had discovered about him over the network. The gangers were hardly inconspicuous and all three had criminal records of impressive length; another conviction would be enough to get any of them a long custody sentence. But Raven had pulled out more data than that. She knew about their drug habits, their squats, she even knew about their families, and she held that knowledge in her eyes as she looked at them. She heard Finn and Jeeva mirror Wraith and Kez's retreat, stepping away from that stare. But she held Melek's gaze, pressing for that extra advantage, waiting for the right psychological moment.

Then it came, a brief flicker, and the ganger's gaze left hers, unable to hold it any longer. Raven allowed herself a slight smile before she spoke.

"I'm the hacker," she agreed. "And you need have *no* doubts about my abilities." She let the statement hang in the air, waiting for their response. Finn's came first, a muttered aside to Jeeva:

"Freakin' skitzo . . ."

But Melek was more controlled, knowing that he had to preserve his confidence or lose the respect of his subordinates.

"You're confident enough," he shrugged. "But that don't count for nothing when the Seccies are on your tail."

"I'm confident with reason," Raven said coldly. Then, having displayed enough ice to alarm them, she allowed herself to relax. "And I'm good enough to wipe you from the Seccie records. . . ." She grinned at their widened eyes. "That's the payoff," she added. "As well as the creds, I'll clean you off the system. Make you invisible."

She didn't wait for Melek's nod. Agreement was a foregone conclusion, the offer irresistible. As the gangers shook hands with Wraith to clinch the deal, she headed for the flitter's controls. Kez seated himself beside her in the front.

"You're not scared of anything, are you?" he said in a low voice. Raven glanced at him as she powered up the craft. She could have told him how she felt about where they were heading, the reasons why she didn't like to think about the laboratory where Ali was trapped. Her fingers flew over the computer unit that formed part of the control panel, her mind sinking into the technology as she renewed the link with Ali.

"No, I'm not," she lied.

Ali felt sick.

Luciel had been unwilling to show her the three surviving victims of the memory experiments but she had insisted, impelled by Raven's insistence that it was important for her to locate them. Now she believed that Luciel had been right and Raven wrong. These children would not be able to tell her anything about Rachel.

Tom had joined them as well, although he was as morose as ever. Ali suspected he had agreed to accompany them simply because she provided a diversion. But she was relieved that he had chosen to come. The three survivors were housed on another floor of the facility and it was obvious that Luciel became increasingly nervous the further away from his room he was. The elevator had two panels. One with option settings for three floors, the other covered with a metal plate with a keylock rather than a computer-coded locking device. Tom had noticed her looking and shrugged.

"Access to the rest of the facility is restricted," he told her. "And they don't want to risk any of us getting computer access. That's why they use outdated recording methods most of the time. You've probably noticed that they take down test results on paper."

Ali had nodded, thinking silently that the computer room—that Raven had claimed existed—was probably on one of those restricted floors. The floor the elevator took them to was almost identical to the one they had left. The only real difference was the nature of the test subjects. Almost all of them were confined to their beds, either because they were incapable of moving, or because they were held there by heavy restraints. Tom led them to the end of the first corridor and opened a door, walking with the minimum of movement and obviously self-conscious about the jerky machine-enhanced reactions of his body.

Once inside, both Luciel and Ali had paused, frozen in place as they looked at the figure lying on the bed. Tom regarded them with a curious satisfaction at their reaction. He had been right when he spoke of Mikhail being covered in more machinery than him. The boy on the bed lay in the midst of a tangle of cables and medical equipment. He was naked, except for a pair of shorts, and Ali could see that the machinery extended further. Metal seemed to have been welded to his skin, giving him an inhuman appearance. And from the flesh that survived, stretched tight over the bones of the skeletal figure, came the unmistakable stench of corruption. The boy was literally rotting away. As she stared in fascinated horror, her eyes met Mikhail's and she realized with shock that his expression was not vacant. Within that living corpse, he was still, against all reason, horribly aware.

Her stomach heaved and she turned quickly, fumbling for the door and escaping into the corridor. Taking deep breaths she sank to the floor, half retching, half sobbing. As her body shook in paroxysms of fear she heard a quiet voice buzz in her ear.

"What happened?"

She couldn't speak as she continued to gasp for breath and Raven's voice took on an edge of what might have been alarm as she continued:

"Ali, your heart rate's gone right up—you're going into shock. Get a hold of yourself and tell me what happened."

"Raven." Ali bent her head and murmured the words into her folded arms. "I saw . . . I saw one of the test subjects for the memory experiments. . . . It was, it was so horrible. . . ." She cut herself off abruptly as Tom and Luciel emerged from the room. Luciel bent to help her to her feet.

"Are you OK?" he asked with concern.

"I think so," she said shakily.

"Then you want to go on?" Tom asked and grimaced a little in response to her nod. "It won't do any good," he said. "We asked

Mikhail about your friend. He didn't tell us anything. He doesn't speak anymore."

"This is pointless, Ali." Luciel looked distressed. "The other two won't be able to tell us anything either. Mikhail won't talk, Esther can't, and Revenge is incomprehensible."

Ali hesitated and heard Raven speak softly into her ear:

"Say you want to go on."

She sighed, wondering how the others would react if she told them she heard voices in her head telling her to continue. Rejecting the impulse she said only:

"I want to see them." Tom and Luciel exchanged glances, but set off again in search of the next patient.

If the gangers hadn't known that Raven was a Hex when they got into the flitter, they must certainly know by now. Wraith frowned when he realized that Raven was making no attempt to disguise her abilities. But he rationalized that the Countess had assured him they would be discreet, and that he would be trusting these people with their lives anyway. However, Raven's use of her Hex abilities made him uncomfortable. Her preference for working in seclusion meant that he had not exactly been aware of what her connection with computers entailed.

Now he found it slightly alarming to see her sitting in the pilot's seat, one hand resting lightly on the controls, her eyes defocused. The flitter weaved past the buildings at high speed, avoiding the rest of the aerial traffic, but the sight of Raven's blank eyes made him tight with tension. The gangers seemed to be similarly affected, if the care with which they had fastened themselves into the vehicle was any indication. The only person who seemed at ease was Kez, who hadn't fastened his own belt, and was grinning with every evidence of enjoyment at the high speeds the flitter was attaining. His absence of alarm seemed to increase his status in the eyes of the gangers. Wraith leaned forward with a deliberate ease to speak to Raven.

"Can you hear me?" he asked.

"Naturally," she replied somewhat caustically. "But there's a limit to how many things I can do at once. I'm not really in the mood for conversation."

"Are you in contact with Ali?" Wraith said, ignoring her tone.

"Yes."

"If you want to concentrate on your link with her, you needn't pilot as well," Wraith suggested.

"I think I can handle it," Raven said, a shade of amusement in her voice, although her eyes remained blank. "If there's a problem I'll hand over to Kez."

"Very well," Wraith agreed, reflecting to himself that, given Kez's propensity for speeding, the exchange would hardly make much difference. As he sat back he caught Melek's gaze and the ganger gave an almost rueful shrug. Wraith acknowledged it with the barest flicker of his eyes, but he sensed the mood in the flitter become less antagonistic.

The second of the patients was no more communicative than the first. But Ali found herself more able to handle Esther's vacuity than Mikhail's consciousness. The girl was one of the oldest patients. According to Tom she had been in her late teens when admitted and was now in her early twenties. He had added, almost without interest, that test subjects rarely survived that long. Ali wondered if Esther's state could be called surviving. Her mind had been damaged by the experiments, leaving her with the mental abilities of a small child. She smiled lopsidedly at a point somewhere behind their heads as Luciel questioned her, and it was obvious to Ali that there was no way she would be telling them anything about Rachel. Raven obviously concurred. After only a few minutes of questioning Esther, her voice came over the com-link again.

"We're accomplishing nothing here."

Ali tried to conceal her frustration. The presence of the others meant that she couldn't point out to Raven that this had been a useless exercise from the beginning. Instead she turned to Luciel.

"Can you show me the third test subject?" she asked.

"Revenge?" Luciel sighed. "I guess so. I suppose you won't be satisfied until we do."

"Come on then," Tom said gruffly, heading for the door. "Let's get this charade over with."

He led the way down the corridor and through three more sets of doors until he halted before a shut door. He moved to open it and then paused, the hum of his machinery dropping to a low purr as he cautioned Ali:

"Revenge is under permanent restraint because she often becomes violent. If she starts acting up, we had better get out of here. I don't want *them* to turn up and start asking us what we're doing here."

"OK," Ali agreed and Luciel added his assent, obviously equally unwilling to come into contact with the scientists. Tom turned back to the door and pushed it open.

A girl was lying on the bed, metal cuffs holding her wrists to the sides of the bed and a heavy over-blanket buckled tightly over her so she couldn't move her body. She had been sitting as far up the bed as the restraints allowed, leaning back against the pillows. But as the door opened her head snapped round and she fixed them with a piercing stare. She looked more like an old woman than a child. Her features were gaunt and her eyes sunken. Her hands clutched the sides of the bed like claws and her wrists were flecked with blood, lacerated by the cuffs. Her hair would have been waist length if it was brushed, but instead it was matted around her head in a dirty mess. Her skin was grimy, and there was dried blood from the scratches on her face and bruises on her neck. In a facility where everything else was clinically sanitized she seemed incongruous. Looking at her injuries Ali felt convinced they were self-inflicted.

Tom approached the bed hesitantly and the girl focused on him with a fearful intensity, her lips drawing back to show her teeth in an animal snarl. Luciel looked nervous and Ali found herself holding her breath as Tom spoke.

"Revenge?" he said soothingly. "It's Tom. . . . Will you talk to me?"

There was a growl. If the girl had been an animal she would

have flattened her ears; as it was she flinched back, looking as if she would bite if Tom came any closer. Ali jumped when a human voice rasped from Revenge's torn mouth.

"You are poisoned," she hissed. "Infected. Get away from me!" Her voice rose to a scream and both Tom and Luciel retreated. Luciel glanced sideways at Ali.

"You wanted to talk to her," he said. "Good luck."

She wet her lips nervously and prepared to speak, wondering what it was Raven expected of her. But before she could say anything a voice spoke in her ear.

"Relax, Ali," Raven told her. *"Repeat exactly what I say."* Ali couldn't respond, but Raven took her assent as read and began softly: *"Ask her name."*

"What's your name?" Ali said obediently and the cadaverous face turned to regard her.

"I am Revenge," she said, looking through Ali in a way that was eerily familiar.

"Is that a name or a threat?" Raven's voice was chilling.

"Uh . . . is that a name or a threat?" Ali asked uncomfortably.

"It's what I am," Revenge whispered, leaning forward ominously. Ali resisted the urge to flinch back as she added: "There is nothing else. . . ." Her bloodied lips parted in a terrible smile, and Ali found herself staring into the eyes of insanity.

Raven's attention was almost entirely concentrated on the link. Lacking Ali's physical presence, she was blind to what the other girl saw. But the words that came through the link resounded in her ears. She perceived the flow of a thousand streams of data as she searched databases all over Europe, concentrating on one word:

> revenge <

> revenge <

> revenge <

The test subjects in the memory experiments had been linked up to a computer database. Which one? What had it contained? Raven was hardly conscious of Ali transmitting her words as she spoke directly to the shattered figure on the bed.

"Who are you?"

There was no answer, but the transmitter reported a rise in Ali's heart rate. And then Raven heard the girl's voice:

"You speak out of the dark. . . ."

She froze. It was impossible for the girl to know that she was speaking through Ali. Impossible, but her words suggested that, somehow, she *did* know. Raven felt the pressure of that darkness, fought against the urge to throw off her contact with the computer network, and just then one of the myriad tendrils of her awareness caught hold of a piece of information and brought it to her consciousness.

> re-venge {ri'ven(d)3} I. v/t. 1. *et,. a. j-n rächen* (*[up]on* an *dat.*): *to ~ o.s. for s.th.* sich für et. rachen; *to be ~d* a) gerächt sein *od.* werden, b) sich rächen; 2. sich rächen für, vergelten (*upon, on* an *dat.*); II. *s.* 3. Rache *f*: . . . <

The association that had lodged somewhere in Raven's eidetic memory had been located. She focused on the dictionary entry for a heartbeat, an eon in the virtual time of the network. Whatever twisted logic had led the girl through the Germanic association of her name to a deadly statement of intent was lost now. But from a chain of half-formed clues Raven had unraveled the truth. She directed a new message to Ali's comlink and as she spoke she acknowledged the reality of what she had discovered.

"Hello, Rachel."

9

THE MORTAL SWORD

"Rachel?" Ali exclaimed. Luciel and Tom turned to stare at her, but before they could say a word they were interrupted by a raw scream. Revenge had lunged for Ali, fighting to escape the cuffs, her body thrashing with effort.

"Raven! Raven, where are you?" she screamed. The two boys looked baffled. But Ali knew that this was the most rational thing Revenge had said so far.

"We'd better go," Tom urged and Ali looked from him to Revenge, uncertain of what to do.

"Ali, speak to her," Raven ordered. *"Repeat after me . . ."*

Ali listened, memorizing Raven's words. Grabbing Revenge's arms she held her down on the bed and lowered her voice to repeat what she had been told:

"Be still . . . Raven comes . . . wait for her. . . ."

"Yes," Revenge hissed, her eyes burning with anticipation. "Tell her, soon . . . she must come soon, or it will be too late."

Raven blinked. The flitter had reached the edges of London. The towering skyscrapers were thinning out. The concrete jungle continued in a line across the countryside, a tangle of roads curving on top of and around each other, bordered by the towering skyrises. Raven guided the flitter out over the highway, careful not to deviate from her course into the no-fly zone over the agricultural lands. As she did so, she slowly drew her mind back from the computer connection, severing both it and the link with Ali.

She took a breath slowly. She wasn't certain of why she was unwilling to speak. But she doubted that her reticence came from anything so basic as a consideration for Wraith. The fact that Rachel was still alive bound them to their purpose, impelled them to break into the laboratory, but the things that Ali had discovered there made Raven extremely unwilling to move any nearer the reach of the CPS. Her right hand clenched into a fist on the controls and the flitter leaped forward with a lurch, shifting into a higher speed. She refused to accept the fear that threatened to control her. Instead she savored the roar of the wind rushing past them and said without emotion:

"We've found Rachel."

"You have?" Wraith sounded tense and Raven turned to meet his eyes. "Is she . . . How is she?" he asked, trying to preserve his mask of control.

"Her mind has been severely affected by the testing," Raven

said dispassionately. "But she appears to retain some measure of sanity."

"Some measure of sanity?" Wraith looked frozen and Raven heard Kez's soft gasp of distress. She felt distanced from both of them, identifying herself with the three disinterested gangers in the back of the flitter rather than with her anxious brother.

"Be thankful she's not brain-dead or flatlined," she stated. "Her condition is better than I thought it would be."

Kez tried to stretch his cramped muscles and frowned. Large as the flitter was, the passenger seat was not the most comfortable place he'd been, especially after the long flight. The gangers and Wraith had room in the back to stretch out, even with the packing cases. But, cramped as he was, Kez hesitated to join them. Melek had been antagonistic to his presence on the operation and he didn't want to provoke the gangers into making their disapproval more immediately felt. As it was he tried to make himself comfortable in his seat and alternated between dozing and looking out of the window.

The latter of these two alternatives was easier to accomplish. Raven had been obliged to keep below the speed limit, since they didn't want to attract the attention of the Seccies with a cargo of armaments, and had therefore increased the volume of her rock music to painful levels. Kez suspected that this was also a function of her wish to avoid conversation. Wraith was clearly concerned about Rachel's condition and Raven just as obviously wanted to avoid the issue. However, every now and then the music paused as Raven changed disks and Kez took advantage of one of these breaks to engage her attention.

"You're still not piloting manually?"

"As you see." Raven shrugged. Her seat was tilted back and her legs stretched out on top of the bank of controls, only one hand resting lightly on a set of controls to her left.

"What would happen if you fell asleep?"

"I'm not certain," Raven said slowly, and then grinned. "Want to find out?"

"I don't think so." Kez shook his head but he was smiling as well. Raven's good humor relieved a little of his anxiety about what they were doing. "Are you tired, though? If you are I can take over." He made the suggestion a little hesitantly, but Raven didn't seem annoyed by it. She shrugged again.

"I'm OK," she said. "There's not much point in changing places now—we're almost there."

"We are?"

"Look outside," Raven suggested, and Kez turned to the window.

It was almost dusk and it was hard for him to make anything out in the dim half-light. Raven seemed to have left the main roadway, and the lights of the buildings that surrounded it were nowhere to be seen; gone also were the running lights of other flitters. But Raven had kept their own lights on and Kez could catch glimpses of the dark countryside, a town or city in the distance lighting up the sky, and below them the black ribbon of a minor road and the streaks of light as skimmers sped by. Up ahead were the darker masses of hills and Raven gestured toward them.

"That's where the lab is. But, according to the transport database, everything on either side of this road is restricted airspace."

"Isn't there an approach road?" Wraith asked.

"We'd hardly use it if there was," Raven pointed out. "But no, there's nothing indicated." She considered. "I expect there is one though, and it'll be in the government databases so their operatives can reach the lab."

"Pull that database," Wraith told her. "We don't want to use that road, but we don't want to stumble across it by accident either."

"Better cut the running lights," Melek added. "Since this is a covert op, best not to get seen."

"I can't cut them while we're still over the main roadway," Raven pointed out, her eyes already defocusing as she connected to the network. "If a Seccie monitor caught us flying without lights they'd order us to halt. But I'll swing off the road in about thirty minutes and cut the lights then. If anyone does catch us entering restricted airspace, we'll send a com message saying we had technical problems."

"A power loss?" Kez suggested. "That would explain why you'd cut the lights."

"With any luck the eventuality won't come up," Wraith said. "Any luck with that road, Raven?"

"Found it," she stated. "There's an exit from the main roadway. Blink and you'd miss it. Then there's about a kilometer from the turn-off to the outer perimeter of the facility."

"Break off from the road before you reach it," Wraith ordered.

"Then bring the flitter down behind trees or something. I don't want us to make the run on the lab until later tonight. We can catch a couple of hours sleep while we're waiting."

Ali lay flat on her back on the bed trying to stay calm. The revelation that Rachel was Revenge had shocked her. She was still trying to come to terms with its significance. The girl's grip on sanity seemed so tenuous that she doubted if even Raven could understand her. But Raven had seemed to know the right things to say to calm her sister down, without arousing Tom and Luciel's suspicions.

Ali sighed. The thought of the two boys was what troubled her most. She was surprised at how confident she was of Raven and Wraith's ability to rescue her. Her only doubts concerned what that escape would mean. She and Revenge were not the only prisoners in the facility. The idea of leaving the others trapped in the lab while she saved her own skin was rapidly becoming unpalatable. Ali could hardly imagine that Raven would take well to her altruistic impulse, but she had to try.

She rolled over to bury her head in the pillow and whispered almost under her breath:

"Raven. Raven, are you there? I have to talk to you." There was no reply. Ali waited, then repeated herself, but still there was nothing. She felt icy fingers grip her heart and had to force herself not to panic. Raven had said that the link was unbreakable. They'd been steadily in contact for hours with no mention of danger. Nothing could have gone wrong. She paused in her rapid calculations as a new thought hit her. It was only logical really. She could hardly be surprised if Raven proved herself human and succumbed to a human weakness like falling asleep. But this was hardly the best time. She sat up, frowning. Then she blinked in surprise at the sight of a face peering through the glass panel on the door.

It was Luciel. He pushed the door open hesitantly, revealing Tom standing behind him.

"Can I come in?" he asked.

"We need to talk to you," Tom added.

"OK," Ali agreed, feeling uneasy. She couldn't help the thought that all three of them were under a death sentence that at present only she had a chance of escaping. "What about?"

"You're going to try to escape," Tom said flatly and Ali started. Luciel was already nodding agreement.

"You're here for Revenge," he said softly. "I don't know why, but I'm sure that's it."

"Are you even a Hex at all?" Tom demanded, although he kept his voice low.

"I am a Hex," Ali admitted, her mind racing as she tried to think of a way to evade the rest of the questions. Where was Raven when she needed her? But the comlink was silent and she had to make the decision of what to tell them on her own. The choice was surprisingly easy. "You're right," she said. "I am going to break out."

"You don't have a hope in hell," Tom said, shaking his head. "There's no *way* you'll manage that."

"She got in, didn't she?" Luciel said. "If she could get in, and find Revenge, she must have a way to get out."

"I'll have help," Ali said softly. "I'm not here on my own. There's a group of people, gangers, who'll be helping me."

"You mean you and Revenge," Tom corrected.

"Yes." Ali nodded.

"Why?" Luciel looked baffled. "Why Revenge? She's brain-fried. What good would she do you?"

"Her brother's one of the gangers," Ali told him. "And her sister . . ." She broke off abruptly, deciding that it would be a bad idea to mention Raven. She'd probably annoy the other girl enough when Raven found out Ali had told them about the rest of the team, without exacerbating that. Ali knew Raven well enough to realize that she wouldn't take kindly to a betrayal of her identity.

But even without mentioning Raven, Ali was worried that she'd gone too far. They were in a high-security facility and a single word to a scientist would be enough to stop the retrieval before it started. Wraith had kept his team small deliberately, planning to use surprise as his primary weapon. If Ali gave away that element of surprise, the team really wouldn't have a chance.

"You mustn't say a word," she cautioned hurriedly. "Please?"

Tom and Luciel looked at each other. Luciel was the first to speak.

"We won't say anything, Ali," he said. "But if you're really escaping . . ."

"We're coming with you," Tom finished. "And so is everyone else kept prisoner here. You won't be going alone."

Kez woke with a start as someone shook him. He opened his eyes blearily to see a ghostlike shadow standing over him. Wraith's gray eyes stared at him, his mop of white hair blowing out around his face.

"Time for an equipment check," he said curtly and Kez nodded, yawning as he sat up. "I need you to explain the functions of those devices of Raven's," Wraith continued.

"Why can't she do it?" Kez protested, glancing over to where the three gangers sat against the side of the flitter. They looked as if they'd been awake for some time already.

"She's still asleep," Wraith told him. "I don't want to wake her until I have to. We'll be needing her tonight."

Kez wondered if that meant *he* wasn't needed. But the fact that Wraith had asked for his assistance suggested he wasn't entirely useless. He got to his feet, pushing away the coat that he'd been sleeping under, and wandered over to the flitter. Raven was stretched out over the front two seats. She looked exhausted, dark shadows under her eyes. He sighed. The success or failure of this operation was essentially resting on Raven. But although they had to put their trust in her she refused to do the same for them. She pushed herself to the limits of endurance rather than rely on anyone but herself.

A hand dropped onto his shoulder, making him jump, and he turned to see one of the gangers standing behind him. It was Jeeva and he was grinning, somewhat to Kez's relief.

"Hey, kid. Does he know you're cruising his sister?" He jerked his head at the flitter. Wraith and the two other gangers were already checking through the equipment.

"I'm not cruising her," Kez objected, and then shrugged. "And even if I was it wouldn't make any difference. Raven's only interested in one person."

"Herself, right?" Jeeva slapped Kez's shoulder and gave him a twisted smile. "So, forget about her, kid. Don't waste the effort on the ice queen. C'mon, let's go."

"Yeah, OK." Kez fell into step with Jeeva, realizing to his own amazement that he had had a conversation with a ganger without getting flatlined.

Wraith only listened with half an ear to Kez's explanation of the explosive charges, concentrating on checking the artillery he would be taking with him. All three gangers had a combat rifle slung over one shoulder and the ammunition for it, as well as handguns hanging from their belts. Wraith had chosen more specialized weaponry, but like the gangers he was wearing extensive body armor. He glanced over at Kez, frowning slightly. The boy was demonstrating how to activate the frequency oscillator which would cause Raven's devices to explode within five seconds. The boy was dressed simply and his only weapon was the laser pistol that hung from his belt.

Wraith wondered if it was too late to forbid Kez to come with them. He seemed more likely to be a liability to the gangers than any assistance. He glanced toward the front of the flitter where Raven was still asleep. Their plan of action called for Kez to act as her cover. If Wraith pulled him off the mission it would affect her the most. He leaned over the back of the seats and looked at Raven. She must be exhausted to sleep so long and he had almost decided not to wake her when she spoke:

"What is it, Wraith?" she asked, her eyes still shut.

"Kez," he said quietly, too low for the others to hear him. "He doesn't have the experience for something like this."

"That didn't seem to worry you too much before." Raven opened her eyes and considered him. "And it's not as if we had a great many options. We needed to keep the team small, and Kez is a streetkid. He can take care of himself."

"What if he can't?" Wraith asked. "We need you to get into that computer system, Raven. If something happens to Kez you won't have any backup, and the rest of us will be relying on you alone."

"I'll get into the system," Raven assured him. "With or without Kez." She sat up and stretched, sighing a little. "Wraith, we've gone over this enough times before. If we change our plans now we'll only be endangering ourselves."

Wraith studied his sister for a few more seconds, but he didn't contradict her. The strategy she was advocating had been his own and he agreed with it. But everything seemed so much colder when it came from Raven. Eventually he acknowledged what she had said with a curt nod. "You'd better get ready," he told her. "We should be ready to leave within half an hour."

The flitter approached the perimeter of the facility, only just above ground level. Raven had relinquished the pilot's seat to Kez, who was concentrating determinedly on the difficulties of the course Wraith had dictated. They could see the gray shape of the laboratory buildings in the distance, beyond the electric fencing. Melek was studying this intently as Kez landed the flitter.

"That's not very sophisticated security for a government facility," he said suspiciously.

"It doesn't need a lot of security," Wraith pointed out. "Almost no one knows it exists, and even if they did, popular feeling is so against Hexes that there's little danger of anyone trying to rescue them from the scientists."

"It's not as innocent as it looks," Raven said quietly. "There are motion sensors and vidcams focused on that fence."

"How do you know?" Kez asked and Raven gestured to the computer console on the flitter.

"The Countess knew what she was doing when she rigged out this thing," she told him. "But it hasn't been able to detect anything behind the immediate vicinity of the fence. As soon as I get into that security system we'll be OK, but until then it'll be hard going."

"Can those motion sensors detect us from here?" Wraith asked and Raven shook her head.

"Not until we're five meters from the fence."

"Right." Wraith turned to the rest of the team. "Don't let those sensors pick you up. We'll have to shoot them out, simultaneously. When they're out of the way we can get through the fence. Stay in contact"—he gestured to the com unit round his wrist—"and try to keep things quiet. We want to get in, pick up Ali and Rachel and get out again. Nothing else. While my group looks for the girls, Raven will hack into the computers and neutralize the security system. Let's make this as quick and as clean as we can. Is that clear?"

"We scan," Melek told him. "Stay chill, brothers." He nodded to Kez, as an afterthought. "Good luck, kid."

"Raven," Wraith said. "Are you set?"

"Everything's under control," she told him, already unlocking the doors of the flitter.

"Then let's go."

The group approached the fence cautiously as Raven pointed out the sensors that would have to be neutralized. Once she had identified them all, Wraith positioned Kez and the gangers ready to shoot them down. With each of them targeted on a sensor, there were still two vidcams to be put out of action and he intended that he and Raven should deal with those. However, it was not until he'd unholstered his gun that Raven reached under her long coat to produce one of her own. It didn't look that different from a long-barreled pistol. But instead of loading it, Raven tapped a key sequence across a panel on the butt of the pistol and it emitted a low hum.

"What is that?" Wraith asked curiously and Raven shrugged a shoulder.

"Electrical energy," she told him. "I designed it. There are certain advantages to it." As she finished speaking she leveled the pistol at one of the vidcams, then turned to look at Wraith expectantly. He turned to the other, trying to ignore the fact that Raven had sighted on her target in under a second, concentrating on his own. He kept his eyes on it as he asked:

"Ready?" There was a low murmur of assent and Wraith continued. "Fire on three. One . . . two . . . three!"

There was a soft roar, then a flash of sparks as the sensors and vidcams exploded on cue. Wraith checked them instinctively. Apparently everyone on the team had made their targets. Melek and Finn were already moving in to attack the wire of the fence, using lasers to cut through a section without being electrocuted.

"Security will have been alerted as soon as those sensors stopped transmitting," Raven reminded them. "We've got to reach the lab building before they catch up with us."

"OK, get going," Wraith ordered as the section of fence collapsed, sprinting for the building. The gangers were immediately behind him, and Raven and Kez brought up the rear.

It was then that Raven heard a voice in her ears, coming through the comlink that she'd left active before falling asleep.

"Raven, can you hear me?"

"Now is not the time, Ali," she hissed as she ran, keeping her voice low.

"I need to talk to you," Ali insisted.

"Are you in danger?" Raven demanded.

"No, but . . ."

"Then, forget it, Ali! We'll be with you soon enough!" Raven snapped and cut contact. The distraction had left her several paces behind Kez and she speeded up, trying to move faster over the uneven ground.

Wraith had the plans in mind as he approached the lab. However much the facility might have changed on the inside it appeared that the layout on the outside hadn't altered substantially.

Over to the right he could see lights and unhesitatingly identified them as belonging to the approach road and the main entrance of the lab. But he led his team to the left and what had been marked on the plans as a service entrance.

They were still two hundred meters away from the door when there was a sudden glare of lights and the sound of an alarm. Wraith swore under his breath and dropped to the ground, waving the others to join him. The gangers were with him immediately and Kez only a second after them. Raven raced up a moment later, her black coat flapping out behind her as she threw herself beside them. For a while there seemed to be no security reaction other than the siren and searchlights sweeping over the ground, and Melek grabbed Wraith's arm.

"Those lights are going to catch up to us real soon," he warned.

"I know. Stay chill," Wraith told him. He was scanning the area carefully, looking for any signs of response, but it was Kez who noticed it first.

"Wraith! Over there," he said urgently.

Three uniformed security personnel were approaching from the direction of the main entrance, carrying rifles. Melek reached for his gun but Wraith pushed his hand away.

"Not yet," he cautioned. "Wait." Melek halted his motion, but Finn was not as circumspect. Either he hadn't heard Wraith's warning or he deliberately chose to disregard it. His combat rifle roared and one of the guards fell. The other two threw themselves out of the line of fire and Raven hissed in annoyance.

"That's torn it," she exclaimed.

"Melek, Finn, deal with those two. Try and get them out of the way before they can call for backup."

"Some chance," Raven said under her breath but Wraith ignored it.

"Raven, you're with me," he ordered. "Jeeva, Kez, cover us." He leaped to his feet and headed for the service entrance, Raven following close behind. This time his instructions were apparently obeyed. Melek and Finn had opened fire on the guards behind them, and as he and Raven were halfway to the door, he heard more gunfire begin. He looked left in time to see two more guards seeking cover from Jeeva and Kez's fire. Then they had reached the door and there was no time for him to worry about what was happening. He had to rely on his team's ability to do their job. Raven was already examining the door.

"It's physically locked from the inside," she told him. "We'll have to blast it open."

"How many?" Wraith asked, grabbing two of the explosive charges from the bag he had slung over one shoulder.

"Not those." Raven shook her head. "We wouldn't have enough time to trigger enough of them. Give me a moment."

She rummaged in the deep pockets of her coat, producing what looked like a net. The firefight went on behind them as Raven unrolled the object, revealing it to be an electronic mesh of circuitry and explosives, and attached it to the door.

"Come on," she told Wraith. "Follow me." They were about ten meters from the door when she turned back and fired her pistol at the mesh. Electricity crackled over it in a glowing net before Raven pushed her brother to the ground. Seconds later the door exploded behind them. As it did so Jeeva and Kez ran toward them. Wraith stood, dragging Raven up with him, and they all headed for the door.

"We got the two who were shooting at you just now," Jeeva told Wraith as they made it inside. Wraith nodded at him and turned on his com unit, keying it to Melek's signal.

"Wraith here," he said. "What's happening?"

"We'll be done here in a moment, brother." The ganger's voice came from the unit, overlaid with the sound of heavy fire. *"You get that door open?"*

"It's down," Wraith told him. "We're going in."

Ali lay in bed, wide awake. Two of the scientists had patrolled the corridors in the evening, making certain that all the test subjects were restricted to their own rooms. Luciel and Tom had been reluctant to leave, but they were better acquainted with the rules of the lab than she was and didn't want to risk arousing the scientists' suspicions. Ali had told them to be ready for anything.

She wore her white coveralls in bed, knowing that she'd need to act at a moment's notice. But she had no idea of what acting would entail. Somewhere outside, the gangers were breaking into the laboratory, in danger of their lives, and she was stuck in a room unable to do anything. She felt useless and more than that, helpless. Her life was dependent on Wraith and Raven's ability to rescue her.

A dark shape moved by the door and Ali caught her breath in

alarm. Then there was a familiar hum of machinery and she recognized Tom. Luciel wasn't far behind him as they slipped into the room together.

"What's going on?" Ali whispered, climbing from under the covers.

"That's for us to ask you," Tom pointed out. "You said your team would be breaking in tonight. Where are they?"

"I don't know," Ali admitted. "But they *are* on their way in. I tried to contact Raven, to tell her about . . . about what we discussed, and she cut me off. I think things are getting serious outside."

"Wait!" Luciel looked stunned. "You can contact them?"

"Only Raven," Ali admitted, wondering when she would hear the last of this. "And we're not in contact right now."

"But something's happening, right?" Tom said. "What are we going to do if your gangers don't know that we're coming with you?"

"I'll tell them," Ali promised. "But I can't do it while they're breaking in. If I distract them I'd be endangering us as well as them. Besides . . ." She hesitated. "I don't think we can take everyone with us."

"What?" Tom looked angry, but Luciel's eyes were understanding.

"There are just too many people, Tom," he said softly. "Not enough of them are mobile. We'd never get out."

"We can only take those who can walk by themselves," Ali said as decisively as she could. "We can't do anything more."

10
STRIDING
THE BLAST

Melek and Finn raced through the door, almost cannoning into Kez and panting for breath.

"We got them," Melek gasped. "But there are more coming!"

"We need to find that control center," Wraith told them. "Find a computer terminal so Raven can locate it." He was already moving, gesturing for Melek to join him. "Finn and Jeeva, bring up the rear. Raven, whatever you do, don't get yourself shot." He heard Raven make a derisive noise behind him, but she seemed to be keeping up.

They thundered down the corridor, turning a corner just in time to avoid gunfire from behind. They were passing rooms which might contain an access terminal but they just couldn't risk the time to search. Another corner loomed and Wraith skidded around it. Finn and Jeeva were firing behind; presumably the guards were getting closer. Ahead of them he could see an elevator, which must lead to the part of the facility which was underground, and the corridor branched in two directions. He was trying to decide which to take when the elevator doors slid open. A scientist in a white lab coat stared at them in horror and tried to close the doors, but Melek forestalled her. He forced them open, pulling the woman out and knocking her unconscious with a swift blow.

"Keep the guards back!" Wraith called to the other two gangers, who stayed at the turn of the corridor, firing a fusillade of shots. Kez grabbed some of his stock of explosives and switched them to explode before lobbing them down the corridor one by one. The resultant explosion was loud enough to make Wraith wince, but it seemed to be successful as Jeeva called to him that there was no one else in pursuit.

Wraith didn't doubt that more guards were on the way but it seemed that there was a problem with the elevator.

"What's wrong?" he demanded as Melek cursed.

"The panel's locked down," the ganger told him.

"Raven?" Wraith asked, but she shook her head. "It's a physical lock. I can't fuse it." However, she did produce a small tool and set to work on the panel.

"What's holding us up?" Finn demanded as he and Jeeva reached the others.

"The elevator controls are locked," Wraith told him and Raven looked up.

"Wraith, try to find another way down," she told him. "There must be emergency stairs. Try to find where they're holding the test subjects." Wraith hesitated for only a second then he nodded quickly.

"Jeeva, Kez, stay with her," he ordered and headed down the corridor with the other two gangers.

Kez looked around nervously, holding the elevator doors open so Raven could work on the panel. Jeeva was watching the corridor warily, holding his gun ready in case more guards should turn up. Suddenly Raven gave a grunt of satisfaction and the panel clattered to the floor of the elevator.

"Get in," she told them. "We've got to go now!" Kez and Jeeva didn't need any more persuasion; in seconds they were in the elevator.

"Which floor?" Kez asked and Raven frowned.

"We'll try this one first," she said, pressing the appropriate button as the doors slid shut. "On the original plans this floor was used for administration—there should be terminals there, even if the control room isn't."

The ride took less than a minute, and as the elevator slowed both Raven and Jeeva readied their weapons.

"Get back," Jeeva warned him, and Kez flattened himself against the right-hand wall of the car next to the ganger. Raven had already moved to the other side. As the doors slid open bullets clanged off the back wall and Raven and Jeeva opened fire simultaneously.

"Explosive!" Raven hissed and Kez quickly switched the one he held to detonate, counted to four, and threw it through the doors. A second later it exploded and there were shouts of alarm. Jeeva quickly leaned out of the elevator and fired several rapid shots. Then he turned to nod at them.

"Three dead," he said. "We'd better get going."

"There must be hidden vidcams," Raven said, looking both ways down the corridor they had emerged in. "Kez, find me a computer terminal now!"

Wraith was having no luck finding a flight of stairs anywhere in the maze of corridors. The laboratory had definitely been remodeled and he couldn't reorient himself enough to locate where the emergency stairs had been on the original plans. They might even have been blocked up by now. Twice they had run into security and had only got free by blasting their way through. That wouldn't work another time. The whole facility was on alert now.

Wraith also wasn't comfortable with killing so many people. But he had forced himself to accept that this was the cost of his sister's rescue. He rationalized that the scientists had killed thousands here over the years; more blood was on their hands than would ever be on his by killing them. But so much death revolted him and he was relieved that the gangers lacked his scruples. His comlink with Raven came to life—the private link rather than the unit he wore on his wrist.

"We're three floors below you, Wraith," she told him. *"But we haven't found a terminal yet. It would seem the scientists put a lot of their findings on paper first."*

"Keep looking," Wraith said aloud and in answer to a glance from Melek, explained: "Raven hasn't found a computer yet."

"*Watch your back, Wraith,*" his sister warned. "*I think there are hidden vidcams all over this place.*"

"Damn!" Wraith exclaimed. "Raven thinks we're being watched," he told the gangers. "We'd better find those stairs fast." There was a sudden yell from Finn as he pushed through a set of double doors ahead of them.

"Over here," he yelled back at them.

"Did you find the stairs?" Melek demanded as they joined him.

"Service elevator," Finn corrected, pressing the panel to summon the elevator.

"Better than nothing," Wraith agreed. "Let's just hope they haven't locked down this one too."

His prayer went unanswered. The controls were covered by the same locking panel. This time it was Melek who went to work on it, while Wraith and Finn watched out for guards. Melek was using a laser to cut the panel off, a delicate task, as it could short-circuit the controls before they could use them. Wraith took advantage of an apparent lack of pursuit to contact Raven on his wrist com unit.

"Raven?"

"*Here,*" she answered immediately. "*No news yet, brother.*"

"That's not why I'm calling. Can you guess where Ali is? We've found another elevator and we need to know what floor."

"*One moment,*" Raven answered. "*I can locate her by her signal. Hang on . . . That's strange.*"

"What is?" Wraith demanded as Melek called out to him:

"Got it!"

"Good work," Wraith told him and he and Finn squashed

themselves into the elevator. Then he spoke into the com unit again: "Raven, I need a floor number."

"She's in another elevator," Raven told him, in tones of disgust. *"God only knows what the stupid kid thinks she's up to."*

"Raven!" Wraith shouted into the unit.

"OK, it's stopped. Five floors down," Raven told him. *"Now leave me alone. I have problems of my own."*

Wraith turned to Melek, but the ganger had already pressed the correct button.

"Sure hope there aren't more guards waiting for us down there," the ganger said fervently. "I don't know how long we can hold out."

"I know." Wraith's expression was set. "But Raven will take out that security system. We just have to give her time."

Ali had been nervous about using the elevator at night, certain that the scientists would detect an unauthorized use. But Tom had insisted that they try to get to Revenge before the gangers arrived. She wondered if his insistence had been partly motivated by the suspicion that, given the opportunity, Ali would leave him behind. She was annoyed by the thought that he didn't trust her, but admitted privately that he had grounds for suspicion.

The person she'd been only a month ago wouldn't have cared less what might happen to Tom. But the events of the last two weeks had changed her. From her encounter with Raven in the network to her capture by the CPS, forces had been in motion compelling Ali to reevaluate her conception of herself and of everyone else. One of those forces had been Wraith. His conviction that the extermination laws were immoral had made her think for the first time of what they actually meant to people besides herself. Her experience in the laboratory had brought that home. She knew she wouldn't try to double-cross Tom or Luciel. But they couldn't know that.

Whatever her misgivings, they seemed to make the elevator trip unnoticed, arriving on the floor where Revenge was without incident. The lights were muted on all the corridors and they passed by the rooms quietly.

"We should wake them up," Tom said at one stage. "Get them ready to go."

"We'd better not." Ali shook her head at him. "When my friends arrive they'll have enough problems without a bunch of kids all over the place."

"You're trying to get out of taking them," Tom accused.

"I'm trying to keep us alive," Ali hissed at him. "And I won't do anything that could prevent our escape." *If I haven't done that already,* she added silently.

Luciel pushed open the door to Revenge's room cautiously and in the dim light they saw a convulsive movement from the bed.

"Who's there?" the girl demanded, her voice rising alarmingly, and Ali hastened to reassure her as Luciel touched the panel by the door to activate the lights.

"It's me," she said quickly. "Ali. We've come to help you escape."

"There is no escape," Revenge told her and Ali groaned inwardly. Obviously this wasn't one of the girl's lucid periods and she wondered how they would escape with someone more than half out of her wits.

"We're getting you out of here," she said as calmly as she could. "Raven's coming, remember?"

"Raven . . . ," Revenge repeated, trying the word out.

"Ali," Luciel said softly, calling her attention to him. "She's still in restraints."

"I know." Ali frowned at them. "I just hope Wraith can do something about that. We'll have to wait until he gets here."

"He'd better get here soon or this escape will end in this room," Tom said gruffly. Then they all froze as a voice behind them replied.

"Your escape is already over."

Kez had run into the scientist as he searched one of the lab rooms, and before either of them had any time to gasp, Jeeva had grabbed the man and shoved him against the wall

"Where are your computers?" he demanded. "Tell us or die!" The man looked wildly at the ganger, clearly terrified, as there was a soft laugh from behind them. Kez turned to see Raven raise an eyebrow at Jeeva.

"'Tell us or die?'" she repeated.

"I can't tell you anything!" the scientist insisted. "We don't use computers!" Jeeva looked appalled, but Raven just shook her head, a nasty expression coming into her dark eyes.

"You're lying," she said softly. "You need equipment to process the results you get from the test subjects. Where is it?"

"I don't know," the man moaned before Raven hit him hard with the butt of her pistol.

"Tell us *now!*" she insisted. "Or I'll let my friend kill you." Her eyes locked with those of the scientist for several long seconds. Kez's heart thudded at the look on her face. He'd never seen anything so utterly malevolent. Raven was clearly furious at the delay in their plans and every ounce of her anger was directed at the man she confronted now.

"It's over there," the scientist muttered, giving in to that cold stare.

"Show us," Jeeva told him, taking the initiative again and pointing the man in the direction he had indicated, setting his rifle against the scientist's back.

He was shaking with fear but led the way through the maze of corridors obediently. They seemed to have halted pursuit for the moment and Kez suspected that the guards were concentrating on Wraith's part of the team. But his suspicion proved false when they rounded the last corner and came face-to-face with six guards in CPS uniforms. Raven and Jeeva opened fire instantaneously, the ganger still holding the scientist in front of him as a human shield. Raven didn't have that protection, but before the guards could take advantage of that she'd retreated, pulling Kez after her. The resulting firefight lasted only five minutes. The guards were professionals, but they couldn't stand against the explosives Raven had devised. Within minutes the corridor was a blackened wreck and all six guards and the scientist were dead, the last an afterthought on Jeeva's part, annoyed by the man's earlier prevarication.

Raven crossed past the dead without blinking, stopping in front of a heavy door.

"This is what they were guarding," she said, kicking it experimentally. It swung open with a clang, the twisted metal attesting to the force of the explosives which had wiped out their opposition. Raven's eyes lit up as she saw what lay inside and Kez heaved a sigh of relief at the sight of the gleaming computer terminals.

"This is it, right?" Jeeva asked and Raven grinned at him.

"This is it," she confirmed. "Watch the door. This'll only take me a minute." With that she swung herself into a chair before one of the consoles and activated a terminal, seemingly at random. Kez stood at her side, watching her hands speed over the keypad before suddenly coming to rest as her eyes glazed over and she entered the computer system.

Ali turned around slowly, her companions following her lead. There was a hiss of rage from the bed as Revenge threw herself against her restraints, but the man who stood watching them ignored her. He was flanked by a detail of five armed CPS guards, but he wore a white lab coat over an expensive tailored suit. He didn't look like the kind of person who would inspire the obvious terror that gripped Tom and Luciel. He was white-haired and elderly, looking mild in comparison to the guards. Ali raised her eyes to meet his, and froze. A steel-blue gaze held her in place, seeming to turn her inside out and dispose of her in a few seconds.

"I don't think you're going anywhere," said the scientist she unhesitatingly identified as Dr. Kalden. "I was notified of an unauthorized elevator use on this floor. Would this escape of yours have anything to do with the group of vandals security has just disposed of?"

"Disposed of?" Ali paled in alarm and she heard Luciel gasp softly.

"It looks very like there's a conspiracy here," Dr. Kalden said, his eyes boring into Ali. "And I would very much like to know why you are attempting to remove this test subject from the laboratory." He gestured toward Revenge casually and Ali glared at him. But before she could speak, Revenge beat her to it.

"She's coming for you!" she shrieked. "Raven's coming to wipe you clean with blood!"

"And who is Raven?" Dr. Kalden regarded Ali coldly. "Another of your ganger friends, Miss Tarrell? Or would she be another mutant?"

Ali didn't answer but she couldn't help an involuntary warning glance at Tom and Luciel, and that was all Dr. Kalden needed.

"I see," he said slowly. Then he turned to one of the CPS operatives. "Advise the rest of security that one of the terrorists is a mutant who will be aiming for the central computer room."

"Oh God," Ali groaned, transfixed with horror.

She'd betrayed Raven and now they were all going to die. She watched as the CPS guard reached for his com unit and then started as a new voice rang out.

"Drop it!" Wraith ordered, leveling his rifle at Dr. Kalden. Two sinister-looking gangers stood behind him, also pointing guns directly at the scientist.

"Wraith!" Ali thought she might faint from the sheer flood of relief that poured through her. "I thought they'd caught you!"

"Not yet," Wraith replied, keeping his eyes on the scientist. "What's going on here?"

"Your break-in has failed," Dr. Kalden informed him, unwavering despite the gun pointed at his head. "Give yourselves up."

"All I want is Ali and Rachel," Wraith told him. "Let them leave and you won't be injured."

The CPS operatives followed the conversation, their eyes going from one speaker to the other as they watched the standoff. Ali had been watching as well, but now she felt she should say something. Wraith didn't know yet that he wouldn't just be taking two of them out. But it was then that Wraith got his first look at his sister.

"Rachel," he whispered, his eyes blank with grief. "Rachel, is that you?"

"Wraith?" For an instant the fury flinging herself against her restraints calmed, sanity returning. But the moment passed. "Let me free!" she screamed at Dr. Kalden. Wraith made a movement toward her, but was halted by the scientist's next words.

"Leave her," Dr. Kalden ordered. "It is *over*. You are outnumbered here, and your mutant friend trying to break into the control room will discover that our system is safe from any intrusion." He smiled chillingly. "There's a virus in that system which is activated automatically when the computers are accessed during a security alert. Your friend Raven won't get past that, however skilled she is."

As Raven allowed her mind to fuse with the laboratory's computer system she tried to concentrate on what her objectives were. Huge amounts of data surrounded her and the lure of those test results was hard to resist. But it was the security system she needed to find.

She flashed through the data streams, calling up information on the security alert. She was vaguely aware that the signals from Wraith's and Ali's transceivers were getting closer and the information scrolling past informed her that they were about to be joined by two different security teams headed toward them.

> **cut power to elevators** < she commanded. > **lock out all access attempts not originating from this room.** < She was moving faster through the security database now, taking steps to terminate its effectiveness.

> **disrupt transmissions on frequencies used by cps operatives** < she continued. > **cut transmissions from vidcams/motion sensors. cut power to electrified fencing.** < Caught up in what she was doing, Raven issued her commands peremptorily, delighting in the way the computers obeyed her every whim. Valuable minutes had passed before she realized that something was wrong. The system was slowing down, taking longer to carry out her orders, becoming sluggish. She tried to identify the cause of the problem and found it hard to focus. Her mind, wrapped around the circuitry, was subjected to the same blight as the computers. Raven tried to pull back some of the tendrils of her consciousness, realizing too late that the system was exercising a stranglehold on her, dragging her down into the depths of its own dementia.

Kez stiffened in alarm as Raven groaned, one hand slipping from the keypad as her eyes rolled back in her head. She was white, her brows drawn together in pain. As if on cue there was a shout from the doorway and the sound of gunfire. He heard the roar of Jeeva's gun and realized that there were more guards arriving.

"Raven!" he exclaimed, catching her arm and shaking it. "Raven! What's wrong?"

Wraith halted, the conviction in Dr. Kalden's voice turning him to lead. He was aware of what was happening but felt strangely divorced from it, overpowered by the realization of his own failure. He had convinced Raven to accompany him here; if he didn't surrender now he would lose her as he had lost Rachel; and Ali and Kez, dragged into something that had nothing to do with them, would die too.

"It's over," Dr. Kalden said again and Wraith lowered his weapon. It was time to end this. Suddenly there was an inarticulate cry of rage and frustration and Wraith blinked as one of the two boys who were standing with Ali launched himself at the scientist. One of the CPS operatives leaped to block him and they went down in a tangle of limbs, Dr. Kalden moving quickly behind his guards. A gun sprang into life as Finn took advantage of the distraction to attempt an escape, Ali screamed and then everyone was firing.

Wraith only had one object in view. He hurled himself across the room, blasting away the restraints that held Revenge down before overturning the bed and using it as a barricade to shelter her from the blazing guns even as he moved to face them, opening fire on a CPS guard. The firefight lasted a few more seconds, cut off as suddenly as it had begun. As Wraith stood he became aware of the sound of running footsteps and glanced at the door.

"It was the doctor," Ali told him, getting up from the floor; a cut on her forehead attesting that she had not been swift enough in seeking shelter. "He got away."

"Forget him!" Finn snarled, one arm hanging limply as he bent over his comrade.

"How is he?" Wraith asked, concerned.

"He's flatlined," Finn said harshly, using his good arm to reach to close Melek's eyes. "They got him."

"I'm sorry," Wraith began, when a movement recalled him to another casualty. He could see for himself that the boy was dead; blood streamed from the bullet wounds that had shattered his skull, staining the metal that encased his body. The second boy knelt at his side and Ali moved to help him up.

"Luciel, are you OK?" she asked.

"I'm OK," he told her, limping slightly as he stood. "I guess Tom would have wanted to go that way."

"What we gonna do now?" Finn asked, turning to Wraith, but it was not the ganger who answered.

From behind the bed a small ragged figure got to her feet, walking like an animated scarecrow. As they turned to look at her, Revenge croaked a response to Finn's question.

"Raven . . . ," she said. "You must warn Raven."

"Raven!" Wraith's face darkened as he reached to flip on his com unit. "I hope it's not too late." He keyed to Raven's frequency and said her name urgently. "Raven, are you there?" There was a crackle and then a voice replied:

"Wraith, it's Kez! Something's wrong!"

"Where's Raven?" Wraith demanded.

"She's right here. But she's totally out of it, I can't make her hear me." Kez sounded frantic. *"And there are guards outside the room. I don't know how long Jeeva can hold them back!"*

"Stay with Raven," Wraith told him. "We'll try to get to you." But his heart sank at the thought. He doubted if they would get out of this facility alive.

A virus. Raven's thought processes finally connected enough for her to identify the source of the problem. Slowly a virus was shredding the computer system, endeavoring to take her with it. Well not this time. With the realization came rage. The fury crested within her as she realized that this had been something she hadn't anticipated and she took the first step to combat the threat. The million strands of her awareness snaked through the system, this time binding themselves to it, battling insanity with reason. Raven knitted the ravaged data streams back together, forcing them to mesh and become whole again.

The progress of the virus slowed under the onslaught of Raven's icy expertise. She controlled the system. Her conviction made it true. As the last trace of the virus disappeared she gradually became aware of other calls on her. Wraith was apparently attempting to use a deactivated elevator, Kez was shaking her insistently, and someone was conducting a battle only meters away. Raven sent the command to unlock the elevator and turned to regard Kez.

"What happened?" she asked.

"You're back!" Kez's eyes were wide as he clutched her hand urgently. "I thought you were out for good."

"It would take more than an amateur computer virus," Raven said contemptuously, glancing back at the terminal.

"Is that what it was?"

"Yes. Do you have any more of those explosives?"

"No," Kez admitted. "I've used all mine."

"Take this then," Raven told him, producing a disk-shaped object from her pocket.

"What is it?" Kez asked, dubiously.

"A more powerful explosive," Raven said calmly. "Flip that switch, count to three, then throw it at the guards. Go now! I'm getting a headache from the noise."

Kez headed for the door and Raven grinned. Still keeping contact with the computer system, she used one hand to activate her com unit, setting it for wide receive so the rest of the team would hear her.

"Hey, Wraith! What's up with you?"

"Raven!" Wraith's voice came from her com unit, the relief in it evident. "Are you OK?" There was the sound of an explosion from the corridor outside, ringing in Raven's ears. She shook her head to clear it.

"I'm chill. You?"

"We've got Ali and . . . Revenge. But we've lost Melek."

"Damn." Raven frowned. "Get up here. We've got to move out soon."

"We'll be with you in a minute," Wraith replied.

• • •

As Raven cut the channel, Kez and Jeeva entered the room behind her. The ganger was wounded, his shoulder bleeding copiously, and he seated himself on one of the chairs to bind it up.

"I spoke to Wraith," Raven told him. "He said Melek didn't make it."

"Melek?" The ganger cursed under his breath, his expression dark with anger, but then shook his head. "There'll be time for that later—for now we've got to get out of this rattrap!"

"Agreed," Raven replied. "But have you any idea how?" She indicated the computer terminal. "The CPS are crawling all over the place. I don't think we'll make it back to the flitter."

11

BLOOD WILL
HAVE BLOOD

Finn raised his gun warily as the elevator doors slid open, but this time there were no CPS guards waiting for them. Instead Kez stood on his own, holding a massive combat rifle that Wraith recognized as Jeeva's, his eyes wide and apprehensive.

"The control room's just down the hall," Kez said instantly. "We should get back there quickly before more guards turn up."

"Lead the way," Wraith agreed, lifting Revenge's emaciated figure into his arms. She was shaking, her eyes flickering wildly from one direction to another, but Wraith didn't have time to worry about her. Behind him Ali was supporting Luciel, whose limp had grown more pronounced, and Finn brought up the rear, keeping his gun trained on the empty corridor behind them.

Raven glanced up as they entered the control center and for a moment her gaze locked with Revenge's. The younger girl stiffened and Wraith released her, setting her down gently in one of the empty chairs. As he did so Raven's attention moved from Revenge to him.

"Wraith, we've got trouble," she said curtly.

"So I see," Wraith agreed, before looking back at Finn. "Finn, Kez, you guard the door." He paused while he looked at the boy Ali was supporting, then added: "You, kid, can you handle a gun?" The boy began to shake his head but Jeeva interrupted before he could say anything.

"I'll go with them," the ganger said, retrieving his combat rifle from Kez. Wraith nodded at him and turned back to Raven.

"What's the stat?" he asked.

"This," Raven replied and all over the control room screens sprang to life. They showed images of the lab from monitors scattered throughout the facility, many of them focused on armed guards. Raven hadn't moved, but her hands lay on a computer keypad, obviating the necessity. Clearly the computer system was under her control. "I've restored some of the lab's security programming," Raven explained, "so we can keep track of the opposition."

"Do you know where the doctor went?" Ali asked, joining them in front of the monitors.

"What doctor?" Raven frowned.

"Kalden," Ali's companion answered her. "He's the senior research scientist here."

"He caught us in Revenge's room," Ali added, "but then he got away before Wraith could stop him."

"I'll try to locate him," Raven said, "but right now we have more important concerns." She paused and then added, "And who is this?"

"Luciel," Ali explained, looking guilty. "He's a friend."

"We were going to free the other test subjects," Luciel said, his eyes meeting Raven's in a strange challenge.

"You're out of your mind," she returned. "We're going to have enough problems getting out of here ourselves, let alone bringing a bunch of kids with us."

The one thing that had sustained Ali while she was held in the laboratory was her knowledge of Raven's abilities. Although she trusted Wraith's promise of rescue, that promise could not have been made without Raven. When Dr. Kalden had claimed that Raven would fail to penetrate the lab's system, Ali had been shaken, but now she knew that Raven had succeeded, Ali's confidence in the younger Hex had increased. Now as Raven sat at the center of the control room, surrounded by flickering screens and the hum of machinery, Ali lacked the necessary conviction to promote her cause. But Luciel, who knew nothing of what Raven was capable of, felt no such restrictions.

"Have you any idea how many of us have died in this place?" he demanded of Raven, addressing her as the leader of the group in a recognition of the power she wielded within it. "How many more will die if you don't do something to help them? What kind of a rescue is this, if you only come for two out of the hundreds of us who are held here?" He paused before adding, in a quieter tone of voice: "A friend of mine was killed trying to help you people—doesn't that mean anything to you?"

"One of our team didn't make it either," Raven pointed out, still not turning away from her computer screens. "And I don't acknowledge the responsibility you're trying to make me feel." Her voice was cold and her eyes unreadable as she concluded: "Am I my brother's keeper?"

For a moment there was silence as Luciel struggled for words, and Wraith watched him as if waiting for a sign. Then from the side of the room a faint voice replied:

"You are his keeper as he is yours."

Wraith and Raven stiffened, before turning as one to look at Revenge, who returned their gaze with the impenetrability of an oracle. It was Wraith who broke that contact first.

"We must at least attempt to do something," he said.

Raven wrenched her gaze away from Revenge's and turned to glare at her brother, her black stare boring into him.

"We?" she queried. "You mean me, don't you? I've paid my dues, Wraith. You came here for Rachel and found Revenge. Now let's leave."

Kez shrank back behind the corner of the corridor as another burst of gunfire slammed into the wall. Jeeva swore under his breath before reloading his gun and angling it blindly round the corner to fire at the advancing guards. Kez glanced behind him. Twenty meters back was the open door of the control center and twenty meters behind that was another turn in the corridor, guarded by

Finn. He too was firing round it, which meant more guards were coming in the other direction. Jeeva ducked his head round the angle of the walls and pulled back even faster.

"They're still coming," he told Kez, and articulated the boy's unspoken thought when he added: "We can't hold out much longer."

"Shall I tell Wraith?" Kez asked, gesturing to his wrist com unit.

"Go tell him in person," Jeeva replied. "Show him we're not kidding."

Kez didn't need any further persuasion. He swung round and raced back up the corridor and into the control room, coming to an abrupt halt as he realized an argument was in full force. Wraith and Raven were quarreling furiously, the girl having left her post in front of the computer keypad in order to argue her point more fervently. Ali and her friend were watching them anxiously, while keeping half an eye on the monitors which showed the advancing guards. Kez grabbed Wraith's arm.

"We've got to go now!" he insisted, ignoring the ganger's cold stare. "We can't hold out against the guards much longer."

"That's it then," Raven said. "We go . . . if we still can."

"If you leave now nothing will have changed," Ali's friend said softly. "The lab will just go back to normal, and the experiments will continue."

"Luciel!" Ali looked desperate. "There are *hundreds* of test subjects. How do you expect us to break them all out, when we're having enough problems getting ourselves out?"

"So there are hundreds of people here," Luciel replied fiercely.

"Have you any idea how many *thousands* have died as a result of the CPS's illegal experimentation, how many have—"

"Wait!" Raven commanded, and Ali and Luciel turned to look at her. "What did you say?" the girl asked, dark eyes fixed on Luciel.

"That there are thousands who have died," he replied. "Surely you know that?"

Raven had already turned away from him and faced Wraith. For the first time since the ganger had arrived she didn't look angry.

"The experimentation is illegal," she said in a considering tone of voice.

"So?" Wraith prompted.

"We can't take the test subjects with us, but we can let other people know they exist," Raven replied. She turned and gestured to the computers. "This database is full of records of the test subjects and the experiments performed on them. I can dump that information straight into the main net and into all the databases of the news channels. With a scoop like this the media will have people here in under half an hour."

"And you think that'll be enough?" Luciel challenged, still not looking convinced.

"It'll have to be," Wraith replied, having made his decision. He pressed two buttons on his wrist com unit and spoke into it. "Jeeva, Finn, can you hold on another fifteen minutes?"

"It's cutting it close, but it'll be chill," Finn replied, followed shortly after by Jeeva's voice agreeing.

"Right then," Wraith said, shutting his com unit off. "Get to it, Raven."

• • •

Three floors below the control center Dr. Kalden addressed a team of guards, while the scientists clustered in an alarmed huddle around him. A penetration of the facility alone might not have worried them, but the revelation that there was a rogue Hex on the loose had thoroughly frightened them. They were used to dealing with cowed children who barely understood what being a Hex entailed, let alone how to use those abilities. But now they knew that, not only were three of their test subjects on the loose, the gangers had brought their own Hex with them.

"She must have broken past our virus safeguards," Kalden was saying angrily. "That means they're in control of the facility."

"There aren't that many of them, sir," one of the armed guards pointed out.

"There aren't that many of us either," a scientist said anxiously and Kalden frowned warningly.

"The intruders must be captured and disposed of," he insisted, "and do it quickly. If word of this gets out, there will be a number of awkward questions asked." A few of the scientists exchanged incredulous glances at the understatement, but most were too horrified by the possibility of discovery to do more than fix the remaining guards with hopeful eyes.

"We'll get them out of there, sir," the guard stated confidently. "A bunch of street trash and a few scruffy kids won't present any difficulty."

"They've already done that," Kalden said curtly. "Now get rid of them."

The security guards headed for the door, but Kalden halted them before they could leave.

"Wait," he ordered, his eyes narrowing to slits as he thought. "Leave the stranger, the Hex, alive if you can. I think she would make an ideal test subject."

Raven stiffened at the words, a fragment of her consciousness alerting her to the conversation picked up by one of the monitors. One of her hands clenched slightly, but she didn't allow herself to become diverted from her purpose.

The laboratory's system was separated from all of the main information networks and she had almost given up hope of getting a message out. The communications lines were sealed against computer data flow, scrambling any signal sent out from the lab's computers. But there was one angle Kalden had failed to cover. It was a residential facility and the scientists required certain amenities. She had tracked the power grid to the residential area of the lab and discovered the vidcoms in almost every room. The vidcoms, used for recreation by the scientists, were configured to handle the data flow from the channels they picked up and send signals out in return. Raven tapped into that connection and began rigging up a physical circuit in the control room to handle the jerry-rigged communication channel while she concentrated on the message she had to send.

She had no difficulty in finding convincing evidence of the CPS's illegal experimentation. From the moment she had destroyed the virus nesting within the system she had been downloading its

data files. The duffel bag on the floor beside her was rapidly filling with disks. But in the course of her rape of the system she had
located the evidence she would need, records of the experiments
performed, complete from original assessments to final autopsy
reports, coupled with a small but chilling selection of video record-
ings of some of the test subjects. She patched the records together
with the location of the lab, the identity of Dr. Kalden, and the
relevant section of European Law that allowed the extermination
of Hexes and imposed the penalties for allowing a known Hex to
live. There was no legislation precluding experimentation, but on
that subclause alone, the CPS would find themselves with a lot of
explaining to do.

The data package complete, Raven dived into her own connection with the network, and streamed toward the main UK direc-
tory. Tendrils of her consciousness snaked through the database,
collecting listings of media channels, humanitarian organizations,
government ministries, and foreign embassies. She intended that
this information dump would be as much of an embarrassment as
possible to the government, which must have colluded in it. Her list
complete, she added it to her information dump, so that those who
received it would know exactly how widespread its release was.

> **send message** < Raven commanded and the system com-
plied, sending out a thousand data pulses in every possible direction, arriving simultaneously in systems across the country.

The Hex's mouth tightened into a grim smile, but she wasn't
finished yet. This time she was heading for the vidchannels themselves, tracking those streaming paths of data to their source. It

was something she'd never tried to do before; the incompatibility of technologies would have made it difficult even when not operating from a separate system, but her use of those channels to send her message into the net gave her the idea of utilizing them more directly. As her consciousness ranged through each of the media vidchannels, leaving a tag on each, she directed the video monitors in the control room to pick up the feed from ten major channels, from news to entertainment. Then with a brief moment of intense concentration she pulled on those tags and released her data package.

Ali gasped as she saw what was happening. Ten of the monitor screens had been showing the images from vidchannels, apparently at Raven's command. But, just as she was about to inquire whether the other girl thought they were in need of some light entertainment, all the vidchannels blacked out for a microsecond, coming back on line simultaneously to show the same image. Pictures of mutilated children passed across the screen, covered by a continuously scrolling text, comprised of the test results. Test subjects followed each other in rapid succession, each image accompanied by a name, details of the experiments performed and the date of death. Raven was flooding the vidchannels with proof that the world couldn't ignore.

As the others stared, Raven detached herself from the computer and turned to challenge Luciel with dark eyes.

"Satisfied?" she asked.

"Not entirely," he replied. "But it'll do."

"My pleasure." Raven bowed ironically and then turned to Wraith. "I'm going to bring the flitter to the roof of this building; we'll have to get up there somehow."

"Is that safe?" Kez asked, warily.

"How can you do that?" Ali demanded, their voices overlapping.

"I left the flitter's com-channel open. The scanning devices here don't pick it up as anything more than white noise, but if you know what you're looking for, and you have the skill, you can hack into its controls." She shrugged. "With running lights off, no one'll see it coming. But we can't afford to cut it much closer."

"Right," Wraith agreed and switched on his wrist com, broadcasting to Finn and Jeeva at once. "Get ready to make a break," he ordered. "The flitter will be waiting on the roof. We have to make it up there."

"OK, get ready to run then, friend," Jeeva's reply came back. "We won't be able to hold them here while we're heading in the opposite direction."

"Raven, can you control the lab system once we've left here?" Wraith asked sharply.

Raven reached into her coat and produced a small black control pad, which emitted a piercing sound, traveling quickly through the upper harmonics before disappearing from their hearing range. She held it in her left hand while her right hand traveled quickly over the keypad and then turned back to nod at Wraith.

"I can keep control for a while, but as soon as the scientists get back in here they can lock me out, *and* trace me by the signal from this."

"They'll be able to trace us anyway, once they've got their system back," Kez pointed out and Raven grinned at him.

"Not for long," she told them. "I'm setting an automatic domino circuit fuser. Once I trigger the right command this system will be irretrievably trashed."

"The data from the experiments will be lost?" Luciel asked.

"Unless they have copies," Raven replied. "But even if they lose it all, I've still got it."

"You downloaded the data files?" Luciel asked, wavering between surprise and disgust.

"The CPS have had access to these files for years," Raven pointed out. "It's about time a Hex got the chance." As she spoke she grabbed the last stack of disks and threw them into her bag. "I'm set," she told Wraith.

The ganger immediately switched on his wrist com and alerted Finn and Jeeva.

"Meet us at the elevator, one minute," he told them. "We're getting out of here." Wraith slung the slumped form of Revenge over his shoulder and handed his gun to Ali. "Cover my back," he ordered and headed for the door.

"Wraith!" Ali's protest was almost a wail, but the ganger wasn't listening.

"Here," said Raven, coming up behind her. "Hold it like this." She adjusted Ali's hands on the weapon, placing one of them lightly on the trigger. "You see anything, shoot."

"But . . . ,"Ali began.

"It doesn't matter if you don't hit anything," Kez told her, reloading his own gun. "The guards won't charge into gunfire, and the important thing is to keep them back."

The CPS guards charged around the corner of the corridor as the sound of gunfire ceased, just in time to see the elevator doors close. The first man to arrive at the elevator pressed the call panel, but it was already dead.

"They're still in control of the system," he announced.

"But they're out of the control room," his leader responded. "Call Kalden and tell him this floor is secure. Have him get his scientists to release the lock on the elevators. Then get after the intruders."

Raven was jammed between Finn and Jeeva in the elevator, one hand gripping her customized gun, the other holding the link to the computer system. Through the transceiver she was aware of the computers still obeying her orders, pumping out the evidence over the vidchannels, locking out the security systems, transmitting all the data they had to Raven. She leaned against the hard white metal wall of the elevator, closing her eyes. They were burning with the pain of sensory overload and she could hear a buzz building up in her eardrums. Raven bit her lower lip hard, trying to concentrate on an easily defined pain, rather than the reality of what was happening to her. She had never engaged in so many complex computer operations at once. Now her body was finally feeling the strain and she knew that she was reaching her tolerance levels.

Slumped against the wall, trying hard not to succumb to the overwhelming flood of exhaustion, Raven didn't notice when the elevator began to slow. But when it ground to a halt, Wraith grabbed her arm, shaking her roughly awake.

"Raven!" he demanded. "What's going on?"

"Wraith." Raven opened her eyes with an effort, not wanting to admit the truth. She concentrated and the elevator started again, the effort causing her knees to buckle. Kez caught her before she hit the floor and held her upright.

"Raven? You OK?" he asked, with concern.

"I'm fine," Raven insisted. She glared at him, but didn't pull away, admitting to herself, if not to her companions, that she lacked the strength to support herself anymore. She had been running on adrenaline and determination; now she had only the determination left. "We've got to get out of here soon," she told Wraith. "I won't be able to hold control over the computer much longer and I don't want to trigger the system wipe until we're safely out of the lab."

Dr. Kalden glanced angrily around the control room as he entered, and suddenly stopped dead. Behind him he heard a shocked gasp, but his consuming emotion was anger. Splashed across the row of security monitors were transmissions from vidchannels, their logos identifying them to be a broad section of the media. All of them were showing information so classified that only senior CPS officials had access to it.

"Our security has been compromised," he said in an icy voice.

"We'll be crucified," one of the scientists moaned and Kalden shot him a steely glare.

"This experimentation was authorized at the highest level," he stated. "If those gutter rats intend to accomplish anything by this, they are gravely mistaken." He studied the computer monitor for a few moments, then gestured to one of his operatives. "Shut down this transmission and get this system back under control. I want the lab's defenses back online now."

The operative seated himself at the terminal and his fingers sped rapidly over the keypad. After a few moments he began to frown.

"The system's acting up," he informed Kalden. "It's not letting me back in."

"She'll have put a block up," Kalden said impatiently. "Break it."

The operative returned to the keypad, watched intently by Kalden, and after a few minutes the images on the monitors winked out.

"I've shut down the transmission, sir," the man said with relief. "And I'm trying to regain control of the security system."

"Can you find out where the intruders are?" one of the guards asked. "If we know that we won't need the defenses—we can go and get them personally."

It was a while before the operative could persuade the computer system to provide him with an answer. Eventually he stated:

"They're on the roof."

"Get after them," Kalden ordered fiercely. "Don't let them leave this complex! That girl's been in this system—if she's allowed to escape she could do untold amounts of damage to our research."

As the security people raced after the gangers, one of the scientists turned to speak to Kalden:

"What if they escape, sir?" he asked nervously. "The media exposure alone . . ."

"There are ways to minimize this damage," Kalden said, cutting him off. "The media won't find anything here to use against us. I've taken precautions against that."

Wraith raced across the flat roof of the laboratory, still carrying the unconscious form of Revenge and closely followed by Ali and Luciel. Raven and Kez were a little behind them, Raven grudgingly accepting Kez's aid. Jeeva and Finn brought up the rear, guns ready for any sign of pursuit. The flitter was waiting for them, and as they approached, the doors hissed open at Raven's command. Only Kez noticed her stagger as they did so.

Jeeva and Finn covered the area while Wraith placed Revenge as gently as he could in the back of the vehicle. He hurried Ali and Lucil in after her, retrieving his gun, and turned back to the others just as a shout rang out from across the roof.

"Guards!" warned Jeeva, and Finn spoke simultaneously:

"They've found us."

"I'm losing control of the system," Raven warned and the gangers ducked as the guards fired at them.

"Into the flitter!" Wraith ordered and Finn and Jeeva piled into the back as Raven took the driver's seat and Kez slid in beside her. Wraith fired one last volley at the guards, who were much closer now, before hurling himself inside, beside Finn. The doors hissed shut and the flitter took off into the air. Raven was using manual controls instead of her link with the machine, but even so the flitter climbed swiftly, out of the range of the guns and rifles.

"We're out of range," Finn stated and Ali breathed a sigh of relief. Two seconds later there was a flash of light and searchlights came to life all over the facility. There was the boom of an automatic gun and the flitter banked to avoid the fire.

"The CPS is in control of the computer system again," Wraith deduced. "Raven, kill it."

Kez turned to look at Raven as her eyes defocused, glazing over as she renewed her link with the lab's computer system. The searchlights went dead and the gun was silenced. Raven's eyes rolled up into her head and she slumped forward over the control panel, as the flitter went into a screaming dive.

"Raven!" Wraith yelled and Ali screamed piercingly. Kez lunged at the controls over Raven's body and forced the flitter back on course. He was shaking with tension as he wrestled with the controls and climbed over Raven to pilot the flitter from the driver's seat.

"Can you handle it, kid?" Jeeva asked, and he nodded.

"Yeah, I think so."

"What's wrong with Raven?" Ali demanded, an edge of hysteria in her voice.

"She's still breathing," Kez assured her. "She must have knocked herself out shorting out that system."

"No sign of pursuit," Finn reported, from his vantage point at the back of the flitter.

"I think we're clear," Wraith responded. "Kez, what are you doing?"

"I can't pilot this thing without lights!" the boy replied angrily. "I'm not Raven. And if the Seccies caught us without lights on the road we'd be pulled over for sure."

"Stay chill," Jeeva told him. "Keep to the speed limit, follow the road. No one knows we were the ones who broke into that lab. There's no alert out yet."

"This place will be swarming with reporters in under an hour," Ali said authoritatively, losing a little of her tension. "We should worry about them as much as the Seccies, if we don't want to be caught on camera."

"When the media gets here Kalden will have a lot of explaining to do," Luciel said with satisfaction.

"I hope so," Wraith was beginning, when Finn gave a yell.

"Pursuit!" he warned. "Get off the road!"

Kez pulled the flitter aside, bringing it to a halt with a jerk and turning off the lights. It hovered there as the cause of Finn's warning became visible to the rest of them. A group of flitters with CPS symbols emblazoned on their side sped past them, not halting at all. In moments they were out of sight, but Ali pointed downward at more vehicles. Skimmers were on the road below them, heading away from the lab at high speed.

"The scientists," Luciel said softly.

"Rats deserting a sinking ship," Ali added.

"I don't like this." Wraith's voice was grim as he watched the lights fade into the distance.

"I guess they don't want to be here when the media arrive either," Kez said, craning back to look in the direction of the laboratory.

It was out of sight, no lights left to show them its location. But all six watched apprehensively, infected by Wraith's foreboding.

And then they saw it. The light of the fireball reached them before the sonic boom of the explosion. Clouds of smoke and fire boiled into the sky, throwing flaming debris high into the air. Then the shockwave hit them and the flitter rocked with the air disturbance as the ground far below shook. Wraith clenched his fists and Ali hid her head in Luciel's shoulder but no one spoke as Kez guided the flitter back over the road, heading back to London while the fireball lit the sky behind them.

12

LIES LIKE TRUTH

The vidscreen was on. It had been on constantly for the past three days since their escape from the lab. Ali sat on the floor of the squat, in front of the battered unit, not looking at any of the others. Barely a word had been spoken since they had arrived back in London, after the long, weary night, and negotiated with the Countess for the use of one of her properties. It was down in the depths of London, in precisely the setting that would in other circumstances have frightened Ali and annoyed Raven. But no one was complaining.

Raven hadn't stayed with them. Wraith had told her about the destruction of the lab but she hadn't said much in response, white and tired from overstraining herself, except to ask if Kalden had escaped. No one knew the answer and when Kez suggested she link up to the net Raven had just shook her head. Once they reached

London she had stated her intention of seeking sanctuary with the Countess and no one had had the energy to argue with her.

The others had been isolated in the three rooms that comprised the squat. Jeeva and Finn had returned once for their payment and to tell Wraith that their gang would not be exacting retribution for Melek's death. Luciel had remained, tinkering with the electronic equipment that Raven had abandoned when she'd disappeared into the Countess's fortresslike building. He didn't speak much, burdened by the weight of his guilt for the lives that had been lost when the lab was destroyed. Wraith was also silent. He spent long hours caring for Revenge, trying to coax a resemblance to the child he had known out of the shattered body of the test subject. Ali already knew that the effort was wasted. But Wraith was trying to salve his own conscience by caring for the child he had managed to save. Kez was still with them, but he disappeared for long hours at a time, wandering the streets of the urban catacombs.

The group had fragmented and Ali blamed it on the absence of Raven. Wraith and his sister had balanced each other, his private humanity providing a foil for her public ruthlessness. Together they had been the perfect leader. His caution and her daring had carried them through the raid on the lab, but having achieved that end the link had been lost. Ali suspected Raven would have disappeared anyway, whatever had happened; the presence of Revenge disturbed her on a level that made it difficult for her to remain. Unlike Wraith, she had never once called her sister by her old name, a tacit recognition of the change that had overtaken her. But the presence of Revenge was not the only reason for the fragmentation of the team. That had come inevitably with the sense of failure that had overtaken them all, once the media coverage had begun.

The appearance of the lab records on every main vidchannel simultaneously had stunned the media as much as the general public, and reporters had been immediately dispatched to the alleged location of the CPS facility. The footage they had sent out had appeared within the hour on every major news channel, showing the gutted shell that had been the lab. But before the reporters could examine the wreckage the Security Services had arrived, with a government injunction, forcing the media to leave. The news channels had continued to speculate on the situation over the next day and their persistence had been rewarded with the announcement of an official investigation. The government had stubbornly refused to comment, and despite the inevitable comments from sources, it became clear that officialdom was stonewalling the media.

The team had watched this from the relative safety of the squat with increasing frustration. Raven had regained consciousness after twelve hours and refused all offers of medical treatment to watch the vidscreen. But she was the first to turn away from the coverage, announcing that she was going to see the Countess and declining Kez's company on the way. Finn and Jeeva had left shortly afterward, declaring that their part of the operation was over.

Jeeva had wished them luck, but Finn had departed without a word, impatient to call an end to their association.

Wraith had lost interest in the coverage in light of Revenge's continuing vacancy. Luciel had done his best to explain what had happened to her and to assist Wraith in taking care of her. But the girl had retreated into her own mind. Her periods of lucidity were rare and came in the middle of incoherent ravings, so that Ali could never be certain at what point reality began for her. She had nightmares too, and after waking three nights in a row to the sound of banshee screaming, Ali's own dreams were displaying the same maelstrom of insanity. Flames licked at her, while the screams rang on, sleeping and waking. She would have left too, but unlike Raven and Kez or even the gangers, she had nowhere to go. She and Luciel were trapped there by the simple fact that any of their old connections would refuse to aid them. As far as their parents were concerned, they were dead, and Ali reflected that the way things were going that was likely to come true before very much time had passed.

Wraith could hear the muted sound of the news channel, even through the closed door. He wished Ali would turn the thing off, but she had seemingly taken root in front of the screen and only removed her gaze with reluctance. At least her obsession with the coverage was preferable to her wandering around the squat, mournfully regarding all she saw as if she were interred in a tomb. Wraith sympathized with her situation, but he didn't feel himself equal to handling it. It was difficult enough to come to terms with the fact that his long search for his sister was over, without the satisfaction of having really found the object of that search. Revenge was an entirely alien creature to him, and he could see little or nothing of what he had lost in the shadows of her haunted eyes.

She was sleeping again, a natural sleep, if disturbed by the dreams that plagued her, and Wraith took the opportunity to check on Ali.

"What's happening?" he asked as he entered the room, gesturing at the scratched screen.

"There's going to be an official statement this evening, given by the Prime Minister, followed by an announcement by the Head of the Security Services. Most of the news channels are speculating on what they'll say, some are rerunning the transmission from the lab, to see if they can detect any evidence of fraud."

"Has that been suggested?" Wraith asked.

"There's been a lot of claims that the data from the experiments and the pictures of the test subjects were fabricated by Hexes in an effort to gain public sympathy. But people don't believe that explanation because the government claims that no Hex can get past the ever-vigilant CPS." Ali's voice was bitter, and Wraith couldn't blame her. It hadn't been that long since her own exposure as a Hex, and unlike Raven she hadn't had time to come to terms with the revulsion in which mutants were held.

If Raven were there she might have made it easier for Ali. Wraith was aware of the mutual antipathy between them, but nonetheless Raven might have been able to help Ali come to terms with her new identity as a member of the criminal underclasses. Perhaps she could even be taught how to use her Hex abilities to survive on the streets. Wraith found it difficult to imagine Ali as a hacker, but she hardly had an abundance of opportunities on offer. However, Raven had disappeared, and he didn't know if she ever planned to return.

Kez crossed the bridge with care. This far down most of them were ruined. The essential base structure of the city was secure, but the government hadn't spent money on the upkeep of areas inhabited primarily by criminals. The area where the squat was located was further down than the depths where Kez had spent his childhood. He rarely saw gangers, who hunted the poorer suburbs where pickings were better. Instead, the few people he saw wandering the deserted bridges and ruined plazas were society's unwanted, those who had given up hope.

He wandered on listlessly, wondering if this was where he belonged. He didn't know what Wraith intended to do, whether he would go back to Denver or join up with the gangers here. Perhaps he would rely on Raven to provide sufficient credit for him to live in obscurity, taking care of Revenge. If that happened, Kez would have little choice but to return to the streets. He had effectively blocked out the memory of his former life; now he felt it returning to claim him. Everything depended on Raven. He was certain of it. Without her, the team was nothing. Her expertise, her ruthless exploitation of her abilities, had given them confidence in her as the main power of the group.

Without realizing it, he had come to familiar territory. The building that loomed beside him was the one where the Countess had her base of operations, three levels up. That was where Raven had been headed when she left them. Kez studied it blankly, wondering if he dared. Then, deciding that he had nothing to lose, he began to climb the stairs that snaked around the skyscraper.

The guards in the foyer looked up warily as Kez entered, and moved to block the door that led up to the Countess's base of operations. Kez approached with equal caution, but the request he made when he reached them was unexpected.

"I want to see Raven," he stated.

The guards looked at each other, then the woman frowned in consideration.

"The hacker?" she asked.

"Yeah, that's her," Kez confirmed. "I heard she was here."

"Wait," the woman said coldly, and turned to speak into the vidcom, too quickly for Kez to make out her words. Finally she stepped back from the unit and gestured him forward. "State your name and business."

Kez didn't know if Raven was at the other end of the vidcom or not. But he assumed that the message would be passed on to her and spoke as if she was there.

"It's Kez," he said. "I need to talk to Raven. It's important."

"Is it personal business?" an unfamiliar voice asked, and Kez nodded. "Wait there," the voice responded and the vidcom clicked off.

"You heard her," the male guard told him. "You can wait over there." He waved Kez away from the door and both guards resumed their alert stance.

Long minutes passed as Kez waited. There was no sign of Raven, and the guards were ignoring him. He wondered if he had made a mistake in coming here. But the compulsion to see Raven had been too strong for him to resist. One of the guards shifted and the motion drew Kez's eyes to the open doorway just as a figure emerged from the shadows. Raven was dressed simply in black, her hair scraped back to reveal her pale face and the dark shadows under her obsidian eyes. She was wearing her duffel bag slung over one shoulder and carrying her long coat, and Kez let himself hope for the first time since the lab had burned to the ground.

"Hey, Kez," she said as he approached. "What's up?"

"Not much," he admitted. "Everyone's just . . ." He shrugged his shoulders, completing the thought with the gesture.

"Fallen apart," Raven concluded. For a moment a brief flicker of something passed across her face and was gone before Kez could identify it. "What did you expect?" She shrugged. "Did you think everyone would be on a high because we'd found Rachel? It's not that easy, Kez. Wraith hasn't won a war, or even a battle, whatever he might think." She shook her head. "In the real world no one lives happily ever after; it's hard enough just to keep living." Kez said nothing and after a moment Raven adjusted the strap of her bag and began to walk off. "Come on, let's go."

"Back to the squat?" Kez asked, falling into step with her.

"For now," Raven answered.

She had been following the news broadcasts when Kez arrived, listening to the speculation about the Prime Minister's statement.

Admittedly, that statement was probably already written and lying in some government database, safe from any but the most electric of hackers. But Raven hadn't entered the net since the night of the raid. Her time had been spent with the data files she had extracted from the lab's computer.

The data on those disks had been collected from the results of sadistic experiments performed over more than fifty years, on thousands of children. But Raven had forgotten that as she read the files. She wanted to know what it meant to be a Hex, what the scientists had discovered. But she learned more about what they didn't know than what they did. Raven had always known that she was unusual. She had known she was a Hex long before any government agency could have guessed and learned to use her talents before she really understood what they were. But, reading through the CPS's files, she realized the flaw in their ruthless policy of exterminating mutants as soon as they were discovered. The test subjects had no idea what they were capable of and, consequently, neither did the scientists. Some of the research had yielded useful results, but most of it consisted of dead-end and blind alley projects, which seemed to miss the point entirely. Dr. Kalden's team had never encountered anyone with abilities that came anywhere near to matching Raven's; the virus they had constructed within their computer system to catch a Hex hacker had told her that. If she could evade the best defenses the lab had, at her age, a more experienced Hex ought to be able to do far more. Raven wondered if any more experienced Hexes even existed, then dismissed the question. The main concern was that she existed and as long as she continued to extend her skills they would surpass any possible expectation of the CPS researchers.

Raven grinned silently. Her experience in the lab had been sobering. She'd never suffered the sensory overload of extended connection with the net before. But, once she had recovered from the experience, the realization that she was just as much of a threat to the CPS as they were to her had reassured her. She felt her confidence building as they approached the squat where the others waited, and her grin didn't fade as Kez opened the door.

Ali glanced up idly as the door opened, and her eyes widened with shock as she saw who it was.

"Raven!" Wraith said, affection and relief in his voice. "How are you?"

"I'm chill," Raven grinned at him. "I see you've made yourself comfortable," she added, glancing ironically around the bare room. "Makes a change from the Belgravia Complex, doesn't it?" This last was addressed to Ali, who blinked, uncertain whether it was intended to indicate malice or camaraderie. "Have you been watching the screen all this time?" Raven continued, dumping her bag and coat and seating herself against the wall.

"Pretty much," Ali admitted cautiously. "Wraith's been looking after . . ." She hesitated and Raven finished for her:

"Revenge." She turned to look at Wraith. "Any improvement?"

"No," he stated flatly.

"I didn't expect there would be," Raven replied.

"I bet you don't even care either," Luciel stated from the corner of the room, where he had been sitting, virtually ignored. His voice was just as cool as Raven's. "You didn't even see the lab explode."

"I've seen the news reports," Raven reminded him. "And I'm not flagellating myself with guilt. Tell me one thing we could have done that we didn't," she challenged. "Just one."

Luciel met her eyes for a long moment, but he didn't speak. Raven held his gaze and then turned away toward the door of Revenge's room. Wraith was the only one to follow her, and as they went inside, he shut the door behind them. Revenge was sleeping, her fragile body collapsed on the bed like a broken doll. Raven studied her for a while in silence until Wraith spoke.

"Will she recover?"

"You know the answer to that as well as I do," Raven replied. Turning her back on Revenge she continued: "Was she worth it? Was finding Rachel that important to you?"

"She wasn't to you?" Wraith replied, his words half question, half statement.

"As Luciel said, hundreds have died. Does the fate of one more Hex make any difference?"

"If you care about hundreds, you have to care about one," Wraith said quietly. "How much do you care, Raven?"

Before Raven could answer him, they heard Ali calling and the sound of the vidscreen being turned up. Raven turned away to join the others and, after a few seconds, Wraith followed her to the next room where the coverage of the Prime Minister's statement was beginning.

"Tonight George Chesterton, the Prime Minister, will address

the House to make a public statement on the recent allegations concerning the Center for Paranormal Studies, the UK body responsible for the elimination of defectives with the mutant Hex gene."

"Defectives?" Ali exclaimed and Luciel hushed her.

"Get used to it," Raven said dryly, not looking away from the screen.

". . . now we go live to the British Parliament, where Mr. Chesterton is about to make his official statement."

The scene shifted to the circular parliament building where a tall man with graying hair was regarding the house with an expression of severe authority.

"Honorable and right honorable members, I come here tonight to quell the speculation concerning the integrity of this government and to speak out against acts of terrorism such as those inflicted upon the British people last week. The invasion of a CPS extermination facility, the fabrication of records from that facility, the publication of those records and eventual destruction of the facility concerned are all acts of astounding terrorism, perpetrated by a group of criminals sympathetic to the cause of illegal mutants. Rest assured these criminals will be caught. In the meantime I would like to state categorically that I have every confidence in Governor Charles Alverstead, the current head of the CPS, and in his operatives, including the head of the facility, who was hospitalized last night after injuries sustained during a valiant defense against the terrorists. His courage and heroism are an example to us all."

The Prime Minister seated himself to cheers from all over the house, and the news reporter broke in on the footage to state that a short announcement by the Head of the Security Services would follow. They all watched the screen in appalled fascination as the cheering continued in Parliament. Kez was the first to speak.

"They're all in on it!" he exclaimed. "It's all being covered up."

"Will the public fall for it?" Wraith asked, turning to Raven, but it was Ali who answered him.

"I'm sure they will," she said. "People will want to believe it. Everyone knows that Hexes are criminals and those pictures of the experiments were hard to take." She swallowed. "Some people might doubt, but not enough of them to sway public opinion."

"She's right," Raven agreed. "I have a great deal of faith in human nature—they'll believe it."

"Every word of it is a lie," Luciel said, but no one replied. The uniformed figure of the Head of the Security Services had just appeared on the screen. He began his announcement without ceremony.

"The Security Services have identified several of the participants in the raid on the CPS facility. Descriptions and artists' impressions follow. If any citizen has been contacted by these people please inform the Security Services immediately. They are terrorists, known to be killers, and all are believed to be armed and dangerous."

Ali's eyes widened in amazement as the screen filled with pictures and statistics.

"Suspect One: Wraith, young male with prematurely white hair and gray eyes, about average height. Suspect Two: young male with dyed blue hair, and green eyes, believed to be of Irish descent. Suspect

Three: Caucasian boy with blond hair and brown eyes. Suspect Four: Raven, young female, known to be a rogue Hex."

The item ended with another plea for anyone with information on the terrorists to come forward, and then the reporter's image appeared on the screen as a panel of hastily assembled political analysts began to discuss the situation over vidcom links. The discussion opened with the reporter asking why mutant sympathizers were engaging in terrorist acts now, when the extermination laws had been enacted 269 years ago.

The vidscreen went dead as Raven leaned forward to turn off the unit and they regarded each other in the sudden silence.

"Why didn't they mention me or Luciel, or Revenge?" Ali asked eventually.

"Because legally you're dead," Raven pointed out. "The CPS have records of your extermination; they can hardly admit that you are alive without confirming the reports of the experiments."

"You're still in danger," Wraith stated. "They may not be admitting to it, but I'm certain the Security Services know exactly who you are."

"There wasn't a description of Raven," Luciel pointed out.

"No one saw me and lived to tell," the girl said grimly. "Jeeva flatlined them all." Then she glared at the screen. "But I've never been this visible before. The CPS never even knew I existed. Now they know my name and they know how much of a threat I am."

"Are you intending to go into hiding?" Wraith asked, knowing that such an action would be uncharacteristic for Raven.

"Are you?" she asked.

Wraith considered, aware that all eyes were focused on him. He thought about the extermination laws, about the things he had seen in Kalden's laboratory, about the broken body of Revenge, and about Raven's continual fight to stay alive. Finally he remembered the official denial, the lies that would be believed unless the government could be forced to acknowledge the immorality of what they were doing and had done ever since the Hex gene was first created. The hopelessness of the past few days was erased as he made his decision.

"No," he stated. "I'm not going to hide."

"What then?" Raven asked, with a strange expression in her eyes.

"I'm going to fight it," Wraith declared. "The government thinks we're a threat, so let's *be* a threat."

"Become terrorists?" Ali asked.

"No." Wraith shook his head. "Don't let them label us that way. Thousands have died because of their lies already. Whatever you do, you mustn't believe them." He paused to study them each in turn. Luciel, Ali, Kez, Raven, and the closed door of the room where Revenge lay sleeping. "Think of what we've accomplished already," he told them. "I think we should stick together."

They looked at him. Ali's eyes were shining with hope, and Kez and Luciel were smiling for the first time since the raid. It was a responsibility that Wraith had not intended to take on. But since he had arrived in London every step had led him inexorably toward the conclusion that this was something he *had* to do. But he knew as well as the rest of them that the decision was not entirely his to

make. They would follow him alone if necessary, but as he turned
to look at Raven, he sensed their eyes follow his.

Raven's head was bent, her eyes hooded as she thought. They
waited for her answer, knowing that while Raven would never
consent to hide, agreeing to fight was quite another thing. Then she
raised her head and grinned wickedly. With an exuberant gesture
she shook her hair free from its confinement and stood up.

"I'm with you," she said. "It should be wild."

The flitter rose slowly through the levels of London, piloted by a
dark-eyed girl whose hands rested lightly on the controls. No one
noticed them as they cruised past the bridges, a Security Services
skimmer remained stationary as they flew over it, keeping to the
speed limit. Three levels further up Raven turned to the figure in
the passenger seat and raised an eyebrow quizzically. Kez looked
back slyly, conscious of Wraith seated behind them.

"Dare me?" Raven asked.

"Go for it," Kez replied and the flitter went into a screaming
climb. Raven's laughter was drowned out by the music that blasted
from the flitter's speakers as they swept out of London, heading for
the sky.

SHADOWS

1
PAINTED HONORS

Alaric swung his flitter past the craft moving to intercept him and guided it into a spinning roll, setting a collision course for the bridge ahead. At the last minute he directed the vehicle upward again and shot over the bridge, instead of into it, allowing the people crowding it to see the words emblazoned across the side of the flitter, proclaiming in brilliant gold: *Power to the People.*

As he guided his flitter around for another pass, avoiding the pursuing Security Services, Alaric glanced at the pandemonium below. The five skyscraper sections that formed the offices of the European Federation Consulate were surrounded by protesters. The bridges and archways that linked the Consulate to the rest of the level were blockaded by skimmers and pedestrians waving banners that carried the same slogan as Alaric's flitter. Portable holo units were mounted on the skimmers, projecting images onto the walls of the EF building. Other units, concealed among the protesters, created phantom images of flitters to distract the Seccies from their real targets. As protests went, it was a successful operation, but Alaric was aware that ultimately all their efforts would be useless. Already EF officials and Seccie operatives were pushing the crowd back from the doors of the Consulate and soon the demonstration would disintegrate.

Alaric was not under any illusions that this protest would change EF policy. It would be enough if news of the demonstration reached the public. Above the confusion, flitters mounted with vid and holocams observed the scene, logos of the media networks painted prominently across the small aerial craft to distinguish them from the flitters of the demonstrators. The media was the real audience and Alaric was well aware of it. After passing low over the bridges he headed upward to tumble past the news crews in a victory roll, displaying to advantage the words on his flitter. Next to the golden slogan was another logo, a red Celtic dragon coiled around a scepter, the symbol of the most prominent political pressure group at the gathering. Alaric's group called themselves Anglecynn and would use any means from peaceful protests to terrorist attacks to expose the corruption and illegality at the heart of the European Federation. The dragon emblem was a warning to the watching masses that the EF could expect more than demonstrations if they disregarded the people who defied their control.

Even as he exhilarated in the thrill of the chase, Alaric longed to do some real damage, to hit the EF hard and fast and show that Anglecynn was a force to be reckoned with. But, despite their standing in the media, the group was too small to tackle the might of the European government on its own. Alaric knew his own limitations, and as he saw the Seccie operatives producing crowd control weapons down below, he knew that for the moment they had been reached. Clicking on his com unit he addressed the protesters in the other flitters:

"Time to pull back, people. They're bringing out the big guns."

The five flitters swept away from the crowds and up past the media crews. Taken by surprise, the Seccies were late in giving chase, and the little flitters took advantage of their delay to split up, each seeking a different path through the skyscraper maze of London to their rendezvous point in the depths of the city.

Several miles away on a level somewhere in the middle of the city a black-clad figure turned away from the holoscreen with a derisive half-smile.

"Amateurs," Raven said, without emotion. "And naïve at that."

"Why naïve?" Wraith asked. He had been watching the feature with the same fixed concentration he gave to all political reports but now he fixed his gray eyes on Raven, who had turned back to the mass of circuitry she had spread out over the blue-gray carpeting of the apartment.

"The machinery of political protest is defunct," Raven replied, with a cynical expression, "rendered obsolete by the microchip and the data pathways of the net." She paused as she searched through a pile of tools for one she needed. "This protest will vanish amid myriad media images, travelling faster than light through the information age. The records we released from Kalden's lab were discredited and eliminated within the week, the media nets moved on to new scandals and no one even blinked. You don't use the media by feeding it, but by controlling it." She flicked a glance at the girl sitting in front of the holoscreen. "Ali should be able to tell you all about it."

Ali Tarrell glanced up at the sound of her name and blushed as she registered what Raven had said. Ali's knowledge of the way the media worked was, at best, tenuous. The life she had had with her media mogul father had ended a year ago, vanishing even as she had become one of the invisible people, slipping between the cracks in the system and officially on record as exterminated for possession of Hex abilities.

Ali turned back to watching the news, imitating Wraith. He found all forms of protest fascinating, as he still hoped that the Hexes could gain legal rights by taking their case to the European Federation which had issued the original law permitting their extermination. Raven was openly contemptuous of such a plan but Ali, coming from a more conventional and law-abiding background, favored the idea. She still aimed to earn the respect of the ganger who had rescued her and her gaze lingered on his features, which could have been chiseled out of white marble, framed by equally white hair. The news report moved on to another story, losing Wraith's interest, and Ali looked away guiltily, glancing back over her shoulder to check that she had not been observed by the other occupants of the room.

Kez was nowhere to be seen, and, to Ali's relief, Raven was

again absorbed in her tangle of components. Although Raven was able to enter the virtual network that connected all computer facilities, she was as interested in the mechanics of machinery as in their data streams. Ali wondered if that was why Raven seemed so much more able than her. Although Ali was two years older than the other girl, her abilities were much more limited. It was a fact that Raven never ceased to remind her of. Ever since their first meeting, Raven had exhibited contempt for someone she clearly regarded as an inferior imitation of herself.

Ali glared silently at Raven, whose long black hair fell over her face as she scrutinized the insides of the computer she was designing. It was particularly galling to recall that Raven was the kind of person that Ali would have despised during her old life on the right side of the law. Ensconced within a clique of popular pretty girls she would have felt safe to sneer at Raven, whose behavior she considered to be almost psychotic. As if she could read her thoughts, the dark-haired girl looked up, her obsidian eyes meeting Ali's challengingly. Ali looked away again, not wanting a confrontation. The younger girl had been in a black mood for days, brought on by an argument with Wraith, which was lifting only now. Ali wouldn't have minded seeing them at odds, but the argument only served to remind her of the fact that, no matter how much they argued, they seemed determined to stay together. Ali had hoped Raven would take off someday but the possibility seemed remote. And Wraith, despite the fact that he condemned the apartment every day, showed no signs of intending to move elsewhere.

The apartment was not as luxurious as the one in the Belgravia

Complex, where Ali had lived until six months ago. It was in a different area of the city and on a different level from her home. But it was desirable and expensive enough for Wraith to worry that they were unnecessarily exposed to the Seccies or the CPS. Raven wasn't worried about the Security Services; they had enough difficulty policing the ganglands without worrying about Hexes living secretly in the heights. But even she admitted that the CPS was a danger, if not to her, then to the others. They still had immense legal powers to kidnap and exterminate anyone with Hex abilities. However she insisted they were better able to watch out for them here than in a place that they would have to defend against more conventional criminals.

Ali might admire Wraith but she was alarmed by the alternative he proposed. She didn't want to move down into the darkness of the ganglands any more than Raven did. However, her reluctance was motivated by fear and she suspected that Raven's was the result of pure stubbornness.

Just then the door to one of the bedrooms slid open and Kez entered. He had been a London streetrat before he joined up with Wraith and Raven. Since then he had changed enough for the brother and sister to trust him not to betray them. But Ali was still uncomfortable with the boy. Partly because of his gangland history and partly because Kez obviously admired Raven and she did nothing to discourage him. But the fact that Kez was able to take care of Revenge was an advantage to his presence as a member of the group.

Wraith and Raven's sister had never recovered from her stint in the CPS laboratories. As far as Ali could understand it, the eleven-year-old's brain had been directly linked up to a computer database with no experience in handling the dataflow. Most of the other children who had been experimented on in this way had been burned out, becoming mindless wrecks. But Revenge, who had possessed a greater potential to become a fully functional Hex, had survived the experience, though not unscarred. Most of the time she could function well enough to take care of herself, but her thoughts were so disengaged from her surroundings, scrambled as they were by the experimentation, that it wasn't safe to leave her on her own. Ali, Wraith, Kez, and Luciel, the boy they had rescued from the CPS lab, divided the responsibility among them. Raven refused, considering the task a waste of her time. She spent hours in further research on the data she had stolen from the lab. From the questions she would occasionally ask them, Ali and Luciel suspected she was devising her own experiments to test the Hex abilities but she had said nothing to either of them, and Wraith was too absorbed in his own project to notice. He was collecting information on the judicial processes of turning people with the Hex gene into criminals, hoping to form a group of Hexes and their sympathizers who could work to challenge the extermination laws.

While Ali had been speculating on her companions Wraith had been thinking about what his sister had said. Turning away from the holoscreen, he crossed the room to sit on the arm of the chair next to her.

"How would *you* organize a protest, Raven?"

"I wouldn't," she replied, not even deigning to look up.

"Why not?" Kez asked curiously, joining the conversation.

"They serve no useful purpose," Raven said. Putting down the tool she was working with, she looked up, her gaze shifting to include Ali as well as Wraith and Kez in her communication. When Raven chose to give her point of view, she always spoke to an audience. While Wraith often condemned her behavior as reckless, he didn't deny that her judgments, when based on her own cynical philosophy of how the world worked, were rarely proved wrong.

"A protest is a public admission of incompetence," Raven said coolly, shaking her hair out of her eyes. "Its purpose is to draw attention to a situation in the hope of altering it. But, except in a few rare cases, the situation does not change because those who would care about the issue are either already alerted to it or, once they become aware of it, because they have seen the protest, believe that something is already done. Demonstrations are just another form of media entertainment. They change nothing."

"The protesters against the European Federation control don't believe that," Wraith pointed out.

"Naïve." Raven shrugged. "As I said." Her expression turned wry as she continued: "But in any case, the anti-EF front doesn't believe in the power of the people any more than I do. Did you notice that wasn't the only symbol the flitters carried?"

"There was a red dragon," Ali recalled. "The reporter said it was the insignia of a terrorist group."

"The group is called Anglecynn," Raven informed her. "They've been flooding the public nets with material for the past few years, combining information about EF corruption with threats of their next attacks." She gave a half smile. "They've actually been quite effective at destruction of property, even a few attempted assassinations. They're a small group, without much cohesion or strategy, but they might yet prove successful. The slogan on the flitter is not the real message, the dragon is. It reminds the EF that Anglecynn don't just rely on the media stunts to get their message across."

The flitters cruised slowly through the darkness. After the chase through the high-rise levels and the tension travelling through the ganglands further down, the silence of the tower levels was almost soothing. The lights of Alaric's flitter slid across the shadows, illuminating the debris that had built up around the roots of the massive skyscrapers. Centuries-old graffiti etched the ancient support struts with faded colors; light gleamed eerily back from the consumer graveyard beneath him; layers of obsolete luxuries sifted like sand into a rubble composed of the discards of the rich, long since scavenged and rejected by the poor and now abandoned like the roots of the city itself. The street lighting had long since failed and the lights from the flitters pierced the darkness like a desecration.

The distant sounds that filtered down from above had gradually melted away and now the silence was complete. Alaric shivered and activated his comlink.

"Alaric to Jordan. My scanners show no signs of pursuit or surveillance. Do you concur?"

"*I concur,*" the girl's voice came back over the channel. "*No spooks or bugs. All scans are spangly and clean, now let's blow this joint and go home.*"

"Agreed," Alaric replied dryly and opened a new channel. "Alaric to Dragon's Nest. My team is back and there's been no sign of a trace. Are we clear to come home?"

There was a buzz of static, punctuated by echoes from other signals before a voice replied briskly.

"Our scanners agree there's no trace. Your team is cleared to approach, Alaric."

Alaric's hands moved swiftly over the control panel, speeding the flitter up as he signalled to the others that they were allowed to approach. Together they navigated the maze of support struts that rose from the sea of debris to become lost in the darkness above. The scenery passed by unchanging until the gloom was broken by a sprinkling of light in the distance ahead. The flitters slowed down as they approached a large plaza rising a little above the rubble and forming the forecourt to a skyscraper section which was not as damaged as the rest. Dim light shone from the windows as the flitters touched down on the cracked and pitted surface of the plaza and lit the way for the five newcomers to enter the building.

Alaric fell into step with one of his companions as they neared the door. Jordan glanced up at him, brushing her untidy brown hair out of her eyes, as he rested an arm over her shoulders.

"You did good work," he told her.

"We all did good work," she said, stopping to wrap her arms around his waist. "But it's back to garbage city for all of us."

Alaric frowned and rested his chin on the top of Jordan's head, drawing her into a hug so he wouldn't have to meet her serious blue-green eyes. The girl's voice was muffled as she continued:

"We all talk big, Alaric, but the EF knows we're not a serious threat. We're flies to them and they're just waiting for the right time to swat us out of the sky."

"Then we'll have to convince them otherwise," Alaric said firmly. But as he took Jordan's hand and led her into the building he wondered how that was ever going to be accomplished.

Anglecynn's headquarters were a safe refuge for the terrorist group. Far from the policed upper levels and ganglands alike, no one could find them in the depths of the city. They could expand through the abandoned buildings without fear of retribution and they had made the area their own. To Alaric and Jordan, Dragon's Nest was home and they relaxed as they entered its confines, secure in the knowledge that the proximity sensors would alert them to anyone approaching long before they neared the refuge. A short corridor leading from the entrance hall of the building took them to a large communal room. As Jordan headed for the battered Nutromac unit in the corner of the room, Alaric collapsed in an equally dilapidated chair and slung his feet up on the table in front of him. Heaving a deep sigh he stretched and sank back into the chair only to be jolted upright again by something landing hard in the center of his chest.

It was a computer disk, and Alaric regarded it with confusion for a moment before its owner appeared in his field of vision.

"Got a job for you, Alaric," Liz said, sitting on the side of the table.

Alaric groaned quietly. Like most of Anglecynn's so-called "administrative" staff, Liz tended to disregard the work of the actual protesters. Unfortunately, the group's efficiency depended on the information that Liz and others like her managed to dig out. Alaric could have pulled rank as a veteran of the group but instead he picked up the disk and looked questioningly at Liz.

"Information came through contacts yesterday," she told him. "Managed to filter through sources to us today. Comes from a sympathizer in the know—I thought you'd better take a look at it."

Alaric had barely assimilated this brusque communication when Liz disappeared again and he was left looking quizzically at the desk as Jordan turned up with two cups of a thick black coffee substitute.

"Thanks," he said absently, taking a sip of the acrid substance, and then got wearily to his feet.

"What's up?" Jordan asked, glancing at the disk Alaric still held.

"More work," he told her. "Hopefully shouldn't take too long. I'll join you in a while and we can grab some food, OK?"

"'Kay," Jordan replied, taking over the chair he'd vacated. "Wake me up when you're ready."

Alaric made a mock grimace at the sight of her relaxed figure, tousled her hair affectionately, and went to find a computer unit and check the disk.

Although most of Anglecynn's real members lived in the city's depths, they had sympathizers and contacts in more exalted surroundings. The disk was marked as being a transmission from a Daniel Hammond, an Anglecynn sympathizer and the son of the recently appointed security minister. According to the appended file he had been approached by an Anglecynn contact and asked to find out what provisions were being made for the prevention of terrorism. This transmission was his response and as Alaric reviewed the file he found it increasingly odd, especially considering the amount of anti-EF activity.

Since appointment of Adam Hammond as Security Minister (4.10.2368) plans have been in progress for a new crackdown on terrorism, especially activities prejudicial to British relation with the European Federation. These plans have been superceded as of 3.1.2369 after a meeting between Adam Hammond MP (Security Minister and Head of the Security Services), Governor Charles Alverstead (Head of the CPS), and a Dr. Kalden (unknown). Minutes of this meeting have been suppressed. The new security strategy is not focused on anti-EF terrorism. It is instead focused on supporting the CPS in their legalized extermination of mutants possessing the deformative Hex gene. The Security Services have pledged themselves to the elimination of all mutants within five years. Their efforts are concentrated on this one aim. Particular emphasis is being laid upon the capture of a mutant known as "Raven" (described as a terrorist with the Hex gene). Transmission ends.

Alaric considered the transmission for some time, trying to understand all its implications. The increase in terrorist activity and the expansion of the ganglands had been the primary motivations behind the British Prime Minister's appointment of a new Security Minister. Now, if this information was correct, that Security

Minister had decided to throw other considerations aside to support an organization that, because of its activities, had a politically unsavory reputation. The combined threat of gangland crimes and terrorist attacks had been ignored in favor of apprehending a rogue mutant on the basis of a single meeting with the Head of CPS and an unknown scientist. Alaric frowned at the screen. Other members of Anglecynn would rejoice in their good fortune in not being the focus of the Seccies' attention for a change, but Alaric found this new development too unusual to celebrate. Still frowning, he left the computer unit on and went to find Liz.

It took him some time to locate her in the rambling building. But he eventually tracked her down to a room several floors up where she and other Anglecynn members were watching a holovid projection of the raid on the EF Consulate. Crossing the room as unobtrusively as he could, Alaric came up behind Liz and touched her on the shoulder.

"Can I talk to you for a minute?" he asked.

Liz glanced at him, looking slightly puzzled, then shrugged and followed him out of the room. Once they were in the corridor, Alaric kept walking, leading her back to the room where he had viewed the disk.

"That transmission you gave me," he said. "Have you had a look at it?"

"Yeah." Liz nodded. "Good news, if it's true. But it seemed a bit dodgy. Do you think it's a fake?"

"No, I don't think so." Alaric thought for a second. "At least if it is, it's very subtle." He paused as they entered the room he had only recently vacated and guided Liz toward the computer unit. "I want you to check something out for me."

If Alaric had wanted to pay Liz back for preventing him from relaxing earlier, he would have been disappointed. Liz didn't raise a single objection as she slid into the chair in front of the keypad, waiting for further instructions.

"I want you to find out about the people mentioned in this document." Alaric told her. "Charles Alverstead, Dr. Kalden, whoever he is, and this mutant, Raven. I want to know what's so important that the Seccies can't be bothered about tracking down an armed and dangerous terrorist group like us."

Liz grinned but she was shaking her head as well.

"I'll do what I can," she said. "But I'm no hacker. I'll find out what's on the public databases, maybe a little more, but don't expect huge results."

"Just do what you can," Alaric reassured her. "Any information would be better than nothing. Tomorrow I'll try and find out something more from this sympathizer: Daniel Hammond."

Daniel was watching the news. His father had been pleased when Daniel joined him, finding his son's serious demeanor a welcome change from his daughter's levity. Caitlin was in her room sulking because the news interfered with watching one of the many amorphous programs that dominated her life. But Adam Hammond had been firm. Not only did he insist that the news was a priority, today there would be an article of special interest to him, since the Security Services had provided it. Unknown to him, Daniel was watching for the same reason. His father's work had never been of much interest to him until Adam's elevation to Minister of Security. Daniel's tenuous connection to Anglecynn had meant that his father's work had suddenly become more compelling, since it meant life or death to Daniel's associates. The transmission he had sent the day before, risking prosecution as a spy, was a reaffirmation of his commitment to the anti-EF front.

He didn't know what was going to be on the holovid this evening that so interested his father. But Adam rarely insisted on his right to watch the news, deeming it not worth Caitlin's complaints at being separated from the vid screen, so whatever it was must be important. However, article followed article without provoking any reaction from his father. The repeat of a feature on the attack on the EF Consulate drew a frown but that was already old news. Daniel shivered at the thought of what his father would do if he ever discovered his son's connections with the same demonstrators he condemned.

The feature came to an end and Adam leaned forward expectantly; Daniel focused on the screen as the next article began.

"In related news, the mutant terrorist with the illegal Hex gene, who was responsible for the destruction of a CPS facility causing the deaths of one hundred and thirty-seven men and women last year, is still on the loose. It is believed that the terrorist, who styles herself 'Raven,' is hiding among the criminal element in the lower levels of the city. Today Adam Hammond, the Security Minister, said that information leading to her capture would be treated in the strictest confidentiality and he warned that citizens should beware

*of approaching Raven, who is probably armed and certainly danger-
ous. Nothing has been seen of Raven or the terrorists associated with
her this year but last year her activities prompted a statement by the
Prime Minister."*

The report cut to a segment of old footage showing the Prime
Minister giving a statement to the House.

*". . . The invasion of a CPS extermination facility, the fabrica-
tion of records from that facility, the publication of those records,
and eventual destruction of the facility concerned are all acts of
astounding terrorism, perpetrated by a group of criminals sympathetic to the cause of illegal mutants. Rest assured these criminals
will be caught. . . ."*

The segment ended and the reporter continued:

*"Despite those assurances Raven has managed to elude the
Security Services and is suspected to be planning acts of even greater
atrocity. Political analysts cite this as an argument for greater EF
control of Britain. The European Federation has the resources necessary to apprehend dangerous criminals of this kind without the risk
to those who capture them. But even without the aid of the Federation it seems the mutant plague will be finally brought to an end.
Mr. Hammond has pledged the Security Services to a widespread
eradication program, supporting the CPS in their mandate to rid
this country of Hexes for ever. Britain will show the way by taking
the first step and encouraging the rest of the world to do the same."*

2

THESE MASKS AND CURTAINS

The vidscreen flickered in the darkened room, the recording frozen on the anonymous face of a news anchor. A pale hand moved against the moment control and the picture sprang to life again:

"*. . . seems the mutant plague will be finally brought to an end. Mr. Hammond has pledged the Security Services to a widespread eradication program, supporting the CPS in their mandate to rid this country of Hexes forever. Britain will show the way by taking the first step and encouraging the rest of the world . . .*"

The screen blanked to black as the control twitched spasmodically in the hand of the watcher and for a while the room was dark.

The silence was broken by the sound of a door swishing open and light streamed into the room from the hallway, glinting off the red hair of the figure slumped in front of the vidscreen.

"Avalon?" a voice said, lifting a little in surprise. "I'm sorry, I didn't think there was anyone here."

"Don't worry about it," the seated figure replied. "Could you turn the lights on?"

"Certainly." The newcomer turned gracefully and brushed his hand across a touch-sensitive panel set on the wall next to the door, causing soft lights to come on all over the room, illuminating the red and gold decoration that gleamed with luxury. "What were you watching?" he asked, glancing at the control Avalon still held in her hand.

"A news bulletin I recorded yesterday," Avalon replied, shifting up against the heavy red cushions to make room.

"May I ask why?" her companion asked politely, arranging himself carefully beside her.

Avalon shrugged in reply, then sighed and replied more explicitly.

"Looking for material, I guess. Seems the media are jazzed up on this terrorism story."

"Is there an angle you want to use?"

"Maybe," Avalon said slowly. "A song with a terrorism theme, perhaps."

"We could put ourselves on dangerous political ground," was the response. "Either we support the government in asking for more EF control or we glamorize terrorism. Perhaps something with ambiguous wording." He paused to consider this and Avalon studied him thoughtfully. Cloud Estavisti cultivated a graceful poise that had catapulted him to fame as surely as his actual talent.

He had an air of untouchability that shrouded him in mystique. Avalon liked to think that in two years of stardom she had learned something about media manipulation but compared to Cloud she was still a novice. From his streaked silver-blond hair and dark blue eyes to the holographic projections that floated in and out of sight around his plain white clothes, Cloud was not so much a human being as glamour personified and even Avalon was envious of such a quality.

Cloud came out of his reverie and raised his eyebrows at Avalon's intent stare. Gesturing toward the vidscreen he said:

"I came to see if you wanted to watch CultRock. They intend to show the new vid tonight."

"OK." Avalon passed Cloud the control and looked back at the screen as it came to life and flipped through a sequence of ephemeral images as Cloud searched for the right channel. With so many media feeds devoted solely to contemporary music, it took him a while to find it, but eventually the split-second images settled into a holographic projection of an alien city, spiderlike creatures moving across the bridges and walkways to spin the buildings out of silk. The music itself made use of so many new effects that Avalon found it difficult to pick out the lyrics from the masking ultrasonics. Cloud set the image to project a meter out from the screen, not far enough to enclose them in the vid, and settled himself back next to Avalon.

Movement in the hallway alerted Avalon to the presence of more people and she turned to see the other members of what was loosely called her rock group clustering in to join them, drawn by the music pouring out from the custom-made speakers. Music was their life as much as hers and it never hurt to keep up on the competition.

"Isn't that Elohim's latest effort?" Lissa drawled, tossing her honey-colored hair for Cloud's benefit as she slid into the seat next to him. "Well, he's always been a little off the planet, but this time I don't think he's coming back."

"Don't knock it, Liss, it sells," pointed out Corin cynically.

"We sell," Jesse corrected, sprawling sideways across an item of furniture designed for three people. "And we don't have to get ethereal to do it."

"Don't get complacent," Corin told him. "We could get knocked off the top of the ratings just as quickly as Elohim."

"Have you noticed how we are being emulated by groups with lesser talent?" Cloud interjected. "Our style could easily cease being original and innovative and become last month's cliché."

"It's all about style with you, isn't it?" Corin demanded belligerently. "You're not a musician, so don't tell us how to work."

The conversation continued argumentatively, band members jostling for position and cutting each other down. Avalon concentrated on the screen and tried to ignore it. They were always this nervous before an important exposure and they had all worked themselves to exhaustion on this new vid. Cloud was right. It was becoming harder and harder to buck the trends, with so many ready to imitate that their music was prevented from ever becoming truly distinctive. Recently they had been making more of the visual aspect, something in which Cloud excelled, to create a unique feel to their vids. But that wouldn't be enough without music to equal it and Avalon had been taking risks to achieve that. She couldn't explain how she did it, how she modified the electronic signals from her guitar to create sounds she knew the instrument should not be capable of, how she played with the equipment in the studio to create just the right sound. But she could put a name to the ability that allowed her to build a sound just this side of impossible and it was an ability that could get her killed, executed as summarily as every other Hex, despite the protecting shield of her fame.

Caitlin Hammond watched her brother with irritation as he shifted nervously in his chair. Daniel was always so jittery, she wouldn't be surprised if he had a secret girlfriend, what with all the hours and hours he spent on the vidcom. Usually Caitlin was too absorbed in her own affairs to pay even cursory attention to the fact of her brother's existence. But at the moment his fidgeting was irritating, distracting her from the vidscreen. She was about to suggest that Daniel go elsewhere when a soft chime indicated that there was someone at the apartment door.

"That's probably Zircarda," Caitlin said with satisfaction, heading toward the door, knowing how much her brother disliked her friend. "We're going to watch the premier of the new Masque vid together."

"Oh, God," Daniel groaned and hastily got out of his chair. "I don't think I can cope with Zircarda Anthony at this time of night. I'll be in my room if anyone wants me."

Caitlin answered the door as Daniel beat a hasty retreat, seeing that as usual Zircarda hadn't come alone. As the self-styled leader of the most popular clique in the Belgravia Complex, she considered it beneath her dignity to go anywhere without a couple of satellites. Currently she was accompanied by Mira, a long-standing clique member, and Roni, her latest protégée.

"Hi, Caitlin," Zircarda said casually and she and Mira came inside, Roni trailing a few steps behind them. "Has it started yet?"

"Not yet," Caitlin replied. "Come and sit down, the screen's already down."

"Electric," Zircarda said lazily, drifting over to the seat right in front of the screen and fiddling with the holo controls.

"Set it for room inclusive," Mira suggested, heading toward the kitchen. "I'm starving, Caitlin—have you got anything to eat?"

"Of course," she replied and spent the next five minutes making drinks for the others while Mira rummaged around looking for food.

Having constructed herself a snack consisting of no calories whatsoever, Mira joined the rest of them in front of the screen.

"Isn't this the channel Ali's father set up last year?" she asked curiously and Caitlin flashed a glance at Zircarda, uncertain of how to react.

"Who's Ali?" Roni asked innocently and Zircarda made an expression of distaste.

"Mr. Tarrell's daughter," she said in a clipped tone of voice. "She used to live here."

"You must have heard of it, Roni," Mira said more conversationally, interested in the sensation value of the story. "It was a big scandal. She turned out to be a Hex and the CPS came and took her away, right here in the Complex and everything."

"And you knew her?" Roni was wide-eyed.

"She was a friend of ours," Caitlin said sharply. "And she can't have known what she was. Ali wasn't sneaky."

"No, but what a way to find out." Mira shook her head in disbelief. "What a nightmare."

"Well, it's over now," Zircarda said firmly, taking control of the conversation again. "Mira, did you manage to get tickets for the premiere of your mother's film?"

Daniel could still hear drawling voices through the closed door of his room and he turned on his sound system to drown it out. He was always amazed by the way the clique could drop people and never appear to think of them again. He vaguely remembered Ali Tarrell. She had seemed much like all the others, a pretty, if spoiled, teenager with too much money and no responsibilities. But she was surely worth more than a minute's conversation, a year after her death, by people who had been her friends.

A shrill chirrup cut through the soothing waveform music emanating from Daniel's sound system, signalling that someone was attempting to contact his vidcom. Daniel silenced the music with a word and hurried over to sit in front of the com unit, touching the keypad to answer the signal. When he touched the control the screen remained black and Daniel frowned, wondering if there was a bug in the unit, until an obviously computer-alerted voice spoke to him.

"Daniel Hammond?"

"Yes, that's me," Daniel said nervously to whoever was watching him from the other side of the vidcom link.

"We got your message," the voice continued.

"You're from Anglecynn?" Daniel asked and then clapped a hand over his mouth in alarm, realizing that if anyone was monitoring this signal he would have already condemned himself.

"Yes," the stranger confirmed. "There's no need for concern, this is a clean transmission." Daniel wondered if he was imagining that a note of amusement had crept into the synthetic voice.

"What do you want?" Daniel asked. "I can't talk to you here—it isn't safe."

"Agreed," the unknown terrorist replied. "We want a face-to-face meet. You will be collected in one hour from bridge 9-75."

"But . . . ," Daniel protested and stopped as he saw the transmission had been cut. He tapped his fingers nervously on the side of the console for a minute before sending a new signal, this one to a public flitter firm. In seconds their operator had assured him that a flitter would be at his door in ten minutes to take him wherever he wished to go.

"And now it's time for what you've all been waiting for . . . the latest from Europe's most sensational rock combo: Masque. The new song's called 'In the Dark' and showing for the first time anywhere. CultRock brings you tonight the electric holovid. . . ."

Ali's former friends would probably have been more horrified

than gratified to know that halfway across the city she was watching the same channel that held them entranced. Although Ali
had changed considerably since joining the renegades, some of
her tastes were still those of the sheltered teenager she had been.
Here, in a comfortably luxurious apartment, submerged in the
images of a state-of-the-art holovid, Ali could imagine herself
safe.

But safety was not the atmosphere Masque had sought to
create with this video. Once it might not have touched Ali with
its nightmare images; now it was a reminder of what lay beyond
the haven of this room. The holovid showed dark passages leading ever downward, a series of half-imagined horrors flitting
from shadow to shadow, a world of terror realized by the shriek
of a guitar. Ali shivered and then jumped as she caught sight of
another shadow out of the corner of her eye. A soft laugh brought
her back to reality.

"Raven!" she gasped, in mixed relief and embarrassment. "I
didn't see you there."

Raven gave her a blank look, then turned back to the holoscreen.

"What is this?" she demanded.

"The group?" Ali asked, puzzled. "Or the song?"

"Whatever," Raven replied, with a touch of annoyance.

"It's Masque, their new vid: 'Into the Dark,'" Ali said nervously. "Do you like it? I've got their latest lasdisk, if you want to
borrow it."

"OK," Raven said, to Ali's surprise. Her dark eyes were distracted and she frowned at the vidscreen as if she was trying to remember something.

"Hang on, I'll go and get it," Ali said and went to the room she had staked out as hers. It took her a few minutes to find the disk but when she got back she saw that Raven had not shifted position, she was still transfixed by the vidscreen.

"I didn't think you liked contemporary music," Ali said. "This latest disk is kind of freaky, though—their previous stuff wasn't like this."

Halfway through what she was saying the final chords of the song signalled the end of the vid and the screen returned to the presenter's face. Raven blinked suddenly and turned away from the screen, her mouth twisted into a half smile.

"The disk," she demanded, holding out her hand for it.

"It's called 'Transformations,'" Ali explained. "That's how come there's all the weird stuff on the holo. But there's a picture of the band on the other side."

"Mmm," Raven responded absently, flipping the disk case over to find it. Ali couldn't remember ever having seen the other girl less antagonistic.

"That's them," she continued helpfully. "The girl with the red hair's Avalon—she's the lead singer and guitarist—and that's Cloud and Corin, and Lissa, the sax-player, and the drummer's called Jesse."

"Interesting," said Raven thoughtfully. She seemed to look through Ali for a moment. "Do you mind if I borrow this?"

"No, go ahead," Ali managed to reply. She stared at Raven, as the younger girl took the disk to her own room and disappeared inside, closing the door firmly behind her. "Weird," Ali said to herself and turned back to the vidscreen.

Kez soldered the last connection and looked critically at the mass of wires hanging out of the flitter's console.

"Hey, El, come and have a look at this!" he yelled and Luciel came round the side of the flitter to look through the open door.

"Are you done?" he asked.

"Yeah," Kez said proudly. "Custom job—nothing'll catch us when this thing's in the air."

"Electric," Luciel grinned and punched Kez's arm lightly. Of all the group he had changed the most in the past year. Since being rescued from the lab he had lost his scarecrow appearance and although his eyes were still haunted by memories of the experiments, he had managed to recover from withdrawal from the drug dependency the scientists had given him. He and Kez tended to spend most of their time together, although Luciel had managed to reconcile Kez and Ali enough for them to feel less uncomfortable with each other.

It was Kez who'd persuaded the gang that working for the Countess would be a good contact for them, and he and Luciel accordingly spent hours working in the fixer's building in the heart of the ganglands, mending electronic equipment for a small fee. When there was nothing else for them to do, they worked on the flitter. Raven had given them the creds to buy it when Kez said he wanted to custom-rig one from the start. She dropped in occasionally, on her way to see the Countess, to give them advice and to give Luciel tools he had asked for. With Kez's practical and Luciel's theoretical science they were learning enough to make themselves useful to the Countess and get the flitter working the way they wanted it to.

"What's next?" Kez asked, looking over the console.

"Not much," Luciel replied. "I've got these power couplings linked up now. That just leaves the locks and the weapons system."

"Yeah." Kez frowned. "Raven said she'd help us with that weeks ago."

"I still can't believe it's possible." Luciel shook his head. "It *shouldn't* be possible. The power system she's designed for those laser weapons is the strangest thing I've ever seen. No one designs a system like that."

"Except Raven," Kez concluded. He sighed. "I wish you could do the things she can, El. We wouldn't have to wait for her to be free."

"She asks me and Ali questions all the time, to figure out what we can and can't do," Luciel replied. "She says she's working out a science of the Hex abilities."

"She ought to be able to teach you something," Kez insisted and Luciel shrugged. "Come on," he continued, "we're done here for today. Let's go back to the apartment—perhaps Raven will have time to help us with the flitter tomorrow."

Daniel wrapped his thick coat tightly around himself. The wind whistled through the towering skyrises and whipped across the deserted bridge. Grayness was all around him, the light of the luxury heights were lost somewhere above him and the slums emblazoned with gang colors were invisible in the depths below. This was a no-man's-land, separating the rich from the poor, an area occupied only by transients, businesses, and people on their way up or on their way down. The hired flitter that brought Daniel here had left ten minutes ago but there was still no sign of his contact. Shivering in the cold, he wondered what Anglecynn wanted with him. He had become a spy for the organization because he was ashamed of his father's connection with the brutal Security Services and he was afraid that greater EF control would be bad for the country. But he still hadn't fully committed to the movement; he lacked the courage of his convictions to break away from his father and the safe sheltered life he had in the Belgravia Complex and officially join Anglecynn. Thinking of the Belgravia Complex reminded him of his sister's conversation earlier; Ali Tarrell hadn't found herself safe there, despite her father's fame and riches. Perhaps he was fooling himself to think that he could support Anglecynn and not be in danger. Daniel shuddered and wondered if the time had come to leave home.

His musings were interrupted by the sound of a flitter swooshing past over his head and pivoting to land on the bridge beside him. The side window slid open to reveal a young man, not much older than a teenager, at the controls of the flitter. Dark eyes regarded him seriously before the stranger spoke.

"You must be Daniel."

"That's right," Daniel confirmed, nervously.

"Get in," Alaric told him. "It's not safe to talk here."

Daniel hesitated for only a moment before crossing to the other side of the flitter as the door hissed open. It closed again behind him as he climbed in, and the flitter started to lift off as he was fastening his safety harness. The Anglecynn member sent the flitter weaving through the buildings and bridges with practiced ease as he began to talk.

"We received your transmission," he began. "You said that the Seccies were concentrating their efforts on helping the CPS."

"Yes, it's true," Daniel agreed, relieved that this was a question he could answer. "Everyone's after the Hex sympathizers who destroyed an extermination facility last year."

"I would have thought the Hexes were just about wiped out by now," Alaric said thoughtfully. "Why would they suddenly start attacking the CPS now?"

"I don't know," Daniel shrugged. "But the government seems to be taking it seriously."

"And so should we," Alaric added. "If these Hexes have the Seccies this rattled, they might be useful to our cause. We need allies and the Hexes have suffered from EF control more than anyone else. I'm surprised no one in Anglecynn's thought of using them before."

"No one really knows what Hexes do," Daniel protested. "They took a girl from my apartment complex last year but no one had even suspected she was a Hex. The CPS keeps all the details secret. All anyone knows is that Hexes are dangerous."

"I'm suspicious of things that 'everyone knows,'" Alaric replied.

"And until I find out why Hexes are supposed to be so dangerous I think I'll give them the benefit of the doubt. In the meantime I'll need you to find out everything you can about this CPS operation and about this Hex called Raven. If we can contact her before the Seccies find her, we might be able to help each other."

"I'll do my best," Daniel agreed. "But I'm not sure how long I can keep doing this. I think I'd rather work for Anglecynn directly than keep spying on my father. It seems dishonest."

"I understand," Alaric said quietly. "The media brands us as terrorists even though we're fighting for their freedom. Sometimes we have to sacrifice our consciences for what we believe in. But if you can get this information it would help immensely. After that, I'll see about finding you a place with us permanently."

"Thank you," Daniel said and meant it. The darkness of the ganglands where Anglecynn operated was no more frightening than the things he had heard since his father became the Security Minister. Some of the darkest crimes happened openly in the light and because they were legal no one protested. The Hex laws were an example of the kind of thing the law permitted: the legalized extermination of an entire group of people.

Luciel and Kez arrived back at the apartment to find it virtually deserted. Ali was sitting in front of the vidscreen in the main room; music pounding from behind Raven's closed door indicated where she might be; but there was no sign of Wraith or Revenge. Ali looked up and smiled as the boys entered and moved up so that they could sit down. Luciel came to sit next to her and Kez perched on one arm of the sofa, still uneasy around the former socialite.

"Hey, Ali, what's up?" Luciel asked. "Have you been watching the vid all day?"

"Mostly," Ali shrugged. "There's not much for me to do around here. Wraith went out to get food, Raven's in her room, Rev—Rachel's asleep, I think."

"You two should ask Raven about teaching you more of this Hex stuff," Kez suggested. "We could get the flitter finished faster that way and it would give you something to do, Ali."

"I don't think Raven's really interested in teaching us," Ali said quietly. "As far as she's concerned she can do anything that needs doing faster and better than us anyway."

"I still think you should ask her," Kez persisted. "If the two of you could do even half the stuff she can, we'd be so much safer. What's the point of being a Hex if you don't know how to be one?"

"A good point," a voice said from the door and they looked round to see that Wraith had returned. The smell of Chinese food drifted across the room from the three bags Wraith was carrying, emblazoned with the holos of an expensive Chinese restaurant in the heights. "Perhaps we should talk to Raven about it," he continued. "Do you think this will coax her out of her room?"

"I expect so," Ali said smiling. "She loves Chinese food and she's not really doing anything much. She borrowed one of my lasdisks and she's been listening to it all evening."

"Really?" Wraith looked surprised. "What disk?" he asked.

"It's 'Transformations,'" Kez told him, having listened to the music seeping into the living room. "The latest release by Masque."

"Well, perhaps you can drag her away from it, Kez," Wraith suggested. "It's about time all of us talked."

Kez nodded and headed for the door to Raven's room. He knocked loudly and was rewarded a few seconds later with it opening to reveal Raven dressed in her usual black, her hair a wild cloud around her face.

"Hi," Kez said nervously, hoping she was in a good mood. "Wraith got Chinese food from Hwang's. Do you want to come and eat with us?"

"Wraith went to Hwang's?" Raven smiled fleetingly and then glanced back into her room. "Yes, I'll join you," she said. "Just give me a minute to finish here." Then she retreated, closing the door behind her.

As Kez went to tell the others Raven would be joining them he saw Wraith disappearing into Revenge's room but he doubted that she would come and eat with them. Revenge spent most of her time sleeping or endlessly playing computer games. She ate food from the Nutromac unit when they brought it to her and she let Wraith and Raven examine her but she rarely spoke to any of them and when she did her words didn't make much sense. Hoping that Wraith wouldn't be too disappointed with Revenge's progress, he went back to join the others. Ali had turned off the vidscreen and was unpacking the food while Luciel laid out plates on the long dining table. He heard the sounds of music cease from Raven's room and moments later she appeared just as Wraith came out of Revenge's room. His expression was bleak but he smiled when he saw Raven and she grinned at him.

"I see you bought dinner in the heights," she said. "To what do we owe the honor?"

"I thought it was time we all talked," Wraith explained, coming to sit at the table. "Did any of you see the news this evening?"

The others shook their heads, Ali with a blush of embarrassment. She would have liked to say yes, but she rarely watched news programs when Wraith wasn't around.

"So, what exciting news item did we miss?" Raven asked, heaping food onto her plate from one of the containers and passing it to Luciel.

"The new Security Minister, Adam Hammond, has vowed to obliterate the Hex threat and has committed the Security Services to helping the CPS in exterminating Hexes," Wraith said succinctly.

Ali went white and Luciel froze in the middle of helping himself to food. Kez shot a look at Raven who, alone of them, still looked calm.

"Really?" she asked. "Why the sudden crackdown?"

"Because of us," Wraith said grimly. "The government still claims we blew up the laboratory and they're calling us terrorists across the media."

"I used to know Mr. Hammond," Ali said softly. "He's Caitlin's father. I can't believe he's doing this." Luciel reached out to squeeze her hand supportively.

"So we're notorious," Raven said with a half smile. "What of it?"

"I think it's about time you taught Ali and Luciel how to use their abilities," Wraith told her. "And I think we should move down into the ganglands."

Everyone turned to look at Raven, expecting her to protest, as she had so many times before, about leaving the luxury of their apartment. Instead she merely raised an eyebrow.

"All right," she said calmly. "It's probably time we moved, and if we're going to recruit more Hexes, a training program would be useful."

The others stared at her in surprise. Kez was the first to speak.

"More Hexes?" he asked.

"Well, one more at least," Raven replied. "I discovered one today."

"Who?" Wraith asked, meeting Raven's eyes seriously.

Raven smiled mischievously.

"A celebrity, no less," she said. "Avalon, the lead singer of Masque."

3
THY KNOWN
SECRECY

The Countess's building was unusually busy when Kez and Luciel arrived there the next day. The Countess herself was supervising operations as her guards loaded crates of equipment into two large flitters. Watching the activity with expressionless black eyes was Raven. Kez and Luciel looked at each other, then crossed the room to where the young Hex was sitting cross-legged on a crate marked *Explosives: Handle With Extreme Care.*

"What are you doing here?" Kez asked curiously as Raven looked up at him.

"Shopping," Raven said briefly. "If Wraith wants to move back into the ganglands we'll need some decent security. The Countess has a building she's not using about ten levels down from here, but the area isn't exactly safe. This stuff is to make it more secure."

"How are you paying for all this?" Luciel asked incredulously and Raven shook her head with a grin.

"Hacked a bank this morning," she replied simply.

Kez was about to ask what was in the crates when a familiar voice called out across the foyer:

"Hey, Raven, you ever wear anything that isn't black?"

Kez and Luciel turned round simultaneously to see two men in blue and gold gang colors approaching, their blue braided hair strung with gold beads.

"*You're* talking?" Raven asked, raising an eyebrow at their gang uniforms.

One of the gangers reached to ruffle Kez's hair and grinned down at him.

"Hey streetrat," he greeted him. "You still tagging along after this schizo?"

"Hey, Jeeva," Kez replied, ducking out under the ganger's hand and aiming a mock punch at him. "Blow up any buildings lately?"

"Can you believe it?" the ganger said, shaking his head. "Half the Seccies are looking for us since that job and those double-dealing scientists blew the place up themselves."

"Try getting the government to admit that," Finn said scornfully and Kez nodded.

Finn and Jeeva had been members of the team that rescued Revenge and Luciel from the secret CPS laboratory last year, the raid in which the third member of their team had died. Kez was surprised to see them again, but relieved that they were no longer as antagonistic as the first time they'd met. The gangers seemed to have decided they could trust them.

"I hear you're setting up in the ganglands," Finn said. "We're your escort into the depths."

"Electric," Raven said with a grin, jumping down off the crate. "I think we're about ready to go."

"Then let's fly," Jeeva replied. "Come and see the place we've got for you. It's not quite five-star accommodation, but I think you'll like it."

"Can we come?" Luciel asked, looking hopefully at Raven.

"If you like," she said with a shrug.

As Finn and Jeeva showed Raven the way to their flitter, Luciel and Kez tagging behind, Kez reflected on the difference between Raven and Wraith. Wraith considered the younger members of the group as his responsibility and was often concerned for their safety, while Raven expected them to take care of themselves. Thinking over what he knew of the brother and sister he decided it was probably something to do with the fact that Wraith used to run with a gang, whereas Raven had grown up on her own. As Finn piloted the flitter out of the Countess's building, Kez wondered whether he preferred Wraith taking responsibility for them or Raven giving them complete independence.

Daniel caught himself glancing over his shoulder as he entered his father's study and shook himself quickly. Although he knew that no one could be watching him he still felt nervous. What he was about to do probably counted as treason as well as espionage and he couldn't help but feel guilty that he was betraying his father's trust. Trying not to think of his doubts, he headed for the computer terminal; Caitlin would be home from school soon and he couldn't afford to be caught logging into their father's private files.

As Security Minister, Adam Hammond had to work long hours both at his office in New Westminster and at home. As a result he had to keep a number of files relating to work on his home terminal. It was those files Daniel was looking for now. Although he wasn't a hacker, he had used his father's terminal before when his own wasn't sophisticated enough for research he needed to do for college. His father had given him access privileges, partly in the hope that Daniel would one day follow in his footsteps and work for the British government. For a long time Daniel had known that was a forlorn hope; he could never work for the government as long as it was under control of the European Federation. But he had never told his father about his doubts and now that conceal-ment worked to his advantage. Sitting in front of the terminal his fingers moved steadily across the keypad as he carried out his task for Anglecynn, searching his father's files for information on the CPS crackdown and on the Hex called Raven they were so deter-mined to find.

Daniel soon discovered that Adam's files were encrypted, most of them using Ministry of Security passwords and code sequences. He copied those files to disk anyway, although he doubted that Anglecynn would be able to break the encryption. Then he started looking through his father's personal notes. They were also sealed with a password but it didn't take Daniel much thought to guess what it might be. Nervously he chewed on a strand of his loose brown hair as he typed in his mother's name:

> FRANCES <

The terminal began to decode the files and Daniel sighed. Ten years after his mother's death she was still helping him. Briefly he wondered what she would have thought of his involvement with the terrorists before shaking his head and returning to his work. His father's notes weren't that detailed but they were informative and the most recent entries concerned the Hex threat.

> **Arrangements for search for Hex named "Raven": post rewards for information, greater surveillance ganglands, crackdown on hackers, regular "stop and searches" by SS and CPS in lower levels. Also seek information on other terrorists' involvement in assault on CPS facility: male—white hair (Wraith); Irish male—green eyes, dyed blue hair; Caucasian youth—blond hair, brown eyes. Also seek information on missing test subjects: Luciel Liechtmann, Rachel Hollis, and Alison Tarrell <**

Daniel blinked and sat back, staring at the screen. As far as he was aware Ali Tarrell had been legally exterminated; his father's notes indicated differently. The term "test subject" mystified him but the implication was clear: Somewhere his sister's friend was still alive and possibly involved with the infamous Hex terrorists. Mechanically he sent the terminal to copy these notes as his mind raced. The previous day he had been thinking about Ali and how her father's position hadn't protected her; now it seemed that even a vacant socialite of a schoolgirl had managed to look after herself and escape the all-seeing eye of the CPS. As he hid the disk copies in his jacket, Daniel suddenly felt hopeful again. If Ali Tarrell could escape and survive, so could he. Turning off his father's terminal and leaving the study, he tried not to think about the fact that Ali might not have survived at all.

Oblivious to Daniel's thoughts about her, Ali was feeling sorry for herself. Finally Raven had agreed to move into ganglands, which meant she would have to move there too. She had no choice but to stay with the gangers; she could never survive in the city on her own and succeed in evading the CPS. But moving into the lower levels meant that she would lose the last of her freedom. It wouldn't be safe to wander those levels on her own and she doubted that the others would give her anything useful to do. Day after day she would be trapped in the same place, a prisoner because of her one ineptitude. All the others could defend themselves and all the others had abilities they could use and trade, all except her and Revenge. She was as much a drain on the group as a brain-damaged cripple.

A tear slid slowly down Ali's face and she wiped it away angrily. Just because the others thought she was useless didn't mean she had to be, she told herself firmly. Raven had said they would try to contact Avalon, the lead singer of Masque, soon. Maybe that was something she'd be able to do better than the others. As long as she could remember Ali had been meeting media celebrities; when they contacted Avalon she'd be able to understand the singer best and that would prove her usefulness. Biting her lip, Ali clung to the hope that through Avalon she'd find some way to prove herself.

The little flitter cruised slowly through the lower levels of the city as Finn pointed out the sights to Raven, informing her which gangs controlled the slums and who led them. The building the Countess had agreed to rent to them was in territory controlled by the Snakes, the gang that Finn and Jeeva ran with. As the flitter sank past broken bridges and derelict plazas, Kez and Luciel stared through the windows at the increasing proliferation of the blue and gold Snake emblem. When Finn finally set down the flitter it was on a slim archway connecting an abandoned plaza to an empty skyscraper section.

"This is it," he told them, touching the door release so they could exit the craft. "What do you think?"

Kez got out of the flitter and looked around. They were in the heart of gangland, the place he had grown up, and he felt his heart sink as he looked at the grime-covered walkways, the burnt-out lighting, and the garbage strewn across the plaza. This was exactly what he had been trying to escape when he first met up with Wraith and Raven and now he had returned to it. Beside him, Luciel looked around curiously, his eyes round with wonder.

"It looks like nothing on earth," he said softly.

Kez looked anxiously to see if Finn or Jeeva had overheard, but the gangers were accompanying Raven along the archway that led to the empty building. Dragging his feet, Kez began to follow them.

The inside of the skyscraper section was equally unprepossessing. It was at least clean, though, and their footsteps echoed softly as they crossed the floor of the foyer. Four doors led off the main entrance hall and Finn showed Raven around conscientiously. The first door led into a large empty room that could be used for vehicles, the other three opened into stairways leading up to more empty rooms. After an initial exploration, Kez and Luciel returned to the entrance and sat down on the cold floor.

"It's not much like the apartment, is it?" Luciel said ruefully.

"I can't believe Raven agreed to move," Kez replied bitterly. "This area looks like a bomb site. We'll have to barricade ourselves in just to avoid the gangs, let alone the Seccies."

The noise of flitters setting down outside alerted them to a new arrival and they looked up to see the two craft they'd seen at the Countess's base being loaded with Raven's equipment. As they watched, some of the Countess's people started taking crates out of the vehicles and began to carry them along the walkway.

"It looks like it's going to take Raven some time to get this place operational," Luciel said.

"The longer the better," Kez replied.

By the time Caitlin returned from the Gateshall school, Daniel had finished packing the small amount of stuff he intended to take with him and had written a note to his father. There wasn't much he could say, other than that he no longer felt comfortable with the privileged lifestyle he led in Belgravia and that he hoped his father would understand. Daniel didn't cherish much hope of that, but once he was hidden with Anglecynn his father would only see him again if they were discovered by the Security Services and he had to find some way to say good-bye. When Caitlin arrived he was waiting for a commercial flitter to collect him, and his sister entered the apartment to find him in the main living room with his bags packed. Caitlin looked at him in surprise when she saw the bags.

"Hey, Daniel, what's going on?" she asked. "Are you moving out or something?"

"I'm going to stay with some friends for a while," Daniel told her. "I've got a letter for you to give to Father."

"He doesn't know?" Caitlin was incredulous. "Daniel, he's going to be furious when he finds out. Who are these friends anyway?"

"No one you know." Daniel sighed, finding it harder than he'd expected to explain himself. "Look, Caitlin, I know you don't think much about politics but try to understand, I'm just not comfortable living here now that Father runs the Security Services. I think that what they're doing is wrong, especially now that they're helping the CPS exterminate Hexes."

"What do you mean?" Caitlin looked frightened. "Working for the government is just a job—why should it matter to you what Father does? Why should you care about Hexes or the CPS?"

"Why should I care?" Daniel felt himself getting angry and attempted to control his temper. "Caitlin, just because we've been lucky doesn't mean the rest of the world has nothing to do with us. All you've ever had to worry about is being pretty and popular.

You've got no idea how many people have to fight to survive every day of their lives!"

"You're crazy." Caitlin looked at him oddly. "Why can't you just be normal, Daniel? There isn't anything you can do about poverty or injustice or anything like that so why do you have to act as if you're better than the rest of us?" Turning her back on him she headed for her room, saying over her shoulder: "Go and be a martyr if you want to be. When you get bored you'll come back."

Avalon couldn't remember a time when she didn't know she was a Hex. Brought up in the glitter and gold of clubland, the part of the city that was a playground for the rich and a prison for the poor, everything about Avalon's life had hovered on the edge of illegality. She'd never known her father, her mother danced in the stage shows the clubs put on, and Avalon spent her childhood between the shining lights where the rich played and the slum apartment on the edge of gangland where the poor starved. Her mother's only gifts were her dancing and her prettiness, and to escape the trap of the slums she hired herself to the clubs. But the drug and alcohol abuse that pervaded the slums and ganglands like a choking fog was also there in clubland, the same scent only sweetened with the tang of money.

She never knew for certain if her mother was aware that she possessed the mutant Hex gene, but throughout her childhood her mother taught her to hide what she was from other people.

"Whether you run with a gang or work for the rich, you can't ever let them know who you are," her mother told her. "Because then they have a part of you. You have wonderful gifts, Avalon, and you can be anything you want, just as long as you never let anyone else decide your future."

And Avalon had done just that. With no official identity or existence she couldn't have found a place in a school and so she learned from the people who worked in clubland. All they had to teach was dance and music and how to sell your talents to the people who paid, but in the end that was enough. When Avalon's mother died, spending their last savings on slum doctors who didn't even attempt to cure her, Avalon had taken her place on stage. But where her mother's gifts had been only just enough to earn her that place, Avalon shone like a star. At fifteen her success had already been assured. From clubs to concert halls and stadia, she had rocketed to megastardom, keeping her secrets for herself. Now she was on the pinnacle of that success, admired by millions, envied by billions, but despite the fame and fortune still afraid that some day she would be found out.

Touching the moment control, she played the news item again. In silence, for by now she knew the words by heart and she whispered them to herself as the pictures flickered in front of her.

". . . pledged the Security Services to a widespread eradication program, supporting the CPS in their mandate to rid this country of Hexes forever."

She touched the control again and the picture froze in position as Avalon picked up the guitar. Her fingers moved softly across the strings, and chords rang out from the amp across the room, melding seamlessly with the images in Avalon's mind. As the music began to form a pattern, she wondered, as she often did, if she needed to touch the strings. But, as always, you never knew who might be watching, or when it was dangerous to forget the rules. So she played conventionally, the only clue to her abilities being the perfection of her music—the way each note seemed exactly right for that moment. The song she was composing was dangerous enough, but she had told Cloud she was thinking of composing something with a terrorist theme and it was time for her to deliver. Lyrics could come later, for now it was a sound she was looking for. Something that would wordlessly express the emotions she would only ever use words to conceal.

Wraith had spent the day with Revenge, as he was increasingly forced to think of her. Even while he called her Rachel, to her face and in front of the others, he had begun to realize that she would never be Rachel again. The image he had held in his mind through all those years of searching, the kid with shining brown eyes and a crooked grin, had been erased by Dr. Kalden's experimentation, leaving behind the gaunt and silent figure he tended now. Revenge was the memory of Rachel and a constant source of guilt. He couldn't even look at her without thinking of how he had failed. He had failed Rachel by not finding her soon enough, failed Raven in allowing her to distance herself from the world, and failed the other Hexes he hadn't been able to rescue in the raid on the lab.

Sadly, he watched Revenge, still enmeshed in a tangle of machinery, although this time it was of her own choice. When they'd first moved into the apartment, Raven had fitted her sister's room with the medical equipment necessary to help her through the withdrawal symptoms of the drugs she was kept on, a bank of vidscreens for entertainment, and a VR Helmet system to play computer games without having to move her wasted limbs. Wraith had argued that they should try to get her to come out and rejoin the world, but Raven had overruled him.

"That might be what you want for her, but it's not what she wants," she told him. "She wants to hide, inside this room and inside her own mind. She's Revenge now, not Rachel—don't remind her of what she can't have."

So now, except for the physiotherapy sessions she had once a day, Revenge remained cocooned in her mechanical world.

Wraith stroked her hand, not expecting a response, and stood up. Ali was still in the main room of the apartment and he knew he ought to spend time with her. He could hardly ignore the fact that Ali was miserable here and he couldn't risk failing her as he felt he had failed so many others.

As he left Revenge's room he heard the sound of an arrival, and glancing at the main door, he saw Raven, Luciel, and Kez enter. The boys looked subdued but Raven was grinning.

"I've found us a place," she informed him, slinging her black rucksack onto a nearby chair and kicking her heavy boots off. "It'll take me a couple of weeks to get it fixed up properly, but after that we'll have a better security system than the Countess. She's already hired me to refit hers when I'm through."

"Congratulations," Wraith said, with relief. He'd always been uneasy living so openly in the heights of the city, especially now that they all had so much to hide. He and Kez were the only members of the group whose existence wasn't illegal and both of them were still wanted for the attack on the lab. Now it looked as if he was going to have his wish and he was grateful to Raven for no longer opposing him. "So, what next then?"

"What about this training program for Hexes?" Kez asked diffidently. "It would be useful if Luciel and Ali could do some of the stuff you do." He looked hopefully at Raven.

"If they can," Raven said dryly, but before the others could protest she held up a hand. "But I agree. We'll start just as soon as I've contacted Avalon. I still need more data on the Hex abilities and my observations indicate that she is a fully functioning Hex."

"How are you going to contact her?" Ali asked, showing an interest in the conversation for the first time.

"Wouldn't you like to know?" Raven grinned mischievously.

"Raven . . . ," Wraith began, warningly, but she interrupted him.

"Stay ice, Wraith, it's under control." She smiled. "If all goes well I should meet her tonight." She looked around at the rest of them. "As things are I think I'll have to go on my own, though—too many of you are wanted criminals."

"And you're not?" Ali exclaimed. She looked at Wraith, hopefully. "I think I should go," she said. "I know media people and how to talk to them."

Raven looked contemptuous but Wraith was thoughtful.

"Wouldn't you be recognized?" he asked carefully. "Your father was quite prominent and your arrest was widely reported."

"I could change the way I look," Ali persisted. "Maybe if I colored my hair. . . ."

"I don't think Raven should go on her own," Kez put in. "I could go with her."

"I don't need protection," Raven insisted. "All I'm doing is going to a party I think Avalon will be at. It's not exactly dangerous."

"Take the younger ones, then," Wraith insisted. "I agree I'm likely to be recognized but Luciel isn't and Kez or Ali could be disguised."

Raven considered this for a moment, then shrugged.

"Come if you want," she said eventually. "But I'm not going to be watching over you all the time—and make sure you don't get in my way. You're old enough to take care of yourselves."

Luciel and Kez agreed quickly, excited to be involved for a change, and after a moment Ali did too. She resented Raven treating her like a kid when she was older than her, but she wanted to be included as much as the others.

"OK, then," Raven agreed. "Don't dress too noticeably and be ready to leave in two hours. If you're not ready, I'll leave without you." And, with that, she stalked off to her room, closing the door decisively behind her.

Alaric was asleep in the small room he shared with Jordan when he was woken by the chime of the vidcom. Dragging himself wearily out of bed, he crossed the room to answer it and saw Liz staring back at him.

"Maggie and Cal have brought in your new recruit," she informed him. "Daniel Hammond."

293

"Oh yeah." Alaric nodded, starting to rub the sleep out of his eyes.

"He's in the debriefing room," Liz added and broke the connection, the vidcom screen going dark.

Alaric got up and stretched. He'd been asleep in his clothes; the building's heat units had been malfunctioning again and everyone was too busy to fix them. Pulling on his battered jacket, he headed downstairs. He'd promised Daniel Hammond a place here; the least he could do was greet him.

The debriefing room was a small office with a table and chairs and little else. Daniel Hammond was standing uneasily near the table, rubbing his hands to keep them warm, a couple of expensive suitcases next to him. A cup of coffee substitute was cooling on the table nearby. For an instant Alaric looked at their base as Daniel must see it. A dreary island in a sea of garbage, cold and inhospitable and reeking of poverty. But he refused to accept the image. His job was to make the new recruit feel welcome and to do that he had to concentrate on the positive aspects of the home they had here.

"Daniel Hammond?" he said with a welcoming smile. "I'm Alaric. I wasn't able to tell you my name when we first met. But now you've officially joined us, you ought to know who we are."

"Pleased to meet you," Daniel responded, obviously trying to look relaxed.

"And there are a lot of people who'll be pleased to meet you," Alaric replied. "Your information has been very useful to us. Why don't you sit down and I'll explain some things, then I'll show you around." As Daniel slid into one of the rickety chairs, Alaric drew another up to the table and began the introduction he'd given to every new recruit.

"As you're probably aware, Anglecynn isn't a large organization—at the moment we number about fifty—but every member is dedicated and prepared to commit themselves to our goals. This is our main base, but we have other contacts in the city and a few sympathizers in the rest of Britain. We don't have a hierarchy as such, but the longer you've been with the operation the more qualified you are considered to be and the greater role you have in deciding our strategies. Not everyone here takes part in the protests and demonstrations we organize; we have about ten administrative staff who are responsible for our research and the preparations for events. It'll be up to you to fit in where you feel the most comfortable. We call this place Dragon's Nest and there's plenty of space for everyone so you can either move into a shared room or find one for yourself. Nowhere's out of bounds and if you get in anyone's way they'll tell you about it. The common room's where most of us spend our free time and hold meetings when there's something to discuss." He leaned back and considered his words for a moment, thinking over what he had said. Daniel was nodding, but he still looked nervous and Alaric decided putting him at his ease was the priority.

"That's about all you need to know now but if you have any other questions ask anyone or come and find me. If you can't find me, ask for Jordan—she's my girlfriend and she usually knows how to get hold of me. She's also one of our veterans and can sort you out on most things herself." Standing up he put a reassuring hand on Daniel's shoulder. "Now, if you want to have a look around, I'll give you the grand tour."

"Thank you," Daniel said, his smile looking a bit more genuine. He reached a hand into his pocket and pulled out a few disks. "What about these? It's the data you wanted—shall I give them to you now?"

"Sure," Alaric replied, taking them easily. But as they left the debriefing room he knew that, once he'd showed Daniel around, he'd have to start work right away on them. It would be a long time before he got another chance to sleep.

4

SUBTLER THAN
VULCAN'S ENGINE

The party Raven had decided to crash was the ultimate in celebrity glitzfests. Held in the infamous Winter Palace, an exclusive club at the peak of one of the tallest of the high-rises, the ostensible purpose of the event was to celebrate Elohim's thirtieth birthday but in actuality the get-together was to convince everyone that the star was still the paramount talent of the day, despite recent ratings losses to Yannis Kastell and Masque. The Winter Palace had been chosen as the venue, not least because it resembled something from Elohim's own holovids. Its crystalline walls, designed to simulate the effects of snow and frost, sparkled in the starlight and a flurry of holographic snowflakes whirled around the arriving flitters, projected by holocams mounted on the towering parapets, spires, and flying buttresses of the palace.

Raven had rented a state-of-the-art customized flitter for the purpose, and as she piloted the small craft in to land on one of the castle's projecting crystalline platforms, her three passengers stared out of the darkened windows in awe. Ali knew all about the Winter Palace but even she had never thought she'd visit it. Kez and Luciel gaped in wide-eyed wonder at the fairy-tale structure. When the flitter landed and Raven stepped out, the others followed uneasily, feeling underdressed and out of place. Raven alone looked at her ease. Wearing dead black as usual, she didn't at first seem to have made any special effort, but in the glittering lights of the Winter Palace the others could see that her clothes were made of a light-retarding fabric that retained its obsidian darkness even under the multiple floodlight reflections, seeming to clothe her in shadows. The others were also dressed plainly and Ali's ash-blonde hair had been dyed a dark chestnut in keeping with their attempt at disguise. Following Raven to the end of the spur that joined the flitter platform to the palace itself, they exchanged worried looks as a burly security guard stepped forward to confront Raven.

"ID please, ma'am," he said, reaching for a small vid-unit hanging at his belt, which undoubtedly held a copy of the invitation list.

"Elizabeth Black," Raven told him calmly, then turned to indicate the rest of them. "Lestan Austen, Annabel Tarrant, and Kester Chirac."

"Thank you, ma'am," the guard replied, scanning through the names on the list. After a brief moment he looked up with a polite smile and stepped aside to let them pass. "Have a nice evening."

The interior decoration of the Winter Palace was equally fantastical, every surface glittering with frosty silver light. For this occasion vidscreens had been mounted all over the walls and cycled through scenes from Elohim's latest vids. Holo units were mounted on balconies and staircases, projecting images of imaginary alien creatures which mixed with the throng of celebrities who filled the halls. Watching this from the high balcony which led to the flitter platform, Raven smiled to herself, then turned to regard the others.

"You can go and mingle," she told them. "Don't draw too much attention to yourselves."

"What are you going to do?" Ali asked curiously.

"Get an introduction to Avalon."

Avalon had made her entrance, with the other members of Masque, in full view of the media. Little flitters circled the Winter Palace, recording the arrival of the various celebrities for the news networks, and a few dedicated fans filled other larger craft that swarmed around the entrance. The phalanx of bodyguards, hired to protect the members of the rock group from unwanted attention, formed a protective knot around them as their flitter touched down on the most secure of the palace's landing platforms.

Once inside, Corin and Jesse peeled off in search of refreshment while the other three surveyed the crowd. Avalon felt almost overpowered by the scene. Elohim had intended this celebration to impress and as his music filled the air and his face flickered from the multiple screens, Avalon found it difficult to remember that she was now as big a star as he was. Cloud evidently had no such problem. Poised elegantly at the side of the main hall, he accepted a glass of pale gold wine from a passing waiter and sipped it casually.

"Quite a show," he said softly. "I'm surprised Elohim wants to remind so many people of how old he is."

"He's not that old," Lissa protested. "It's not as if he's exactly losing his looks, even if his talent is a little in doubt these days."

"You know that, but does he?" Cloud replied speculatively. "At thirty I'd start to get just a little nervous about birthdays."

"Are you going to tell him that?" Lissa asked, her eyes sparkling at the thought of a confrontation.

"Certainly not," Cloud replied, beckoning to another waiter and gesturing to him to serve Avalon and Lissa. "I shall be perfectly gracious. There's no need to say anything. Everyone here knows that we're at the top of the ratings again." Ignoring Lissa's attempt to continue the conversation, he took Avalon's arm and began to lead her across the room. "Don't look so nervous," he said quietly. "Remember you're a megastar."

"I don't like this kind of thing," she replied, under her breath. "I feel like the main dish at a banquet."

"Elohim's the dish of the day," Cloud said. "He's over there with his dedicated admirers, all paying court to the Prince of the Vidscreen."

Avalon turned to look at Elohim, dressed in silver and white, smiling generously at the host of admirers who clustered around him. Her gaze lingered on the group for a moment then, almost against her will, was arrested by a dark figure making her way across the hall toward Elohim. Alone in this glittering company she wore black, and, against her pale skin and onyx hair, it made her look as if there was no color to her at all. Other heads were turning and Avalon recognized how that much blackness would inevitably catch the eye in a room full of light.

"Who's that?" she whispered to Cloud.

"No idea," he replied. "Looks like she's lost the way to a funeral."

"Elohim seems to know her," she continued as the dark-haired girl was greeted by the megastar. Cloud shrugged, and with one last glance at the stranger, Avalon turned away.

Across the room Ali had also noticed Raven's progress toward the megastar, at first with alarm and then with a surge of jealousy as Elohim greeted her with a warm smile of recognition. Thinking back to a life that seemed decades ago, she remembered how Elohim had put in an appearance at one of her father's parties. Raven had been there as well, masquerading under a pseudonym, the first time Ali had met the young Hex. Ali had never imagined that Elohim would actually remember her but now he was talking to Raven and smiling as if he'd known her all her life, while Ali was left in the corner unrecognized and unnoticed. It didn't do her any good to remember that she'd deliberately come in disguise; she doubted that anyone here would have given her a second glance if she'd introduced herself as Ali Tarrell. But Raven had the gift of being noticed and a supreme confidence in her own abilities. Ali's eyes defocused as she watched the crowd blindly, wondering if she would be in Raven's shadow for the rest of her life.

• • •

Meanwhile, Elohim was leading Raven across the room, toward Avalon and Cloud. There was a touch of pique in his voice as he asked:

"Why do you want to meet her anyway? Masque have made a few disks but they're hardly known outside this country."

"I'm researching a program on minor European groups," Raven replied with a sideways smile. "I heard about Masque recently and thought they might be useful material."

"I see." Elohim lost his frown as he guided Raven toward Avalon, acknowledging other people's greetings with an expansive smile.

Pacing beside him, Raven's dark eyes were alight with amusement. It had all been so easy. Hacking into the system which held the invitation list was the work of moments and reviving her Elizabeth Black identity had secured her an introduction to Avalon and the status of knowing Elohim. The fact that the megastar was obviously interested in her only served to increase her amusement and she had to prevent herself from grinning as they came close to Avalon.

Avalon wore dark red, the same color as her flame of crimson hair. As she looked up to see Elohim approaching, Raven felt a shock of recognition. She felt that she would have known Avalon as a Hex even if she hadn't already surmised it from Masque's music. Watching as Elohim greeted her, Raven attempted to clarify her own impressions, trying to understand her own certainty about Avalon. But, apart from that sensation of recognition, she had nothing to go on and she filed the incident away for further study.

Elohim was introducing her and she had to concentrate on the business at hand.

"This is Elizabeth Black, a friend of mine," Elohim said proprietarily.

"I'm assistant producer for AdAstra," Raven continued. "It's a pleasure to meet you. I've been following your career with great interest."

"Really?" Avalon studied Raven with candid consideration. "What do you think of it?"

Elohim drifted away toward a group of holo executives, uninterested in a conversation about Masque's music, as Raven began to answer.

"I assume you want more than a personal criticism," she said and smiled as Avalon nodded. "In that case, my main impression is that your apocalyptic imagery suggests that Masque is on the brink of a transformation, although apocalypse usually signals an ending rather than a beginning."

"You think Masque's career is ending?" Avalon said quickly, her violet eyes darkening.

"No," Raven corrected her. "I think you do."

"Masque has no intention of splitting up," Avalon replied, stating categorically in case her comments got back to the media.

"The future is always uncertain," Raven replied before adding quietly. "And none of us is ever really safe. Even me, though my associates would be surprised to hear me admit it."

"What do you mean?" Avalon said quickly, glancing around to see if anyone else was nearby.

"We're alone," Raven replied. "In more ways than one." Her dark eyes met Avalon's levelly. "But, if you let me teach you, you won't be defenseless." Reaching into her jacket she produced a small metal card. "My com signal's encoded into this," she explained, passing it to Avalon. "Ask for Raven."

Before Avalon could reply she had stepped away, a shadow drifting through the brightness of the crowd.

Kez and Luciel were watching the party from an upper balcony. They had seen Raven approach Elohim, and Kez explained that Raven had met the megastar before, even though he was amazed at her audacity. They continued to watch as Elohim took Raven to meet Avalon and had seen the young hacker give something to the singer before turning and coming back across the hall toward them. They came down the staircase to meet her and she greeted them with a grin.

"I've seen her," she said. "Shall we go now or are you enjoying the experience?"

"I don't think we should push our luck," Luciel said, reluctantly. Kez was more decisive.

"Let's leave," he said. "These people don't seem real at all. It's like watching them on a vid."

"I'm not sure many of them can tell the difference either," Raven agreed. "Where's Ali?"

"Over there," Luciel pointed out. "She doesn't look like she's enjoying herself much."

"Probably missing the high life," Kez said.

"Go and get her then, Luciel," Raven instructed. "We'll fade and meet you at the flitter."

Alaric pushed his chair back from the computer terminal and stretched painfully. Glancing at the chronometer he realized he'd been working for hours, checking and rechecking the information Daniel had brought them. The reference in the Security Minister's notes to extra surveillance in the ganglands and increased Seccie "stop and searches" had worried him, but it was the information on the Hex terrorist faction that had been the focus of his work. The description of the terrorists and the name Raven had appeared on the newscasts, but the reference to missing test subjects was a new factor.

He'd searched the net for more information on the "CPS facility" the terrorists had allegedly destroyed and found no information even on its existence until it had been blown up, when its location was given and it was described as an extermination center. The mention of test subjects caused Alaric to doubt that and also explained why the group had chosen to target that particular facility rather than any of the hundreds of others scattered across the country. Even more interesting was the note Daniel had appended to the files mentioning that Ali Tarrell, described as a missing test subject, was a teenage Hex who was listed as legally exterminated by the CPS. It looked to Alaric as if the "terrorist raid" had in fact been a rescue attempt and it made him increasingly eager to make contact with the group. Unfortunately, if the group had half the resources they would have needed to mount an assault on a test lab no one even knew existed, they would be difficult to track down.

Alaric considered the problem as he made arrangements for countering the increased Seccie activity, instituting new recognition codes and protocols and restricting all members of the group to Dragon's Nest except for essential business. Eventually he decided he couldn't think of anything but turning the problem over to the fixers. Throughout the slums and ganglands there were fixers who claimed to be able to set up any contact or provide any equipment. Chances were the Hex group had encountered one of them and could pass on a message. Starting with fixers in London, Alaric sent a coded message to each of them, indicating Anglecynn's interest in meeting up with the Hexes.

Finally leaving the terminal, he went to find Jordan. She and Daniel were in the main common room and Alaric was relieved to find that the new recruit was looking a bit less nervous. Although Daniel was slightly older than him, Alaric had spent half his life on the edge of the law and he knew how protected from reality those who grew up in the heights were. Jordan was one of the best people to help him come to terms with the life in the depths of the city. She'd come from the heights herself; studying politics at school had involved her in a number of political protests and got her into trouble with the Seccies. By the time she'd met up with Anglecynn she'd already had a hard lesson in what the city was actually like. As he sank into the chair beside her, Alaric felt himself begin to relax. Even in the depths of the darkness he still had hope.

• • •

Revenge, immersed in her own personal and private darkness, had no hope at all. She existed in shadows now and everything she experienced seemed to take place a long way away, receding from view like light seen from the end of a dark tunnel. Even Wraith was like a phantom to her, more memory than reality. But Raven was real and sometimes Revenge could convince herself that she *was* Raven, able to drive the darkness away. Somewhere out in the dark Dr. Kalden was looking for her and he wouldn't stop looking ever. The only thing that prevented her from whimpering in fright was the thought of revenge, that next time she would be stronger. Now as she lay on her back she repeated her incantation.

"I am Raven," she whispered into the dark, "and Raven is Revenge." The darkness seemed to lift a little and Revenge's breath calmed. If Kalden was looking for her, she would hunt him, and this time there would be no escape.

Wraith, looking in on the sleeping figure of his little sister, was startled to see the smile on her lips. Allowing himself to hope it was a sign that she was recovering, he gently pulled the covers over the sleeping figure. Turning on a small light by her bed, he keyed down the main lights, remembering how hysterical she'd been the one time he'd turned them all off at once. In the dark he could see that the lights of the room's computer terminal were on and reminded himself to speak to Raven about it. If Revenge felt able to use the net it might be a sign that the scars, from her experience in the lab, were fading. As he left the room, he felt the burden of guilt he carried lift a little.

• • •

When Raven returned to the apartment with the others she didn't show much inclination to talk. Wraith hadn't waited up for them and Ali had quickly headed for her room. While Kez and Luciel turned on the holovid, Raven had left them for the privacy of her room. For the next few hours she worked in silence with the tangle of circuitry she was gradually assembling into a computer link of her own design. Only her occasional glance at the terminal betrayed that her attention was divided. It was late into the night when the com signal finally chimed and Raven crossed the room to touch the keypad. She had given Avalon a coded signal, the circuitry in the card sending her message through multiple relay stations before bringing it to Raven's attention, all in the space of microseconds. She hadn't thought the singer would want to betray herself by reporting her, but Raven didn't trust anyone entirely.

Her fingers dancing across the keypad, she instructed the unit to key the incoming signal while suppressing the outgoing visual signal. Avalon's face appeared on the screen. Her red hair was disheveled but her expression was calm.

"Is that Raven?" she asked quietly, dim light in the background indicating that she was making the call in secret.

Through her link with the system, Raven checked that the signal was not being monitored and keyed the terminal to display her image.

"This is Raven," she confirmed. "I've been expecting your call."

"Are you really the hacker?" Avalon frowned. "Elohim said your name was Elizabeth."

"I am Raven," she replied and wordlessly extended her consciousness through the link. She felt the sensation of speed as part of her identity raced through the same convoluted route as Avalon's signal, tracing the link back to its point of origin. Although Avalon had not consciously entered the data network, part of her mind responded automatically to the presence of the circuitry, her Hex gene giving her a part of the symbiotic union Raven had with the network. It was enough for Raven to touch her mind through the terminal, confirming her assertion with the wordless message:

> i am raven <

Avalon tensed, her eyes glazing over for a fraction of a second before returning to reality.

"What do you want from me?" she asked and through the network Raven sensed > fear <.

"To learn from you," Raven informed her, not attempting to conceal her intentions. Unlike Wraith, she doubted the possibility of forming a solidarity group of mutants but the existence of another functioning Hex fascinated her.

"I want to understand more about the potential of our kind," she told Avalon. "In return I offer to teach you what I know."

"What do you think you can learn from me?" Avalon asked.

"You use your talents more artistically than me." Raven gave a half smile. "My interests have been in other directions. Why shouldn't we learn from each other?" Reaching into her link with the net, she added:

> i can teach/show/give you this <

"What would I have to do?" Avalon asked, her expression unreadable.

"Meet with my associates?" Raven suggested. "There are things you might want to know about the CPS."

"It sounds dangerous," Avalon said seriously.

"You can decide on a meeting place," Raven told her.

Avalon was silent for a minute, obviously thinking, before she spoke again.

"The Carlisle Hotel, tomorrow at midday," she said eventually.

"I'll arrange a room," Raven confirmed. "You can find me under the name Aria Draven."

As Avalon cut the connection, Raven withdrew from the net, then hesitated. Within the terminals connected to the apartment she felt a difference. Tracing it back to its source, her awareness concentrated on the terminal in Revenge's room. Unused since their occupancy began it was now showing signs of use. Drawing closer Raven found the traces of activity; some of the operating code had been changed. The alterations were confusing; a babel of new code threaded through the system. Disappearing and reappearing as Raven tried to track it down. Raven raised an eyebrow. Apparently the Hex abilities the CPS had found in Rachel were resurfacing in Revenge after lying hidden since her rescue from the lab. Raven recorded the snatches of code on her own terminal, simultaneously imprinting them on her eidetic memory, and slid out of the net. She would have to talk to Revenge soon, she told herself, before crossing the room to fall asleep in seconds.

• • •

By the time Ali got up the next day, the others were already planning their meeting with Avalon. Wraith was insistent that recruiting her would be the first stop toward a campaign on behalf of the Hexes. Raven was more skeptical but the fact that she'd convinced the megastar to meet with them had let loose a new enthusiasm in the other members of the group. Luciel took advantage of the opportunity to ask Raven when she would start teaching them to use their Hex abilities.

"After I've spoken to Avalon," she replied. "The things I intend to tell her will be the basis for your education as well."

"It sounds as if you've progressed in understanding Hex abilities," Wraith said carefully.

Raven grimaced, then shook her head.

"Not enough," she said. "The disks I took from the lab were worse than useless. They spent too much time exploring blind alleys of experimentation and all their subjects were too immature."

"They were kids," Luciel said sharply.

"I'm not being callous," Raven said coldly. "I am criticizing the scientific methodology, which is separate from ethical considerations. In any case," she continued, "I got a little information from the tests—although mostly what avenues not to follow—some ideas from talking to Ali and Luciel and a little more from Revenge. Discovering Avalon has been useful as well. What I'll say to her today includes my current hypothesis concerning the Hex gene." Swinging her boots down from the table she headed toward her room, turning over her shoulder to add: "By the way, someone should stay with Revenge today. It could be unwise to leave her on her own."

The door of Raven's room closed, making it clear she didn't consider herself a candidate for remaining behind. The three younger members of the group glanced at Wraith and then at each other. Kez was the first to reach the obvious conclusion.

"Wraith and Raven have to go and you two are Hexes," he said. "I guess I'll stay behind." Luciel flashed him a smile but Ali's expression was glum. To his surprise Kez found himself wishing that he carried the mutant gene, now that it looked as if Raven was going to start teaching others. Looking at Ali's expression he couldn't understand why she wasn't more enthusiastic about the idea. As it was, looking after Revenge at least didn't present much of a chore, he told himself. It wasn't as if she was likely to go anywhere.

The suite Raven had booked at the Carlisle Hotel was luxurious and secluded and the hotel had a reputation for discretion. While Raven used the terminal to access the hotel's security system, in order to watch for the approach of Seccies or the CPS, the others tried to make themselves comfortable. They had arrived some time before they were due to meet Avalon, and Wraith began scanning the newsfeeds for any more information on the Security Services' crackdown.

Ali and Luciel had nothing to do but wait. Neither of them was sure what Raven intended to say to the megastar or to them.

"It's hard to believe Avalon is a Hex," Luciel said quietly. "The CPS seem to catch most of us as kids."

"They didn't catch Raven," Ali said, with a touch of bitterness. "That's probably why she's so interested in Avalon. We were both caught but she managed to stay unnoticed."

"You think that's why?" Luciel asked, lowering his voice even further.

"Do you remember what I told you when we first met in the lab?" Ali asked.

"Something about Raven?" Luciel frowned, then shook his head. "Sorry, I don't remember."

"I told you what she told me," Ali replied softly. "Anyone able to escape the CPS wouldn't want to burden themselves with people who aren't." She glanced over at Raven, but the younger girl appeared to be completely absorbed in the terminal. "She didn't even want to take the other test subjects with us when she left the lab."

"She couldn't have," Luciel protested. "I know what I said at the time, but I didn't know how small your group was then. I still feel guilty that we didn't try. But we couldn't have saved them. And Raven *did* contact the media."

"I know." Ali's expression was bleak. "But she didn't care, did she? Not like us, and not the way Wraith does."

"She's just different," Luciel said, but his voice was edged with uncertainty.

"Look at all the effort she's going to just to meet Avalon," Ali pointed out. "She doesn't care about us because we got caught or about Rev—Rachel, because her brain is fried. But she thinks Avalon is worth the effort."

"Raven cares about some people, like Wraith, or Kez—she rescued him from the streets."

"No, she didn't," Ali insisted, her voice rising. "Wraith did. Kez just thinks Raven did it because he has a crush on her."

"What about Wraith then?" Luciel continued. "Do you really think Raven doesn't feel anything for him? He's her brother."

"Rachel is her sister, but she doesn't seem to feel anything for her," Ali replied. "She thinks of her as a test subject, just like—" She stopped abruptly when Luciel interrupted.

"Like Dr. Kalden? No chance," he insisted in a furious whisper. "I know you don't get on with Raven and I admit she doesn't seem to think much of us as Hexes. But you weren't in the lab for long, Ali—you don't know what Kalden was like. Raven might be cold, but she's not *evil*."

Ali looked away for a moment and then sighed.

"I'm sorry," she said quietly. "I don't mean to be unfair. I'm just tired of being so useless."

Silently Luciel took her hand and held it. There wasn't anything he could say and they both knew it.

Avalon arrived three minutes after midday. Raven saw her arriving through the hotel's security cams. She was alone, pulling up in a plain black skimmer, her distinctive red hair tucked under a cap. Raven watched her passage through the hotel, different holocams picking her up in the foyer, elevator, and corridor on their floor.

She was impressed by what she saw. Avalon betrayed no sign of nervousness. Only Raven, familiar with the constant anxiety of having to hide her mutation, would have been able to see any tension in the star's deliberate movements. Smiling to herself she turned away from the terminal.

"She's on her way up," she said. "No one accompanying her, no signs of pursuit or surveillance."

"Good." Wraith relaxed perceptively and turned off the holovid, crossing to sit with the others in the suite's lounge area. Ali and Luciel were looking apprehensive and neither of them met his eyes as he joined them. Raven continued to watch the terminal for a few moments more. Then she got up, the terminal switching itself off without her apparently touching it, and crossed to the doors. She was halfway there when they heard a soft knock, sounding as loud as a hammer in the suddenly silent room.

Raven opened the door and the others looked up expectantly as she ushered Avalon in, closing the door behind her. The star's eyes skimmed across the group quickly before coming back to Raven.

"These are your associates?" she asked. "I was expecting something more militaristic."

"We're not terrorists," Raven replied. "Despite our reputations." She gestured to Avalon to sit down. She came to sit next to Wraith. "This is my brother, Wraith; and Ali Tarrell and Luciel Leichtmann; both Hexes."

"Avalon," the redhead said politely, nodding to each of them.

"We're pleased you could find the time to meet with us," Wraith began, taking charge of the situation. "As Raven pointed out, our reputations are against us. I know that she has promised you certain information. But I'd like to begin by explaining how we came to possess it."

He looked expectantly at Avalon, who nodded.

"I'd rather have the full story," she said calmly.

"In that case I'll begin by saying that Raven and I have a younger sister and we first came to this city to discover what had become of her. . . ."

Avalon listened in silence as Wraith recounted the results of their search for Rachel, Raven's discovery of the illegal experimentation, and their meeting with Ali. Reluctant to remember the past, Ali briefly explained how she had acted as a spy in the laboratory and left it to Luciel to describe the facility and the details of the experiments. Wraith took up the story once more to describe their attempt to expose the CPS by calling in the media and the subsequent explosion that had destroyed the lab, resulting in the government branding them as terrorists.

"Everyone died," Luciel couldn't help himself from adding. "Dr. Kalden destroyed the evidence so that no one would find him out."

"We don't know it was Kalden for certain," Wraith interjected.

"It's not as if it makes much difference," Ali said. "Everyone blamed it on us."

"And now the government has vowed to eliminate all Hexes as a result," Avalon concluded.

5

COVER HER FACE

Kez was trying not to feel bored, but it was difficult when the others had gone to meet Avalon and all he had to do was look after Revenge. He'd checked on her four times, apart from taking her breakfast or lunch, but each time she'd either been wired up to her VR Helmet or her computer terminal. Despite Kez's attempts, she hadn't spoken to him once and he wondered, as always, if she would ever have a chance of leading a normal life. Shaking his head he returned to the living room, dialing himself a snack from the Nutromac.

"Raven, Wraith, and Revenge," he said under his breath. "What a family." To his surprise the thought cheered him up. Revenge might be weird, but he was starting to believe that Raven and Wraith could do anything. Kez had never joined a gang when he was living on the streets, distrusting the loyalty gang members claimed to have toward each other. But since he'd met Wraith and Raven he'd felt for the first time as if he belonged to something. His friendship with Luciel and even his quarrels with Ali were beginning to feel routine and familiar, like something he'd miss if he left the group.

"Like this apartment," he reminded himself. While he'd been uncomfortable at Elohim's celebrity glitzfest, places like the Belgravia complex and this apartment were luxuries he'd be unwilling to give up. The talk of a move to ganglands had alarmed him, but remembering Raven's own taste for comfort he hoped they'd be able to refit the building to something like the luxury they had here. All the same, he'd still miss it. With a sigh, Kez stretched out along one of the sofas and reached for the moment control, telling himself he might as well enjoy it while he could.

"Everyone's in danger," Raven said. "And we are one of the causes." She looked around at the others. "But I am the primary reason for the government's crackdown. Dr. Kalden studied Hexes for most of his life. If his knowledge had been greater or his methodology more sound he might have discovered what he was searching for—a way to turn unwanted mutants into military superiority. He suspected that the Hexes possessed a capability to interface directly with electronics, something which would be of immense use in the art of war, but he never proved his theories. His subjects were too young, too few escaped detection as children, and those that did were never found."

Avalon's eyes were fixed on Raven; Ali and Luciel were similarly transfixed. Wraith watched the tableau silently, listening as the pent-up fury that was always present in Raven found release in her catalogue of discoveries.

"The only thing Kalden did discover was how to spur the Hex gene into action. Usually our capabilities are dormant. That accounts for the number of Hexes disposed of shortly after birth as a result of routine medical scans. But sometimes the gene passes undetected and Hexes are caught before adolescence, when anomalies are discovered during their interactions with electronic devices or as a result of further medical testing. These first two groups accounted for most of Kalden's subjects. Through what amounted to torture he found ways of unlocking that potential, which is what happened to Rachel—she had no use of her abilities until after Kalden's experimentation. In a few cases his victims were teenagers who had begun to use their abilities themselves as a result of a particular interest in electronic media.

"But Kalden never had the opportunity to experiment on a subject who had reached adulthood and gained the full possession of their abilities. Avalon is the one person I know of who's even approached those criteria."

"What about you?" Luciel interjected and Raven shrugged.

"I took my age into calculation when I started looking at Kalden's results. I discovered my abilities when I was nine and have been using them ever since. According to Dr. Kalden's test results, my abilities significantly exceed those recorded for any age group. This is based on my study so far. Once I've attempted to teach you what I know, I'll be better able to reach a conclusion as to whether the extent of my abilities is unique or if the things I have learned can be taught to any and all Hexes."

Turning to Avalon she concluded:

"I am already committed to instructing Luciel and Ali, but your contribution would give me more information to go on, apart from proving useful if this new initiative leads to your discovery."

Avalon was silent for a while, frowning to herself. Never before had she been inclined to go against her instincts and share her secrets with another person. But Raven seemed to know them already.

"I was a child when I found out I was a Hex. I can't ever remember not knowing. But I've known how to use it, not as you do. I feel it sometimes in my music, in the way I use instruments, but I've never dared take it any further. I suppose my success has protected me from having to find out what I could do." She looked at Ali and Luciel. "Do you want to be able to use it? From what you've told me this could be more dangerous than any of us imagine."

"I want to learn," Luciel assured her. "The government is wrong to think the mutation is harmful. Sure, it could be used for harm and the world relies on the security of the networks. But it's wrong to kill us for possessing a talent most people don't have. I want to learn to use it so I can prove that. Before this happened I was going to be a scientist. The only person I can experiment on is me."

Ali listened to Luciel enviously. Discovering she was a Hex had seemed like the end of her life and she wished she could see the potential he did in the discovery.

"I just want to protect myself," she admitted. "The CPS caught me once—next time I want a chance to escape. If they're going to hunt me until I'm dead for being a Hex, I want to know what I can do to defend myself."

"Wraith, you should answer too," Raven said softly. "It's possible that since Rachel and I had the potential, you do as well. There are tests I'd like to do."

"Of course," Wraith answered immediately. He looked at the others. "If I am a Hex it won't make much difference to my life. Besides I'm already committed to fighting the government as long as the extermination laws exist."

"You make it sound like the only possible decision." Avalon smiled wistfully. "I'm going to have to think about it. I've been hiding this all my life and if I start to use it, I don't know where I'll stop."

"It has to be your decision," Wraith agreed, but Raven's eyes were dark with premonition.

"You've begun already," she said. "When you're ready to admit it, contact us."

Revenge wasn't even aware of Kez's presence although she noticed every once in a while that someone had brought food. She ate it without interest. It was the computer terminal that drew her attention. She had seen it when they first brought her to this room, squatting in the corner like a spider waiting for a fly. She wanted to use it, to touch it, but for a long time she had been able to escape its trap. The monitors by the bed were frightening but Raven had put them there and Raven was safe. Raven had also brought the helmet and that was safe too. With the helmet she didn't have to be Raven or Revenge, she could just be, in a world of color where it was never dark. But the helmet wasn't real, the terminal was real and Kalden was real and as long as there was the terminal to trap her, Kalden could find her.

Remembering that Raven would use the terminal she had forced herself to test it and realized for the first time what lay beyond it. They called it a net and it was the net Kalden would use to trap her. Revenge's identity spun through the data networks, careening through nodes and systems, breaking through security protocols with the power of her fear. Everywhere she traveled she found lists, of names, numbers, dates, and times, lists which said where everything was supposed to be, lists which would help Kalden to track her. The net was made of light, the only places its tendrils didn't extend were the depths of the city, the slums and ganglands where the sun couldn't penetrate and the lighting burned out. But the depths of the city were dark and Revenge recoiled from their threat. Racing away from the edge of the net she shot through it again. Everywhere she travelled she closed doors behind her, blocked off junctions, ceased the flow of data. Behind her, systems fell silent, the fear of the dark spurring her on to move faster. The tide of her presence was felt across the city as systems shut down, the inaudible murmur of information slowed and began to stop.

The lights flickered and Raven shivered suddenly, breaking the tension in the hotel room.

"Something's wrong," she said and the lights went out. The

others froze but Raven was a blur of motion, darting toward the window and opening the thick curtains.

"Look," she said and the others hurried to join her, blundering blindly into objects as they crossed the room.

It was midday and the hotel was on one of the higher levels, so some grey light from the sun gave them a view of the city. But nothing else did. From the depths upward the lights had gone out, from every walkway and archway, every window in the skyscrapers was black and the darkness was spreading. Further up into the heights lights were still going out. Holo-projections disappeared like ghosts and silence muffled the city.

"It's like the end of the world," Avalon whispered, staring out at the suddenly strange scene before them.

"Check the vidscreen and the terminal," Wraith instructed.

"No use," Raven replied from out of the darkness but Luciel fumbled across the room anyway.

"They're both dead," he confirmed after a few moments. "Nothing doing."

"It has to be a Hex," Ali exclaimed.

"Unfortunately, yes," Raven agreed and moved back across the room toward the vidcom. Suddenly the screen lit up with a soft glow and the others could see Raven's pale fingers lightly on the screen. "It's difficult," she said quietly. "Everywhere systems are shredding. It's like a virus replicating throughout the net." Before she could continue the screen sprang to life with an image of Kez, looking scared.

"Raven!" he exclaimed, *"What's going on? Everything's stopped working!"*

"Check on Revenge," Raven instructed.

"That's what I mean!" Kez looked frantic. *"It looks like she's had some kind of fit and the monitors aren't working."*

"Is she still breathing?" Wraith demanded, his body tense with shock.

"Just about." Kez looked at him. *"But I don't know what to do!"*

"Do the best you can," Raven instructed. "I'll be with you shortly." She took her hands from the vidcom and the signal winked out, leaving the unit as dead as before. She was already moving toward the door.

"Wait!" Wraith called after her, moving to catch up.

"Not you," Raven replied, turning to halt him. "Revenge didn't know enough to hide what she did. The CPS could already be on their way. Stay here with the others. If I can't stop them, you won't be able to help."

With that she was gone, the door closing behind her as the others were left in the darkened room.

Across the city a pair of needlelike blue eyes stared out through the levels.

"It's her," he said to himself. "I'm certain of it." Turning to the man behind him, whose uniform marked him as a senior officer in the security services, his lined skin wrinkled in a rare smile.

"Have your men stand ready," he ordered. "Once we've re-initialized the network, your team can track the disturbance to its source. Then it will be your job to apprehend the Hex responsible."

"A Hex did this?" the officer exclaimed, his surprise betraying him into informality.

"So I suspect," Dr. Kalden replied. "This incident will persuade the government to give me the resources I need to eliminate them."

Raven's flitter cut through the chaos of the city like a shark in the depths of the ocean. Thousands of flitters and skimmers clogged the bridges and archways, the loss of the city net depriving them of lights and direction. A few attempted to navigate with only their own lights to guide them but were making slow progress across the complex tangle of bridges. Raven passed them at the flitter's top speed, its lights flashing across the confusion. Without the network to guide her, she was forced to pilot the craft on eyesight and the speed of her reactions alone, trusting to her eidetic memory to furnish her with directions back to the apartment.

One pale hand lay dormant on the console as she used the other to pilot the flitter, keeping track of the situation within the net. It had fragmented, but the powerful computers which held it together had only been wounded by the loss. Slowly they were coming back on line, repairing themselves, ready to launch their own attack. All the broken tendrils of the net led back to one source and as the net was restored that source would become increasingly obvious. Raven's only chance to save Revenge lay in reaching the apartment before the CPS and the console told her that she would be too late. Whispers of information were starting to echo across London again.

If she'd allowed herself more time to consider, Raven might have decided Revenge and Kez were already lost. But she didn't allow herself the luxury of consideration. Her pride exhorted her to challenge the limits of possibility, and she refused to recognize the possibility of arriving too late. Turning the flitter on its nose she dived through the levels, before sweeping in a curve that brushed the flitter against one of the colossal skyscrapers and skimming past the bridges. The area was still dark but the net was back on line and Raven threw herself out of the flitter as it touched down, leaving the power running. She raced up the stairs to the apartment; the elevators were powered by the network and their lights were off. The door to the apartment was locked and she knocked on it hard.

"Who is it?" Kez's voice was high and frightened.

"Raven."

The door was opened and she saw the room beyond was dark.

"Here," Kez said, shutting the door behind her and taking her hand to lead her across the room. "She collapsed in front of the terminal. I went to find her when the lights went out and . . ."

"She's shorted out the entire city network and the CPS will be here any moment."

Kez's gasp was silenced by a short harsh scream which suddenly cut off. Raven made her way to the sound. Revenge lay on the floor, curled into the fetal position and whimpering to herself.

"What is it?" Raven demanded. "Revenge, where are you?"

The whimpering continued, then became words.

"In the dark," the child whispered and Raven swore under her breath. In under a second the lights came on and Kez could see Raven kneeling on the floor next to Revenge. The whimpering stopped and the girl's eyes glazed over under the lights as she clung to Raven with skinny arms and legs. As Raven stood, lifting Revenge's slight figure without any difficulty, a siren began to wail in the street, joined by a chorus of others in the distance.

"Close the curtains," Raven hissed and Kez ran across the room to do it. As he pulled back the heavy drapes he glanced outside and turned to look at Raven.

"There's three Seccie flitters out there!"

"Stay chill," Raven said softly, shifting Revenge's weight in her arms to reach into her jacket, and produced a pistol.

Nodding silently, Kez started to move toward the door then froze at the sounds of footsteps in the corridor.

"Drop your weapons!" an amplified voice demanded.

"Come and make me!" Kez snarled back.

"This is the Security Services," the voice boomed. *"You are under arrest. Drop your weapons and come out with your hands up!"*

Raven leveled her pistol at the door, then to Kez's surprise lowered it again. Her eyes were fixed on the door.

"Checkmate," she whispered as the gas started to roll under the door. Revenge began to cough and Kez ran for the window.

"No use," Raven told him. "Strengthened glass." She lifted Revenge higher, above the clouds of gas. The little girl's lips were blue and she was choking. "She's dying," Raven said softly. "The dosage is too strong."

"Should we surrender?" Kez asked. Raven shrugged.

"Not much point for me," she told him. Revenge had lost consciousness and Raven laid her down gently on one of the chairs, sitting on the floor as the gas rolled over them both. "Good-bye, Kez."

It was hard to breathe and Kez felt dizzy as he tried to move toward them. He had to crawl the last few inches to take Raven's hand. It was cold but her fingers brushed his lightly as he sank unconscious to the floor.

Wraith paced up and down the hotel suite. The lights had come on again fifteen minutes ago and still there had been no word from Raven. Luciel was scanning the newsfeeds but, while every channel carried the story of the unexpected blackout, there was no clue as to what might have happened to Revenge. Avalon, unwilling to intrude on their private affairs, had offered to leave but remained when Wraith said that Raven's fate concerned her too. All of them knew that without Raven their greatest asset was gone, even though no one was ready to acknowledge it, still hoping that she would return safely. Now Avalon was talking quietly to Ali, listening to the teenager's story of how she had found out she was a Hex. It hadn't taken the megastar long to realize that Ali was jealous of Raven and her feelings of inadequacy had been exacerbated by this current situation.

An exclamation from Luciel had them all clustering around the vidscreen as one of the media channels abruptly changed to a view of their apartment.

"We're now coming to you live from the source of this after-noon's disturbance," the news anchor was saying. *"Half an hour ago SS and CPS operatives surrounded this normal-looking apartment and captured two members of the dangerous terrorist group that threatened the security of the country with their destruction of a*

CPS facility last year. A third individual was taken directly to Saint Christopher's hospital and pronounced dead on arrival. Although the Security Services have not yet made any official statement it is widely believed that one of the apprehended criminals is the terrorist named Raven who the Prime Minister vowed would be caught.

"As you can see here, SS officials have closed the crime scene and have apparently brought in additional CPS specialists to study the area. Meanwhile the terrorists are undergoing questioning at a secure facility and the mutant, Raven, is expected to be terminated later this evening. We now go to the studio for an in-depth analysis of these latest events."

Luciel muted the vidcom and turned to Wraith.

"I'm sorry," he said and was echoed by Avalon. Wraith looked stricken. There had been no mention of Revenge in the broadcast and he knew what must have been her fate. As for Raven, the guilt seemed more than he could bear. He seemed to hear Ali's voice as if from a great distance away.

"They won't exterminate her."

"What?" Luciel frowned at her.

"Raven said Dr. Kalden never had the opportunity to study a functioning Hex," Ali reminded them. "Well, he's got one now, hasn't he? I bet there are lots of tests he'll want to do."

"Better if she had died," Luciel said coldly, voicing the thought the others were thinking.

"But . . ." Ali looked confused. "Aren't we even going to try to rescue her?"

"How can we?" Wraith said bleakly. "Without Raven we couldn't have had a chance last time. What hope do we have without her now?"

Such resignation was untypical of the white-haired ganger and Avalon seemed to realize that as well as any of them.

"We can't decide here," she said firmly, taking charge of the shell-shocked group. "You'd better come back with me."

"No," Wraith protested. "We're a liability."

"Without Raven you're without resources, right?" Avalon insisted. "And we have a lot to talk about anyway. Come on—who's going to look for you with me?"

"I think you're right," Luciel agreed, turning off the vidcom. "It's not as if we have a lot of other options."

Avalon's residence was at the top of a skyscraper section on the edge of London. She shared the fifty-odd rooms with the other members of Masque but sometimes they didn't see each other for days at a time. As she escorted Wraith, Ali, and Luciel into the residence there was no sign of the other band members. Wraith showed no reaction at all to the opulence of their surroundings but Ali and Luciel were wide-eyed. The rooms they passed through were lavishly decorated in deep lush colors; Egyptian artifacts and artworks were scattered across surfaces and elaborate masks hung on the walls.

Avalon took them into an extensive living room and made drinks of a sweet fruit juice.

"I'd offer you alcohol," she explained. "But I think you have a lot you need to decide and so do I." She smiled politely but already she seemed more distant than when they had waited together for news of Raven. "I'll leave you alone now, if you don't mind. There's a lot I have to think about."

With that she departed and the two younger members immediately turned to look at Wraith.

"Ali's right," Luciel began. "We have to try to save Raven."

"Of course." Wraith had recovered something of his composure, his gray eyes no longer like shattered glass. "But it will be difficult."

"Raven can probably do something toward saving herself," Ali put in. "She's told us often enough not to underestimate her."

"She could be injured." Wraith looked concerned. "And the news bulletin indicated that Kez was taken too—that is, if Rachel was the casualty."

"We might be able to get more information on that," Luciel suggested. "The Countess has contacts who could find out."

"And she provided men for the raids on the lab," Ali added. "Perhaps we could do that again?"

"There's the building Raven rented from her as well," Wraith remembered. "That would be a better place to plan than this. We shouldn't rely on Avalon's generosity, especially now that we are a danger to her."

"I think we should try to bring Avalon in," Luciel contradicted, surprised to hear himself take such a stand in planning their future. Now that Raven was absent and Wraith affected so badly, he felt for the first time as if his counsel was needed. But his conviction that he was doing the right thing gave him the courage to make his views felt. "Avalon could be an asset to us. We're supposed to be trying to fight for the rights of Hexes—we should try to recruit as many people as possible who carry the gene."

"We don't know how many Hexes there are," Ali reminded him. "Or if they'll want to join us." She, like Luciel, was also experiencing a new freedom to express her opinions and the feeling that she was actually a part of the group.

"We could try to find out," Luciel insisted. "And let people know that we exist and might be able to help them."

"We shouldn't get too hasty," Wraith warned. "Right now it's as much as we can do to help ourselves. But getting word to the Countess sounds like a good idea. And I think that we should leave for the new residence as soon as possible."

"We should rest first," Ali said. "And probably eat something. The city's probably still dealing with the effects of the blackout. It might be a good idea to wait until things have calmed down."

"There must be a Nutromac somewhere here," Luciel suggested. "I'm sure Avalon won't mind if we use it."

Avalon sat on the floor in the middle of her sumptuously appointed bedroom. It, like most of the residence, had been decorated by professionals hired by the band's manager. The four-poster bed and the gold inlaid furniture suited Avalon's idea of the megastar but she always felt a little as if the room belonged to someone else. Despite media adulation she hadn't changed that much from the clubland musician, sharing rooms with a group of other hopefuls waiting for the big chance to prove themselves. She had succeeded, but megastardom didn't sit so easily on her shoulders as it did on

Elohim's. Or even Cloud's, she thought to herself. Since joining Masque, Cloud Estavisti was becoming a star in his own right and Avalon knew how capably he would deal with it. And on that thought there was a knock on the door.

"Come in," she called, expecting one of the ill-named terrorists but instead it was Cloud, dressed in holo-weave clothing the same dark blue as his eyes.

"I hope I'm not disturbing you," he said lightly. "But you seem to have mislaid some visitors. I found one of them wandering around looking for a Nutromac and directed him to the kitchen."

"Oh, yes," Avalon sighed. "Thank you, Cloud. They are my visitors but I needed some time alone for a second."

"Shall I leave?" he offered.

Avalon shook her head. "Perhaps you can give me some advice."

"If I can," Cloud said with a thoughtful smile, seating himself on the floor beside her. "You rarely seem to need advice."

"Although you give it anyway," Avalon returned. "Now I need it." She sighed again. "My visitors need help and I feel obliged to provide it. For various reasons I think they have a claim on me. But if I help them I can't stop at basic necessities—I'll need to give up more than that. Probably all of this." She gestured at the room.

"I see." Cloud raised an eyebrow. "Or rather, I don't see. Why do these strangers have that sort of claim on you? You haven't been doing anything ill-advised, have you? Even if you think it can break your career, something can probably be arranged. I've never heard of a blackmailer that couldn't be bribed one way or another."

"No," Avalon said quickly. "It's nothing like that. But they're . . . they're freedom fighters of a sort, and I believe in their cause."

"Their cause?" Cloud looked incredulous. "Avalon, in all the time I've known you, I've thought you had the discipline to survive the occasional insanity of this kind of life, the feeling of power that encourages so many of us to destroy ourselves. But now you're suggesting sacrificing everything you've worked for all your life to help some political terrorists. Even if you do believe in their cause surely you can use your position to help them more than you can as another starving freedom fighter?"

"Then your advice is to abandon them," Avalon said sharply.

"And to save yourself." Cloud stood up. "I'm sorry if it's not the advice you wanted. But they'll drag you down, Avalon, and us with you if you don't break from them now." Turning in a whirl of shimmering blue light, he left the room, and Avalon looked after him, wondering if he was right.

All three of them ate sparingly of the meal Luciel had dialed from the Nutromac when he eventually found it.

"There's a whole kitchen as well," he added. "I didn't think anyone cooked for themselves any more."

"They probably don't," Ali told him. "Although my father and I had a Nutromac we had a kitchen as well and hired people to come and cook for us. Home-cooked food tastes better but it's expensive and anyone who can afford to install a kitchen can usually afford to hire professionals to cook for them."

"I saw Cloud Estavisti as well," Luciel told them. "He doesn't exactly look real, does he? I felt like I was talking to his holo."

"He's very talented," Ali said defensively. "Next to Avalon he's the most famous member of Masque."

"It's light-years away from the kind of life we're leading," Luciel replied. "It's hard to believe Avalon is one of us."

"Raven didn't seem to think so," Ali reminded him. "You heard what she said—she didn't want to teach us but she wanted to teach Avalon."

"Raven said she was committed to teaching you," Wraith corrected her. "And that was a large concession for her to make. She's always preferred to work alone. If she felt special sympathy for Avalon it might well have been because she's shared something of Raven's experience, growing up knowing she was under sentence of death."

Ali fell silent and Luciel tried to break the tension.

"Do you think Raven would like it here?" he asked from where he stood at the window looking down at the city. "She seems comfortable wherever she is."

"I don't think Raven cares where she is," Wraith replied. "Except now."

Luciel nodded and began to move away from the window. Suddenly he froze, then moved back quickly and silently.

"Wraith," he said urgently. "There are a lot of Seccie flitters out there all of a sudden."

"You don't think Avalon would have—" Ali began but was cut off by Wraith.

"I'm trying not to think it," he said, taking his laser pistol out.

To Ali's surprise Luciel produced his own. As he was checking it over the door opened and both of them turned to face it. Avalon blanched as she found herself staring down the barrel of a gun.

"What's going on?" she demanded.

"There are armed flitters out there with Seccie ID," Wraith told her.

"Oh no." Avalon ran over to the window and looked out. "I promise I didn't call them," she said quickly, realizing their probable thoughts.

"How did they find us?" Luciel asked. "No one else knew we were here."

"Cloud!" Avalon exclaimed, her shock obvious to the rest of them. "I can't believe he'd do this."

"We'd better find him," Wraith said.

6

VIRTUE AND FORM

The slim ethereal figure of Cloud Estavisti confronted the Hex grouping in Masque's opulent residence. Alone and unarmed he had the best defense against them. Wraith couldn't have shot him, even if he felt the dancer deserved it.

"Cloud, how could you?" Avalon's voice was hopelessly confused.

"You couldn't do it yourself," Cloud told her. "And it needed to be done. I told the Security Services you were being held hostage. You won't be connected with them."

"I am connected with them," Avalon raged at him. "And you've forced me to admit it. I can't risk the SS arresting me any more than they can. If I do, I'm in danger of my life." She turned to Wraith. "You have to leave now, if you still can. Will you take me with you?"

"Of course," the ganger said courteously.

"Avalon, this is unwise," Cloud protested but she rounded on him, violet eyes blazing.

"Betrayer," she flung at him. "I can trust strangers better than you. I suppose you'd have sold me to the CPS too if you'd known what I was." Turning her back on him, she stalked across the room. "There are flitters on the upper level," she announced. "We can probably outrun them for a while."

"Is there anything you'd like to take with you?" Wraith asked, also turning his back on Cloud. Luciel moved to follow them and only Ali hung back. Cloud's expression was unreadable and for a moment he reminded her of Raven. Then he noticed her standing there and looked derisively at her.

"Go on, then," he said. "You don't want to be left behind, do you?"

"No, I don't," she said angrily and turned to catch up with the others, thinking that Wraith or Luciel should have at least incapacitated him to prevent him from further mischief.

Ali caught up with the others on the roof. Avalon had somewhere acquired an electric guitar, which she wore slung over one shoulder. The flitter bay was full with luxury craft and Avalon had led them to a sleek black vehicle that looked designed for speed.

"I'll pilot," Luciel volunteered. "Wraith, can you hold them off with your pistol when we go out?"

"I can attempt it," the ganger said wryly. "Give your pistol to Ali."

"There's no point," Ali said. "It's not as if I can use it."

"I can," Avalon interjected, to their surprise. "Give it to me." She took the weapon with a surprising ease and smiled at their expressions. "Not everyone is content to rely on the protection of bodyguards," she explained. "Besides, I grew up in the slums."

Ali climbed into the back, beside the singer, and watched as Luciel operated the controls to the bay door and began to pilot the flitter out. Wraith and Avalon slid down their windows and sighted down their pistols, waiting for the first sign of pursuit.

Alaric watched the news item in silence. Other members of Anglecynn looked up expectantly when he turned off the battered vidcom. Since he had issued instructions that everyone should remain at Dragon's Nest, almost the entire group was there. Sixty people, of which only five including himself were founding members and only another fifteen were veterans of over two years.

"It looks like that's it," Alaric told them. "I had hoped to discuss the possibility of sharing some resources with the Hex group but it seems the idea comes too late."

"Why not discuss it anyway?" Geraint asked. Next to Alaric he was the oldest member of the group and to anyone else the remark would have constituted an order.

"It's possible not all of them were captured," Jordan added.

"Well, what would be general feelings on forming an alliance with the rebel Hexes?" Alaric asked, throwing the question open.

"As long as they're against the EF, I'm for them," Maggie announced, drawing noises of support from some of the others.

"Hell, they've got even more reason than us to be against it," one of the younger members added. "Stands to reason they'll want to get rid of extermination laws."

"I don't know." Geraint looked uncertain. "We don't know anything about the Hex powers. I've heard them called witches and demons. I think we ought to know what we're getting into before we consider involving ourselves with them."

"Excuse me?" To Alaric's surprise, Daniel Hammond was signaling for attention and he waved the others silent for a moment. "Thank you," Daniel said nervously. "I know I'm a new member but I think you ought to know I once knew someone who I think could be a part of their group. She was one of my sister's friends, a bit spoiled and a little vain, but she certainly wasn't any kind of demon. I don't think she could have even known she was a Hex and she must have been terrified when they took her away. I don't know how she escaped. But I'm glad she did."

"Daniel's right," Jordan agreed. "The legalized extermination of Hexes is one of the laws we should be fighting. Otherwise we sanction government-authorized murder of children with no other fault than a genetic anomaly they couldn't help having."

The meeting broke up almost immediately into smaller discussions as everyone attempted to debate the idea at once. None of the veterans intervened while the discussion went on, taking part in it equally enthusiastically. But after about fifteen minutes, Alaric glanced at Geraint, who nodded.

"I think we ought to take this to a vote," Geraint suggested, his voice effectively silencing the others. "How many in favor of making some contact with what might remain of this group, with a view to further discussion?"

About half the room raised their hands immediately and were followed after a few minutes by most of the others.

"Would those opposed like to speak?" Alaric asked and the first of the dissenters stepped forward. As he began to outline his arguments, Jordan leaned forward and squeezed Alaric's hand.

"I think it's carried," she said in an undertone. "There's already a majority in favor."

"Let's hope when we've decided there's still someone left to contact," Alaric replied.

Shots ricocheted from the side of the flitter and it lurched alarmingly as Luciel attempted to swing it away from the pursuit. Leaning dangerously out of her window, Avalon fired off a couple of blasts at random and leaned in again as Luciel swung the craft round, aiming for a space down to the next level. Wraith leaned out of his window, firing more deliberately, and Ali called:

"They're falling back!"

"Not far enough," Luciel replied, diving down a level and flipping the light vehicle round a bridge support.

A fusillade of shots confirmed his words as the Seccie flitters continued the chase, fanning out in an attempt to encircle him. Luciel accelerated again, swearing to himself.

"How do I lose them?" he exclaimed involuntarily.

"Head for the ganglands, then pull off through the slums and come back again," Wraith instructed. "If you have to, go right into the depths, but watch out—there's no lighting at all down there and a lot of arches have fallen." He leaned out through the window and fired again, holding back the Seccies as Luciel attempted to get a lead on them, piloting the flitter in a crazy spin across the level. Avalon was firing as well but few of her shots hit.

"It's not like my training," she excused herself.

"You don't need to shoot to kill," Wraith replied. "Just scare them a little, make them fall back."

"I'm trying," Avalon assured him, then spun to look at him as the ganger gave an odd curse.

Wraith collapsed back in his seat and Ali saw blood staining his jacket.

"What happened?" she asked, her voice shrill with alarm.

"Dropped the pistol, dammit," Wraith said succinctly. "Took a hit in my right arm."

"How bad is it?" Ali asked, desperately trying to remember the first aid course she'd taken at school.

"I've taken worse," Wraith replied raggedly. "But it's bad timing."

"Maybe not that bad," Luciel said with relief. "We're pulling ahead."

The flitter shot through the levels, pursued by the Seccie swarm, but as the greasy lights of gangland drew near, Luciel executed a fast turn that sent their flitter spinning a dive down the levels, before yanking the craft back up with a jolt. They swung past a building that loomed alarmingly close, then sped back up through the levels again.

"Can you see them?" Luciel demanded and Ali clung on to her seat as she attempted to look back.

"Not any more," she replied and Luciel immediately cut the speed, sending the flitter cruising more comfortably through the more respectable slums.

"They'll have our description," Wraith warned.

"Next level down we'll dump the flitter then," Luciel replied. "Once we've stolen another we should be relatively safe."

It was an anxious ride that seemed excruciatingly slow to all of them until Luciel spotted an alternative craft and pulled in. The others waited inside while he walked casually toward it and attempted to disable the lock. A few years ago he wouldn't have had any idea how to pick a lock, but since customizing the flitter he'd worked on with Kez, he'd learned a few things. After five minutes that felt like an eternity he cracked it open and turned to signal the others. They hurried over to the new vehicle, Ali supporting Wraith, who looked even more pale than usual. Once they were inside, Luciel got the flitter moving at a fast but just legal speed and they headed back toward gangland.

"Once we get to the building we can see about fixing you up," he told Wraith. "I just hope Raven managed to include some medical supplies in that inventory of hers."

The room was cold and gray. A dim light glowed from a panel high above, shining into Kez's eyes as he awoke. He felt nauseous and the first breath he drew made him cough. Dragging himself roughly upright he saw for the first time the other figure in the room.

Raven lay against the wall, looking like a broken doll, her face white and still. Crawling toward her, still shaken by hacking coughs, Kez reached for her wrist and tried to feel a pulse. After a few bleak seconds he found it, fluttering lightly under Raven's almost translucently pale skin. Pulling himself up again to sit next to her, Kez took Raven's shoulders and shook them lightly.

"Raven," he whispered, his voice rough and hoarse. "Wake up!"

The older girl stirred slightly, then opened ebony eyes and began to cough. He helped her sit up and she leaned back against the wall of their cell as she tried to stop herself choking. Finally she stopped and, catching her breath, began to look at their surroundings.

"Are you all right?" Kez asked anxiously.

"More or less," Raven replied. She looked around the room again before saying to herself. "And here I am again."

"You've been here before?"

"Hardly," Raven replied. "But places like this." Stretching out her legs to make herself more comfortable on the cold floor, she continued: "Back in Denver, I grew up in an asylum blockhouse. A standard punishment was locking us in a room something like this one."

"What did you do?" Kez asked.

"Nothing," Raven replied. "Waited." She shrugged. "I'm sure this cell is well enough designed that I couldn't get out of it by any conventional means and nothing unconventional comes to mind right now. So we wait and sooner or later someone will turn up and we'll find out a little more."

"They will?"

"Sooner or later," Raven confirmed. "Either to question us or torture or just stand there and laugh."

"That doesn't sound too good," Kez said uneasily.

"It isn't too good," Raven replied. "Being dead might be a better option but that didn't happen, so we wait."

"Don't you have anything that might help?" Kez asked hopefully.

"If there was a lock I could probably pick it," Raven told him. "But there isn't one on this side."

"Aren't you scared?"

"It wouldn't be productive." Raven's eyes met his seriously. "Fear isn't going to help us get out of here."

When the flitter touched down in front of the gangland building everyone was tense with nerves. Ali helped Wraith out of the flitter and Luciel led them toward the building. As they approached the main entrance, Luciel paused, looking at the blue and gold Snake emblem that was slashed across the door.

"This wasn't here before," he said warningly. Cautiously he tried to open it. "It's locked."

"Can you open it?" Avalon asked.

"I think so," Luciel replied. "Unless Raven's been playing with it, in which case I don't have a chance."

Ali helped Wraith to the side of the building so he could lean against it and slumped down at his feet. She felt grimy and bruised from the ride and almost impossibly tired. Luciel was fiddling with the lock while Avalon covered them with his pistol.

"This might be it," he said after a few minutes.

"Wait a second." Avalon put her hand over his, gesturing for silence. "Can you hear something?"

The others listened. Traffic noises filtered down from the upper levels but there was nothing nearby.

"Inside the building," Avalon insisted. She frowned, her head half-tilted to catch the faint noise, then stepped back, waving the others off. "Someone's coming," she whispered.

Silently, Luciel took the pistol from her and levelled it at the door. Still leaning against the wall, Wraith reached into his jacket and revealed a lethal-looking knife and held it toward Avalon. Then he pushed himself upright and took a fighting stance. Fumbling in the garbage Ali grabbed hold of a short metal pole, broken off from some piece of machinery, and got to her feet. Then the door opened and Luciel found himself pointing a pistol at a man with a machine gun.

"Chill, kid!" Jeeva said quickly. "Ain't no call to be shooting."

Ali almost collapsed with relief and tried to disguise it by taking Wraith's arm as he also sagged against the wall.

"Jeeva!" Luciel said with relief. "Thank God. We need help."

"Looks like it," Jeeva agreed, slinging his gun and moving to support Wraith into the building. "What's going down?"

"Raven's been caught, and Kez," Luciel explained. "Wraith was shot while we were escaping from the Seccies."

"I scan." Jeeva set Wraith down on an empty crate in the main room and hurried to lock and then bar the door. Crossing the room he opened one of the doors leading up to a set of stairs and called up it: "Hey, Finn! Get down here!"

Booted feet rang on the stairway and Finn appeared in the

entrance hall. He went immediately to Wraith and motioned the others aside so he could inspect the injury.

"Bullet wound," he said to himself. "Not a blaster. It'll have to be taken out." He looked round the group and focused on Ali. "Is anything major going to go down in the next few minutes or can we have this taken care of properly?"

"I think so," Ali replied nervously, looking to the others for reassurance.

"Then in that case we'll take him upstairs," Finn decided. "Jeeva, get on the com to the Countess. Tell her we need a medic and probably more backup. Where's Raven?"

"Captured." Luciel told him. "Kez as well."

"Tell her that too," Finn instructed. "And get her to send over some more technicians—we'll need to get this place up and running fast. You scan?"

"Understood," Jeeva said briefly and left the room at an easy loping run.

"We'd best get Wraith upstairs," Finn continued. "Help me carry him," he addressed Luciel. "You two get up to the control room and start getting stuff uncrated."

Ali and Avalon glanced at each other as Finn lifted Wraith into a standing position.

"Thank you," he said faintly. "I appreciate this."

"Don't sweat it," Finn replied. "Raven hired us to get this place operational, you've just made it a bit more urgent, that's all." Hoisting Wraith up between him and Luciel he started to head back toward the stairs.

"Wait a moment," Avalon called after him.

"What?" Finn didn't look back.

"Where's the control room?"

"Second door along, up the stairs, straight ahead there's a room full of crates. That's it."

With that he disappeared up the stairwell and Ali and Avalon were left alone.

"I suppose we go upstairs then," Avalon said ruefully. "Though I'm not sure what we're supposed to be doing."

"Neither am I," Ali admitted. "Maybe we'll find out when we get there."

The door opened so smoothly that Kez didn't notice the difference until a shadow fell over his face. Looking up quickly he saw the door blocked by four uniformed men. As they spread out and took guard positions around the room a fifth entered. Unlike the others he was elderly, his hair white with age and his face lined. But his blue eyes were bright as he entered the room, closing the door carefully behind him and coming to face the two prisoners.

"This is an unexpected pleasure," he said pleasantly. "I'm not certain of your identity, young man, but you must be Raven—or do you prefer Miss Raven?"

"Just Raven," the girl replied, still seated on the floor, with Kez crouching uneasily beside her.

"Raven," Kalden confirmed. "Well, my dear, it looks as if you've made an unfortunate mistake."

"It does appear that way," Raven agreed. "But you'd be wrong to think so."

"Then you planned to find yourself here," Kalden suggested with an edge of sarcasm.

"Not exactly, but I'm finding the experience instructive."

"Then we shall endeavor to provide you with further opportunities for your education," Kalden replied coldly. "I trust you will find them equally instructive."

"I hope so." Raven stretched out her legs and looked up at the scientist with a dispassionate interest. "But I'm often disappointed. If I were you I'd have us both executed now."

"I'm sure you would, Miss." Kalden smiled, showing his teeth. "But I am not so foolish as that. I expect to learn a lot from you." Turning on his heel he opened the door again and the guards moved to cover him as they exited the room. Less than a minute later the door swung shut again, sealing with a dull clang.

"No one ever takes what I say at face value," Raven reflected. "Perhaps we should try and get some sleep. From the sound of it Kalden is planning a busy schedule for us." She shifted position to lie flat on her back on the smooth floor.

"Raven?" Kez asked, attempting to compose himself similarly.

"Yes?"

"Did you mean that? About executing us?"

Raven laughed quietly. "Does it matter?" she asked. "He won't do it."

"But would you?"

"Of course," Raven replied. "If a threat exists, it should be removed immediately and effectively. If a threat does not exist, any action taken to circumvent it is futile. Now go to sleep."

Raven's credit with the Countess was obviously better than the others had imagined because in less than an hour the fixer had sent over five of her guards and two technicians as well as a street doctor whose credentials Finn vouched for. While he was attending to Wraith's arm, Finn took the technical experts to the control room where Ali and Avalon had successfully uncrated all the equipment and had stacked it up around the room. Neither of them had understood much of it. There were banks of panels and monitor screens as well as a lot of seemingly random electrical components and power cabling. But the technicians, a man and a woman who introduced themselves as Cy and Selda, seemed to know exactly what was intended.

"Monster of a security system," Cy commented, looking around the room at the assorted components. "Let's start getting it set up." Selda grabbed a coil of the cabling and Ali and Avalon found themselves relegated to a corner of the room as the technicians started wiring parts together. Avalon watched them intently but after a while Ali slipped away and went to find Wraith. He was asleep on a pile of blankets in a suite of empty rooms, with Luciel watching over him.

"Hi," Ali said softly as she came in and sat on the floor beside them. "How is he?"

"Doctor said he'd cracked the bone and lost a lot of blood but he should heal OK if he's easy on it. That's how come the bandaging. He'll need a sling once he gets up."

"What do we do without him?" Ali asked nervously.

"I don't know," Luciel shook his head. "But we'll have to try." He grinned ruefully. "Technically you should be in charge now."

"Why me?" Ali looked alarmed.

"Apart from Kez, you've known Raven and Wraith the longest," Luciel explained. "You know what they'd do better than me."

"I'm not sure about that," Ali contradicted. "And even if I did, what good does it do to say that Raven would hack some secure system and Wraith would storm it with guns blazing? I can't do any of that."

"So we'll have to think of something else," Luciel replied. "Maybe Avalon can help."

"Maybe." Ali looked doubtful.

"By the way," Luciel added, "we might have something to go on. The Countess passed on a message from some group who want to open negotiations with us. Says they're called Anglecynn and they're anti the European Federation."

"What do they want with us?" Ali asked.

"No idea." Luciel looked blank. "The implication was that we have to start negotiations before we can find out."

Kez was asleep and Raven listened thoughtfully to the even sound of his breathing. She suspected the only reason he was still alive was that Kalden thought he might be a Hex. Revenge was almost certainly dead already.

Laying her palm flat on the floor she concentrated. Somewhere out there the net still existed, even with no apparent way to reach it.

But it was far away and she couldn't even sense its presence. She let her mind go blank, reaching out as far as she could. There. A flicker of familiarity. A random datastream intersecting momentarily with her consciousness. She reached for it and lost it. Reached out again and found nothing. But it was there. She stared up at the ceiling. She would need to conserve her energies and she doubted that the task ahead would be easy. But she had no intention of surrendering herself to Kalden's experiments.

She wasn't a child any longer. Hadn't been a child since she'd escaped from the asylum and forced the use of her abilities. But that night while she slept Raven dreamed of being alone in the city and everywhere she went the streets were silent.

7
A FEARFUL MADNESS

Ali awakened from an uneasy doze as someone shook her by the shoulder. Sitting up quickly, her nerves still on edge since the blackout, she looked up to see Cy, the male technician, taking a hasty step back.

"Didn't mean to startle you, Miss," he said politely. "I just came to tell you that your system's up and running and you might want to test it out."

"Oh." Ali got out of the battered chair she'd been sleeping in and stood up.

The room she'd been in was unchanged, but as they walked toward the control center, she could see the corridor had changed. The battered wall panels had been removed and replaced by a smooth black surface which gleamed slightly with a dark red light. As they entered the control room she could see that the changes extended much further. Every wall was covered with vidscreens, large and small, and a semicircular bank of computer terminals commanded the center of the room. Avalon, Luciel, and Selda were standing in the center of the semicircle, looking at a bank of screens showing different vidcam images.

"The cams form a sphere around the perimeter of the immediate area of the building," Selda was explaining. "And the others are in the building itself." Seeing Ali, she turned to include her in the explanation. "All three stairways and the approach corridors to the control room are force shielded and the staircases have hidden explosives as well."

Ali took a seat in the middle of the control bank as Selda and Cy continued to explain the system to them. Avalon was listening intently and Luciel even asked a few questions but Ali found most of the technical descriptions went over her head. This was what they needed Raven for, she thought to herself. The teenage hacker had designed this security system herself and the rest of them would be lucky if they could understand it well enough to use it. Ali found Raven difficult to get on with but she admitted to herself that the group needed her more than they'd ever needed Ali. Once the technicians had finished their explanation and left, Ali turned to look at the others.

Avalon was frowning as she studied the terminals, her lips moving silently as she repeated some of the instructions they'd been given.

"I didn't catch most of that," Ali admitted. "This is really Raven's system."

"I know." Luciel sighed. "The computer system doesn't even

have basic security protocols yet. Raven must have been planning to do that all herself." He looked hopefully at Avalon. "How much did you understand?"

"Not enough, I suspect," she said seriously. "But at least we have a system now, even if we don't understand it properly. That's better than nothing at all."

"You're right," Luciel agreed. "So what do we do next?"

"Is Wraith still asleep?" Ali asked anxiously.

"Looks like it," Luciel replied. "The doc gave him some tranqs when he left and they seem to have knocked him out."

"Perhaps we could try and make this place more habitable." Avalon suggested. "Right now Wraith doesn't even have a bed."

"Raven would probably go on a shopping spree," Ali told her. "She likes to be comfortable."

"Let's borrow the large flitter Finn was using earlier," Luciel said. "We can go and pick up some furniture and try and make Wraith more comfortable."

"Is it safe?" Ali asked.

"Take Finn with you for protection," Avalon said. "He looks as if he can take care of himself."

"OK." Luciel was heading for the door when he thought of something and turned back. "Thanks for all your help, Avalon. I'm sorry we seem to be causing you so much trouble. I don't think Raven meant all this to affect you."

"Don't worry too much about it," Avalon told him. "This is Cloud's fault more than yours. If it wasn't for him Wraith wouldn't be out of action now when you need him."

. . .

The group of scientists were checking the equipment for the third time, quietly murmuring their results to each other so as not to disturb the trio who observed them. Dr. Kalden wore an annoyed expression as he considered the makeshift laboratory.

"The facilities are highly inadequate," he complained to his companions. "This subject could represent an important breakthrough for my work and I need specialized equipment to study her. I need more people, more resources, and a proper laboratory to work instead of this basement."

"I appreciate your concerns, Doctor," Adam Hammond replied. The Security Minister looked just as exasperated as Dr. Kalden. "But under the circumstances I consider the Security Services have been more than reasonable." He nodded toward the third man who as yet had said nothing. "Governor Alverstead has informed me that the European Federation considers your experiments a matter of state secrecy. Therefore I cannot allow you any more assistants than those who have already been involved in this project. My people are working on supplying the equipment you've requested but that much specialized technology cannot be provided immediately. As for the location, this building is the best maximum security facility there is in this city. The subject is considered a dangerous terrorist with unknown abilities. I cannot allow you to remove her from this location especially since she was directly responsible for the escape of test subjects from the facility which was under your sole control."

"An attack that occurred at a time when the government was

refusing me additional funding on the grounds that my project served no useful purpose!" Kalden exclaimed angrily. "Now I've been proved right! The girl does have abilities which would be of use to the Federation and to your Security Services, Mr. Hammond. But still I'm being denied the resources I need to continue."

"Dr. Kalden, Minister." Charles Alverstead's voice cut smoothly through the argument. "The Federation Council appreciates the effort you gentlemen have put into the work of my agency." The Governor of the CPS turned to consider the scientists flocked around the room. "This equipment may be far less than you deserve, Doctor. But I am certain a scientist of your caliber will obtain valuable results from it nonetheless. Equally I feel certain that the Minister's security precautions are necessary measures even if they do hamper the experimentation." Smiling urbanely at both of them he paused to consider his wrist chronometer. "Since other duties call me away and it appears your team have completed their tests, Dr. Kalden, I will leave matters in your capable hands. Please contact me once you have some results from the subject."

Raven had been giving Kez a history lesson when the guards arrived. Since their cell was certain to be monitored, they couldn't discuss anything that might compromise the others. But there was nothing to do except talk. Raven had attempted to take advantage of the opportunity and the occasion had come out of a question Kez had asked about Wraith's politics. Raven had found herself explaining the structure of the European Federation to him, something Kez had never given any attention to during his childhood on the streets.

"How come you know this stuff anyway?" Kez asked her, interrupting her explanation of Federation law. "You always say politics is a waste of time."

"There's no need to be ignorant," Raven replied. "Even if intervening in the political situation is futile, it's to our advantage to understand the world we live in." She smiled wryly. "But the reason I know this is the same for most hackers. In order to find the right computer system to break into, you need to know who controls it. It's a waste of energy to spend time and effort cracking a computer that doesn't have the information you want because it's the responsibility of a different agency." She laughed quietly as Kez looked up warningly at the ceiling, which probably concealed the monitors.

"Kez, considering I'm under the sentence of death for suspected mutation and due to be experimented on at any time, it's not going to make much difference if the CPS know I worked as a hacker."

"I guess not," Kez admitted and they returned to the lesson.

Ten minutes later the guards arrived, pointing their stun guns warningly at the prisoners as they ordered Raven to get up.

"Where are you taking her?" Kez demanded, trying to stand up as well.

"No questions," one of the guards said roughly, pushing him back down as two of the others took Raven's arms.

She frowned warningly at Kez as they led her out of the cell and he subsided, watching impotently as the door closed behind her.

Raven let the guards march her down the corridor. It was blank and featureless, only a few heavy doors along the way giving an indication of the building's function. Other cells, she speculated, and wondered if they also held prisoners. Her fingers twitched in the handcuffs the guards had put on her. Somewhere beyond the walls of this corridor was a computer system. The only problem was reaching it. Her mind worked on the problem as they marched her down the corridor and into a large windowless room. White-coated scientists were making adjustments to what looked like a hospital diagnostic bed surrounded by a bank of machinery. As she was brought into the room, Dr. Kalden turned to give her a sharklike smile.

"I see Raven has arrived," he said cheerfully. "So pleased you could join us." Raven ignored him and Kalden smiled even more broadly before ordering the guards to strap her onto the bed. Raven allowed them to do so, noticing that Kalden was amused by her cooperation, thinking her numb with fear. She had to clamp down on her emotions to keep from grinning with excitement.

Stupid, ignorant, and unimaginative men, she thought to herself. *Surround me with the most sophisticated technology available and you think you're safe because there's no computer terminal in this room.*

She stared blankly up at the ceiling as they attached wires and electrodes to her skin, wiring her up to the machines that surrounded the bed.

"Turn the test equipment on," Dr. Kalden ordered and Raven's body convulsed as electrical impulses ripped through her mind.

The pain was incredible. She'd read about this experiment in Kalden's files. The equipment was supposed to provide a map of her brain by recording her synaptic responses to different energy signals. She'd laughed at it at the time, amused by the way Kalden seemed to think this sort of testing would help him understand the working of the Hex abilities. Now it wasn't so amusing as pain tore through her body with each new signal.

Ignore it, she ordered herself. She forced herself not to remember that it was equipment like this that had left Rachel a shred of her former self. Instead she concentrated on the machines. In a universe the scientists were unable to comprehend, the equipment was sending messages all the time, chittering its results to itself. Raven reached out with her mind.

> **there!** < Behind the chatter of the equipment was a silent force, empty of words, a river of power flowing toward her. She reached out for it. Power cabling, piping energy to Kalden's test equipment.

> **and beyond . . .** < She reached further, nerves screaming in agony as she attempted to ignore the pain. The power cables thrummed with a constant force, providing the city with the power it needed, running into every building, every aspect of city life, endlessly supplying energy. She let her mind be carried with a wash of energy, taking her further and further away from her suffering body.

> **almost** < She felt at the edge of her perceptions, the link to the net. The power lines carried her toward it but too slowly. Suddenly there was nothing and the cessation of the pain brought

her back to her body as she realized the equipment had been turned off.

"What happened?" Kalden demanded, turning dials on the test equipment.

"I've no idea, sir," one of the scientists replied nervously. "It just stopped giving results. All we've got for the last three minutes is static."

Kalden looked suspiciously at Raven but the girl had collapsed back on the bed, her face gray with pain as she attempted to catch her breath. Kalden knew from experience how the equipment affected his subjects. He could have designed it to be less traumatic for them but he considered that the fear of torture kept them under control. It seemed to have done the same for Raven and he rejected the momentary fear that she could have caused the equipment failure.

"Take her back to the cell," he ordered the guards. "We'll need to check this over before we can perform any more tests."

Raven was still gasping for breath. But at least the link had revealed where she was being held: the EF Consulate.

Wraith woke up to find himself in unfamiliar surroundings. Someone had moved him while he slept, the drugs the Countess's medic had given him preventing him from waking up. Sitting up in bed he looked around the room. It wasn't elaborately furnished but a thick carpet now covered the floor and simple but attractive furniture was scattered around the room. Getting out of bed he arranged the cloth he found waiting for him to form a sling for his injured arm. Then he left the room and began to explore. He was amazed at the changes that had taken place in just a few short hours. All the rooms in this part of the building had been furnished. The layout was similar to the design of the apartment they'd been living in. But, instead of the heavy crimson and russet colors that Raven favored, the furnishings were in softer greens and blues. One undecorated corridor drew his attention. The black shielding gave him an idea of its purpose and he wasn't entirely surprised to find it led to a control room, although the scale of the equipment inside astonished him.

Finn and Avalon were inside, seated at a semicircular bank of terminals. The angle of the door prevented them from seeing him and they were evidently absorbed in conversation.

I didn't realize how much I relied on Cloud until he betrayed us," Avalon was saying. "I never realized I trusted him until I trusted him too much."

"If you run with a gang you have to trust your brothers," Finn replied. "But even then you make mistakes. You're not to blame."

"And I'm very grateful to you," Wraith added, coming to join them. Avalon smiled but Finn shook his head with annoyance.

"Hidden cams all through this place and we didn't even see you coming, Wraith. We've got to get more people up here to monitor that kind of thing."

"We?" Wraith asked, taking a seat beside them. "Are you joining us, Finn?"

"Don't get excited," Finn replied. "The Countess made a deal with Raven to supply support for this place until it's working and at the moment that support is me. But when it's done, the Snakes are gone. Otherwise you might start getting ideas and take my brothers on another schizo rescue mission."

"Raven's still a prisoner," Avalon reminded him and Finn shrugged.

"The way I see it, Raven can probably rescue herself. She's an electric hacker and a Hex. Whoever's holding her won't know what hit them." He grinned suddenly. "But if you do get round to breaking her out I might come along to see if there's anyone left for you to fight."

Wraith didn't stay talking for long. Excusing himself he went to find Ali and Luciel. As he continued to explore the building he tried to take comfort in Finn's belief that Raven would be all right. Even though she had proved herself self-sufficient in the past the image of Revenge haunted him. Whenever he thought of Raven being held prisoner he was almost overcome by the fear that he would find her, as he found Revenge, destroyed by Dr. Kalden's horrific experimentation.

Kez rushed to Raven's side as the guards dropped her on the floor. Blood trickled from her mouth where she'd bitten her lip, and her face was gray and lifeless. As the door closed behind the guards he checked her frantically. She didn't seem to be breathing. Taking her wrist, he tried to find a pulse, cursing himself for not knowing more first aid. A dry rasp startled him as Raven suddenly breathed and he almost collapsed with relief.

"Stop crying and help me sit up," Raven said faintly. "I'm not dead yet."

Flushing with embarrassment Kez helped her sit and lean back against the wall.

"What happened?" he asked her. "I thought they'd killed you."

"They didn't even complete their first batch of tests," Raven told him. "That man is a sadist. I'm going to positively enjoy killing him."

"Killing who?" Kez asked, startled.

"Dr. Kalden, of course," Raven replied, with an edge of annoyance despite her weakness. "Unless you know of any other sadistic experimenters who require my immediate attention."

"But how?" Kez asked. "He's almost killed you already."

"No he hasn't." Raven frowned. "I'm just not used to being wired up to a live electric current. There's a significant danger involved in experimenting on people whose abilities you don't understand. Now leave me alone, I need to think."

Raven closed her eyes and Kez moved away. Although Raven still sounded confident, her appearance worried him. He was also annoyed with Raven. If Wraith had been caught, he would have been a more considerate companion. Raven seemed annoyed by his concern for her, and even though he was sure she was planning something, she kept her own counsel. He also didn't understand why he was being held here. At first he'd thought it was because Dr. Kalden thought he was a Hex. But no one had attempted to run any tests on him. He caught his breath as an unnerving thought occurred to him.

"What is it?" Raven asked irritably. Kez blanched at her tone but he couldn't keep silent.

"I just thought," he said haltingly. "Maybe they're keeping me here because they can use me to get to you. They could torture me to get me to tell them about you."

"Or to persuade me to help them to save your life," Raven added. "It had occurred to me."

Kez took a deep breath, embarrassed by what he was going to admit.

"I don't know if I can handle torture," he said. "It scares me."

"That's the point of it," Raven replied unemotionally. Then she gave a half smile. "Don't worry about protecting me, Kez. Or the others. Tell them whatever you want."

"I don't want to tell them anything!" Kez protested. "I owe you."

"No you don't." Raven looked surprised. "Why would you think that?"

"Because if it wasn't for you I'd still be on the streets!" Kez exclaimed. "Of course I owe you."

Raven looked at him silently for a moment. Some color was returning to her face and she regarded him seriously.

"No, you don't owe me," she said quietly. "Since meeting us your life has been in danger almost constantly. Even the penalties for helping a Hex are high. Now you're in greater danger than you've ever been before. There's no reason to think you owe me anything."

Kez thought for a while before answering. Then he said slowly, "You gave me something to do with my life. Don't I owe you for that?"

"Maybe," Raven said thoughtfully. "Obligations are a decision you have to make for yourself. However, I'd rather you didn't try to risk your life for me."

"You risked yours," Kez insisted. "When you came back to the apartment."

"I know," Raven said. "It was unwise. Especially since I didn't succeed."

"Why did you come then?" Kez asked.

"I don't know." Raven looked annoyed. "Sometimes I don't understand myself."

"Sometimes no one else does either," Kez replied.

"At the moment that's probably to our advantage," Raven reminded him. Then, to his surprise, she grinned fiercely. "Dr. Kalden has a lot to learn," she said.

Wraith, Ali, and Luciel had been discussing the message from Anglecynn. Although the two younger members of the group had attempted to sort out the arrangements for the base they were still uncertain about what to do next. Rescuing Raven and Kez was the important thing, but with no way of knowing where they were being held it seemed almost impossible to achieve.

"Perhaps this group could help us?" Luciel suggested. "They probably have resources we could use."

"They're terrorists," Ali objected. "And we don't know anything about them."

"The government considers us terrorists," Wraith reminded her.

"And Raven told us something about them," Luciel added.

366

"She said they were naïve amateurs," Ali remembered.

"But they're against the European Federation," Luciel insisted. "And that includes the Hex laws."

"The fact that they've attempted to get in touch with us suggests they might support the Hex cause," Wraith agreed. "But we would have to be careful in contacting them and I don't know where would be a safe place to meet."

"Isn't here safe enough?" Ali asked, alarmed. "Finn and Jeeva said this was one of the best setups they'd seen."

"In negotiations like this it's generally considered unwise to reveal the location of your home base," Wraith explained. He didn't want to put Ali down but he was aware that despite her efforts to help the group she was still inexperienced. "Customarily one arranges a meeting on neutral territory."

"Then maybe we could go through the Countess," Luciel suggested, thinking quickly. "She passed on the message originally and her place is well defended. Perhaps we could meet Anglecynn there."

"It's a good idea," Wraith said approvingly. "If the Countess will agree."

"I'll go and ask Jeeva," Luciel said. "He's supposed to be heading back to her building. He can ask her if she'll be a go-between."

"All right," Wraith agreed. "Once you've done that you should try and get some sleep. There's nothing more we can do today and we'll need to be alert tomorrow."

"What about you?" Ali asked. "You're still recovering."

"I've already rested," Wraith replied. "And we'll need to take shifts in the control room, just in case the CPS or the Seccies have managed to track us here."

"I still can't believe Cloud betrayed us," Ali said quietly. "He must hate Hexes."

"A lot of people do," Luciel said softly. "The government tries to make us seem dangerous so no one will object to the extermination laws. No one really knows what Hexes are like."

"It's really Avalon he betrayed," Wraith said. "The rest of us didn't even know him but she trusted him. That kind of betrayal is difficult to accept."

The officials from the Security Services had left hours ago but Cloud still sat where they had interviewed him. The other members of Masque had returned that evening to find Security Services operatives searching the residence while Cloud was questioned in a private room. Once the Seccies had left they tried to find out what had happened but all Cloud had told them was that Avalon had gone. Corin and Jesse had tried to get him to tell them more but Cloud stayed silent and Lissa's concern for the future of the band had infected them all.

"Without Avalon we're nothing," she had exclaimed bitterly. "What are we supposed to do without her?"

Cloud had left them arguing and returned to his room. The Security Services had asked him to turn off the holo images that normally swam through the air and without them his room was stark and empty.

Avalon had accused him of betraying her and he knew she was

right. The questions the Seccies had asked him had made it clear that the strangers had not only been terrorists but Hexes as well and suddenly Avalon's final words to him had made sense. He'd meant to protect her from a foolish decision. Instead it seemed he'd endangered her life. Even if the Seccies didn't yet suspect that Avalon might be a Hex as well, they would soon. Then she'd be in greater danger than if he'd just allowed her to leave with the strangers and made up some excuse for her disappearance. Avalon's face was known across the world. There was hardly a person in the city who wouldn't recognize her, and once she was known to be a Hex, every hand would be turned against her.

That's my responsibility, Cloud thought to himself, staring blankly at the walls of his white room. *And there's nothing I can do.*

8
TWO CHAINED BULLETS

The call came through just after dawn. Alaric got up sleepily as his com signal chimed and he answered it, yawning.

"Alaric here," he said, rubbing the sleep from his eyes. "What's up?"

"This is Liz," the voice on the other end of the signal informed him. "You have a message from a fixer called the Countess."

"I'm on my way down," Alaric informed her and turned the wristcom off. Jordan was still asleep, and he dressed quietly so as not to disturb her and headed down to the computer room. To his surprise Liz was waiting for him with a cup of coffee substitute and she seemed unusually communicative.

"I'm sorry to wake you," she said. "But everyone's stirred up since the discussion about joining the Hexes and I thought this might be relevant."

"I hope so," Alaric replied, taking the cup and seating himself at one of the terminals. "But they might not be interested in meeting with us."

He called the message up, using his personal cypher to access the message. When it came it was terse and to the point.

"Negotiations can commence at your convenience. Location: my premises. Each group may bring four members. Weapons to be surrendered on arrival."

Alaric moved aside so that Liz could see the screen and she nodded approvingly.

"Good conditions," she said. "You going?"

"I think I should," Alaric replied. "Who else do you suggest?"

"Geraint," she said instantly. "It balances opinions since he is still uncertain."

"And if he's uncertain he needs to see what they're like," Alaric agreed. "If he changes his mind most of the other dissenters will as well and if he doesn't there's probably a good reason for it."

"What about Daniel?" Liz asked. "He knows one of them."

"He's still a new member," Alaric replied. "I'd rather take people with more experience. Maybe Jordan."

Liz smiled and Alaric felt annoyed. Jordan was an experienced member of Anglecynn. He wouldn't have suggested her otherwise. He was surprised when Liz said thoughtfully:

"Jordan might be a good idea. She doesn't look like a terrorist."

"And I do?"

"Don't be dense." Liz looked irritated. "Jordan's obviously less of a threat—she's young and female. If they're alarmed by us, she might convince them to be forthcoming."

"Conversely then, the fourth member of the party should be someone who does look like a terrorist," Alaric suggested. "Just in case they're not alarmed by us and think of trying something."

"Good idea," said Liz approvingly and moved away from the terminal. "I'll leave you to organize it."

With that she left the room and Alaric turned back to the message, composing an equally brief reply. A meeting like this had to be arranged as quickly as possible in case anyone else got to hear of it. The Countess's reputation was good but the longer he waited to commence negotiations the greater the chance her security might slip and compromise the meeting. Tonight, he decided, keying a reply on the terminal.

That way there'd be the cover of dark in case anything went wrong.

"*Twenty-two hundred hours. Will comply with conditions.*"

He sent the message and turned off the terminal. He'd need to discuss this with some of the other veterans before he officially decided who should go. He hoped they'd be as relieved as him that the Hex group made contact.

Avalon was on duty in the control room. The other members of the group had taken shifts through the night and Finn and Jeeva had left saying they'd be back in the morning with the Countess's reply. Avalon had offered to take the dawn watch and was spending the time familiarizing herself with the security system. She was impressed by the effectiveness of the system Raven had designed and she wanted to understand how to use it. She suspected the group had little use for a musician and she needed something to do. She'd noticed how inexperienced the young Hexes were and how useless they'd felt when Wraith was out of action. Now they seemed to be taking more of a role in decision making and Avalon didn't want to be left behind as a worthless member of the group.

She was still trying to get to know the others but so far she'd only talked much to Finn, who wasn't really one of them. She'd found herself liking the Snake gangers for the way they'd instantly taken charge of the situation when they arrived at the base. The Hex group had obviously been thrown by the loss of Raven and Avalon suspected it was because the dark-haired girl had made most of the decisions. From their discussion in the hotel room it seemed clear that she'd taught the others very little, if anything, of what she knew and they were handicapped without her.

Is it that she doesn't trust them, she wondered. *Or does she deliberately try to keep them dependent on her?*

They were a disparate bunch of people without very much in common. But something held them together as a group despite their seeming differences. The arrangement reminded Avalon of Masque. None of the band members, except perhaps Corin and Jesse, had very much in common. Lissa had been a child star and in the music business all her life in various different groups, never sinking very low or rising very high until she joined Masque. Corin and Jesse were both talented musicians who'd grown to be friends in the group but played very different styles of music. Avalon had worked her way from the slums to megastardom in a meteoric leap and Cloud came from the upper echelons of society, where he'd been privileged all his life.

Thinking about Cloud gave Avalon a sinking feeling. All her life she'd been careful not to trust other people too much and the one time she'd really needed to follow that rule she'd discarded it. She knew Cloud had thought that in some strange way he was helping her, but he had also unequivocally rejected the Hex group as terrorists. If he'd known she was a Hex as well he'd probably have sold her out too to save himself. Thinking about Cloud reminded Avalon that there might be media coverage of her disappearance.

Does everyone know I'm a Hex now? she wondered. *Or haven't the CPS guessed that's how I was involved?*

She fumbled with the notes she'd made about how to operate the control system, searching for the correct keypad. Eventually she found it and a large vidscreen turned on, showing a transmission from one of the entertainment feeds. She channel surfed for a while, trying to find some form of news, and stopped when she saw an image of Masque's palatial residence. There were media flitters clustered around it and a few other craft marked with the logo of the Security Services.

"*. . . still searching for the singer Avalon,*" the newscaster was saying, "*. . . who disappeared yesterday in mysterious circumstances from her home in the heights of London. The Security Services were on the scene today but declined to give any statement, although sources within the Ministry of Security have suggested that the singer's disappearance is connected to the capture of the terrorists* *responsible for yesterday's blackout. However, other members of Masque have strongly refuted those claims."*

The image cut to an interview with Lissa, Corin, and Jesse. They all looked worried and harassed. Avalon could imagine how the media networks must have been badgering them to give some kind of statement.

"Avalon wouldn't have had anything to do with the terrorists," Jesse was asserting fiercely. *"In all the time I've known her she's never done anything like that. A lot of people in this industry have tried to bend the law in one way or another but Avalon's completely honest."*

"I can't believe anyone would suggest that," Corin agreed. *"At the moment we think Avalon may have been kidnapped and if anyone has any information about her whereabouts please call our record company's hotline. We're very worried about her."*

"How will this affect Masque's future?" the interviewer asked and Avalon frowned to herself as she watched.

"Avalon is still the lead singer of Masque," Lissa said quickly, *"and we're all anxious to have her back—but she's not the only member of the group and we're all still involved in creative projects of our own. Until Avalon returns we'll be concentrating on those for a while."*

The vidscreen cut again back to a news anchor standing in front of Masque's residence.

"Cloud Estavisti, Masque's enigmatic dance and holo-artist, was unavailable for comment today. Despite repeated requests from the media he has declined to give any statement. Perhaps his silence

suggests another reason for Avalon's absence: could the two megastars have quarrelled? Perhaps this signals a split for Masque. We now return to the studio to discuss the implications of this breaking story."

Avalon turned off the vidscreen decisively. She had no wish to see what conclusions the media were going to jump to. Lissa seemed to have made it clear that the band would be trying to survive without Avalon before their news value disappeared. Cloud's absence confused her. She had been expecting him to throw her to the wolves. But perhaps he was being questioned since he had called the Seccies in the first place. She found herself hoping that they made his life as difficult as possible.

Sir Charles Alverstead regarded the dancer dubiously. He had hoped that the capture of Raven would prevent any further action by the Hex terrorists but the disappearance of Avalon had gravely concerned him. He had ordered an immediate check on the megastar's medical records only to find that Avalon had never seen a doctor in her life. Her background was known to be from the slums of the city and she had missed out on the routine medical examinations normally performed on children. In the circumstances it was highly possible she was a rogue Hex and he disliked the possibility that the terrorists had lost one dangerous member only to acquire another. He had sent for Cloud Estavisti to attempt to find out more about the singer but Cloud was being uncooperative.

"This is a matter of the highest security," he informed the dancer coldly. "Failing to provide the Security Services with information is a crime under Federation law."

"I've told you all I know," Cloud replied. Despite the questioning he had kept his composure even when Alverstead had refused to allow him a lawyer present. "I discovered a group of armed strangers entering the residence and called the Security Services immediately. By the time they arrived the strangers were gone and so was Avalon. I've given you their descriptions. There's nothing more I can tell you."

Alverstead looked annoyed.

"I'll be honest with you, Mr. Estavisti," he said. "More honest than I suspect you are being with me. Avalon is currently under suspicion of possessing the Hex gene and I suspect you know more than you are telling us. The Federation Council allows the CPS wide powers of jurisdiction where Hexes are concerned and if you are not more helpful I have the power to hold you here until you are."

"I understand that, Governor," Cloud said calmly. "I could point out that the CPS would become the focus of a lot of media attention if you continue to hold me here. But, as it is, I shall simply say I can give you nothing more. If I could help you further I'd be glad to—this sort of speculation isn't going to do my career any good. But there's really nothing else I can tell you."

Alverstead considered Cloud carefully. He couldn't rid himself of the belief that the dancer knew more than he was saying but Cloud's continued calm caused him to doubt his instincts. He was also aware that the CPS depended on the media's lack of interest in their activities. If he did hold Cloud it might lead to unfortunate questions about the way the agency operated. If the general public were to find out about the experimentation Alverstead's job would become much more difficult. He decided not to risk it. Kalden had promised that there would soon be results from the experiments he was performing on Raven. In the circumstances this matter of the missing rock star couldn't be allowed to interfere.

"Very well, Mr. Estavisti," he said. "I will release you for the time being. But make sure you are available for future questioning. I wouldn't want you to disappear as well."

"I assure you I do not intend to," Cloud replied, before being ushered out of Alverstead's office.

Cloud was escorted back to his luxury flitter by armed guards but he didn't lose any of his composure. His chauffeur opened the door of the flitter for him and he stretched out inside, looking through the window at the European Federation building. Armed guards surrounded it, giving an ominous appearance to the dark skyscraper section.

"Where to, sir?" the chauffeur asked politely.

"Back to the residence," Cloud replied. "But take a long route." He wasn't eager to return home, what with the media watching the place like hawks and the suspicion that the Seccies and the CPS would probably be keeping an eye on him. The other members of the band were still pestering him for an explanation of Avalon's disappearance. He had told them the same story he'd told Alverstead but they didn't believe him any more than the CPS Governor had seemed to. The other members of Masque were used to Cloud's unruffled appearance. Lissa had once asked him if anything ever surprised him. Cloud was frequently surprised but the image he projected of cool unconcern was a part of his mystique. He had cultivated it, aware that people found mysteries fascinating. Now it seemed that pose of indifference had saved him from being locked up in a CPS cell until he provided Alverstead with more information. Cloud was relieved but he didn't trust that the reprieve would last. Alverstead was still suspicious. Under the circumstances Cloud would have left the city, maybe even the country, until the mess could be sorted out and the media had forgotten the incident. But Alverstead had warned him not to drop out of sight.

Watching the view of the city flash past his window, Cloud considered the problem. Ideally, he would like to warn Avalon of the CPS's suspicions but in the circumstances she was probably aware of her danger. Danger that he had caused. Cloud wrenched his mind away from that thought and tried to concentrate. He had warned Avalon against the terrorists honestly. Now he was caught up in the kind of mess he'd hoped he could help her avoid.

Poetic justice, he thought to himself. *But what do I do next?*

Raven had expected the experiments to begin again the next day but when the guards arrived to open the cell they came with two strangers, men in expensive dark suits who looked at the prisoners with faint disgust. Dr. Kalden was with them and looked annoyed at the interruption of his experiments. Kez looked at them in alarm but Raven considered them carefully. She recognized Adam Hammond the Security Minister almost immediately. She'd seen him on newscasts and wasn't entirely surprised to see him now. The other man took her longer to identify. The CPS tended not to issue many statements and most of its officials tended to remain anonymous. But Raven had been understandably interested in the subject and after a few minutes she placed the second visitor as Sir Charles Alverstead.

"This is her then?" Alverstead asked. "She doesn't look more than a child."

"This is Raven," Kalden confirmed. "She may look young but she's one of the most interesting subjects I've ever had."

"She's been confined here since her capture, sir," Adam Hammond added. "I hope the arrangements are to your satisfaction?"

"They seem to be adequate," Alverstead agreed. "Who's the other child?"

Kez looked with concern at Raven who silenced him with a warning look.

"Another dangerous prisoner," she said dryly. "Who doubtless will also be executed once you've contravened European law in twenty different ways by experimenting on him as well."

Alverstead looked at Raven in surprise.

"You're very certain of yourself, girl," he said coldly. Raven laughed.

"Between this cage and the activities of your paid torturer, I don't have much more to fear," she said wryly. Unlike Kez she hadn't got up when they arrived and she looked at Alverstead sarcastically from where she sat cross-legged on the floor. "But I'm sure I'll be a model prisoner once Dr. Kalden has finished his experimentation."

Alverstead looked shocked and Adam Hammond looked quickly at Dr. Kalden. Kalden's blue eyes narrowed angrily. But his voice was level when he spoke.

"Perhaps you'd like to look at my initial results, Governor?"

"Yes, I think so," Sir Charles agreed, turning away from Raven. Kez said nothing as the visitors left the room and Raven also watched them leave expressionlessly. Her diversion had prevented Alverstead from inquiring too much about Kez but sooner or later Kalden would decide he was worthless as a test subject. She doubted that Kez would be released. As a streetrat there wasn't any record of his existence anyway; it wouldn't be difficult for the CPS to dispose of him quietly without anyone finding out.

Jeeva and Finn arrived at the base at mid-morning with more equipment. The group were reaching the limit of their available creds but there'd been enough left for some more basic necessities like the Nutromac unit the Snake gangers unloaded from their flitter. Luciel set it up in the apartment suite upstairs and immediately dialed a meal for everyone. They ate in the sparsely decorated dining room and Wraith began the conversation by asking Finn if the Countess had agreed to host the meeting with Anglecynn.

"She says it's chill," Finn told him. "They've asked to meet this evening. The Countess says you can bring four people and so can they."

"We still don't even know what they want," Ali said cautiously.

"Then we'll find out tonight," Wraith replied. "For now we need to find out more about what happened to Raven. We don't even know if she's being held in the city."

"Most dangerous prisoners are taken to London prison," Finn

said thoughtfully. "But there are other jails in the city and CPS facilities as well. She could really be anywhere."

"The newsfeeds said she would be exterminated," Wraith said uneasily.

"The government would never waste an opportunity to study someone like Raven," Luciel said confidently. "Not after the effort they put into the experiments on us."

"If the CPS are performing experiments on her she'll be at one of their facilities," Jeeva put in.

"But not all the CPS know about the experiments," Ali told him. "The government tries to keep them secret."

"Then she'll be held somewhere secret," Avalon suggested. "That's not going to be easy to find out."

"I'll contact the Countess and ask her to compile a list of possibilities," Wraith said. "Although the fee will probably take the rest of our creds."

"Ali and I can do it," Luciel suggested. "The information's probably all on the net—we don't need to be hackers to find it."

Wraith glanced at Ali but she didn't raise any objections to being volunteered so he nodded.

"All right," he said. "We'd better get to work then."

"Before you start," Avalon interjected, "there's something I'd like to suggest." The others turned to look at her and she continued: "If you . . . we are going to try and break Raven out of wherever she's being held, Ali and Luciel will need some more weapons training and so will I."

"She's right there," Finn replied. "I've seen Wraith in action and Raven's a dead shot. But these kids can probably use work and I doubt you're much of a sharpshooter."

"I can get by," Avalon said seriously. "But I'd like a little more experience before I get involved in an assault on a maximum security prison."

"Jeeva and I can help you out there," Finn told her. "How about Ali and Luciel start work on the net while we show you some of the tricks of the trade. Once I see how you shape up we'll start working with the other two."

"I'll monitor the control room," Wraith offered. "It's about time I had a look at what kind of system my sister's set up for us."

The tests didn't begin until the afternoon. The guards had brought them a plain meal at midday but neither Raven nor Kez felt much like eating. It wasn't long after that they came to collect Raven for more experiments. She didn't object as they escorted her out of the cell and to Kalden's makeshift lab. The equipment was different today although they strapped her down to the same bed. Even before the machinery was turned on Raven was reaching out with her Hex sense. The testing was less painful than before. The scientists inserted thin needles into Raven's skin and fed data through them, using a bizarre helmet filled with more needlelike spikes to measure activity in her brain. The needles kept giving Raven electric shocks but, compared to yesterday, that wasn't anything she couldn't handle.

As the needles probed her she felt for the tug of the power cabling and found it, letting its flow soothe her as she was carried toward a connection with the net. It was far away and faint. If it wasn't for the needles connecting her to an electric current Raven doubted she would have found it at all. Her phantom presence slipped through the data streams of the net, observing them but unable to affect them.

Observe then, Raven told herself firmly and fell further into the net. She passed through unknown systems like a ghost, leaving nothing behind. Through routes she'd travelled thousands of times before, made suddenly unfamiliar by her strange fragile connection to the net, she made her way back to her old computer terminal. The sleeper programs she'd left in place were still running although there'd been some clumsy attempt to break her security precautions. In contrast Revenge's terminal was a riddled corpse. The CPS operatives had been through the girl's programming like locusts and there was little left to suggest what Revenge had done to cause the blackout. Raven left it and moved on, drifting toward the edge of the net, the part that belonged to the gangland systems. Everything was darker here and bulletin board systems issued warnings of the increase in Seccie activity.

Not my problem right now, Raven thought and slid onward through the data paths. She was looking for the Countess's system but as she moved slowly toward it her attention was arrested by something unusual.

To Raven's Hex perceptions most of the systems which interfaced with the net were crude and ugly. Only a few had any trace of elegance or subtlety. But as she drifted across the network her attention had been caught by one spider-silk filament, tenuously connecting a computer system to the net. She reached for the silk only to feel it slip away. But now she was certain. She had spun this web herself. It was with a sense of coming home that she relaxed into it and followed its path to a system she had designed. There was no security at all, no ice to keep intruders out. But the system was hard to find, the delicacy of its pathways making it almost invisible in the crowded world of the net.

Raven floated inside the system, watching it. Only one terminal was in use, one connecting the system to the network, and someone was scanning slowly, painstakingly slowly, through the net's public databases.

Looking for prisons, she thought with some amusement. *I could save you the trouble if I wasn't so far away.*

But distance didn't have to matter. She'd studied the Hex abilities more thoroughly than Kalden ever had and she'd yet to find any proof that distance limited them. It was the test equipment that was blocking her, filling her brain with extraneous signals that she had to ignore even as it gave her access to the electronic universe. Deliberately Raven removed her own blocks, allowing herself consciousness of all those random signals of gibberish being fed into her body. Pain stabbed at her like hundreds of tiny knives. She didn't ignore it. She just refused to allow it to interfere with what she was doing. Then, carefully, she reached out and *touched* the system.

She could image the panic of the user as the system suddenly froze, the keypad no longer inputting search parameters into the terminal. Meticulously careful, she sent the message she wanted to the screen.

> **identify yourself** <

There was a pause while Raven freed the system again and watched. The other user did nothing and she called upon her patience to send again:

> **this is RAVEN—identify yourself** < She was almost certain that the unknown user was a member of their group but if not, no one from the CPS would believe she was Raven if they knew her to be in custody.

> **this is ali and luciel** < The reply came haltingly, tapped slowly into the keypad. > **raven, is that really you?** <

If she'd been there in reality Raven would have shaken her head at the sheer stupidity of that question. Instead she sent the information they needed.

> **with kez in ef consulate, will make escape attempt shortly, give details of your situation** <

> **you must prove your id first, you could be cps** <

Rage flooded Raven at the answer even though intellectually she could approve of their caution. But the anger threatened to tear her away from the link with the net and she controlled herself. Reaching for the system with all the energy left to her she caused her image to appear on the terminal screen. Black hair in elf locks, black eyes shadowed with exhaustion, dead white skin. No hacker or CPS operative could have done this. The image she spun could only be caused by a Hex. She made the lips of the image move then blanked the screen and sent her message once more with the last of her strength.

> **i am RAVEN** <

Then the system, the shining lines of the net, the world of the Hex, shattered and collapsed into darkness as pain exploded in her head and Raven mercifully blacked out.

Ali and Luciel looked at each other, then Luciel tentatively touched the keypad, tapping out an inquiry. There was no response and he sat back in his seat.

"She's gone," he said. "I wish I'd asked if she was all right."

"She probably wouldn't have appreciated it," said Ali numbly.

They looked at each other for a long moment. Neither of them had the skill or experience to do what Raven had done, spinning the strands of the web from confinement to reach them, but in receiving her message they had had their first glimpse of what the other Hex had experienced. The terminal had become a gateway, stretching into uncharted territory, and across that unimaginable distance Raven had reached out and touched them.

"At least she's well enough to use the net," Luciel said finally. "I wonder how she got to a terminal."

"Maybe she didn't." Ali stood up. "Raven wouldn't let that stop her. Come on, we'd better go and find Wraith. This is something he needs to know."

"You're right," Luciel agreed. "And our search is over anyway. Raven's given us the information we needed."

9

LIGHTNING MOVES SLOW

Everyone was on edge when they set off for the Countess's building. Ali and Luciel had recounted their visitation from Raven and everyone was feeling somewhat stunned by it. Wraith was relieved just to know she was alive but he worried that they hadn't been able to make any real arrangements for her escape. Luciel was concerned that Kalden might have experimented on her and Ali was simply awestruck by the extent of Raven's abilities. Only Raven could have contacted them from a maximum security facility and she doubted that she would ever be able to use her Hex abilities that well herself. Avalon was uneasy about being recognized. She wore a woollen cap to disguise her red hair and a long army coat Jeeva had lent her.

Jeeva and Finn piloted the flitter that took them to the Countess's center of operations. There were two armed guards on the bridge across to her section of skyscraper and they watched expressionlessly as the group got out of the flitter. Wraith took the lead with Finn; Ali and Luciel followed, both armed with the laser pistols they'd been practicing with; Avalon and Jeeva brought up the rear. The guards on the bridge stopped them but only for a cursory word; everyone except Avalon was already known to them. There were more guards inside the building, some barring the route up, others scattered around the main foyer. Three of them were Snakes, with the same dyed-blue hair as Finn and Jeeva, and two gangers melted away from the party to join them. The others removed their weapons and allowed the Countess's people to search them. Then they were led up the mirror-shielded staircase to the Countess's main room. She was waiting for them, in the middle of the customary litter of electrical components, her body covered with remote controls and mini-terminal units.

"Come in," she told them, as the mirrored panel began to slide shut. "Your contacts haven't arrived yet but that's as it should be." She gestured to them to sit down at an oval table in the corner of the room, around which eight chairs had been placed. "Once Anglecynn are here I'll leave you to biz," she said. "But while you're waiting you can tell me how the new place is working out."

"It's going well," Wraith assured her. "The building is perfect for our needs and the security system Raven designed was set up by your technicians yesterday. We're very grateful for your assistance."

"Nonsense." The Countess's eyes gleamed brightly. "Raven paid me in advance for setting you up. If I didn't fulfill my contracts what would happen to my rep?" Her eyes flitted across them and came to rest on Avalon. "You've got a famous face," she remarked, "for all that you're dressed like Raven. Are you intending to replace her?"

"From what I've seen and heard so far, I think Raven's almost certainly irreplaceable," Avalon replied. "But I suppose I'm standing in for her."

The Countess nodded quickly, her movements quick and birdlike.

"That's true enough," she said. "And since you're with friends I'll tell you something for nothing. The Seccies are on your case. They've been looking for you since yesterday afternoon and word on the streets is they're freakin' serious about it. I'd stay disguised if I was you."

"I intend to," Avalon assured her but she looked alarmed and Ali smiled at her reassuringly.

"They've been looking for us for a year," she told Avalon. "And, if it wasn't for Revenge—and she couldn't help herself— they wouldn't have found us yet."

"And Cloud," Avalon reminded her. "He's to blame as well for this mess. If it hadn't been for him no one would even know I'd left."

"There's no point in dissecting it now," Wraith interrupted and the Countess agreed.

"No point at all," she said. "Especially since your contacts seem to have arrived."

The others clustered around her to watch the vidscreen image of the foyer. A sleek customized flitter had arrived and people were getting out of it. The first to emerge was a large muscular man, his arms tattooed with a pattern of entwined dragons.

"Stupid," the Countess snorted. "Why not just write the word 'terrorist' on your head if you want to be noticed?"

She fell silent as the rest of the Anglecynn members got out, four in total. There were two more men, both quite young and not as burly as the first, and a teenage girl carrying a gun that looked incongruous against her slight frame. The guards stepped forward and all four surrendered their weapons and allowed themselves to be searched. Then the guards waved them onward and the small party began to move toward the staircase. The Countess touched a keypad and the image disappeared. She checked over the various controls she wore as armbands and then bobbed her head at Wraith.

"They're clean," she said and as she spoke she touched a control and the door to the stairway slid open. The Anglecynn members were revealed on the other side and the Countess waved them in. "Come in," she told them. "No need to block the door. Since you're all wanted criminals let's not waste time with formalities. You can introduce yourselves." She turned to Wraith. "You've got one hour, so make your conversation count. I'll be back then."

With that she turned and left the room by another door that opened as she approached it and slid shut behind her.

Wraith watched her leave then he faced the newcomers. Extending his hand, he introduced himself.

"I'm Wraith, and this is Ali, Luciel, and Avalon."

One of the Anglecynn members reached to take his hand and shook it.

"Alaric," he said politely, "this is Geraint, Bryson, and Jordan."

There was a pause as all eight of them assembled around the Countess's oval table, then Alaric opened the negotiations.

"I was hoping to meet Raven," he began. "I was sorry to hear of her capture. She had the Seccies on the run for a long time."

"That hasn't changed," Wraith replied. "Despite what you may have heard, Raven is still alive."

"I'm pleased to hear it," Alaric replied. "Especially since it was largely because of Raven that I decided to contact you."

"It was?" Wraith asked with polite curiosity and Alaric nodded agreement.

"My group is often interested in forming new contacts," he explained. "But what led us to meet with you is information we received from one of our agents. He came into possession of details of the latest Security Service orders. We'd expected there to be increased attempts to eradicate Anglecynn because of our recent protests but as it happened your group proved to be the focus of their latest campaign. When I checked out your details I was sure there was more to your story than the official government version." He looked straight at Ali and smiled. "And if you are Alison Tarrell, I believe my suspicions have proved true."

"How do you know about Ali?" Luciel said protectively. "What's she got to do with this?"

"My information made reference to 'missing test subjects' and Alison Tarrell's name was one of them, as was the name Luciel

Liechtmann," Alaric explained. "A member of Anglecynn identified Alison Tarrell as being the name of a teenager who was taken
by the CPS last year for possessing the Hex gene and officially registered as legally exterminated. Since no one who was exterminated
could be considered missing and nothing I know about the CPS
says they can use Hexes as test subjects, I reached the conclusion
that there was more to your group than is commonly known. That
led me to think that the lab you blew up last year wasn't a regular
CPS facility at all."

"All that may be true," Wraith replied. "But what has it got to
do with you?"

"Anglecynn is dedicated to fighting EF control," Alaric told
him. "That includes the Hex laws. I was hoping we might pool
some of our knowledge and maybe resources as well."

"We'd like to know something more about you first, though,"
the man named Geraint added. "The prejudice against Hexes may
have been propagated by the government but even so none of us
know anything about you, or what you can do."

"That seems to be a common problem," Luciel whispered to
Ali and she giggled. Wraith turned and glared at them.

"We don't know much about you either," he replied. "Perhaps
we could share the history of how our respective groups were
formed?"

"Sounds good to me," Bryson said cheerfully and Jordan
smiled glowingly.

Wraith began the account with the same story he had told
Avalon. Although it was only a day ago, it already seemed like

forever. The Anglecynn members all listened intently; Alaric in particular seemed surprised at Wraith's admission that he was not a Hex. Ali, Luciel, and Avalon all appended their own stories and Wraith ended the account with the blackout, Revenge's death, and Raven and Kez's capture. When he finished no one spoke for a while.

"Our story seems mundane in comparison," Geraint said finally. "We haven't had quite so rough a ride as you."

"Geraint and I founded Anglecynn three years ago," Alaric explained. "We were still in college and studying politics. We got to reading Federation law and decided we didn't like the sound of it. So we ran a couple of student protests against EF control. We didn't take it very seriously back then but the government obviously did."

"We were sent down from university and were put on Seccie files as political agitators. After that we decided that was exactly what we wanted to be. Alaric came up with the idea of Anglecynn and we started recruiting. We've been involved in a lot of demonstrations and a few more forceful protests but we generally try not to hurt people unless it's absolutely necessary."

"At the moment there are about sixty of us," Alaric explained. "Although that includes the administrative staff who support our cause but don't get involved in protests. We've plenty of firepower but we're lacking information and, from the sound of it, that's what your group can provide."

"Under normal circumstances," Wraith agreed. "Although at the moment we're lacking Raven, which curtails our sphere of influence considerably."

"So how would you feel about an agreement of mutual assistance?" Geraint asked. "Seeing as we have a common enemy."

"That would depend on how your people feel about Hexes," Wraith replied and Geraint looked uneasy.

"I admit to having some qualms myself," he said. "But so far what you've said seems to check out. Most of Anglecynn seems keen on the idea."

"That's true," Jordan agreed. "And apart from us, you've done the most harm to the Federation. A lot of our people admire you for that. And we're always sympathetic to people who've been persecuted."

Dr. Kalden hissed with irritation. Another routine experiment with equipment that had been tested extensively and now the subject had lost consciousness. One of his team hurriedly checked Raven over while the others rechecked the equipment.

"I think she fainted," the scientist said after a while. "It must have been the electric current. Maybe she's not in as good a condition as some of our earlier subjects or maybe she's just unusually sensitive to the test equipment."

"Interesting," Kalden mused, losing his flinty expression. "If it's a matter of sensitivity this could represent a breakthrough for us. But we can't continue the testing if she's going to pass out like this all the time. We obviously need another approach."

He looked at the slim black-clad figure lying on the bed and wondered what secrets the mutant's mind held. She was indubitably his greatest challenge, he thought. If only she could understand the importance of science she would be proud to sacrifice herself to his experiments.

"But they never do understand," he mused out loud and noticed the other scientists looking at him oddly. "Take her back to her cell," he ordered. "I need time to consider a new approach."

When the hour the Countess had stipulated was up the two groups parted and agreed to meet again in the future. Alaric had things to discuss with the rest of Anglecynn and the Hex group needed to make plans to rescue Raven. However, both sides felt that the meeting had gone well. The last thing Alaric said before his party left was that he would try to persuade Anglecynn to make the Hex right to life a central point of their constitution.

"After that, if there's one thing we're experienced with it's media manipulation," Alaric said. "People deserve to know the truth about the way the Hexes are treated."

Once the flitter had left the Countess's building and was sailing back to the depths of the city, Alaric noticed Geraint was silent and thoughtful.

"What did you think of them?" he asked quietly and the other veteran shrugged.

"They seemed honest, and those Hex kids they have certainly aren't any kind of threat."

"But . . . ?"

"It's Raven I'm wondering about," Geraint admitted. "From the sound of it, she worked out that lab existed then planned a military assault on it. But she didn't think of a way to rescue the other children in the experiments. From the way they talk it sounds like all of them are in awe of her, except maybe Wraith. That worries me."

"I thought Raven sounded wonderful," Jordan said quietly. "The anti-EF front needs heroes and she's the kind of person we could admire. I always thought no Hexes ever escaped extermination. But Raven saved three or four people from it and risked her life over and over again to do it. That's real heroism. It just makes it better that she's not much more than a child herself."

"It didn't sound much like heroism to me," Geraint objected but Bryson interrupted him.

"I like the idea of having a hero, some kind of symbol for the cause. Sounds to me like this Raven would be a good candidate."

"Even though she's a Hex?" Alaric asked curiously.

"That's good too," Jordan said enthusiastically. "Knowing that someone you thought was normal is a Hex is a shock for people. But heroes are supposed to be extraordinary and have special powers. People won't mind that Raven's a Hex, they might even start thinking about Hexes differently when they hear about her."

Daniel had been thinking about going to sleep when Alaric arrived back at Dragon's Nest and sent out the call for a general meeting. Instead he staked out a place in the common room and waited for everyone to arrive. As the room filled rumors began to circulate about the purpose of this meeting.

"Alaric went to meet the Hexes," he heard a girl called Maggie saying. "Maybe he's brought one of them back with him."

"Not without consulting everyone," someone else contradicted. "But I bet this is to tell us about them."

Daniel wondered whether Ali Tarrell had been one of the Hexes Alaric had met. He found it hard to imagine one of his sister's socialite friends as a member of a dangerous terrorist group. But then he found it hard to imagine himself as one either. Yet here he was, part of Anglecynn's private councils, living in a deserted slum in the city's cavernous roots. His mind drifted as he wondered what Caitlin and his father were doing now. Caitlin was probably watching a mindless holovid program, while his father worked late at the Ministry. He was surprised not to feel any nostalgia for his past life; already it seemed years ago.

He snapped back to reality as Alaric came into the room. Geraint, Jordan, and Bryson arrived at the same time and all four of them found seats near the center of the room, other people moving up to give them more space.

"I'm sorry to have to call a meeting so late," Alaric began. "But I know a lot of you have been anxious to know the results of the negotiations with the Hexes and we have a lot of new information you should hear about." He gestured at the three people sitting close to him. "All four of us went to the meeting so all I'm going to give you now is a summary of what happened. Then we can split up for discussion and we'll tell you more about what their group was like. After that there are some questions I'd like to take to a vote."

"Get on with it then!" someone called from the back and everyone laughed. Alaric smiled in return and began his account.

The members of Anglecynn were used to stories of atrocities. That was one of the reasons they'd chosen to fight the European Federation. But they were shocked when Alaric told them the story of the CPS lab the Hexes had attacked and the experiments performed on children. Daniel felt sickened by the tale. What had shocked him the most was that until recently he hadn't even thought about the plight of the Hexes. But for years they had been murdered, tortured, and shunned without anyone lifting a hand to stop it. Across the room there were murmurs of disgust, echoing his own feelings. None of them questioned the truth of the tale. Some of them remembered the pictures of the test subjects that had been broadcast across the media before the government news blackout. At the time it had seemed like just another scandal. Now Alaric depicted it as a crime of epic proportions.

"I feel personally guilty for not thinking about this before," Alaric admitted. "I tried to get in touch with the Hexes because I thought they could be useful to us. I still think that but now I'm certain we owe them our help as well. We're supposed to be fighting EF injustice but we didn't even notice this."

The mood of the meeting was subdued when Alaric finished his account and it took a while for the usual smaller discussions to begin. When they did, Daniel took advantage of the opportunity to ask Alaric about Ali.

"Yes, she was there," the veteran said. "She didn't say much apart from her part in the plan to infiltrate the laboratory. They all looked tired. I think being without Raven's been hard on them."

"I was just thinking I can't imagine Ali Tarrell as a terrorist but then I realized I can't think of myself as one either," Daniel admitted.

"Good." Alaric smiled at him. "I don't want people here to think of themselves as terrorists. Terrorists are people who deliberately spread fear. We're fighting for a cause we believe in. We try to spread enlightenment and the people who are afraid of that are the ones who call us terrorists."

Daniel nodded and then asked, "What proposals are you going to put to a vote?"

"I think we should try and finish what the Hexes started," Alaric explained. "Release the records of what the CPS has been doing to the media, start getting people to think about the fact that under EF law Hexes have no rights and that most Hexes the CPS catch are children who don't even know what crime they're punished for."

"The Seccies won't like that," Daniel warned.

"Since when did the Seccies like anything about us?" Alaric responded and Daniel had to admit that he was right.

After a while the room calmed down enough for Alaric to put forward his proposals. Most people agreed instantly. Quite apart from the justice of the cause most of them were tired of being cooped up in Dragon's Nest and were eager to start a new campaign. But there were a few dissenters as usual.

"It's madness to get involved with this just when the Seccies aren't interested in us," one of them pointed out. "Right now they couldn't care less about Anglecynn, they're all too busy helping the CPS catch Hexes. But if we start getting involved they'll be all over us like falling garbage. We'll never get rid of them."

A few other people agreed but the vast majority of members were overwhelmingly in favor of a new campaign on behalf of Hexes. The final vote came out as fifty-three to seven with four abstentions. Only then did Alaric finally call a halt to the meeting and people departed for bed.

Alaric contacted Wraith first thing the next day on a coded frequency to tell him about Anglecynn's decision and to ask for any more information about the CPS's treatment of Hexes. They had exchanged com signals so as not to have to go through the Countess every time. Wraith agreed to send all the information they had and in return Alaric promised to try to get Anglecynn help with rescuing Raven.

"I haven't put it to them yet," he explained. "But I'm certain they'll go for it. The way Jordan was talking the other day it sounds as if she thinks Raven qualifies for sainthood, and the administrative staff are already talking about the good a known hero would do for our movement."

"We'd be grateful for any help you could give us," Wraith said honestly. "We're under strength at the moment and breaking into the EF Consulate is a major operation."

"Agreed, but we might have some info that can swing the balance," Alaric told him. "One of our members is Daniel Hammond, the son of the Security Minister. He's been to the Consulate and part of the information he gave us included rough maps of the building. That might just give you the edge you need, with or without Anglecynn."

Wraith's private thought was that "with Anglecynn" seemed the better option. He'd been impressed by what he'd seen and heard of the group and he remembered that Raven, while dismissive, had not been entirely contemptuous of their operation.

Personally he preferred the idea of going on as part of an established well-trained group who were used to working together. It had been a long time since he'd missed his days in the Kali; the gangs had held too many bitter memories. But Finn's words to Avalon about trust the previous day had connected with him. He had trusted Ali and Luciel and even Avalon, although he barely knew her. But he knew they were all inexperienced and he missed the sensation of knowing someone competent was guarding his back.

When he told the rest of them about Anglecynn's plans they were enthusiastic. Luciel went off on his own to record a vidtape account of his experiences in the lab so he could send it to Anglecynn.

"You could do something like that, as well," Ali suggested to Avalon. "Lots of people admire you—maybe they'd listen to you if you told them you're a Hex too."

"I'll think about it," Avalon replied. "But I don't know if I can. I'm not sure if people are interested in what megastars have to say. Mostly they just want holosheets to stick on their walls."

Ali didn't allow Avalon's cautious reply to spoil her good mood. She'd been cheerful ever since hearing that Daniel Hammond was a member of Anglecynn. She didn't remember him much; he'd been Caitlin's bookish older brother when she'd known him before. But the idea that Caitlin's father had announced a campaign against Hexes had hit her hard and knowing about Daniel's defection made her feel better about her involvement with the group. He seemed like a link to her old life and she hoped she'd have a chance to see him before too long and reminisce about the Belgravia Complex. It didn't occur to her to think that Daniel had left the Complex voluntarily, whereas she'd been forced to leave by the CPS discovering what she was.

Anglecynn worked fast. The media blitz began that day and the protesters took their flitters up into the city to begin the campaign at the EF Consulate. Armed with banners marked *Stop the Torture* and holo projectors with images of the child test subjects, they began their protest with a bang. The media turned up in under ten minutes and the Seccies seconds later. While the Anglecynn members bombarded the building with pictures and fact sheets, which soon started to litter the ground and blow through the city, the Seccies desperately tried to get them off the premises.

Inside the Consulate, Raven and Kez were unaware of the commotion. Raven had been sleeping ever since the guards had brought her back to the cell, and Kez stayed awake to watch over her. He knew the experiments were hitting Raven badly, even though she still seemed confident that they would escape. Kez had seen what had happened to the kids in the laboratory and he wondered what Kalden was doing to Raven to leave her so weak and drained all the time. Raven had said that Kalden was doomed and Kez was beginning to dream of killing him himself. Raven and Wraith were the two people he cared about most in the world; Kalden had almost destroyed Wraith by torturing Rachel and now he was torturing Raven too. In the small cell Kez silently vowed revenge, just as Rachel must have done before him. If Raven didn't find a way to kill Kalden, he would.

10

HEAVEN
DOTH REVENGE

Raven woke knowing today was the day she would have to escape.
The experimentation was taking a heavy toll on her. She hadn't
anticipated that she would find using her Hex abilities so painful
during the experiments. Now she realized that if it continued any
longer she wouldn't have the strength for an escape attempt. She
would have to do it today or not at all.

With her eyes still shut she stretched herself out on the floor
of the cell and concentrated. That whisper of the net she'd caught
before would still be far away. But now she had found it twice during the experimentation. She hoped that with nothing to distract
her mind, her abilities would be stronger now. She reached out as
far as she could and felt a single thread of the net slip by. That was
enough. Wordlessly she sent her message, directing it to follow the
path she couldn't take, all the way back to Wraith. Then the thread

slipped away from her and she let go. There was nothing more she could do. From here on she had to conserve her energy for the escape attempt.

Across the room Kez didn't even realize that Raven was awake. He was making plans and discarding them as he had been all night. There was no way he could overpower the guards and no way out of the cell without it. He knew as well as Raven that they would have to escape soon. But he could see no way to accomplish it.

Outside the Consulate the Anglecynn protesters had allowed the Seccies to drive them off for a while and moved on to the New Houses of Parliament. The media went with them. Most of them were just interested in the spectacle but a couple of the channels were beginning to investigate what Anglecynn was protesting about. A few smaller pressure groups who had seen the newsfeeds joined Anglecynn at the Houses of Parliament and some of the regular people listened to what they were saying and joined in as well. It wasn't exactly a spontaneous outpouring of sympathy for the Hexes but the size of the demonstration made it difficult for the Seccies to break it up.

Avalon watched the protests on the newsfeeds. Her disappearance was still the main story on most of them. One of the channels was speculating that the reason for all the Seccie interest in Cloud was that they suspected him of Avalon's murder. Avalon felt awkward about that. Although Cloud had betrayed her she was annoyed at the media making up such a complete fantasy. She doubted any of them actually suspected Cloud was capable of murder. But now the story would spread and might harm his career.

Her musings were interrupted by a chime from the com system. She wondered vaguely about it as she touched the keypad to bring up the message, then felt her body stiffen as she read it.

> **come today. as soon as you can** <

It had to be from Raven—no one else would have sent it—and its brevity worried Avalon. If Raven hadn't had time to send more than this it must be urgent. Accordingly she headed down the corridor to the apartment suite. She was certain to find the others there and they'd need to know about the message as soon as possible. She found Wraith first, also watching the news channels on a battered old vidcom he'd salvaged from the litter in the building. He looked up as she entered and immediately spoke:

"Avalon, what's wrong? You look concerned."

"We've just had a message from Raven," she explained. "She wants us to come now, today, as soon as we can, she said."

Wraith looked worried.

"We're not exactly ready to move yet," he said. "What can we do with only four people?"

"You said Anglecynn would help us," Avalon said quickly. "They're already causing a huge diversion. Let's get them back to the EF Consulate and mount the rescue attempt during the protest."

"We'll have to," Wraith replied. "I can't think of anything else to do."

Alaric had just been relieved from duty when the call came in. He'd been part of the demonstration at the EF building and the Houses of Parliament and had come back to Dragon's Nest for a break. But he'd only just got there when the administrative staff summoned him to answer Wraith's call. He'd not been expecting it and he hadn't had time to sound Anglecynn out about rescuing Raven but the other veterans there were willing to try. He told Wraith he'd be at the consulate building in an hour with as much firepower as he could provide and then closed the channel. Apart from the admin people there were only twelve people in the building and he asked them to assemble in the common room.

"I wasn't expecting this to happen so soon," he told them. "But I've had word from the Hex group that Raven is being held in the EF Consulate and she's managed to get a message out saying she can't hold out much longer. Wraith has asked for our help and I think we should give it to them. However, there isn't enough time to call a general meeting."

"Just do it then," Bryson encouraged him. "We shouldn't waste our time having meetings when someone needs help—and everyone voted to help the Hexes last night anyway."

"Not everyone," Liz put in. "But it makes sense to go. There won't be any objections."

"In that case this is what I suggest," Alaric said with some relief. "We send the protesters back to the EF building but this time with some of the crowd-control weapons. We keep everything as confusing and troubled as we can and provide cover for a small group who'll attempt to enter the building from one of the service entrances."

"How small?" Bryson asked. "The place seemed quite well defended to me."

"No more than twenty," Alaric said. "We'll want to move swiftly once we're inside and that means not too many people."

"Twenty sounds good to me," Geraint agreed. "We'll take enough weapons for twenty people and Liz can put out a call for volunteers on the com frequencies."

"Let's get going then," Alaric announced and the group scattered to get ready.

Alaric went to arrange weapons. Most of the time Anglecynn members only carried light arms but this mission would require something heavier. After considering for a while he decided on standard military blasters. They weren't the most advanced weaponry he had but all the troops had trained extensively on them and Alaric decided familiarity was the most important issue. He uncrated twenty blasters and checked each of them over carefully; then added another five in case of accidents and collected some crowd-control weaponry. Other Anglecynn members helped him load two flitters with the weapons and Liz met them in the flitter bay.

"I've got you your volunteers," she told him. "They'll be waiting two blocks away from the Consulate with the current protest coordinator. I've also sent word to the Hex group that's where to find you."

"Thank you," Alaric replied. "Sure you don't want to come with us?"

"I prefer my excitement less lethal," Liz replied and headed back to her work.

Meanwhile work had continued loading the flitters and Alaric took advantage of the opportunity to check over his people. They'd all found light body armor from the group's somewhat motley collection and loaded more into the flitter for the volunteers. Alaric questioned them quickly on the use of the blasters and looked over everyone for any sign that they'd be a danger to themselves or to their teammates. Once everyone checked out they got into the flitters and headed out from the Nest.

It had been over a year since Anglecynn had mounted a military-style attack. But the troops were excited as they set off and Alaric realized that someone had been spreading stories about Raven. If the team members didn't precisely consider her a hero they were certainly proud to be rescuing her and curious about meeting the other Hexes. As the flitters climbed through the city he tried to keep his part of the team in a good mood. It was important to be calm when you went into battle and not overexcited. He concentrated on projecting confidence, knowing that people relied on him to be strong, but he wasn't as calm as he looked. He remembered what Geraint had said about Raven and wondered if the other veteran was right. Raven was too much of an unknown quality for him to be entirely complacent about meeting her. But he had to help save her. If he didn't he was betraying what Anglecynn stood for and without their principles they really would deserve the name of terrorists.

Jeeva had been giving Ali a lesson with the laser pistol when Wraith came to tell her that they were moving to rescue Raven. He didn't say much and politely excused himself as they began the preparations for departure. Wraith tried not to be disappointed and concentrated on making sure that Avalon, Ali, and Luciel were capable of defending themselves. He'd satisfied himself that they'd at least be shooting in roughly the right direction and was about to get into the flitter when Jeeva returned with Finn close behind him.

"Heard you're having some trouble," Finn said. "You going to break Raven out?"

"That's right," Wraith told him. "Want to come along?"

"Only if you don't," Finn replied and the others looked at him in surprise.

"What do you mean?" Wraith asked defensively, even though he had a good idea what the ganger was talking about.

"You're not qualified to go," Finn told him. "If you were one of my brothers I'd order you to stay behind. You're injured, you can't shoot anything, and you'll be a liability to your people. Since I can't order you to stay behind I'm asking you. If you wait here Jeeva and I will go with your people. That's two men who can shoot to replace one who can't."

"And if I go?" Wraith challenged.

"Then we don't," Finn told him. "But I reckon you're smarter than that, brother."

Wraith considered for a moment then he sighed.

"All right, you win," he said. "I probably wouldn't be much use anyway."

"You're right about that," Finn agreed, taking Wraith's place in the flitter as Jeeva got in the back. "Catch you later. We'll bring them back safely."

Wraith didn't doubt that. But as he watched the small group

depart he was conscious of feeling guilty that he wasn't with them. He controlled himself. Finn's decision had been the right one and Wraith should have made it himself. The Snake ganger had made things easier for him, knowing Wraith's judgment was suspect where Raven was concerned. Wraith was surprised how much he had come to trust the gangers but they had proven themselves dependable over recent days and Raven had considered them trustworthy as well. As he made his way back to the control room he tried to have confidence in his team, even though he wasn't a part of it.

As the little flitter left, Avalon looked back at the dark hulk of the building, wondering how Wraith was reacting to being so suddenly deposed.

"That was a generous thing to do," she said to Finn.

"Wraith's a brother even though he doesn't admit it," Finn replied. "We've been in action together. By my code that means we owe each other. No one lets a brother go into a fight he can't possibly win."

"That puts you in command," Luciel told Ali and her eyes widened.

"No it doesn't!" she objected. "Finn knows more about this sort of thing."

"But I'm not part of your group," Finn told her. "There needs to be a chain of command. If you've got seniority, you're in charge."

"But what do I do?" Ali demanded. "I don't know anything about strategy. The last time you did this I was the one being rescued."

"Ask for advice when you need it and ignore it if you don't," Jeeva told her. "You'll get used to it."

Ali subsided. She wasn't confident that she'd be able to see this through but she didn't want to let Luciel down and she supposed she could ask Finn for advice most of the time. She suspected there would probably be a bit more to this mission than just ordering everyone to find Raven and then ordering them out again. She concentrated on checking her gun over the fifth time. At least that was one thing she could probably do. She might not be a great shot but she was much better than she had been. Luciel touched her arm reassuringly.

"You'll be fine," he told her. "You've been doing OK so far."

"Well, just remember if I get it wrong the job's yours," Ali told him.

Sir Charles Alverstead looked out of one of the Consulate windows at the rabble assembled below. Earlier it had looked as if they were departing. But now they were back in full force, chanting and yelling and generally causing trouble. He wasn't worried about the demonstration. The EF Consulate guards had been instructed to leave the problem to the Security Services and so far they weren't having any real problems with the protesters. He supposed this was some attempt on the part of the Hex rebels to strike back after Raven's capture. He was relieved that their reaction was something as negligible as a protest. All the same the publicity was irritating. It was fortunate that most of the protesters were from known terrorist groups. That would discredit their testimony considerably.

He was more concerned about the fact that Kalden still hadn't got any useful results from Raven. He had reported that she was showing an unusual sensitivity to the equipment, which would have to be recalibrated before further tests. But sensitivity wasn't what Alverstead was interested in. Kalden had been running his experiments for years and he was apparently no nearer to providing any useful results. Alverstead had considered replacing him when the main testing laboratory had been destroyed but had decided against it. Kalden's lab had been the only one performing experiments and had been sited in Britain because the country was considered an insignificant power within the might of the EF. That meant Kalden was the most experienced of all the scientists who had worked on the problem. But Alverstead had been irritated by Raven's antagonistic attitude. Usually Kalden's subjects were overcome by fear of him. Raven's attitude appeared to be contempt. He hoped he hadn't made a mistake in leaving Kalden in control of the project.

A roar from the demonstrators drew his attention back to the crowd below and he was alarmed to see a thick blue smoke rolling toward the building. Most of the protesters had retreated to the safety of their flitters although some could be seen amidst the smoke, wearing masks to protect themselves from its effects. The Seccies had no such protection and uniformed officers were staggering out of the blue clouds, bent over with fits of choking. Alverstead looked for the EF guards and saw them retreating back to the building. Crossing quickly to the vidcom unit he called their commander.

"Why are your men pulling back?" he demanded.

"We thought it was advisable—" the Commander of the Guard began, but Alverstead interrupted him.

"Have you had any orders from the Consul?"

"No, sir."

"In that case get out there and find out what's going on. You must have gas masks, man. Use them!"

"Yes, sir!" the Commander said sharply and signed off.

Alverstead returned to the window and looked out at the crowds again. Almost all his field of vision was obscured by the blue clouds of smoke and he tapped his fingers against the window in irritation.

Raven had no way of knowing if her message had got through, but when the guards arrived to collect her for the next set of tests she noticed they looked on edge. Something was obviously going on, even though she had no idea what. When she arrived in the lab room Kalden also looked distracted. Raven couldn't take much comfort in that. Her attention was caught by the test equipment. It was all too familiar, having been the subject of her initial research into the files she'd taken from Kalden's lab. It had formed the most important part of the memory experiments. The same experiments that had left Rachel mind-wiped. As she was strapped to the diagnostic bed, Raven attempted to control her instinctive fear. Rachel had not been an operant Hex. It was this equipment that had triggered her Hex abilities and turned her into Revenge.

But Raven was in full possession of all her abilities and she was determined that this equipment shouldn't master her.

As medical nano-probers were attached to her head she allowed herself to sink into the trancelike state she felt when she was using her Hex abilities, but this time she didn't actively try to use them. Instead she observed what the scientists and technicians were doing and waited to see what the effect of the machine would be. When it came, it came like an avalanche. She felt as if her mind was being forcibly opened and streams of data poured in. Door after door, in the innermost recesses of her brain, was being thrown open and searchlights glared in as data flooded her consciousness. Raven fled from the flood of images, retreating through the electronic machinery of the test equipment and back along the power cabling until she had left her body completely and was no longer conscious of what was happening.

Her mind was being systematically shredded. Kalden might call himself a scientist but he had no idea of how to proceed. If this experiment was a success it would turn Raven into a brain-dead zombie, capable of nothing except retaining information, and even that would probably be garbled by the procedure he was using. Raven's fury crested and she knew she would have to return to her body before Kalden destroyed her mind. She was frightened, and furious with herself for her fear. The net stretched before her, shining with a tantalizing light, and she wondered if she could just leave her tormented body behind and sink forever into its gleaming strands. Then she remembered Kalden and anger achieved dominance over her fear. She brought her thoughts together into a fist and *slammed* back into the test equipment. It halted and juddered at the force of her fury. She tore apart the programming linking the data signals to her body and inserted a new set of operating parameters into the machine. This time it would be set for a wide receive signal and she increased the power accordingly. That much data pumped into her mind could kill her but its effect would be even more devastating on someone without her resources. Using the machine's sensors as an aerial, she turned it back on and poured energy into it. She thought she could hear screaming somewhere in the distance and increased the power further until there was silence again. Only then did she return to her body and open her eyes.

The room looked like a bomb site. All the scientists had collapsed where they were standing, their hands clutched tightly to their heads. Kalden had fallen beside the machine, one hand reaching to turn it off. But he had lost consciousness first and Raven craned her head to look at him. Blood trickled from his nose and he looked as if he was dead.

"Looks" isn't good enough, she thought to herself and began to struggle with the restraining straps. It took her about five minutes to wriggle out of them. When she did she immediately checked Kalden's prone figure. There was no sign of a pulse.

That was really too kind, she thought to herself. *He deserved it to take longer.*

The two guards who had brought her to the room were also unconscious and, like Kalden, they had no pulse. Stripping the smaller one of his military fatigues, she put them on. The uniform was several sizes too big but it would pass a cursory inspection.

She searched both guards quickly for weapons and slung two machine guns and a light pistol from her belt. One of them held the keycard for her cell in his pocket and she took that as well. She also took a slim knife from one of the guards and held it loosely in one hand as she activated the controls to open the door. Outside, the corridor was empty and Raven closed the door again behind her, locking it to prevent immediate discovery of what lay inside.

Then she headed down the corridor that led to her cell.

Despite his lack of experience, Daniel had been eager to be included in the assault team and there weren't so many volunteers that he had been rejected. So far though he hadn't even loosed off a round from his gun. He had been one of the last to enter the Consulate, under cover of the rolling smoke, and by the time he got inside, the guards on the service door had already been dealt with. He caught a glimpse of Ali Tarrell talking quietly with Avalon, the rock star, and a man with blue hair threaded with gold beads who looked like a ganger. Then his group leader had ordered them forward and he'd begun his creeping progress through the building, checking carefully around every corner, as they searched for Raven. So far there had only been two outbursts of gunfire. Once when an opening elevator surprised them and the guard inside squeezed off a couple of shots before Jordan dropped him. The second time one of the lead scouts had seen a party approaching from around the corner and opened fire on them. Geraint, their group leader, was carrying a wrist terminal belonging to one of the EF guards and he said there hadn't been a major alert yet. With any luck that meant the EF still didn't know they were in the building. Daniel was relieved. He'd volunteered hoping to be a part of the action but now he wasn't so sure it had been a good idea. They'd lost a man in the second firefight and Daniel was well aware that had he been further forward, that could have been him.

Theirs was only one of the three groups searching the building, each assigned separate sections. Every now and again one of the other groups would call in but so far they'd found nothing. The group assigned to the top floors had pulled back, claiming they were certain no prisoners were being held up there and unwilling to start searching offices and alerting people to their presence. The group Daniel was with was searching the lowest levels and so far they hadn't come across anything more interesting than storage rooms. But the look of the corridors was beginning to change and one of the scouts had been deputized to take out the hidden cameras which were turning up on every corner. Daniel took a firmer grip on his gun and moved forward in the group. He might be afraid but he didn't want to be a coward.

Kez had started when the door opened so soon after the guards had taken Raven away. When he recognized the uniformed figure he jumped up in surprise.

"Raven!" he exclaimed and she slapped a hand over his mouth, pointing in annoyance to where they expected the monitors were. Handing him a machine gun, she beckoned him toward the cell door. In seconds they were out and standing in a long corridor, painted in military gray.

"Keep quiet," she said softly. "There are hidden cams everywhere and we'll need to take them out. Move carefully." Then she set off down the corridor and, numb with surprise, Kez followed her.

11

PURGE
INFECTED BLOOD

Sir Charles Alverstead wasn't used to waiting. The demonstrators still hadn't been dispersed, despite his sending out more guards to control them. The EF Consul was away, so he had jurisdiction over the building, but it wasn't helping him solve the problem. The Commander of the Guard still hadn't called him back and Dr. Kalden, who had promised him results this morning, was over half an hour late with his report.

That's something I can deal with, Sir Charles thought. The other problems were annoying but this one was downright insulting. He was Kalden's superior in the CPS and the doctor had no right to keep him waiting. He tapped the code for Kalden's lab into the vidcom and waited. There was no answer and he frowned. Tapping in another code, this time one for the security station, he tried again. Again there was no answer, and fuming with anger he called the Commander of the Guard.

"Commander, why haven't I heard from you earlier?" he demanded. "And why has the security station been left unmanned?"

"It wasn't left unmanned, sir," the commander said with a trace of alarm. "But we had to leave a skeleton staff because most of my men are out dealing with the demonstrators."

"Then get them back in here," Alverstead ordered. "And check on the prisoners. There's something going on here and I want you to find out what it is!"

Cloud had been watching the demonstration on the news and he had little doubt of what it meant. These were the people Avalon had joined and for some reason they were mounting an attack on the EF Consulate. He thought of Sir Charles Alverstead under siege and smiled slightly. But he didn't take his eyes off the smoke-filled view. Somewhere in that mess Avalon was hiding, he was certain of it. It was no use. The smoke was only getting thicker and it was impossible to make out individual people, let alone who they were. Cloud turned off the vidcom and stood up. For a while he stood motionless in the center of the room, considering the wisdom of what he was about to do.

"Hell!" he snarled suddenly in the middle of the empty room. "At least this way I won't feel like a murderer for the rest of my life."

Making up his mind he headed for his own private flitter and flung himself into the front seat with a feeling of relief. Most of the media people had stopped watching the residence, lured away by the demonstrations. But two flitters took off and started to follow him as he guided his away from the building. He paid them no attention. When he got to his destination they wouldn't be able to follow him any further.

The security station had given Geraint the first clue they were in the right area. It was empty and they fanned out to search for some idea as to where the guards had gone. Daniel was the first to find it, a monitor screen showing a heap of bodies, and he called the others over quickly. Geraint opened a com signal to the other groups.

"Attention all units, attention all units, this is group leader three, we may have found something."

As confirmation signals came back along the line, Geraint began to describe what they could see on the screen.

"We've found some kind of security control room down here but it's empty. One of the monitors is showing some sort of hospital room. There's a heap of bodies wearing lab coats inside, and two guards. They all look dead."

"Group leader three, this is Ali," a voice came back over the link. *"We think you've found the right area and we're coming to join you. Go and find those missing guards. With any luck they'll lead you to Raven."*

Geraint clicked off the com unit and waved the team out of the room. Their progress was more purposeful now that they knew they were heading in the right direction. Daniel moved up to the leaders, watching for any sign of disturbance ahead.

The corridors were silent but they were watched by the persistent hidden cameras. The leading scouts were becoming adept at spotting them and taking them out. Three corridors on they heard the sound of gunfire and a couple of leaders started ahead.

"Wait!" Geraint commanded. "Proceed with extreme caution. Scouts, get on ahead and look for cameras. We don't know that the room we found is the only security linkup. Everyone else: ready your weapons."

Daniel inched forward slowly, holding his gun ready but not sure if he'd have the experience to fire it at the right moment. The sound of gunfire stopped and the group moved on cautiously. The scouts ducked back around a corner and waved the rest of the team forward. Geraint went up to join them and they held a whispered conversation. Then Geraint moved to the angle of the corridor and called out:

"Raven!"

"Who's there?" a female voice called back and Daniel glanced out at his teammates. They were all focused on the end of the corridor and Daniel looked back that way as well.

"This is Geraint," their team leader called. "We're here to rescue you."

"Come out then," the voice called back and Geraint looked at the rest of the team. "Move slowly," he told them, "and don't make any sudden movements." Then he stepped round the angle of the corridor and the rest of the group held their breath. There was no sound and after a few seconds the scouts followed, then the rest of the team.

As Daniel moved after the scouts he found himself in another similar corridor, this one with four dead guards bleeding onto the shining floor. A girl dressed in military fatigues carrying a machine gun stood over the bodies facing Geraint. Beside her a young boy with wide scared eyes held another machine gun pointed at them.

"We're members of Anglecynn," Geraint explained. "We're your allies."

"Glad to hear it," Raven replied, not lowering her gun.

"If you speak into this com link you'll be able to talk to your friends," Geraint suggested. "They're on their way down right now."

"OK," Raven agreed and extended her hand.

Geraint tossed the com link and she caught it easily before switching it on.

"This is Raven," she said into the speaker. "Who's there?"

"Raven?" Ali's voice came over the line. *"Raven, are you all right?"*

"Don't ask stupid questions," Raven said sharply. "Nice rescue, though. When are you going to get down here so we can leave?"

"We're on our way," Ali replied. *"But group two reports increased guard activity on the upper levels. Finn thinks we might have difficulty getting out."*

"Isn't that always the way?" Raven replied. "See you when you get there." With that she clicked off the unit and threw it to Geraint. "Well, ally," she said to him, "we'd better start looking for a way out of here."

Ali's group was heading for the lower levels of the building when the klaxon started to wail.

"That's torn it," Luciel muttered and Finn readied his gun ominously.

"Looks like getting out is going to be a hell of a lot harder than getting in," he said.

"At least we've found Raven," Avalon said with relief.

"What about Kez?" Luciel asked. "Is he OK?"

"I didn't think to ask," Ali blushed. "But I'm sure Raven would have said if he wasn't." Luciel looked disappointed and Ali mentally kicked herself for her mistake. But there wasn't time to worry about it now. The wailing alarm might bring guards toward them at any minute. Their team thundered down a set of service stairs, trying to meet up with Raven and group three. Two levels down they heard gunfire and approached slowly until Finn identified Alaric.

"I heard Geraint's located Raven," he said. "We were moving to meet up with them when this guard squad charged at us." He looked over his group with concern and Ali could see several of them were being attended to by teammates bandaging up bullet wounds. There were two dead bodies on the floor not wearing military uniforms.

"This is getting bloody," Avalon said and Alaric nodded curtly.

"I think it's time we got out," he said. "But it looks like the guards are moving back into the building."

"Why don't we move on down quickly and meet up with the others," Ali suggested. "We'll stand more of a chance together."

"Agreed," Alaric replied and Ali was surprised to see people moving instantaneously into position.

The two squads moved on, keeping to a rigid formation with the injured team members in the middle of the group. Ali found herself with Luciel and Alaric at the front while Avalon, Finn, and Jeeva brought up the rear. Ten minutes later they encountered one of group three's scouts and were led on to where Geraint, Kez, and Raven were waiting. Kez and Luciel greeted each other with relief, exchanging stories quickly while the groups converged. Raven didn't acknowledge anyone in particular but Ali saw her with relief.

"Raven," she said urgently. "Do you want to take over? Wraith couldn't come because he was injured so I'm supposed to be in command but . . . "

"Don't be ridiculous," Raven told her. "I don't even know who any of these people are. I'm in no state to start taking over."

"We're Anglecynn," Alaric explained, overhearing. "And I'm Alaric."

Raven nodded to him briskly before asking:

"Do you know what's happened to all the guards?"

"We did have people outside distracting them but now it looks like they're coming back in," Alaric explained.

"We need to find some kind of way out," Ali said and to her surprise Raven grinned.

"I can see at least twenty people carrying blasters," she said. "Twenty blasters can make their own way out."

"Good idea," Alaric agreed. "Someone find an exterior wall."

"I'll do it!" Jordan said, speaking up for the first time. Alaric winced slightly but didn't try to prevent her.

"Take someone with you," he ordered and Daniel stepped forward instantly.

427

"I'll go with Jordan," he said. "I know this building a little."

"Get to it then," Geraint told them and they both took off instantly.

Ali looked after them. She recognized Daniel and admired him for stepping forward. She found herself hoping that he hadn't seen her try to hand command over to Raven. This was probably the only opportunity she'd ever have to look as if she was important.

"I'd better contact the people outside and find out what's going on," Alaric said. "Watch my back."

The people nearest to him readied their guns as Alaric flipped open his communicator and entered the com code of the protest coordinator.

"This is Alaric," he said. "What's up out there?"

"It's like a war zone," Carl's voice came back. *"There are thousands of Seccies out here and we're running out of gas. I don't know how much longer we can hold them."*

"What about EF guards?"

"Most of them are heading back inside but it's hard to tell how many are left," Carl replied. *"The Seccies have been shooting pretty indiscriminately and I reckon they got quite a few of EF people as well as some of the media snoops."*

"The Seccies shot media people?" Alaric asked incredulously.

"Looks like quite a few," Carl replied. *"And they don't look happy about it. More of them have turned up than were here this morning and they're filming the whole thing."*

"Useful to know," Alaric replied. "Thanks, Carl. You can pull back soon now but I want you to hold the flitters ready. We'll be coming out of the side of the building and we'll need collecting if you can."

"We'll do our best," Carl replied. *"Don't take too long."* Then the line went dead and Alaric holstered the com unit. As he did Geraint's unit chimed.

"Geraint," he said, answering it.

"Jordan here," came the reply. *"We've found an exterior wall. West of your position but we'll have to come back and show you the way."*

"Good work," Geraint replied. "Get back here as quickly as you can. He turned off the unit and looked at the rest of them. "Looks like we're moving," he said.

Cloud's flitter streaked past the final bridge and swung down in an elegant curve toward the thick blue smoke. It wasn't as enveloping as it had been on the news earlier. A troop of Seccie police with riot shields and gas masks were advancing on the protesters, opening fire on the flitters in which the demonstrators hid. Cloud watched the confusion, circling around the building to lose his media escort. On the second circuit he ducked his flitter down below the smoke and waited. Three seconds later the media flitters swung past above him and he smiled to himself, moving the little craft slowly forward while keeping out of range of the shooting Seccies.

From his vantage point he was ideally placed to see what happened next. The last of the protesters reached their flitters and they started taking off, still belching blue smoke down on the Seccies.

Then, as the Seccies were firing on the flitters, not making any attempt to distinguish between those belonging to the demonstrators and those with media slogans, the side of the building exploded. Half a level of the EF Consulate opened up as its exterior wall fell open and debris showered on the crowds below. Half of the Seccies turned to fire on the building just as a troop of EF guards ran out of the main doors with the same intention. The two groups opened fire on each other as the rest of the Seccies shot at the flitters.

The demonstrators were taking advantage of the opportunity to skim their flitters up to the side of the building, risking the ricocheting shots as they helped people on board. Cloud watched as about half the people from the Consulate were pulled to safety and the flitters that rescued them took off. It was then that he saw the distinctive swirl of red hair he'd been looking for. He didn't know what Avalon was doing halfway up the side of the EF building but he intended to find out and he edged the flitter upward, trying to stay out of sight of the Seccies and the EF guards. He was wise to do so because the confusion was being sorted out below. Although about half the forces on the level were still shooting at each other, taking revenge for the deaths of their fellow officers, the others had identified the real enemy and were blasting flitters as the demonstrators tried to pull their friends to safety.

It wasn't going to work. Cloud could see the flitters being hit and gradually they pulled off, taking the people they already had on board to safety. Five people remained standing on the blast area, firing back at the Seccies as the last remaining flitter hovered, waiting to take them to safety. One person managed to get on and Cloud recognized her as the blonde girl who had been in the residence. Then the flitter was hit by a direct shot and tumbled almost the entire level before stabilizing. It swung around as if its pilot intended to return but then circled back in another direction, leaving the scene. Avalon and her companions backed away from the ledge, heading back into the building.

Cloud's hands were on the flitter's controls before he realized what he was doing. If Avalon went back into the building she was almost certain to be captured or killed by the EF guards. Even if she found another way out, more Seccies were arriving all the time. Cloud's flitter hurtled up through the dispersing smoke and headed directly for the side of the building. He heard blaster shots sizzling past him and then felt the flitter lurch as one hit the small craft. Forcing the vehicle to greater acceleration he hurtled up the side of the building and through the hole the terrorists had made in its side. The corridor on the other side of the hole was narrow and he pulled back on the controls forcing the flitter to slow its progress as it shot between the walls, a finger's breadth away from them. It came to a halt just before the next turning and Cloud hit the door release. As he exited the flitter he came face to face with four figures, standing astonished at the end of the corridor.

Avalon stared as the flitter rushed toward her, blackening the walls of the passageway with the heat of its passing. When the door opened and Cloud stepped out she was literally speechless with surprise. Finn and Geraint didn't have the same problem.

"My God!" Geraint exclaimed, awestruck by the sight.

"Freakin' insanity," the ganger murmured behind him. "Who's this schizo?"

"Cloud Estavisti," Raven informed them, already heading toward the flitter. "How fortunate. I was beginning to doubt the success of this rescue."

"Cloud's not part of the mission," Avalon warned, finding her voice at last. "He tried to betray us to CPS. He's probably here to do it again."

Cloud's dark blue eyes met hers with an unreadable expression. Then he turned to Raven.

"I am here to help you," he told her. "Despite what may have happened in the past. And you don't exactly have a lot of options."

"Succinctly put," Raven acknowledged. "Everyone get in the flitter."

Avalon hesitated for a second but, as Raven had already admitted, she couldn't think of an alternative. Finn and Geraint climbed in beside her but Raven continued to face Cloud.

"I'll drive," she informed him. The dancer looked as if he was about to protest, then he shrugged and stepped aside, allowing Raven to take the pilot's seat as he crossed to the other side of the craft and took the seat next to her.

Raven touched the controls and the doors hissed shut.

"How are you going to get this thing out again?" Finn asked cynically. "There's no room to turn."

"Then I won't turn," Raven replied and her fingers sped across the control in a blur of movement. As they did so, the flitter took off. Hurtling backward through the cramped corridor, charring the walls once more as it passed by, the flitter shot out of the building without even grazing the sides. A fusillade of shots exploded around them but Raven was still backing off and the flitter streaked past the rain of blaster fire before coming about in a tight turn and shooting for the sky.

By the time the sounds of pursuit began behind them, Raven was already five levels up and still accelerating.

"Where are we going?" Avalon asked in bewilderment as the young Hex guided their craft further upward.

"Gangland," Raven replied curtly, her fingers still flying over the control board.

"Down is in the other direction," Cloud said diffidently and Raven flashed him a smile.

"Just a diversion," she said, still smiling. "Seccies never have any sense of perspective."

"Perspective?" Geraint said quietly, looking at Avalon.

The megastar shrugged and then blinked as a wash of sunlight fell across her face.

The flitter shot out of the city heights, sailing up into the cold winter sky. Below them they could see the tops of the skyscrapers, reaching up toward the clouds. Then Raven pulled the flitter around in a dizzying turn and they circled around the city. The towers were immense; it was impossible to see their entire height from any one point, but at the edges of the city some of them were shorter, still beginning their course toward the sky. Raven guided the flitter toward these stunted giants and once more the darkness of the city enclosed them. Once more they were in the depths of London, heading toward the ganglands.

"No sense of perspective," Raven repeated. "They saw us go up, so they go up. It'll be at least a week before they realize they've lost us."

Wraith paced anxiously across the floor of the control room. He'd been watching the events at the EF Consulate unfold on the news. The government had attempted to impose a news blackout when they realized what was happening but for once the media networks had resisted. Five reporters had died during the firefight, all of them felled by Seccie or EF weapons, and the news networks were in no mood to censor the story.

As a result Wraith had watched as the side of the building exploded and the demonstrators had attempted to haul the rescue party to safety. He had scrutinized the images for any sign of Raven but he hadn't seen her until the last flitter pulled away, leaving four pathetic figures marooned. He cursed Raven for remaining behind while the people who had come to rescue her left and was within an inch of running for a flitter himself, however late he was about to arrive. It was then that the luxury flitter had streaked up the side of the Consulate and into the gaping hole in the building's side. By the time it reappeared the newsfeeds had identified it as belonging to Cloud and were speculating excitedly on what this might mean. A news anchor began to explain their current theory.

"It's a dramatic ending to the story of Avalon's disappearance but now the answer seems clear. This is a picture of Avalon, left behind

after the attack on the EF building that has been raging for the past three hours. Now Cloud Estavisti, who has refused to talk to the media about the reason for the megastar's disappearance, has appeared as well. Two of the members of Europe's leading rock band appear to have joined an underground terrorist group known as Anglecynn. We can only speculate on the reasons why, since it doesn't look like they'll be giving any press conferences any time soon."

A picture was flashed up of the four people who'd been left behind and the anchor added:

"As to who these other people are, again we can only guess. We don't even know the reason Anglecynn attacked the EF Consulate today. But the multiple fatalities we have seen today did not come at their hands. While we don't know the reason for its attack we can see its results. Vidcam images broadcast earlier have shown that the protesters were unarmed, even if their counterparts inside the building were not. They attempted to hold off the combined might of the EF and the Security Services with peaceful means and many of their number were brutally shot down as were those five brave reporters who attempted to bring you the truth of these events."

Wraith was curious to see what the media would say next but the anchor's speech was interrupted by another live broadcast of the events unfolding at the Consulate. Wraith watched as Cloud's flitter flew out of the building backward, curved around, and disappeared from view. As he watched, his body relaxed from its state of tension. There was only one person who drove like that.

12
A GENERAL ECLIPSE

The flitter came to rest inside the gangland fortress and Wraith ran to meet it. As the doors opened and Raven appeared he swept her into a one-armed hug. For a change Raven didn't resist his spontaneous show of affection but after a few moments she stepped away and he released her.

"I thought we'd lost you," he said quietly and Raven looked at him gravely.

"I wasn't sure myself," she admitted. Then she grinned. "Looks like we've caused a lot of trouble," she said. "The government won't find it so easy to cover this up."

"That's true," Wraith agreed. Then, remembering something, he turned to Cloud. "I don't know how to thank you," he said simply. "But it looks like I'll have time to find a way. You were recognized by the media."

"I was expecting that," Cloud replied, looking unfazed by the thought. "It's not a problem as long as you're prepared to take me in."

Avalon looked anxious and spoke pleadingly to Wraith.

"Cloud's made up for his betrayal, hasn't he?"

"As far as I'm concerned, he has," Wraith agreed and looked at Raven for confirmation.

"He can stay," she said with a shrug. "One more megastar doesn't make a lot of difference—it's the fifty terrorists who surprised me."

"Anglecynn!" Geraint exclaimed. "We have to contact them! We don't know how badly the Seccies hit them."

"I'll contact them immediately," Wraith agreed, leading the way to the control room.

Kez had been one of the first to be lifted off and he watched the arrival of the other flitters anxiously. Although there were mercifully few dead, many of the Anglecynn members had been badly injured during the Seccie attacks, and as the flitters unloaded their passengers at Dragon's Nest, the administrative staff hurried to give them medical attention. In the confusion, Kez searched for his friends among the wounded and their helpers. He found Ali talking to Daniel Hammond as he was being treated for blaster wounds. To Kez's surprise Ali smiled when she saw him.

"I'm glad you're all right," she told him. "It wasn't the same without you and Raven."

"Have you seen Raven?" Kez asked anxiously. "I can't find her anywhere."

"No." Ali's eyes darkened. "I hope she made it out. Things got kind of crazy at the end."

"I'll keep looking," Kez said quickly, already turning away.

"Tell us when you find her," Ali called after him but Kez was already gone.

He hurried through the ranks of people, asking everyone if they'd seen Raven and getting increasingly panicked when no one had. Luciel and Jeeva had arrived on one of the later flitters and had only been able to tell him that Avalon, Raven, and Finn, as well as some of the Anglecynn members, had still been in the building when they left. Finally he came to a halt. No more flitters were arriving and he'd spoken to everyone in the room. The grim certainty that Raven hadn't made it was beginning to sink in when Alaric strode into the room.

The terrorist leader's clothes bore blaster burns and he was bleeding from a cut on his head but he had evidently considered his injuries too light to attend to at once. Now he called for Anglecynn's attention and everyone turned to look at him, save for the medical workers who were still attending to the injured.

"I've just had a call from Wraith," he announced. "It seems Cloud Estavisti turned up to lift out the last people from the building. They're all right."

"Does that include Raven?" Kez asked quickly, and Alaric nodded.

"Raven, Geraint, Avalon, and Finn," he said. Then he looked around at the assembled company. "I'd like to thank everyone for the part they played in today's operation," he said. "I know no one expected to have to engage in a mission of that nature on such short notice. But your work today almost certainly saved the life of someone who may help to save many more. Together we grieve for our dead but I'm grateful the casualties were not more heavy. No one, especially myself, expected that the Seccie response would not only be so violent but so undisciplined.

"Everyone will need to be debriefed and I'll arrange a meeting with the Hex group as soon as is feasible. But for now I'll leave you to have your injuries attended to and to get some sleep. However, those who are not wounded will be called upon for the usual watches and everyone should be aware of the possibility of Seccie reprisals. I don't believe that anyone was followed here but I'd like you to remain cautious just in case."

With that he finished speaking and a murmur of conversation resumed. Alaric crossed to where Kez was standing.

"Wraith is sending a flitter to collect you," he said. "And Ali, Luciel, and someone called Jeeva."

"Thank you," Kez said and looked at the terrorist leader with genuine gratitude. "For everything."

Alaric smiled at him then looked over at the injured people.

"I must go," he said. "Please remind Wraith I would like to meet with all your group as soon as possible."

"I will," Kez promised and Alaric hurried back to his people.

Although Wraith urged Raven to sleep she refused to rest until she'd looked over the new base and especially the control room.

"The Countess sent over two technicians to put everything

together," Avalon told her. "Since then we've been trying to understand how it all works."

"You've done reasonably well," Raven replied, running her fingers over the central terminals. "Although I'll have to install a security system before someone trashes the entire computer network." She turned away from the terminal and rubbed her forehead briefly.

"You look tired," Wraith said sympathetically "You've seen everything now—go and sleep for a while. We can talk when the others get back."

"All right," Raven agreed, with uncharacteristic submission. "We'll talk later." With that she headed off to the apartment area, leaving them in the control room.

Cloud watched her leave, then turned to speak to Wraith.

"Perhaps there's somewhere I could wait, as well," he suggested. "Since there are doubtless matters you would like to discuss in my absence."

Wraith and Avalon exchanged a glance. Neither of them was prepared to deny that they would have to discuss Cloud's admission to the group in greater detail. But equally they didn't want to seem ungrateful for his involvement.

"Why don't you wait in the apartment suite, then," Avalon said finally. "You could just relax and watch the vidscreen for a while."

Raven slept deeply without dreaming. She didn't even wake up when Finn returned with the others and they gathered in the apartment's living room to exchange stories. She slept through their discussion of Cloud's role in the group and the decision to give him a chance as one of them. She eventually awoke late the next day when the building was mostly silent.

Emerging from the room she had claimed as hers, Raven wandered through the building. Wraith and Avalon she found in the control room, and the vidscreens showed her Luciel and Kez dismantling a flitter in the vehicle bay and Jeeva giving Ali and Cloud a shooting lesson in the main hall.

"You found a good place," Wraith commented and she smiled slightly.

"For now," Raven agreed. "But I imagine things will change."

"The story's still all over the media," Avalon told her. "There hasn't been an official statement yet though."

"Probably still trying to decide how to cover everything up," Raven replied. "But it won't be easy. The Seccies have been out of control ever since this initiative to wipe out the Hexes came in and I doubt it's going to get better. Not after what the CPS learned from me."

"What did they learn?" Wraith asked quietly. "I hoped that they wouldn't experiment on you immediately."

"A forlorn hope," Raven told him. "They started testing me almost immediately but they didn't learn anything from that. What the CPS have discovered is that a solitary Hex is capable of neutralizing the best resources they have. I killed Kalden and most of his scientists. It will be a while before they can duplicate his work and now that work has proved useless against me they may not want to." She looked thoughtful. "I suspect the

CPS might now decide to adopt a more drastic solution."

"More drastic how?" Avalon asked and Raven shrugged.

"We'll have to see," she said. "But I think, in the circumstances, I might need to start teaching the rest of you sooner rather than later."

"I agree," Wraith added. "What happened yesterday is bound to have an effect. Anglecynn are certainly worried about that."

"Yes, our terrorist allies," Raven said. "I still don't exactly know how they come into all this."

"Neither do they," Wraith told her. "That still has to be decided. They helped with the rescue attempt because they were persuaded that the extermination laws are wrong. But after that I don't know how much support they'll want to give us or how much we should give them."

"Alaric wants to meet with us tonight," Avalon told her. "He seems to be their leader and he's anxious to gain an advantage for Anglecynn through working with us."

"I've no objection," Raven replied. She glanced at the vidscreen when Ali and Cloud were firing rounds at a battered target, hitting it about one shot in ten. "They might be terrorists but at least they can shoot straight."

"Is that going to be important?" Avalon asked carefully. "So far your group has tried to avoid violence."

"I designed this place with self-defense in mind," Raven told her. "It's intended to be a fortress. The Seccies and the CPS aren't going to go away and the European Federation surely sees us as a threat. In the circumstances, some kind of martial expertise would be useful and Anglecynn seem to have that."

"We'll talk to them about it this evening," Wraith agreed. "Maybe by then there'll be some more news."

Sir Charles Alverstead wasn't eager to release anything to the media. He met with Adam Hammond and the Prime Minister, George Chesterton, at the Houses of Parliament. The EF building was still a wreck after the terrorist attack and had been closed down until the EF Special Forces had arrived to determine what had gone wrong. Alverstead had a feeling that he might lose his job over this, although he hoped he might be able to blame the whole fiasco on Kalden. The doctor was dead as a result of his underestimation of Raven, and his experimentation might have to die with him. In the meantime Alverstead's priority was saving his own skin and that necessitated a media cover-up.

"The media aren't being very cooperative," the Security Minister was explaining. "In fact they've been flooding my department with demands and complaints. They claim that the Security Services used unreasonable force on the demonstrators and they're threatening to sue because of the media deaths."

"Can't you find some way to blame that on the Hexes?" the Prime Minister asked. "The last thing this country needs is a scandal in the Security Services."

"Perhaps the last thing this country needs is media that cannot be controlled," Alverstead suggested. "The EF has already discussed bringing in stronger regulatory measures. Perhaps they could be brought forward."

"Good idea," Chesterton agreed. "The Federation Council will back us up if necessary, I'm sure. I only hope they don't blame us for allowing this Hex threat to occur in this country."

"At least the media have helped us in one area," Adam Hammond told him. "We now have reliable vid images of the Hex named Raven. We should be able to trace her background with that."

"All the same, they need to be brought under control," Chesterton said. "Inform the controllers of the newsfeeds that they will be expected to comply with Federation law and issue a gag order on all reports concerning the Hex problem other than official statements. Let's not give these terrorists a platform to address the world."

The Hexes and Anglecynn met by mutual consent at Dragon's Nest. Avalon had volunteered to remain behind to guard the Fortress but Wraith had insisted that they all be there. Finn and Jeeva, who had returned to working for the Countess, had been hired instead to watch the control room. As Alaric's people issued them permission to approach, Wraith looked around the group with satisfaction. Raven was still looking weary but there seemed to be no lasting effects from the experimentation. Ali and Luciel were both looking more confident and Kez was more talkative, sharing their conversation without looking intimidated by Ali. Cloud Estavisti was still a mystery. He talked quietly to Avalon but Wraith couldn't make out their conversation. Raven seemed to guess the direction of his thoughts as they coasted through the depths of the city toward Anglecynn's base.

"I think it'll work out," she said. "It could even be fun."

"I'm not sure I want to be responsible for so many people," Wraith said quietly.

"Then don't be." Raven shrugged and lay back in her seat. "Let them be responsible for themselves. Everyone's here because they chose to be, after all."

"Even you?" Wraith asked. "I recall you said forming a solidarity group was a waste of time."

"I'm here for the time being," Raven told him. "And I've been revising my opinion a little. Let's just see what happens."

The members of Anglecynn were waiting for them in their main common room and Alaric greeted the Hex group with a smile.

"I'm impressed with your base," Raven told him. "The depths of the city are generally considered uninhabitable."

"It's something we take advantage of," Alaric replied. "But it makes expansion difficult. We can only hide so many people here."

"You seem to have done well," Wraith said. "The Seccies must be furious you've evaded them for so long."

"We might not be able to evade them much longer," Alaric said grimly. "We have sources in the city who sometimes pass us information. Word is the government is going to use the events at the Consulate as an excuse to introduce more EF controls. Our fight just got a lot harder."

"Maybe not necessarily," Raven told him. "I'm getting tired of the way the CPS is hunting me. If your group is prepared to support us there are things we'd be willing to give you in return."

"We've discussed this amongst ourselves already," Geraint said, speaking for the first time. "Most of us feel your cause is something we can commit to but we still don't know exactly what you can offer in return."

"How does complete control of the net sound to you?" Raven asked and the Anglecynn members exchanged glances.

"Is that something you can do?" Alaric asked, looking doubtful.

"Not quite yet," Raven told him. She turned to glance at Avalon, Ali, and Luciel. "But yes, I think it's possible and it's something I intend to work toward. I think it's time that Hexes made things difficult for the CPS and I can teach any Hex how to use the net, although it will be a while before they can use it as well as I can." She didn't say there was a possibility that it might never occur. She still didn't know how unusual her own abilities were, and although the other members of the group might not be able to emulate her, she hadn't discounted the chance of finding new Hexes who could.

"Is that something we're prepared to work for?" Alaric asked turning to address the whole of Anglecynn. Heads nodded across the room. Even those who were still uneasy about working with Hexes were swayed by the prospect of control of the net. The agreement seemed, for the moment, to be unanimous. "It looks like we're with you," Alaric told Raven.

"You've already assisted us immensely," Wraith told him. "I'm sure none of us will regret the decision."

"At the moment we need all the allies we can get," Geraint said seriously. "The EF is getting stronger all the time. If we can't move against them soon, we may never be able to."

For a while the room was silent as everyone present considered the possibility. Raven was the first to speak.

"They have more to be afraid of than we do," she said. "We know what they're capable of. But they don't have the slightest idea what we can do to them."

The Federation Council buildings at Versailles were as imposing as the ancient palace which still formed a small part of them. The glittering towers and battlements now hid an array of twenty-fourth century weaponry and the center of the EF dominated Europe as the French kings had once controlled France. The Council's word was law across the states that fell under its protection. Although there were occasional problems when groups attempted to shake off the yoke of the Federation these seldom caused the Council any real concern.

Now a new threat had developed. The Hex problem, supposedly contained centuries previously, had broken out anew in an alarming fashion. It had been years since a rogue Hex had survived to adulthood to trouble the EF with their presence, although such threats had occasionally occurred. Now another mutant had escaped and destroyed not only the secret experimentation program, known only to the governments of Europe, but also the balance of power in the British government. Britain had been one of the last nations to come under EF control. The Federation had not yet imposed the full force of its dominance. The Hex threat meant that things would have to change and the British Prime Minister had accepted that EF control was the only choice to combat a possible rebellion.

In other EF-controlled countries the CPS had worked effectively with the local peacekeeping forces to eradicate the Hex threat. In Britain this policy had obviously failed. Now it was time for a new approach. With Federation troops stationed in Britain, upholding the government and supporting the CPS, there would be nowhere for the Hexes to hide. The rebellion could be crushed and this latest mutant leader eradicated. Within the jewel-covered might of the Federation Council buildings, plans were being set in motion to strike against the threat they only knew by the name of Raven.

GHOSTS

1

TRIED IN THE FIRE

Drow dropped off the edge of the walkway, landing with a jolt that knocked the breath out of his body. A blaster shot zinged past his head and he didn't waste time on catching his breath, staggering to his feet, and running to where the arches sloped down to a lower level. He heard more shots around him but the Seccies were falling behind. A street kid wasn't worth the trouble of an extended chase and he was heading into the depths of the ganglands now.

The lighting on the next level was damaged, flickering erratically and creating odd shadows against the skyscraper sections emblazoned with gang colors. This was Spider territory: not far from home, but Drow kept to the shadows anyway. The Spiders wouldn't cause him a hassle as long as he didn't mess with them—it was their style. Their territory was the rec complexes that surrounded Drow now: vice-joints, dream palaces, and gaming 'cades.

They catered to the low-wagers who couldn't afford to move up to the heights of the city but could spare the creds for a cheap thrill. The locals paid protection money to the Spiders and the gang patrolled the streets, but while they would get tough if they needed to, they didn't waste their time shaking down anyone wearing the wrong colors.

Drow weaved his way through Spider town, checking back over his shoulder casually every once in a while. As far as he could tell, the Seccies had cut their losses and decided not to follow him into the ganglands. But that didn't mean he was safe. They had holocams on their flitter and a record of him running away. If they picked him up later they'd be able to ID him as the kid who'd stolen a case of data disks from the Fractured Image. For now though he was as chill as you could be on the streets. Heading down through the levels of Spider territory he mapped out the route ahead in his mind. He had two choices and neither gave him much of a buzz. The way back home to his own gang's sector lay through Katana space. The knife gang wouldn't like his colors and if they caught him shortcutting through their turf he might not only lose the disks he'd lifted but wake up dead tomorrow. The alternative would take longer, circling Katana territory through the Ghost area. However, the Katanas were a menace Drow understood—no one knew anything about the Ghosts.

Catching sight of his own reflection in the grimy windows of a black-market tech store, Drow made up his mind. The fragments of shining circuitry braided into his black hair and the silvery mirror lenses in his eyes marked him as a Chrome, and a lone ganger was a target on the streets. The Katanas were expanding their area and any stranger would be fair game to enhance their rep. The Ghosts were known to be hard as ice and no one gave them trouble but they were a secretive gang and didn't need to prove themselves all the time. They controlled levels and enclaves all over the sky-rises and starscrapers of London but never displayed their colors or openly hung out on the street. Ghost territory was a no-go area and gangs who tangled with them suffered runs of bad luck that made them suspicious of the Ghosts and wary of trouble. Standing in line for a public grav-tube to the levels lower down, Drow tried not to remember the other stories he had heard about the Ghosts. It was rumored they stole children to increase their numbers and that they were anarchists trying to bring down the city through terrorist action. It had been reported on the holovid that the Ghosts were linked to Anglecynn: a terrorist faction that engineered net crashes and gang attacks on European Federation agencies. But whenever the Seccies made a move on Ghost enclaves they arrived to find everything abandoned, not even trash left behind. Meanwhile, the Ghosts started up in some other wasted section of the city gang-lands and the local gang steered clear.

The other people waiting for the grav-tube gave Drow side-long looks. Two kids wearing Spider colors, at about thirteen just a couple of years younger than him, gave him lazy salutes. Trying to act it up like they were real hard men but chill enough not to try and prove it, Drow thought. The rest of the tube-riders were mostly low-wagers looking at Drow shiftily until they dismissed him as too young to be a threat. That wasn't true, any street kid had to be able to take care of himself, but Chromes didn't fight for thrills and Drow ignored the looks. The grav-tube car arrived with a low hiss and Drow dropped a three cred piece into the slot, receiving a piece of scrip for three levels down in return. Behind him the line shuffled along and the car filled quickly with people. Just before it took off another two people hurried aboard and Drow blinked in momentary surprise. The boy didn't look to be much older than Drow but he held himself with a self-assurance that made him seem much more experienced. Drow felt certain the stranger was a ganger, although he wore no symbols or colors on his clothes. But it was the girl who really drew his attention. There was no way a girl like that could be a ganger. She wore white, an unusual color down in the slums since it attracted notice and was quickly stained by the grimy streets, and her shining pale blonde hair and graceful stance made her look even more out of place. Drow couldn't take his eyes off her as the grav-car sank down through the levels and it was with a jolt that he realized that they had reached his destination and both the strangers were disembarking ahead of him.

Drow stumbled off the grav-car and onto the level. The strangers were already some distance ahead of him but Drow forgot about them when he noticed the silence of the streets. No other gang territory was ever this deserted. All the skyscraper sections on this level were shuttered up but they didn't look abandoned so much as closed off. Garbage and debris littered the streets but the areas in front of the buildings were swept clean and the doors were sturdy enough to be blast-proof. Glancing around warily, Drow realized that some buildings were empty, doors and windows damaged or gone. Those empty doorways worried him. Anyone could be hiding within: sentries watching for intruders into Ghost territory. Drow only hoped that he looked unthreatening enough for them to leave him alone. That thought suddenly reminded him of the couple ahead and he lengthened his stride to catch up a little, trying to keep them in sight. The girl's long white coat flapped in the still air behind her and the boy's hair glinted bronze under the streetlights. No sunlight filtered this far into the depths but Drow found the artificial lighting eerie. Despite the emptiness of the level the Ghosts obviously chose to keep the lights working. Instinctively, Drow scanned the area for holocams: the Seccies had them placed all over the upper levels to keep an eye on people. At first he could see nothing, but then a small black box on the side of a building caught his attention. Beside it someone had scrawled a graffiti image of a black bird with outspread wings. Across the street and lower down there was another slightly differently shaped box with the same bird emblem next to it. Drow's heart rate began to speed up as his eyes flickered across the scene. Black birds seemed to leap out at him from all directions and he realized that, if each symbol meant some kind of surveillance tech, he was under more complete observation than when he ventured into the Seccie-patrolled upper levels of the city. He checked ahead for the figures of the two strangers but they had crossed the plaza ahead and rounded the corner of a building. Drow followed their route cautiously just in case there was an ambush ahead. But when he got to the spot where they'd disappeared there was nothing. Not a sound stirred across the level, although in the distance he could hear the thrum of activity above and below. The strangers must have been Ghosts, Drow realized uncomfortably, and he was lucky they hadn't taken exception to his presence in their area. With that in mind he picked up his speed and kept to a smooth run across the level, heading as fast as he could back to Chrome territory.

As the door slid closed behind them Ali frowned to herself and then glanced at Kez.

"Was he following us?" she asked.

"Don't think so," Kez replied. "But let's check." He touched the keypad on his wrist-com lightly while Ali waited. They were standing in the foyer on one of the larger building sections that their group claimed and, in contrast to the deserted streets outside, the large room was a hive of activity. A flitter was parked in the middle of the space and three gangers in blue and gold Snake colors were unloading crates of equipment. Over to one side a larger group of Anglecynn members were going through a final weapons check and Geraint, their leader, flipped Ali a brief wave when he noticed her. The Ghosts were an unusual alliance of different groups and in the two years they had spent hiding from the Seccies the gang had grown hugely. Ali had begun to like the feeling of being an important part of the group and she found herself smiling as she looked around the room.

Even more reassuring was the feeling of safety that came from being part of a large group. Despite their attacks on the brutal laws of the European Federation, no member of the group had been captured. The Hexes used their ability to interface with the net to gain information that the group could use. Their consistent attacks on EF facilities and their release of restricted information made it increasingly difficult for the government to cover up how much the regime was hated. Most important to Ali were the young Hexes they had successfully rescued from extermination. Despite the Civil Protection Service's best efforts to keep their records secret, the Hex group found them and tried to get to the victims before the CPS could. To some of these children their Hex abilities came as a complete surprise but to others who, like Ali, had lived in fear of discovery for almost all their lives, the Hex were the first real Ghosts because they aimed to be uncatchable and because none of them had any legal identity. They took their safety seriously and even minor threats, like the ganger boy who had followed them down to Ghost territory, were responded to quickly and efficiently.

Kez had stopped speaking into his wrist-com and Ali looked at him inquiringly.

"Jordan's reviewing the surveillance holos but she thought the kid was just taking a shortcut," Kez explained. "I don't think we have a problem."

"In that case we'd better get going," Ali replied. "There's a briefing in an hour's time, we have two rescue attempts tomorrow, and Alaric's team have a plan to sabotage Seccie communications."

"Electric!" Kez grinned, and as Ali smiled back she realized he was enjoying life as much as she was. Two years ago they'd disliked each other, Kez resenting her for her privileged upbringing and she despising him for growing up on the streets. But now the group was so much larger the differences between them no longer seemed important and there was always too much work to do to waste time quarreling.

As they headed up through the building, friends and allies greeting them briefly as they went about their work, Ali thought about the rescued children who were the main focus of her own activities in the group. There were almost two hundred of them now, ranging in age from five to as old as Ali herself. It was Raven's responsibility to teach them to use their Hex abilities but Ali, Kez, and Luciel were responsible for the rest of their education and for any other needs they might have. It was demanding work. Wraith and Raven virtually ran the Ghosts and one of the few things they agreed on was that the Hex children should grow up with every possible advantage the group could provide. As a result Ali was having to relearn things she'd never paid any attention to at school in the luxurious Belgravia Complex just to stay one step ahead of her students. Kez soaked up knowledge like a sponge, Luciel experimented constantly with new teaching methods and ideas, and between the three of them they had constructed an education course that covered everything from philosophy to firearms. Their reward was that the children liked and trusted them, although they were still wary around Raven.

The thought of the group's leader caused a shadow to pass over Ali's cheerful mood. The children weren't the only ones to have been trained by Raven: the older Hexes relied on her to give them the benefit of her experience. Luciel had progressed by leaps and bounds; his ambition to be a scientist had been revived by what Raven taught him of his abilities and he was trying to write a study explaining them. Avalon, the former rock singer, had successfully integrated her powers into her music and was still entranced by the idea of being a Hex. Although she remained on the sidelines of the group, her celebrity continued to gain the Hex cause prominence in the media. But Ali, despite her best efforts to understand Raven's teaching, was intimidated by the net. She had progressed sufficiently in her studies that she could wander happily through databases and nodes. But secured systems alarmed her and the infinite depths of the data network made her feel scared. She sometimes wondered if Raven was more like the net than a human being. The dark-eyed Hex with her cold summaries of people and the situations and her dizzying mood swings reminded Ali of the dark, unknown expanses of information which frightened her.

The flitter hung like a bird above the city and Raven stared down at her domain. She came here more and more often now, watching the starscrapers linked by a glittering network of bridges and arches sinking into bottomless depths where no light penetrated. Up here she felt like a Ghost, unseen and intangible, with the cityscape spread out beneath her like an array of complex circuitry. While the others had found fulfillment in being part of a group, Raven felt increasingly stifled. None of them was any match for her, in abilities or imagination, and as she trained the legion of Hex children she wished that just once they would find a Hex who had struggled as she had had to and triumphed.

"What are you thinking?" a voice asked quietly and Raven turned to regard her companion. Cloud Estavisti was the least likely member of their group. Cloud had fallen from the pinnacle of fame with Avalon and had tried to save them both by betraying the Hexes. He'd made up for his treachery when he'd saved their lives, but most of the Ghosts still felt uncomfortable around him. However, Raven saw in him a foil for her own black moods and a companion in her isolation.

"That maybe Kalden was right," she said softly.

"Kalden?" Cloud raised an eyebrow. "The scientist who experimented on all those children? I thought he was supposed to be renowned for his evil."

"To simply say something is evil means you refuse to understand it," Raven replied, turning to look back down into the maze of the city. "Research like Kalden's cannot be dismissed, no matter how twisted its origins."

"So why was he right?"

"For the wrong reasons," Raven replied. "He was trying to exterminate the Hexes but the trauma he subjected them to unleashed their potential in a way my training hasn't been able to duplicate." She swore suddenly under her breath, her fists clenching with frustration. "We just don't have the knowledge," she hissed. "There's so much we don't understand and I can't even teach all I know."

"Are you advocating torture as part of the training program?" Cloud asked ironically. "I can't see Wraith liking that option much."

"No, I'm not advocating it." Raven's voice was drained and lifeless. "But it was being forced to struggle that made me what I am and so far I am unique."

"Poor Raven." Cloud laughed mockingly. "Only godlike powers and the European Federation living in fear of you. What more does life have to offer?"

Raven grinned, her mood changing suddenly at Cloud's irreverence, and her dark eyes flashed.

"Damned if I know," she said. "Come on, let's fly."

Smiling back, Cloud touched the controls lightly and the flitter fell like a hawk toward London.

Night was falling across Europe but in the glittering splendor of Versailles it brought anything but peace. Sergei Sanatos, the Federation President, scanned the ranks of his advisers with barely hidden fury. The most powerful men in Europe struggled to maintain their equanimity in the face of his rage.

"Sir President," the Governor of the CPS began cautiously. "We have taken all possible precautions—"

"Enough!" Sergei slammed his fist down on the table with a crash that made all the advisers jump. "You speak of possibilities and precautions. I want facts. I want this rogue Hex caught and for the past two years you've failed to give her to me!"

Charles Alverstead took a deep breath. He wanted Raven caught almost as badly as the President did. It had been during his governorship that she'd escaped from them, despite security measures he had personally approved. He'd been able to blame her escape on Kalden, the scientist studying her, but now he was running out of excuses.

"The situation is difficult," he began again. "England was one of the last countries to be brought under EF rule and our attempts to tighten up security there have caused deep resentment. It seems the Hexes have formed some sort of alliance with an established terrorist group, and despite sending Federation troops to work with the Security Services we have no way of combating an enemy who knows our every move in advance."

"We've tried keeping records off the net," the Minister of Internal Affairs added. "But our system would collapse if we attempted it on a large scale. We can't control the Federation without instantaneous data transfer. Information is the currency in which large governments deal. We've worked for years to prevent a Hex from gaining power over the net because without it we are crippled."

"I know we are crippled," Sergei said softly and dangerously. "Your continued failure to deliver this Hex tells me that much at least."

"Sir President, we will capture her," Alverstead said quickly. "There have been threats to international security before and we've overcome them. There were other mutants before this—"

"Wait!" Sergei held up a hand and Alverstead stopped speaking as the President's cold gray eyes narrowed in thought. "There have been threats before this," the President mused. "How did we combat them?"

"Those events occurred during your predecessor's rule and the information is classified, Sir," the Minister for Internal Affairs began but as Sergei's expression grew dangerous he added: "But doubtless we can find it."

"Does no one know anything?" the President snapped in annoyance and around the table the senior ministers shook their heads.

"Sir President?" a measured voice spoke up and they all turned to regard the elderly Minister of Propaganda, the man who controlled all European communications and media agencies. He was nodding to himself, a slight smile playing across his wrinkled lips. "The events you speak of are known to me. It was my department that handled the subsequent cover-up. The Federation was threatened by a mutant once before, twenty-five years ago. Listen and I will tell you how it happened. . . ."

The cloak of the night fell over England and France like velvet wings and moved to capture the rest of Europe in its darkness. South and east of the palace of Versailles, night touched another palace where water lapped through the once splendid hallways and the crumbling wrecks of other ornate mansions surrendered to the inevitable triumph of the sea. From the top of the golden stone palace Tally looked out across the grand canal and gazed on the ruin that was once Venice in the last rays of the dying sun.

It was the only home she had ever known, although most of her life had been spent fleeing from one country to another. It was to Venice that her mother had brought them, exhausted by the chase and looking only for safety and silence. While their mother had tried to make a home for them in the ruined palazzo, Tally and her twin brother had discovered the forgotten history of Europe, explored the art galleries and museums with their treasure-trove of ruined beauty, and moored their boat to the pinnacle of St. Mark's Cathedral while they watched the sun set over the island city the sea had reclaimed. Now their mother was dying and Tally couldn't see the magic of the city any longer. The life she had known was coming to an end and she was afraid to admit it even to herself.

These last few months Tally and Gift had immersed themselves in the past, but the romantic splendors of doomed Venice were as alien to the world of the twenty-fourth century as the life they had lived up to now. Amid the technological sophistication of EF-ruled Europe they had lived in the shadows of the system, camping in the wilderness abandoned or rejected by the technocracy and avoiding the vast datahives of the urban megaplexes. Only briefly had they even seen cities—while being smuggled through and around them by allies or gangers bribed to assist them. Even in so precarious an existence, their mother had educated the children to the best of her ability, but Tally knew when her mother died it might be too late to learn the familiarity with the high-tech world that the city-dwellers took for granted.

Her brother's voice came floating up from the floor below and Tally got reluctantly to her feet.

"Tally!" He was still calling her, his voice high and anxious. "Tally! Come quickly!"

"I'm here!" Tally broke into a run, jumping down through the hole in the broken roof to land on the floor below. Inside the palazzo darkness and dust seemed to cover everything. But in one of the once luxurious suites her brother had kindled a fire and the light was like a beacon as she made her way through the dark.

"There you are!" Her twin appeared suddenly from the shadows like a confused mirror image. Her own golden-brown eyes stared back at her from his face, framed by the same auburn hair. "I was scared you weren't coming back."

"Where would I go, Gift?" she asked. "There's nowhere left to run to."

"Then perhaps it's time to stop running," a weak voice said softly and Tally turned to face the bed where her mother lay.

Her name was Harmony and she had been a beautiful woman once. The rich auburn hair she had bequeathed to her children hung limply around her gaunt pale face and the same golden eyes watched them tenderly. But what she retained of her beauty was little enough. The years of fear had worn away at her and sapped her strength until she couldn't go on any longer.

"Mother," Tally said softly, her voice breaking. "How do you feel?"

"No worse, darling." Harmony tried to smile and lifted a thin arm toward her children. "Come here and kiss me."

The twins came to sit on her bed, each taking one of her hands, and Harmony again tried to smile, comforting them as best she could in the little time that remained to her.

"I must talk to you now before it's too late," she began. "There are things you need to know. . . . "

"His name was Theo Freedom and he was the danger we had always feared," the Minister for Propaganda explained. "Listen closely, for this is a story I had never thought I would need to tell.

It begins with the greatest secret of all: of how and why the Hexes were created."

Around the table the assembled dignitaries leaned closer as the Propaganda Minister lowered his voice. Even the President looked around warily, although none knew better than he how safe the security was here at the political heart of the Federation. Past governments had shrouded the events of their rules in secrecy, as did the current administration, and none of them had any direct experience of the Hex threat. The object of their fear fascinated and repelled them as the old man related how a Hex might shake the Federation from its foundations.

"Our ancestors were misguided in their march toward progress. They experimented with genetics and created mutants intended to be a fusion of mind and machine, technological wizards who would guide us into a new age and some day out into the stars."

The Propaganda Minister snorted contemptuously.

"They were fools and dreamers and they thought to play God. It has taken centuries for us to undo their work. They released the Hex gene into the world, wanting to give everyone the 'benefits' of the mutation. They didn't think of the dangers. There is such a thing as too much knowledge. Our society is founded on privacy, there are secrets that must be kept hidden for the good of humanity."

The President of the Federation nodded and around the table there were murmurs of assent. All of these political leaders had secrets they wished to hide: abuses of power and privilege and petty injustices against the people they had been elected to serve.

"However, there were some who had doubts, who understood that the Hex gene was an abomination that never should have been allowed to exist, and politicians campaigned strenuously to make the use of the Hex abilities illegal. Once those laws had been passed it was the next logical step to make the mutants themselves illegal, to deprive them of any standing in the Federation. And, of course, when they did not know how to use their abilities it was easy to hunt them down.

"I would not know this tale myself but twenty-five years ago what we feared came to pass. A mutant in full control of his abilities single-handedly waged war against the Federation. Theo Freedom was a scientist, a brilliant young researcher without the slightest suspicion of treason ever attached to him. He had the highest levels of security access and the best laboratory facilities the Federation could provide. We had hoped to use him to create a plague that would wipe out the Hexes forever. But we made a mistake.

"Theo was a Hex himself. A mutant clever enough to hide his true nature from everyone who knew him. For five years he studied the Hex gene and the Hex abilities and *taught himself how to use them.*"

The Propaganda Minister paused and looked significantly around the table. Charles Alverstead, the head of the CPS, shuddered. Keeping the Hexes from ever understanding their abilities had been the purpose of the Federation government for generations. Now he feared that the elusive Raven, the Hex he had captured and lost, was as great a threat as Theo Freedom had ever been. He had seen Raven himself. She had seemed barely more than a child and her black eyes had regarded him with a cool disdain as if she had known even then she would escape him. If a child Hex could evade the forces of the Federation government for so long and incite rebellion against the government, what more could she achieve when she was an adult?

"We had no knowledge of this, of course," the Propaganda Minister was saying. "We found out too late that Theo had not only studied the Hex gene but had passed on the knowledge to his son, who also carried the mutation. When a suspicious lab assistant reported that Theo Freedom was using the laboratory to carry out unusual tests on himself and his family we sent a team to investigate. Theo was captured and interrogated but his son had disappeared and not even under torture would he confess the young man's whereabouts.

"More importantly," and here the Minister's creaky voice sank to a whisper, "Theo's research had also disappeared. Enough data to write a book about the Hexes was copied to disk the day his son vanished and neither it nor he have ever been located.

"There have been false leads and suspicions but the son was never captured. Our only hope is that he is dead and the information he carries lost forever. We have no way to combat an active Hex, and with Theo Freedom's research a Hex could destroy us."

"And so your grandfather gave the files to your father and when he sacrificed himself so that we could escape, your father gave them to me."

Harmony coughed raspingly and Tally hurriedly filled a glass of water and held it to her lips.

"Thank you," she whispered, after she had sipped a little of it, and she tightened her grip on her children's hands. "I have never shared your abilities but I have held the files in trust for you so that some day you might learn to understand them. I never thought that we'd be running so long that there would be no time to even teach you the basics. I hoped we'd find some place safe where I could teach you how to use the knowledge the files contained. Your father named you in hope that eventually the Hex gene would be recognized, not as a mutation, but as something to be treasured: a Gift, a Talent . . ."

The twins looked at each other. Their mother's story had filled them with longing for the father they had barely known and the grandfather they had never met. Tally voiced both of their thoughts when she asked:

"But what should we *do* with them? Can we learn to use them on our own?"

"Perhaps you don't have to do it alone," her mother said softly. "Two years ago terrorists attacked the Federation. A Hex escaped from the Federation Consulate in England. Just as your grandfather did, Hexes are again trying to strike against the Federation and his knowledge will help them to succeed."

"Terrorists?" Tally asked dubiously but Gift interrupted her.

"We've been running from Federation troops all our lives," he said fiercely. "If this gives us a chance to strike back we should take it. We've never even used our abilities but the government would kill us if they knew what we are. If these other Hexes understand the files they can use them to protect all of us."

"I hope so," Harmony said quietly. "I wish I could keep you safe myself, my children. I don't want to leave you alone." Her eyes closed and an expression of pain crossed her face.

"We'll be all right, Mother," Tally said quickly, pretending a confidence she didn't feel to comfort her mother. "We know what we have to do." She looked at Gift for confirmation and he nodded.

"We'll make you proud," he assured. "Don't worry about us."

Tally turned to look at her twin. They were both on the brink of tears but neither of them cried. The journey ahead consumed too much of their thoughts. The road before them was long and dangerous and neither of them was sure how to begin.

2
BEGOTTEN
OF THE DEAD

Drow didn't arrive back in Chrome territory until night had fallen.
To a rival ganger the lonely streets decorated with Chrome symbols
and colors would have seemed threatening but to him they were
home and he felt himself relaxing. After he'd made his way through
Ghost territory, mercifully unchallenged by the mysterious gang,
he'd almost run into a Seccie patrol and he'd lain low again,
crouching in the shelter of the bridge while skimmers hummed
past, waiting for the cover of night to bring him safely home.

Now he threaded his way through his own streets, still carrying
the disks he had lifted, eager to show his haul to his family. The route
he was following brought him into a wide plaza and two shadowy
figures stepped out in front of him. Drow tensed but relaxed almost
immediately. The two men wore Chrome colors and the silver
threaded into their braids shone faintly in the flickering lighting.

"It's Drow," he said quickly and added the password. "Chrome untarnished."

"Drow!" One of the men moved forward into the light and Drow recognized Innuru, his sister's husband. "You've been gone too long. The family was concerned."

"I ran into some Seccie trouble," Drow explained, proud to look so calm about it in front of the older gangers. "I had to cut through Ghost turf to get back."

Innuru looked surprised for a moment, then he grinned.

"Brave boy," he said, putting an arm around Drow's shoulder. "Come home and tell us about it. Your sister was worried."

The other ganger disappeared back into the shadows and Innuru and Drow headed toward the building their family had claimed as a home. As they passed through the familiar passageway and heard the sound of music thumping from further inside the building Drow fumbled in his jacket for the disks. There were ten of them, carefully slotted into the plain black case marked with the logo of the Fractured Image datastore.

"Lifted some disks," Drow said casually. "New programs straight off the rack: access programs and encryption algorithms for the net."

Now Innuru did look impressed and he whistled softly as he looked over the disks.

"Your father will be pleased—" he was saying as they entered the main room and the rest of his words were cut off as Electra instantly ran to take Drow in her arms.

As he assured his sister he was all right, Drow looked around the room. His family had obviously been worried. His father was looking up with a smile of relief from his work table, loaded as usual with half-finished circuitry, and his other sisters, Selver and Arachne, looked equally relieved.

"Drow had some problems with Seccies," Innuru said darkly and Drow's father scowled. "But he got us some disks with electric programs, pure gold dust."

As Electra released him, saying she would find him something to eat, Drow basked in the approval of his family as his father carefully unpacked the disk case and commented on the haul.

"You've a good eye," he said with a pleased expression. "You couldn't have picked a better selection. There are programs here that won't be on the net for weeks."

Drow's heart sang and he could barely wait to connect to the net to see the programs in action. But Electra fussed over him relentlessly until he sat down and ate the dinner she dialed from the Nutromac unit. Electra watched him to stop him from bolting his food but he was still finished quickly and his father beckoned him to the row of computer terminals at the side of the room and handed him two of the disks.

"See what you can get out of these," he suggested. "But don't do too much tonight. We have plenty of time."

Drow barely heard him. The terminal drew him with an irresistible fascination. As his hands played the keypad like a musical instrument he could feel himself sinking into the trancelike state the net always caused in him. His father said he had a natural talent for hacking but Drow suspected it was more than that. He couldn't describe the feeling he had when he was connected but he imagined that flying must feel something like it. He soared with the net and it lifted and carried him through its endless data pathways.

The net hummed with life like a city and Drow sped along its familiar pathways. On his own he could only travel so far. The net seemed to multiply the deeper he wandered, every junction or turning offering a dazzling multiplicity of choices, but now the access program he carried with him navigated the virtual city and remembered the path he had taken, so that looking back he could see the route he had taken laid out as a silver vein through all the twists and turns of the moving datastreams. The network was a shining place this evening: a phantom city exuding light and life, in contrast to the shadows that lurked in the physical reality. But as Drow traveled its pathways he could feel shadows in the net as well. There had always been darkened places where access was restricted or the flow of information slowed. But tonight he could feel a darkness as a tangible presence clouding the edge of his perceptions. It hung around the edge of the network as the night did around London, fogging the edges of the furthest datastreams, swirling through the remotest nodes like a contagion and never settling anywhere for long.

Puzzled, Drow paused in his exploration. Then cautiously he extended his perceptions, feeling for the darkness. It lurked in the distance and, relaxing, Drow flew toward it. The sense of wrongness it gave him was his only guide as the moving flows of data buffeted him in different directions like air currents. Then, all of a sudden, he had fallen through space to the heart of the darkness and the life of the net seemed lightyears away. Everything was dead here and silent but he could feel the black fog, of which he was now a part, reaching out tendrils to still the heartbeat of the city.

> **where am i?** < he wondered, not expecting an answer. But his question rang back to him from every direction like a tormented echo unable to stop.

> **where? where . . . ? where . . . ? am i? where am i? where am i? am i am i am i am i am?** <

He tried to screen out the endless repetitions and eventually felt them dying away, the words descending into meaninglessness as they receded further and further into the gloom. Confused, he tried again, more carefully.

> **what/where is this?—everything is dark/dead/lifeless— why—?** <

This time the echoes rang in his head like a scream and he was no longer sure if they even were echoes.

> **darkness . . . darkness . . . where? where? darkness . . . dark/ dead/dark down in the darkness of death . . . where . . . w . . . h . . . e . . . r . . . e . . . ? we here? hear? darkness . . . death . . .** <

Drow pulled himself away. Somewhere in the dark there was a glimmer of consciousness and as the echoes rang on and on, the words melding with each other to become a speechless wail of despair, a shiver crossed his mind. Someone else was here in the net with him and they were insane. The darkness was the shreds of their mind.

He steeled himself for another attempt at communication but then froze where he was, hanging in virtual space at the center of the cloud. It was searching for him, he could feel it. Tracing his position by the thoughts or echoes of thoughts he had set off. Without him to begin the pattern it could barely think, but like a giant amoeba searching for a brain it was hunting him with the words it had stolen from him.

> **where? where? where? am i/you? i am? where????** <

Wrenching himself away, he threw his mind out of the dark wildly, spinning in all directions, thinking only to get away. Until his consciousness came to rest in a river of light: a vast datastream flowing through the electronic maze and soothing him with its murmuring data until he came to shore at a node he recognized and, half-dazed, found the current that carried him home.

Disengaging himself from the terminal, he shuddered and manually ordered the program to forget the location it had mapped for that dark cloud. Whatever it was, he wanted no part of it or its images of darkness and death. Although he didn't know what it was there was something he was sure of. Darkness and death were parts of its nature. It had fed on them and made them part of itself. As he wiped the record of the cloud from his terminal he wondered with a shudder how such a thing had ever penetrated the net.

It was late at night when Ali finally stopped working. Wraith had been adamant that the Hex children weren't to be housed together, the way orphans had been in the asylum blockhouse where he and Raven had grown up. Each adult in the community had to take the responsibility of caring for one of the children, he had said, and despite some hitches the plan had worked well. Some of the Ghosts didn't have the time to spare to care for a child and Raven had flatly refused. But others were prepared to look after two or three and the result was a thriving community of unconventional family groups in which each child had at least one "parent" to look after them. However, it meant that Ali, Kez, and Luciel had to make sure that every single one of them was collected at the end of the day. Since the Ghosts were scattered through several enclaves across the city, that meant making several flitter trips, each time evading any Seccie patrols. Ali had become skilled at piloting a flitter, but by the time her shift was over she felt ready to collapse.

She went through the routine security checks on autopilot as she guided the flitter into the Fortress: the building Raven had purchased from the Countess to be their center of operations. Despite the strangeness of the arrangement she had never felt comfortable with moving away from the living space she shared with the other members of the original group. As she made her way up to the suite of rooms that she had designed Ali found herself wondering how long she would continue to call the Fortress home. Working for the group had been the focus of her life so much recently that she didn't often think about the future. Things had changed so much for her that the Fortress was the only real stability she knew and she was nervous of losing it.

Upstairs the sound of music filled the air, Avalon's voice mingling with a blend of multiple melodies that seemed to burn their way into her brain. As she entered the main living area the music died away and Avalon looked up, smiling. She was plainly dressed, her flame of red hair tied back in a long braid, but she still looked exotic, surrounded by a web of wiring connecting her and her guitar to a cluster of electronic devices.

"Hi," Ali said, flopping lifelessly into one of the chairs. "I hope I'm not disturbing you?"

"No." Avalon shook her head. "I'm just fooling about. Nothing serious yet."

"You're sounding good though," Ali replied, trying to persuade her tired mind to say something intelligent about the music. "It's haunting, as if I've remembered it before I've heard it. . . ."

Avalon looked thoughtful and she picked out a few chords on her guitar before replying.

"Maybe you have," she said slowly. "Raven's idea was for me to try to portray the Hex abilities in music. Teaching the blind to see, she called it."

"That's it." Ali nodded. "It sounds like that's what you've done."

"Not just me." Avalon shook her head. "Raven wrote some of the lyrics."

"She did?" Ali's surprise was echoed by another voice overlapping with hers from the doorway and she turned to see Wraith, looking almost as tired as she felt. "I had no idea," he said, frowning a little. "Is this for the disk you're going to release to the underground?"

"That's right." Avalon fingered a few more chords silently. "A sequel to 'Transformations.' Of course, the record company would sue me if they could, but being hunted by the government is no reason to stop making music."

"I didn't realize you were going to release it," Ali said, feeling herself waking up a little. "Whose idea was that?"

"Cloud's," Wraith explained. "He said Avalon may as well make the best of being a pariah and use her skills to the advantage of the group. The plan is to release it over the net and use Avalon's popularity to promote our cause."

"It's a good idea," Ali agreed. "But I'm surprised Raven's involved." She felt a flash of an old jealousy as she added: "I didn't realize she could write lyrics."

"I don't know if that's what I'd call them," Avalon said thoughtfully. "But you know how Raven talks, as if she's descending from another sphere where they communicate differently. I asked her what she thought about Hexes and wrote down what she said. It seemed to work."

"When are you releasing it?" Wraith asked and Avalon shrugged.

"Soon, I think," she said. "I've recorded all the tracks. Raven said she'd release it when the time seemed most auspicious, but that could mean anything."

"Where is Raven?" Wraith asked, glancing about the room as if he expected her to suddenly appear.

Ali and Avalon both shrugged. Aside from teaching sessions and mission briefings, Ali didn't see very much of Raven anyway. She didn't think anyone did.

Raven was at Dragon's Nest. The old Anglecynn base was in the depths of the city and because of its gloomy position in the heart of

London's darkness, half-buried under the fragmentary detritus of the hundreds of levels above, it was the safest of the Ghost enclaves. Nowadays few people lived there. It was a base for what had once been Anglecynn's administrative staff: those people who preferred to fight for freedom from behind the lines. The rambling buildings had become the security center for the Ghosts. Every piece of data picked up from the surveillance tech, with which Raven had decorated every Ghost enclave in the city, ended up here; it was studied, discussed, reported on, and filed.

It was also here, in the old meeting room, that Alaric had chosen to discuss his plan to sabotage the Security Services' communications network. He, Geraint, Jordan, Raven, and Cloud sat on the ancient furniture, drinking coffee from a damaged Nutromac and discussing how to strike against the security arm of the Federation.

"The real problem as I see it," Alaric explained, "is that the Seccies don't get their orders from a single source."

"Surely they do?" Jordan looked confused. "Seccies are responsible to the Minister for Internal Security, just as Fed Troopers are responsible to the Minister for Peace. Orders from Versailles in both cases."

"The Minister just formulates policy," Geraint objected. "Actual orders come from the civil service, they're just as culpable when considering Seccie crimes."

"I thought we were considering communications," Cloud pointed out and earned himself a narrow look from Geraint but Alaric continued as if none of the interruptions had occurred.

"Policy comes from Versailles and so do direct orders," he said. "But all actual communications travel a variety of routes through the net. It's not possible to stop messages getting through when they fly night and day, twenty-four hours. Seccies in England are connected to the rest of Europe. We make a move and their best minds are on to us."

"Surely the Hexes are an immense advantage?" Jordan said, looking anxiously toward Raven who had not spoken yet and was watching the byplay with unreadable obsidian eyes.

"An advantage when there are enough of them, maybe," Alaric said slowly. "But at the moment, forgive me, Raven, there just aren't enough. We have to bypass increasingly sophisticated security to find out the CPS execution dates, which doesn't leave much time to keep watch on the Seccies and still less to strike back against them." He looked ruefully at Raven. "I know *you* can hack any system ever created," he said. "But there's only one of you."

"An indubitable fact," Raven agreed. "Cut to the chase, Alaric. What are you suggesting?"

"You know more about the data network than I do," Alaric said with a shrug. "But if there was some way to cut the communications line between Versailles and London the Seccies here would be blind and stumbling. No orders. No arrests."

Raven drummed her fingers on the side of her chair, thinking. The others looked at her hopefully. It was a look she was coming to recognize. These people came up with ideas but as usual they relied upon her to implement them. To them she was a sorceress, her capabilities a mystery, and the thought of her failing was impossible. It was a look Kez had given her when the CPS had captured them: behind the fear an absolute certainty that she would survive. Raven accepted it but she didn't encourage it. She relied on no one and it was independence she respected. But Alaric's idea was promising and her mind was already constructing a plan.

"The net is our problem as much as theirs," she mused aloud. "While their communications are always vulnerable to a Hex, the network is so vast a mesh that we can't control enough of it. Revenge burnt out when she tried to control just the section in this city and EF communications span the world."

Alaric nodded, thinking of the net stretched across the world like prison bars—controlling information, money, and politics. "It's colossal," he said. "And they can send messages anywhere."

"Anywhere," Raven echoed. "But—"

"But?" Jordan was grinning admiringly, certain that Raven had an idea, and dark eyes turned to meet hers with an amused glint.

"But . . . ," she continued, "there is a stop every message from the EF makes, no matter where it's coming from or going to."

The others looked blank but Cloud was frowning thoughtfully. "The orbitals!" he exclaimed suddenly and turned to Raven for confirmation. She was smiling.

"Data doesn't travel along roads," she said. "It flies. Bounces off the earth and back thousands of times a second across the orbital satellite network."

"How many satellites are there?" Jordan asked, wide-eyed.

"About five hundred," Geraint replied automatically. "Different sizes and specifications, naturally."

"But all those satellites are controlled from one place," Raven reminded him.

"The EF Space Operations Center," Cloud added, and they all paused for thought.

"It's brilliant," Alaric said finally. "The EF aren't interested in space—the drive for the stars was abandoned over a hundred years ago as uneconomical. The American continent tried for a little longer but not much came of it. Some mining projects was all and then their program shut down as well."

"No one considers space," Geraint agreed. "I hadn't even thought of it myself. But you're right. Everything goes through the satellites and Space Ops controls them."

"There are problems though," Raven pointed out, bringing them all back to reality. "The Space Center is a shielded system. High security. And the computers that control the satellites aren't linked to the net. They function differently."

"We'd have to go there," Alaric said slowly and Raven nodded.

"To Transcendence," she said softly. "That's where it is."

"Transcendence?" Cloud raised an eyebrow. "That won't be easy."

Raven didn't answer him, her mind was already miles away. Transcendence: the European megaplex, the largest city in the world. A sprawling conglomerate of finance and politics where EF law ruled every inch of its gleaming spires and snaking corridors. In Transcendence artifice ruled; nothing was left to nature and everything came under the all-seeing eye of the electronic cyclops, constantly under surveillance by Seccies. But the thought of it drew her irresistibly. It was the triumph of the information age and, to her, the ultimate challenge.

It was almost dawn by the time Raven left Dragon's Nest. They had stayed up for hours discussing possible ways of getting to Transcendence but had finally adjourned, knowing that nothing could be decided before other senior members of the group had been consulted. As Raven and Cloud headed out of the room Jordan caught them up and touched Raven's arm lightly.

"Do you have a few more minutes?" she asked hopefully. "A security matter."

"A few minutes won't make much difference," Raven replied. "What is it?"

"We had a minor alert earlier today," Jordan explained, leading them toward the vast observational room. Vidscreens were mounted on every wall, currently showing nighttime views of the city. "A ganger kid wandered through one of the Ghost enclaves. Nothing major. But he could have been a scout for a serious incursion."

"Doubtful," Raven replied. "But show me anyway."

Jordan touched some keys on one of the terminals and a large vidscreen brightened, showing a display of a Ghost enclave on the edge of ganger territory.

"Kez called it in," Jordan explained. "There they are now."

Raven and Cloud watched silently as the small figures of Ali and Kez walked down an abandoned street. Neither of them looked at the surveillance cameras, absorbed in their own discussion. Then another figure appeared, dressed in black and silver, moving cautiously across the level.

"Give me a close-up," Raven said and Jordan expanded the image to focus on the boy's face. Silver eyes turned to regard the watchers and Jordan whispered:

"He looked directly at several of the surveillance devices. Remember it was a policy that some should be made obvious for intimidation purposes?"

"Good-looking kid," Raven commented, the blend of human and machine appealing to her.

"There seems to be a computer terminal nesting in his hair," Cloud said dryly and Jordan grinned.

"I asked some of the people here if they could ID him," she said. "One of the Snakes said he looked like a Chrome. Have you heard of them?"

Raven shook her head. For the most part gangers didn't interest her. Their posturing and struggles for dominance bored her and she had no need for the sense of group identity they offered.

"I've heard of the Chromes," Cloud said, to their surprise. "They're a hacker gang somewhere in the middle levels."

"How would you know that?" Raven asked curiously and Cloud smiled.

"All megastars have their vices, don't they? Mine was holocam tech. I bought some items on the black market a few years back from the Chromes."

"Did they work?" Raven asked, a thoughtful look in her dark eyes.

"Like a dream," Cloud told them. "Had to leave it all behind though."

"Interesting." Raven turned back to the vidcam still. "What else does he do?"

"After he looked around for a while he got scared and ran off," Jordan told her, keying the image into motion so they could watch the boy's flight across the level. "What do you think?"

"I think you were right to disregard it as a threat," Raven replied. "But it's interesting nonetheless. I think I may have occasion to find out more about this gang."

Looking consideringly at the vidcam she regarded the Chrome boy with an almost avaricious expression. She smiled to herself as she added:

"It's been a long time since I met a hacker who wasn't a Hex."

3

FLED INTO
THE WILDERNESS

Tally awoke a little before dawn. Last night they had given her mother's dead body to the sea. Now she sat on the roof and watched the remorseless waves lapping against the palazzo as if trying to claim her and Gift as well. The rising sun stained the sky a bloody red, bruised streaks of light emanating from one glowing point in a velvety dark night. Turning her back on it, she looked northwest, toward England. It seemed like an impossible journey through the heart of the Federation's power. Gift was confident they would make it but Tally had doubts. Sometimes when she closed her eyes she could feel the data net in the air. Strands of information stretching like tentacles to encompass the world. But she couldn't touch it or control it, and without that ability it would find her and destroy her.

She shivered at the thought of it, huddling deeper into her blanket and heard Gift speak behind her.

"You shouldn't come out here so early if you're cold."

"I'm not cold. I'm worried," she corrected him. "I'm concerned about this journey we've got to make. This journey which we have no idea how to start."

"Don't be so negative," Gift reprimanded her. "Look what I've found." She turned to look and saw him extending a small silver case toward her. "I found it last night," he said, lowering his voice to a whisper despite the deserted city.

Tally touched an almost hidden catch on the side of the case and it slid open to reveal a single computer disk, held in place by two clips. It didn't look particularly special but Gift was gazing at it with a kind of reverence.

"It's useless if we can't access it," she pointed out and her twin frowned, snatching the case back.

"It's our legacy," he objected. "Weren't you listening last night? With this we can rule the world."

"I don't want to rule the world!" Tally objected fiercely. "I want to be a normal kid who goes to school and has parents and doesn't have to run halfway across Europe because people want to kill me for a power I don't even know how to use!"

Realizing that her voice was rising to a shriek, she clapped a hand over her mouth and stopped speaking. For a few moments Gift said nothing. Then he put an arm around her gently.

"It's OK," he said soothingly. "We'll find a way. Come on, Tally. You're as smart as I am and I need you to help me. This is something we have to do. Help me think of how to do it."

Tally resisted the urge to snap that she'd thought he had it all planned out. She knew that he had lied to their mother as much as she had, pretending a confidence neither of them felt so that Harmony could die in peace. But now she had never felt so alone and she stayed silent for a while as she gathered the energy to begin again.

The sun rose slowly while Tally thought. They had been hiding for most of their lives in abandoned cities or in the few wildernesses left in the technological age. Ignorant of the secret history behind their flight, they had known only that they were hunted. Through those long years Gift had fueled his rage against the Federation and vowed many times to strike back in revenge for the death of their father, murdered by Seccies while Harmony had escaped with the twins. But Tally only felt weary and she wondered where she would find the strength to obey her mother's last wishes. The Hexes in England seemed immeasurably distant and she didn't even know if they had the knowledge to help them. But with that thought suddenly her muddle of ideas resolved themselves.

"If these other Hexes can help us when we get to England perhaps they can aid us before then," she said slowly. Gift looked confused.

"How?" he asked. "They don't even know we exist yet."

"Yes, but we could tell them," Tally replied. "If we can access a computer terminal we could send them a message. Tell them who we are and that we need their help."

"But we don't know who they are," Gift said, shaking his head. "It's a good idea but I can't see how it would work, Tally."

"Mother said a Hex could set their mind free in the net. That we have the ability to send our consciousness into the data network. If we were to do that—"

"We might find one of them!" Gift said, completing her thought. "Tally, that's brilliant!"

"It won't be easy." Tally mused. "We'll have to get access to a terminal first and figure out how to use it. But it'll be a lot easier than trying to cross Europe on our own and it might just work."

"We should go to Padua," Gift said decisively. "It's the nearest city and we'll be able to find a terminal there."

"But we'll have to be careful," Tally said firmly. "If anyone were to find out about the disk we'd be in greater danger than ever before."

It was late in the morning when Ali woke up to the sound of her vidcom chiming and the realization that she had overslept. Stumbling out of bed, she found the key to activate the unit and blinked sleepily as Luciel's face appeared on the screen.

"Late night?" he asked sympathetically.

"Yeah," Ali said, rubbing the sleep from her eyes. "Is it me or are Seccie patrols getting more common?"

Luciel laughed as he replied. "You're not spending enough time with Alaric, obviously," he said. "He's been talking about nothing else for weeks. According to Jordan he had a meeting with Raven last night about what to do about it."

"I heard he had some kind of plan," Ali admitted. "But I didn't know it had anything to do with Raven."

"Everything has something to do with Raven," Luciel pointed out. "Like today's mission for instance. The one you're running late for?"

"Mission," Ali frowned, trying to remember what was on her schedule for today.

"The extraction?" Luciel prompted. "Another game of beat the Seccies to the Hex?"

"Right," Ali said, remembering. "Sorry. How late am I?"

"Seeing as Raven has yet to put in an appearance you can have a whole ten minutes to suit up," Luciel said with a grin. "See ya soon."

The vidcam image dissolved into black and Ali hunted through her closet for her combat fatigues. Once she would have taken hours getting dressed in the morning, designing her outfits to conform exactly to the current dictates of fashion. Now she struggled into the loose fatigues without a second thought, scraping her hair back with a hasty plait, and holstering the regulation issue blaster. Catching a glimpse of herself in the mirror as she headed out the door she grinned, imagining what her old clique of popular pretty friends would say if they could see her now.

She ran down the stairs and emerged in the main room of the building just in time to add herself to the end of the line for equipment checks. Luciel was conducting the check-through, and as Ali waited for her turn, she glanced down the line to see who else was part of the extraction team. There were more and more Ghosts she didn't recognize. But Daniel grinned at her from halfway down the line and Ali smiled back. Daniel had joined the group through

Anglecynn, voluntarily throwing away a life of luxury for his principles and giving enough government secrets to the terrorists to
ensure that he could never go back. Ali liked him partly because
their backgrounds were so similar. No matter how close she had
become to the other Ghosts she still sometimes felt adrift in the
urban wastelands many of them had come from.

Her attention was called back when Luciel came to a halt in
front of her and she quickly offered her weapon for inspection.
The equipment checks were for their own safety and had quickly
become part of the established routine after the Hexes had joined
up with Anglecynn. The terrorist faction had changed the character of the group by bringing a military precision to arrangements
that made this extraction seem like routine.

Also routine was the fact that Raven was late. She appeared
in the flitter bay just as Luciel pronounced the check complete,
dressed in black as usual with equipment of different shapes and
sizes tucked into the voluminous pockets of her loose overcoat.
Luciel didn't ask to check her equipment and Ali didn't expect him
to. Raven was a law unto herself where regulations were concerned
and no one was willing to push the point. Not even acknowledging
their presence, her dark eyes unreadable as usual, Raven slung herself into the pilot's seat and turned to glare at the other members
of the team.

"Well?" she demanded. "What are you waiting for?"

"Nothing," Luciel replied quickly, answering for all of them
and hurrying the group forward into the flitter. "Let's get moving, people." He turned to Raven to add: "The CPS haven't picked

up on this one yet so it should be easy in and out."

Raven only grunted in reply, and making haste to get into the flitter, Ali realized with a jab of discomfort that as the last to board she had been left with the unenviable position of sitting next to Raven. Swallowing her misgivings she strapped herself into the seat, knowing Raven's reputation as a pilot too well for comfort. The black-haired Hex was already powering up the streamlined flying craft as its doors hissed shut and, without any signal from the team, the main doors of the Fortress opened in perfect synchronicity.

Ali glanced quickly at the younger Hex. One thin pale hand was resting on the control panel of the flitter, the other was drumming impatiently on the armrest as the bay doors opened slowly to their full extent. Raven used her abilities casually and, despite her obvious bad mood, the team relaxed slightly. An extraction mission, no matter how routine, was often tricky but Raven's presence lent them confidence. To many of the Ghosts, especially the newcomers, she was already a legend. Ali had heard Kez telling some of the younger children stories that made it sound as if Raven had single-handedly saved every Hex in the group and beaten half the Federation army while doing it.

"It's harmless," Luciel had said when she objected. "Regardless of her flaws, Raven has achieved more than any of us. Seeing her as a legend encourages people and we should use every advantage we have."

Ali hadn't pursued the subject any further, not wanting to appear jealous. But, looking at Raven now, she wondered if she had been wrong not to continue the argument. Raven looked immeasurably distant, her mind linked to the net, and for the first time Ali wondered if Raven had become so much of a legend that she was no longer real to any of them.

A sudden jolt threw her back into her seat as the flitter took off, Raven judging the moment perfectly so that the aerial craft swooped through the bay doors with only an inch of clearance and shot out into the ganglands. Ali heard a couple of muffled exclamations in the back of the flitter, probably from team members who had never experienced the way Raven drove before. Used to the dizzying speed, she tried to relax and concentrate on the mission ahead as Luciel ran through the mission brief one last time.

"We'll be going to a closed community in the heights called Fairseat," Luciel explained. "There won't be much Seccie surveillance because it has its own security for all the VIPs who live there but we will have to evade them once we're inside."

"How are we getting inside?" a team member Ali didn't recognize asked and Luciel replied:

"The plan is to go through the service entrance."

Ali frowned at that. She'd lived in a similar complex until a few years ago and it wasn't as if the place had been swarming with service personnel. Even if it had been, she reflected, they wouldn't have looked much like the team she was with now. It was too late to raise objections but if she'd been in charge of the mission she would have made more of an effort to construct a team that could blend into the background in the milieu of the ultra-rich.

"Our target is a twelve-year-old Hex named Charis Weaver," Luciel was continuing. "And if her family's movements are consistent, she'll be in today and her parents won't be. Should be easy, like I said."

"Well, stop saying it," Raven cut in suddenly. "I'm not working with a team that thinks an extraction is a breeze, you scan?"

"Sure, Raven," Luciel said in a mollifying tone. "I understand."

"You had better," Raven added and glanced across at Ali as if to enforce her command. But Ali had no disagreement with the order and met the black eyes seriously. They regarded her searchingly for a moment and then, to Ali's surprise, returned to the view ahead without Raven saying anything.

The rest of the team had fallen silent and they remained so as Raven guided the flitter up through the levels of the city and settled down to a slow cruising speed as they reached the heights. As they approached a five-level high complex faced in gleaming white stone and surrounded by gated walls, Ali had a sense of foreboding. Most of the extractions she had been on had been from poorer areas of the city. This castlelike edifice was an entirely different proposition. Fairseat was truly a closed community, without the usual conduits and grav-tubes for people and vehicles to enter from the levels above and below. Instead, the complex rested on a huge flat expanse of gleaming plazas and gardens and was closed off at the top of its levels by a similar shining ceiling. No natural light would penetrate into this community but Ali somehow doubted that the inhabitants considered that a priority. They lived in the heights for the prestige of the location, not to be closer to the sun.

Raven cruised around the side of the complex and then moved away again, circling up and around to the next level. Ali could hear random clinks and jingles as the team adjusted their weapons and equipment. Then, as lightly as a feather, the flitter touched down at the side of a graceful archway and Raven cut the power.

"We're here," she said quietly. "The service exit is just behind this arch."

The doors slid open with a soft sigh from the hydraulics. The level they were on was almost deserted and the team climbed out quietly, wary of disturbing the peace. Luciel ushered them around the side of the bridge as Raven keyed the flitter's security system on, and following the rest of the team, Ali came to a halt in front of a large metal door. It had no obvious lock and she wondered how they were expected to get in, but Raven, appearing behind her, gave a low laugh.

"Computer-controlled," she said with a wry smile. "Lucky for us they don't learn." She looked at Ali for a moment and then at Luciel. "One of you want to give it a go?"

"I don't think so," Ali said quickly and Raven raised an eyebrow ironically.

"Luciel?" she asked and the boy stepped forward, placing the palm of his hand against the door.

"Good," Raven acknowledged. "Now feel the circuitry. It runs through the entire door and leads back to a controlling security system. Follow the flow of current back to the system and order the door to open."

Luciel closed his eyes and the rest of the team watched silently as they waited for him. He was biting his lips, his expression anxious as he attempted to feel his way to the net: a skill that Raven had attempted to teach all of them but without much success. Finally he broke away from the door and opened his eyes.

"It's no good," he said, shaking his head. "I can't reach it"

"Very well," said Raven expressionlessly. "Move out of the way."

Reaching toward the door she rested her fingertips on it lightly. The rest of the team held their breath and almost instantaneously there was an audible click and the door swung open.

"Why didn't she do that in the first place?" someone muttered behind Ali and was rapidly hushed.

"Come on," Luciel said, to cover the moment of awkwardness. "Let's go." Then, leading the way, he entered the long curving tunnel ahead of them. Ali trailed behind the rest of the team, last except for Raven who closed the door behind her. The dark-haired girl regarded her in the dim light.

"You should have tried," she said.

"If I spent my life learning how, I could still never do what you do," Ali replied, keeping her voice low. "You know that."

For a few moments there was silence, broken only by the sound of the team trooping down the corridor. Then Raven spoke, her voice almost a whisper.

"If the responsibility for failure isn't yours, it's your teacher's," she said softly. "And I don't want it."

Then, like a shadow, she moved ahead in the line, disappearing down into the darkness ahead where Ali could no longer see her.

There was an elevator at the end of the corridor and Luciel was able to summon it by fiddling with the keypad that controlled it.

"This leads down to the ventilation system," he explained.

"And the kid's sure to be wandering around the ventilation system," Ali muttered under her breath and received a sharp look from Raven.

"You see a flaw with the plan?" she asked softly, as they crowded into the elevator.

"I hope not," Ali replied quietly, reluctant to say anything but convinced that if there was a problem Raven should know about it. Leaning closer to Raven so the others wouldn't hear she continued, "This kind of complex doesn't like to have a lot of staff wandering about. They like to be served invisibly and from a distance. And security looks really tight here."

She looked at Raven, half hoping the other girl would tell her she was wrong but she had narrowed her eyes thoughtfully.

"You may well be right," she murmured. "But stay chill." Then she moved away and rested a hand on the side of the elevator car, her eyes glazing over as she sank into communion with whatever computer system was controlling it. Ali watched her anxiously, hoping that Raven would know what to do if they did run into trouble. Luciel was a good team leader but he didn't have Raven's experience or her inventiveness, and despite her uncomfortable relationship with the younger Hex, Raven had saved both their lives with her skill before.

The elevator touched down and the doors slid open, revealing an empty room. The team fanned out around it and Luciel moved to the door and opened it cautiously, one hand on his stun gun.

"It's clear," he said and the others moved to join him.

The room beyond was obviously a control room—banks of terminals were set into the walls at intervals and screens showed complicated readouts, which Ali assumed pertained to the ventilation system. A single grav-tube led down into the complex itself. The room was dominated by one large window and she moved to it instinctively.

Taking a look outside, her throat clenched with alarm and she looked back at the others, still inspecting the terminals.

"Raven?" she said. "Come and look at this."

The other girl moved to join her at the window and together they looked down on the Fairseat community. It was like a miniature city, bringing back memories for Ali of the Belgravia Complex in which she had grown up. White buildings flowed into each other in a stylish architectural design, linked by balconies and walkways softened with a cascade of greenery. Slender trees grew up from the floor, five levels below, and almost reached the ceiling.

"Remind you of home, Ali?" Daniel said suddenly from behind them. "Looks so restful, doesn't it?"

"Yes, it does," Ali admitted. But the anxiety hadn't left her and she was watching Raven for a response.

"Luciel," Raven said, summoning the boy over from the other side of the room. "Tell me again where our target lives."

"Westview Tower," he replied, coming over to join them at the window. "Second level." He looked out across the complex, orienting himself. "Just over there," he added, waving an arm to indicate one of the white skyscraper sections. "We'll cross that archway and then go in through that portico."

"You have to be kidding," Ali blurted out. "We'll be seen!"

"There's plenty of cover," Luciel replied, pointing out the trees beneath them. "And we'll be moving fast."

"We'll be dead meat," Raven said and Ali sighed in relief that the other Hex agreed with her.

"What do you mean?" Luciel protested and Raven turned to face him.

"Even if we're not seen by a single human being, this kind of complex has surveillance specifically intended to prevent strangers from breaking in. The second a vidcam sees us we'll be locked in and it will take all the firepower we have to blast our way out again.

"Should we go back then?" Daniel asked.

Raven thought for a moment and the others watched her expectantly. Even Luciel knew that if Raven didn't want to continue there would be no point in carrying on without her. Finally the Hex shook her head.

"No, we can go on," she said. "But carefully. And only a few of us."

"What about the surveillance?" Ali asked and Raven smiled slightly.

"I think I have an idea to prevent it from seeing us," she said. "If it works out it may prove useful in another mission Alaric is planning. Ali, you and Daniel come with me. Luciel, you and the others stay here and start hacking into the system. If there is an alert we'll need you to keep this way out open for us."

"Understood," Luciel replied. "Good luck then."

Raven nodded and then turned to Ali and Daniel.

"Come on," she said and led them toward the grav-tube.

As they descended into the Fairseat complex Raven closed out all external distractions and concentrated on her link to the net. Without touching the security system she could feel it surrounding her like a cage. Invisible eyes watched the complex from all directions and the path they would need to take across it would bring them into full view of the hidden vidcams. Although she could easily block those signals, preventing the cameras from seeing anything but static, that would trigger an alert as much as the sight of their intrusion. So instead she reached for those cameras and concentrated on what they should be seeing. The visual images they transmitted were encoded as data and delicately Raven reached for that datastream. It flowed smoothly and irresistibly toward the security control room for the complex, buried deep in the maze of graceful buildings. With infinite care Raven reached out with her mind toward the net and diverted the path of the stream, bringing it around in a loop and then feeding the loop back to the control room. By the time the grav-tube had touched the floor of the complex the vid-cams were under her control, showing only empty space where they walked: their true transmissions blocked by the loop she had created.

"We'll have to move fast," she said, and her companions nodded their assent.

They crossed the complex like ghosts, unseen by the vid-cams and ducking smoothly out of sight when another human approached. Staying under the cover of the trees they moved toward Westview Tower. As they entered the ornamental portico that concealed the entrance, the doors ahead slid open at Raven's unspoken command and they hurried into the cool confines of the complex. The corridor ahead of them was lavishly decorated with carefully placed ornaments chosen for their expense as much as their beauty. Here they couldn't hide from people and all three of them concealed their weapons, trying to walk as if they belonged there. Raven continued to fool the vidcams but she knew that if one of the passersby raised an alert her work would have been futile. However, although they received a few puzzled looks, no one stopped them and challenged their right to be there. Raven led them unerringly toward the apartment where Charis Weaver lived and within ten minutes they stood outside the door.

"Security system registers one person inside," Raven said. "Young female, twelve years of age, looks like our target."

"Let's go and get her then," Daniel said with relief and Raven keyed the apartment doors open.

They stepped inside to find themselves in a suite of rooms no less lavish than the rest of the complex. A vidscreen in front of them was showing a popular drama Ali vaguely remembered: a vid program about a group of kids who helped Seccies catch criminals. It was not a promising omen and the girl who stood looking at them in the center of the room was even less promising. She was dressed with a casual style that was too perfect to be anything other than expensive and her honey-blonde curls were caught up in an artistically tumbled heap. Her blue eyes were wide as she looked at them but her voice was cool and controlled as she asked:

"What are you doing in my apartment?"

"We've come to rescue you," Daniel began. "We know you're a Hex and we—"

"Well, I don't want to be rescued," the girl told them firmly. "Go away or I'll call security."

"Don't do that!" Daniel exclaimed. "Please, hear me out?"

"Okay," she said slowly. "But don't come near me." To lend emphasis to her words she crossed to the terminal, where she could summon security if she wanted to.

"Raven?" Ali asked quietly, wondering if the other Hex's control over the system was strong enough to prevent the girl from getting a message out.

"Possibly," Raven replied, under her breath, understanding what Ali wanted to know. "But don't expect miracles."

Daniel was trying to stay calm and he extended his hands as unthreateningly as he could toward the kid, showing her that they were empty.

"It's okay," he told her. "We're not here to hurt you, really." He hesitated. "You are Charis Weaver, aren't you?"

"Yes, that's me," the girl replied warily.

"Okay, Charis," Daniel continued. "Look, we want to help you. If the CPS find out you're a Hex, your life will be in danger. But if you come with us you'll be safe."

"I don't want to come with you," Charis told him definitively. "My parents will look after me. I don't need you."

"Charis—" Daniel began, but she was shaking her head vigorously.

"No!" she said, her voice rising slightly. "I don't want to. Just go away!"

Daniel swung around and looked at the others with an expression of helplessness.

"Raven," he said. "You tell her."

"Dammit, Daniel, leave me out of it!" Raven snapped, her eyes flashing black fire. "Just for once don't expect me to solve all the problems. If the kid wants to stay, let her stay. Maybe she'll be safer here. What am I supposed to know about it?"

"Raven!" Daniel's voice was exasperated but Ali stopped him from continuing.

"Be quiet," she told him, her voice unexpectedly firm. "Raven's right. This isn't her problem. It's mine."

4
THE VOICE OF
MANY WATERS

Tally and Gift had traveled the route between Venice and Padua
before—concealed in the back of an ancient skimmer whose owner
had been paid almost all their mother had to transport them with
no questions asked. Now they would have to travel alone, and from
the edge of the massive road Tally watched the traffic pass and
wondered how they would manage it. The skimmer expressway
wound its way through the sleepy Italian countryside like a roaring
monster. Thirty lanes of traffic coiled around each other in a helix
of sound and speed overlooked by the flitter lanes above where tiny
silver specks made a ribbon of light in the sky.

All the possessions the children owned were tied up in a dirty
backpack and Gift carried the precious data disk next to his heart.
No one could see them from the expressway, but even if they had,
two scruffy children would attract no attention. That would be

different in the city where beggars and transients would be stopped and questioned by the local Seccies. Turning away from the monstrous flood of skimmers, Tally looked at Gift.

"This is useless," she said. "We'd better turn away from the expressway and head for one of the smaller country roads. We might find someone willing to give us a lift."

"Mother always said that wasn't safe," Gift objected.

"Well, she's not here to say that now, is she?" Tally snapped. "And how are we expected to cross Europe walking? Last I heard, England is still an island."

"OK, OK," Gift said placatingly. "But let's be careful. Do you have your knife somewhere you can reach it?"

Tally checked the thin blade tucked into a sheath at the side of her boot and adjusted it slightly.

"I have it," she said. "But I hope I don't have to use it."

"On Seccies?" Gift said with a grim smile. "I'll look forward to it."

"And that will make us *so* much better than them," Tally said sarcastically. "Don't joke about killing people, Gift. It isn't funny."

"Maybe I'm not joking," Gift replied, his voice low and dangerous.

Tally sighed, not wanting to get into another argument about it.

"Come on," she said. "Let's go and find another road."

Gift hoisted the backpack and they set off, but as they walked, Tally worried about her brother. She was sure that his hate for the Federation would get him into trouble and she didn't know if she'd be able to help him when it came.

• • •

Ignoring Raven and Daniel, Ali concentrated on the child in front of her. She knew how Charis felt with an empathy that surprised her. None of their other extractions had been this difficult. Most of the time they arrived seconds ahead of the CPS and the children were grateful to be rescued. Sometimes their parents had thanked the Ghosts for taking them, other times they had cursed their children for being mutants. In both cases the parting was difficult but Ali had never encountered a Hex who didn't want to be rescued before. However, looking around the apartment that reminded her so much of her old home, Ali could understand why.

Concentrating her attention on Charis, she tried to focus her thoughts.

"I understand why you don't want to leave," she said. "I used to be just like you. Nothing ever goes wrong here, does it? Within these walls you're perfectly safe."

"Yes, I am," Charis insisted. "I don't even know how you got in here."

"We were able to get in because we are Hexes," Ali said quietly. "And there's no computer system in the world that's safe from us, even the security system of Fairseat."

"Then I'm *not* like you," Charis said, with an expression of relief. "I can't do things like that. I'm just good with computers, that's all. I'm not really a Hex."

"No, you can't do things like that," Ali agreed. "But you are a Hex. In the eyes of the European Federation, the CPS and the

Seccies, you *are* a Hex and you should know what that means as well as we do."

"You think I'll be caught," Charis replied, "but what if I'm not? She said I might be OK." She glanced at Raven nervously.

"Yes, you might be fine," Ali told her. "You might be able to live the rest of your life being perfectly safe within these walls. But then again you might not."

She took a long breath, remembering how she had felt when Raven revealed that she knew her secret. She'd thought she was trapped but it wasn't until she'd joined the other Hexes that she had realized she'd never been free before.

"Charis, I was once just like you and I thought I could keep my secret forever. I didn't want to leave home either. But one day the CPS came for me. They took me away while my father watched and there was nothing he could do."

She didn't go into detail about the experimental lab they had taken her to. There were some things that could be explained to Charis later if she chose to come with them and there were others that were too horrible to speak of.

"Raven rescued me, Charis," Ali explained, turning to look back briefly at the other girl. "She saved me from the CPS, she saved a friend of mine, and she's saved hundreds of other kids since then. Raven's the best there is. Even the government knows it and some day she'll force them to give us our rights as real people. But in the meantime you're *not* safe. You won't ever be safe so long as you're a Hex and trying to keep it a secret. Wouldn't you rather come with us now than wake up some morning with the CPS at the gates of Fairseat and know that we can't save you in time?" She looked at Charis straight in the eyes as she finished. "We can't force you to come with us and we won't try, but they can and they will and there will be nothing you or your parents can do about it."

Ali stopped speaking, realizing that she'd said everything she could, and just waited. Charis looked back at her, her face pale and serious as her eyes moved from Ali to Daniel to Raven. Finally she spoke.

"Can I leave a letter for my parents?"

"Yes, if you want to," Ali replied as Daniel heaved a sigh of relief. "But please be quick, we don't have much time."

"I'll go and pack," Charis said and headed for one of the doors leading out of the room.

Once she had left, Ali sat down on the side of one of the chairs, feeling immeasurably tired.

"Well done!" Daniel exclaimed. "I've never heard you talk like that before."

"Thank you," Ali said with a smile but it was Raven she turned to look at.

"Congratulations," Raven said softly and Ali felt a smile spread across her face as she looked at the younger Hex.

"You mean that?" she asked.

"Of course." The old snap was back in Raven's voice as she added: "I always say what I mean. Now go and hurry that kid up before this security system realizes what games I've been playing with it."

• • •

Alaric was already making plans to strike at the heart of the Federation's power. Raven's mention of the satellite network and the Space Operations Center in Transcendence had enthused him with a new passion for the cause and it was a natural move to seek out the only other member of the Ghosts with a similar fixation. He found Wraith in one of the smaller Ghost enclaves on the edge of the city with a group of the older Hex children. The slender ganger with his wild unnaturally white hair was an icon for the kids who were old enough to strike back against Seccie persecution. He taught them how to use weaponry and they imitated him almost slavishly dying their hair white to conform to their own image of what the Ghosts should be.

Watching Wraith surrounded by children with serious faces, holding their weapons of destruction with a practiced ease, Alaric was struck by how many of these kids there were now. They *are* the Ghosts, he thought to himself. Much more than the members of Anglecynn or the original Hex group ever were. These children outnumber us now and if we don't succeed in finding them a future they'll do it themselves. The thought was a little daunting and it made him pause as he watched the kids taking turns at blasting at targets. Eventually the gunfire came to a halt and Wraith ordered them to stand down their weapons. As the kids obeyed his instructions he came over to meet Alaric.

"Didn't expect to see you here," he said with a smile. "I thought you were busy plotting to take over the world for us."

"Something like that," Alaric grinned wryly, then glanced over at the children. "I have a feeling these kids might get there first though. You've taught them well."

"Too well, perhaps," Wraith replied seriously. "You lose something in your innocence when you're trained to kill, even if you never use that knowledge."

"But if the choice is between innocence or survival . . . ," Alaric replied and Wraith shrugged acceptingly.

"Agreed," he said. "We have no choice."

"Maybe not, but we do have options," Alaric replied. "And that's part of what I want to talk to you about. I think I may have an idea. . . ."

Drow hadn't used the net since he'd first noticed the darkness, and he was curiously reluctant to touch the computer terminal. The black cloud that had ensnared him had haunted his dreams and he was constantly assailed by visions of drowning in pitch. But his father expected him to help test out the capabilities of the programs he had stolen and so he had resolved to face his fears.

Slotting another of the stolen disks in, he keyed on the terminal in his room and dived into the net. He was supposed to be fortifying his family's own computer system with the new encryption algorithms, setting up an unhackable password protocol, but after about an hour of work his mind began to drift, drawn by the strange affinity he felt for the network. Almost unconsciously he let his mind slip further and further away from the terminal he was working at, out through the computer system, and on to one of the major highways of the net. Data traffic sped past him and he watched it flow by, simply enjoying the color and life around him. Sliding into a datastream he allowed himself to be carried along, soothed by the constant flow of information. Then, suddenly something off-kilter jarred him back into full awareness. Nearby, an information node slowed and stopped winking as if it had been suddenly obscured. He turned to regard it, holding it in his mind, and saw it return. But in data milliseconds away a tendril of nothingness was curling past the datastreams, enfolding them in darkness and then sliding on.

Drow shivered, not wanting to follow that black tendril back to where it came from. The contagion was plainly spreading through the net and he didn't even know what it was, let alone what to do about it. He wondered about speaking to one of the other Chromes but he knew that none of them would interface with computers the way he did. The few times he had attempted to explain what he felt to one of them she had looked blank, unable to understand what he was describing. But maybe there was someone out there who could understand, somewhere in the vast reaches of the net. Withdrawing from the terminal, he considered the possibility. What he needed was to send the message to anyone who saw the net the way he did, a message only another person with his abilities could read. Slowly an idea began to occur to him and he sank back into the net as he considered it.

In all the net he was the only conscious entity that he knew of, unique among the mindless data signals. Using the skills he had learned while programming for the Chromes, he constructed a search program that would look for other anomalies, creatures in the flow of data that didn't behave the way data should. When his search program found one it would give them his message and where to look for him—a prearranged location in the net that he would check every day for a response. His search program complete, he keyed in his message.

> **to those who the net sets free—something here is different— what is it that spreads darkness like a virus?—bring me your answer—if you exist <**

Cloud knew something had changed when the team returned. He had been watching for them in the Ghost enclave, wanting to talk to Raven about her plan to go to Transcendence, but when the team returned he realized it might be the wrong time to speak to her. The others climbed eagerly out of the flitter, escorting a self-composed child carrying an expensive-looking sling bag. Daniel and Ali were chattering enthusiastically to her about Ghosts and Cloud watched the group pass him, completely absorbed in their own affairs. Once they had gone by he walked up to the small vehicle. Raven was sitting in the pilot's seat, staring into space, and after hesitating for a fraction of a second, Cloud swung himself into the seat beside her.

"Successful mission?" he asked, and black eyes tracked slowly across to regard him.

"We rescued a child from dreams of luxury and offered her despair," Raven said bleakly.

"Sounds fairly standard," Cloud replied, trying to bring a measure of humor to the conversation. When Raven didn't reply he stayed silent, thinking.

"Why do you despair, Raven?" he said eventually. "What do you care for children's dreams?"

"I don't despair," Raven corrected him, an edge in her voice. "But I don't dream either."

"So our magician is a realist after all?"

"If only I can discover what is real," Raven replied.

"Sometimes I'm not certain you're real," Cloud told her. "So many of the others persist in thinking of you as a legend that I wonder if we invented you."

"I invented myself in the net and outside it I have to remember to exist."

"In that case you had better go and find some reality," Cloud suggested. "Aren't you planning to unleash Avalon's new release on the world? Now's as good a time as any."

"Yes, I'll do that," Raven said definitely, moving gracefully out of the flitter. "It may well be time her words were heard."

"Her words or yours?" Cloud asked, but Raven was already leaving and if she heard him she didn't answer.

Avalon was idly retuning her guitar and watching the holovid with the sound turned off when Ali and Luciel arrived in the Fortress, cheerful about having rescued another Hex.

"She's so self-possessed," Ali told her. "I'm sure she's going to be a really strong Hex."

"You just say that because that's what Raven's like," Luciel pointed out. "And the word isn't self-possessed, it's 'cold.' Even Wraith says he hardly knows her."

Avalon turned to look at them and Luciel caught her eye.

"Don't look disapproving," the singer told him. "I was just thinking about what you said. But if Raven's difficult to know it must be because she wants it that way."

"Why would anyone want to be that isolated?" Luciel objected. "Just because she likes it when people are afraid of her?"

"I'm not afraid of Raven," Ali objected. "Well, not much anyway."

"I don't believe Raven wants people to fear her," Avalon said and Ali nodded her agreement.

"Well in that case, what does she want?" Luciel asked.

"I think it's more a case of what she doesn't want," Avalon replied. "She doesn't want to be connected to other people. She resists it even with Wraith and he's the only family she has left."

"And that's why," Ali added, with a sudden flash of understanding. "Because he *is* the only family she has left. If she was connected to people she might lose them." She thought of her own father whom she hadn't seen since the day the CPS took her away.

"I don't think it's that simple," Avalon replied, shaking her head. "Although maybe that's part of it."

"What *do* you think then?" Luciel asked and Avalon shrugged.

"Raven was very young when she had to fend for herself," she said slowly. "I don't think she was able to form the normal connections to other people that most of us feel. I think she connected to the net instead and that's why her Hex abilities are so strong. The net is her natural environment and the rest of her life is just marking time."

The others were silent as they considered the concept and Avalon continued to play with her guitar. After a few minutes Luciel opened his mouth to speak but was silenced when the holovid news feed suddenly displayed an image of Avalon.

"Where's the moment control?" he asked quickly, forgetting what he had been about to say. "You're on the vid, Avalon!"

Ali spotted the control first and keyed it on so that the news anchor's voice was projected into the room in midsentence:

". . . *the singer Avalon, now a renegade on the run from the CPS since she joined a known terrorist group last year. Less than an hour ago a collection of music was released into the web on a variety of public bulletin boards and data feeds. The collection is entitled 'Deliberate Disguises,' a possible reference to the work of a twentieth-century poet, and the music is consistent with Avalon's style. Although the collection is almost certain to be proscribed by the government seeing as it is allegedly the work of a criminal, this station was able to access it before any ban comes into effect and our expert analysts are convinced that both the music and the voice of the singer belong to Avalon. However, the lyrics of the songs are wildly dissimilar to any work produced by Masque, the band to which Avalon previously belonged."*

Ali and Luciel were glued to their seats as the commentary unfolded, fascinated by the news item as much because nothing like this had ever happened before as because it was something they were involved in. Having grown up in the world of media, Ali knew that the release of an underground music album was a rare event. The release of an underground album by a rock star turned terrorist who had disappeared from view at the peak of her fame was a sensational event. Cloud had been right to suggest that Avalon's music was the greatest gift she could ever give to the Hex cause. The news feeds wouldn't be able to resist a story like this and every time it was mentioned it lent prominence and even respectability to the Hexes.

"We go now for comments from the other members of Masque: Lissa, Corin, and Jesse," the announcer was saying and the vidscreen shifted into an image of the three musicians.

"I'm just relieved to know Avalon's alive," Corin said seriously, looking directly into the camera. *"We've all worried, not knowing what became of her or of Cloud. Now we know that, wherever they are, they're safe and still creating music. Avalon's still the most talented musician in the business and nothing's going to change that."*

"She's also fighting for something she believes in—" Jesse added but was cut off abruptly by the interviewer who asked:

"What about you, Lissa? What do you think of the album?"

"I wish Avalon was with us," Lissa replied, with a sorrowful expression. *"She's an electric musician but without the rest of the group she's missing something. Masque complemented Avalon. Together we created something beyond what any of us could have done individually. I'm sorry that she's given that up."*

"It's been suggested that she's collaborating with someone new," the interviewer pointed out. *"Do you believe that Avalon wrote those lyrics?"*

"Most definitely not," Lissa said firmly. *"Those words are pure*

sedition. Avalon would never have described Hexes as 'prophets of possibility.' She wasn't even political."

"Her views may have changed since she discovered she was a Hex—" Jesse began to say, but then the image shifted again and returned to the face of the news anchor.

"The disturbing content of the album means that we are unable to play it to you here but Avalon's album seems certain to rock the music world on its foundations. In this collection of songs she has achieved sounds beyond what has ever been created before. Our analysts are still unable to state what instruments are being played. . . ."

The sound on the vidscreen died as Avalon touched the moment control and Luciel and Ali turned to look at her.

"That's great!" Ali said, smiling. "It's really had an effect."

"I hope it's enough," Luciel added cautiously. "The news feed seemed very reluctant to actually discuss Hexes."

"People will be discussing it though," Ali pointed out. "Discussing it and speculating about what it really means to be a mutant. People loved Avalon. A lot of them won't stop just because she's a Hex."

"You think so?" Avalon sounded wistful and Ali touched her hand lightly.

"I'm sure of it," she said firmly. Then she added, more hesitantly, "Do you miss it? The success?"

"Yes, I miss it," Avalon admitted with a rueful grin. "I enjoyed my fame. But I don't regret the decision I made to join you. And I still have the music. Regardless of what Lissa was saying, I think that collection was the best work I've ever done and it was you who made it possible. Especially Raven—what she taught me has taken me to another level of achievement and I'm immensely grateful."

"We all owe Raven," Ali said honestly. "But she doesn't want our gratitude. She doesn't care that she's becoming a legend to us."

"Oh, I think she does care," Cloud said, entering the room with customary unconscious grace. "But Raven never asked to be turned into a myth and a pedestal isn't an easy place to stand."

On one of the back country roads of Italy, Tally had found what she was looking for. An elderly couple driving an equally ancient float-truck, a design of vehicle rarely used now that skimmers were so cheap, had stopped for them when Tally waved. In broken Italian, taught to her by Harmony, she had explained that she and her brother wanted a lift to Padua and promised that they would be no trouble. The old man had seemed doubtful, looking at their worn clothes askance. But his wife had overruled him and let the children aboard.

All they had wanted was to rest and think about the difficulties that lay ahead, but the old woman had obviously let them ride with her because she wanted someone to talk to and the twins had been an unwilling audience for her endless flood of chatter. As the float-truck wound its way up and down the rolling hills, Tally listened to what seemed like the old woman's life history. Her name was Julietta and in her long life she had accumulated enough relatives that her stories looked likely to continue throughout the entire journey: three sons and two daughters had produced nine grandchildren, the eldest of which was about to have children of her own. Tally's mind sank into a half-daze as the old lady's fluid Italian droned on telling her about Ricco and Maria and Grego and Georgiana until she couldn't remember which was which and wondered how the old lady could keep them all straight herself.

Gift's Italian was better than hers though and he seemed able to chatter back to Julietta whenever she gave him the chance to get a word in edgeways. When the old lady finally asked them about their own family it was Gift who was awake enough to think of a clever answer.

"Our parents are English, on a visit to Padua," he explained. "But Tally and I wanted to see Venice so we left them a note and begged a lift there. They'll be angry when we get back but we couldn't come to Italy and not see Venice, even if it is ruined now."

Tally couldn't understand Julietta's reply but it seemed to be something about how the English would do any crazy thing but that Venice was a grand old city, didn't she remember how it had finally been abandoned and she hoped that their parents didn't punish them too hard, although they were wicked children to run away. All of this was accompanied with chuckling laughter and Tally relaxed, realizing that Gift was doing a good job of charming this old lady. Her brother always got on with people better than she did. While Tally worried and fretted over their future, Gift's moods went from black anger to sunny good humor with an ease that she admired, although sometimes it alarmed her. Even now, while they were in greater danger than they had ever been in their lives, Gift could sit here chatting away as if he hadn't a care in the world.

Gift was asking a question of the old lady and Tally realized that she had lost track of the conversation again. It didn't seem to bother them any more than it concerned the old man. Although he seemed to have forgotten his original distrust of them he said very little, concentrating on driving the truck and staring ahead at the curving road. Suddenly Gift pinched her and Tally jolted awake, turning to him with a surprised look. He wasn't looking at her though, all his attention was on Julietta, but his hand gripped her wrist tightly and Tally tried to concentrate on the conversation.

"Grego's a good boy," Julietta was saying approvingly. "Still comes to see his old mother although he has enough work on his hands for three nowadays with his job."

"Grego's bar must have a computer terminal," Gift said cautiously and Tally stiffened, realizing what he was trying to do.

"A terminal?" Julietta snorted. "He has five, my boy. Even our old house has one. Have had for years, Maria's husband had it installed the summer they stayed with us. . . ." Her voice rattled on and Gift listened politely but at the first opportunity he took up the thread of the conversation again.

"Do you think Grego would let us use a terminal when we get to Padua?" he asked. "So we can send a message to our parents to tell them where we are."

"I don't see why not," Julietta said easily. "Grego's a generous boy, always has been. He offered to buy us a new skimmer but Georgio and I don't travel as much as we used to and this old thing's always been good enough for us. . . ."

She was off again and this time Gift didn't try to interrupt her. Squeezing Tally's hand he flashed her a brief smile and she smiled back. Gift had a knack for turning situations to his advantage and it looked as if meeting this friendly old lady had been a double stroke of luck. But Tally's relief didn't last for long. Now they had found a terminal they would still have to use it, and Tally had no idea how they would send a message to the Hexes in England.

5

THE WEIGHT OF
A TALENT

Alaric officially unveiled his plan that afternoon. The most senior members of the Ghosts had gathered at the Fortress for their regular weekly meeting. Usually not all of them could spare time in their busy schedules for more than a few words as they passed or even make all the meetings and briefings that were constantly being held. Because of this Wraith had instituted the custom of having a regular Council of War and even Raven was expected to attend, however busy she was.

There were eleven of them gathered around the Council table. Anglecynn was represented by Alaric, Geraint, Jordan, and Daniel, three of whom already knew about the plan. The other members of the meeting were Wraith, Kez, Ali, Luciel, Cloud, Avalon, and Raven. Typically Raven was the last to arrive and she turned up just as the others were discussing the release of Avalon's album.

Alaric decided not to speak at once. It was reassuring to wait for a while, watching the interactions between so disparate a group of people, reminding himself that they had already achieved incredibly ambitious aims. He knew that what he intended to suggest at this meeting would alarm them and disturb the fragile equilibrium they had found but he was compelled by an increasing certainty that if they didn't move soon, it would be too late.

The last few years had been almost comfortable. In evading the Seccies and stirring up trouble for the Federation the Ghosts had grown almost complacent. But Alaric knew that if they truly believed in their cause they would have to go further. They had made promises to those children they had rescued, promises of safety and freedom. Many of them were still haunted by the thought of those children they hadn't been able to rescue: mutilated at the orders of the Federation which didn't see any evil in abusing or killing Hexes. More importantly, none of the new Hexes they had discovered had Raven's skill. Whenever they asked her about it she had said only that some of the youngest children were promising and that, with her teaching, they would become more accomplished Hexes than Ali or Luciel. But they all knew the truth. No one could equal Raven and it was possible that no one ever would. That meant that the time to strike was now; before the group grew too large to hide any longer and before some accident took Raven away from them.

While Alaric had been musing, the others had still been discussing Avalon's music, and he tuned in just as Wraith was mentioning the news coverage the collection had received.

"I've seen coverage on every news feed," Geraint was saying approvingly. "Most of them try to avoid any discussion of the Hex issue but some of the smaller channels have mentioned it."

"I've seen something even more interesting," Daniel added. "Ali, your father's corporation owns Populix, doesn't it?"

"Yes," Ali replied warily. She tended to avoid anything on the vidscreen that reminded her of her father. He still thought she was dead and she had never dared to contact him, afraid he might despise her for the life she was now living.

"Well, Populix lost two reporters a couple of years ago when you were rescuing Raven from the EF Consulate, not that she needed much rescuing." He glanced up to smile at Raven, who arched an eyebrow at the comment. "The reporters died when the Seccies and the EF troops opened fire on the crowd. The channel didn't give much coverage to the event at the time, obviously they thought it wasn't worth antagonizing the government, but Populix has never been quite as sycophantic as some of the pro-Federation channels since then."

"Could that be something to do with you, Ali?" Luciel asked gently. "Perhaps your father resents the government because of what happened to you?"

"Maybe," Ali replied but she didn't look convinced.

"Anyway," Daniel continued, "Populix certainly isn't following government orders now. Although the album hasn't been banned yet, all the news feeds know it's going to be so they haven't been playing it. Populix has decided differently. I didn't realize what I was seeing at first because I didn't realize Raven had released vid images along with the music—"

"You did?" Wraith interrupted him, looking at Raven and Avalon with surprise. "You didn't mention that."

"It was Cloud's idea," Avalon explained. "But I honestly didn't think anything would come of it."

"I thought it might be interesting if Raven could depict in a visual form what she imagines the computer network to be like," Cloud explained. "Since that was what she and Avalon tried to do in words and music, I thought it would be unfortunate to leave visuals out."

"I included a set of images with the data package I posted across the net," Raven added. "Just in case."

"Well, it worked!" Daniel told her. "Populix has been showing it across the clock. It's strange material but it's incredible. Cities built out of light and with rivers of color running through them. Graphically it's the best work that's ever been done—at least that's what Populix is saying."

"How can they be playing it, though?" Geraint asked. "Despite Ali's father, the Tarrell Corporation depends on the goodwill of the government and the Federation. They can't really allow one of their channels to openly oppose its wishes."

"Populix has been very careful," Daniel explained. "They regularly state that they have no interest in disseminating sedition or rebellion against the EF but they also claim that true art doesn't have an agenda and that the music and images can be appreciated without considering their content."

"But the content's what everyone's going to be thinking of, nonetheless," Luciel exclaimed triumphantly. "That's electric!"

"It gave me an idea too," Jordan added, somewhat apologetically. "I didn't mean to do anything without your consent but seeing as it's something we were doing anyway—"

"Spit it out, Jordan," Wraith said kindly. "What did you do?"

"Well, you know those tapes you and Raven gave us from the illegal laboratory? The ones with the details of the mutilations Kalden performed on the test subjects?"

"What about them?" Luciel asked. His voice was a little ragged, unsurprisingly since he had been one of the victims of those experiments.

"Well, one thing we do is regularly broadcast them to the news feeds," Jordan explained. "They never show them but we hoped if we kept sending them someone might wonder about the government cover-up and if the lab was real after all. So, since Populix seemed to be going against the government, I made an anonymous call to them today and asked them if they would broadcast the tapes again."

"And?" Wraith asked eagerly.

"They said they would," Jordan replied. "Not all of them, because the subject matter was so disturbing, but they said the tapes would make an appropriate accompaniment to some of the more disturbing songs on the album and they thanked me for the suggestion."

"That's good news," Wraith said approvingly. "And it was a clever idea, Jordan. It looks as if our message might finally be getting out."

"And there's never been a better time to make a strike against the Federation," Alaric announced, and everyone fell silent to look at him.

It was a moment before Alaric spoke. He knew that he had the attention of the entire council and he wanted to plead his case as well as possible. He looked around at the company as he gathered his thoughts and then, taking a deep breath, he began.

"There's never been a group like this," he said. "In all the time Anglecynn opposed Federation rule we heard of a few centers of rebellion but the Federation always found them and put them down. Until now. We've spoken of this before, of the advantages we'll have when we finally make an attempt to threaten Federation power. But we've always considered that time to be far in the future. I think that day has come now.

"It may be sooner than we expected, but if we continue as we have been, how long before the Federation decides to unleash its full force and eliminate us? If we strike a decisive blow now it may take them years to recover and those are years we can use to our advantage.

"Raven and I have discussed a plan to cripple one of the Federation's greatest assets: their communications network. We believe there's a way to either take out or take over the orbital satellite network. If we can do that the entire Federation would be reeling and then maybe we'll be able to topple it forever."

Alaric stopped speaking and Wraith took over from him.

"The Space Operations Center from which the satellite network is controlled is not one of the Federation's more heavily guarded facilities. They aren't interested in space travel and the center doesn't do much more than process information from the satellites and occasionally service them so they don't break down.

Alaric has discussed with me the possibility of sending a team to Transcendence and I think the idea's a good one."

"What about the danger?" Avalon asked, voicing everyone's thoughts. "For one thing, it almost certainly couldn't be done without Raven, and we can't afford to lose her."

"You're going to, one way or the other," Raven answered her and everyone turned to look at the young Hex. She regarded them coolly in return, her onyx eyes giving them no clue to her thoughts.

Raven wasn't the thrill-seeking hacker she had been when they arrived here. She was an oasis of perfect calm in their midst, her previous rages contained by her search for the truth about Hexes. Even her wild mop of black hair had changed, tamed into a silken veil that shrouded her face as she spoke.

"I never asked for this," she told them. "It was Wraith who wanted to change the world. I've stayed for this long because I was interested but now I'm not anymore. Alaric's right when he says things have to change, and this is one of them. You need me, and I'll serve your ends while they're also mine. I'll take this fight to the Federation if that's what you want but I won't be a figurehead for a group that does nothing."

Wraith realized as he studied her that the younger sister he had persuaded to come to London with him was the only member of the group who hadn't committed herself to their cause. She had fought when she had to and they had come to rely on her but he suddenly remembered her saying: "Anyone good enough to escape the CPS isn't going to want to load themselves down with people who aren't."

"You really don't have any loyalty, do you?" Geraint asked, sounding disgusted.

"Is it loyalty to sacrifice yourself to someone else's wishes?" Raven asked and everyone realized that she hadn't answered Geraint's question. Silence fell across the room and persisted until Cloud spoke.

"I know I'm only here on sufferance, so I'll be brief," he began. "But do any of you have a right to resent Raven for this? She said she didn't ask for the role you've given her but even so she's done everything you've asked for a long time. Everything you've created here has been accomplished with her aid. Why should she watch it wither and die because you refuse to act? She's offered to strike at the Federation. Isn't that good enough?"

"No it isn't," Wraith answered him. "Because Raven's commitment to us matters more than her gifts. But it will have to do since we're not going to be offered anything else."

Avalon reached out and took his hand sympathetically. They all knew how much it hurt him that Raven was prepared to desert the group. However, they also knew that the crucial decision had been reached, and when Alaric asked for opinions on whether to attack the Space Operations Center, everyone voted in favor.

Once the vote had been taken the Council meeting moved on swiftly, all hoping to gloss over Raven's announcement.

"If we're decided that we should go to Transcendence we should discuss who'll be on the team," Wraith told them, taking charge of the meeting. "Will it be a small group or a large one? What skills are most necessary?"

"I think Raven's most qualified to judge that," Geraint replied, with a cold edge to his voice. His eyes were hard as he looked at the young Hex and asked levelly, "What would be your preference, Raven?"

"A small group," the girl replied. "Well-armed, able to respond swiftly and independently to trouble and including at least two other Hexes."

"Ali and Luciel seem the most obvious choices for that role," Wraith said. "They've been trained for the longest."

"No, not me," Ali said, and when it looked as if Wraith might be about to object, she pressed on. "I'm not really a natural Hex. I don't have the strength or the bravery. I'll help the group however I can but I don't think I'm a good choice for this mission. I don't think Raven could rely on me to come through."

"You're sure of that?" Luciel asked her seriously. "You're a lot better than you think you are, Ali."

"Maybe, but that's the important point, isn't it? I *don't* think I'm good enough and if you're honest you'll admit I'd be a liability."

"Ali has proved herself in other ways," Raven said unexpectedly. "I won't take her if she doesn't want to go."

"Very well," Wraith agreed. "What about you, Luciel?"

"I'll go," the boy replied. "I want to and, next to Raven, I'm probably the most skilled."

"What about the other Hex?" Alaric asked. "Should Avalon be the one?"

"I don't think so," Avalon replied. "I'm not good enough with weapons or computers."

"Like Ali, you have other skills," Wraith told her. "Perhaps Raven can find a second Hex among the trainees?" Raven nodded and he continued. "What about the other members of the team? I'll only ask for volunteers but I'll go myself."

"I'm not sure you should," Ali told him. "Someone has to be in charge while you're gone."

"There are enough skilled people who can do that," Wraith assured her. "Yourself for one," The others agreed and Ali smiled, looking down at her hands. She had been worried that they would be annoyed with her for turning down the mission but instead they showed that they had enough confidence in her abilities to trust her with an equally important role.

"Geraint and I can't both go, though," Alaric said. "We have too many duties, and if you're agreeable, Gerro, I'd like to go."

"I'd like the chance to take the fight to the Feds," Geraint said. "But I think you're right and that you should go." He glanced at Raven and the others realized that he was uncomfortable with taking her orders.

"I'll go too," Jordan said and Daniel echoed her.

"Jordan perhaps," Wraith said. "But, Daniel, I'm afraid you don't have the necessary skills. We'll need more experienced fighters and there's also a danger that you might be recognized."

"But I'm going," Kez said suddenly and the others realized that he had been silent for a long time. "And don't say I'm a kid. I'm one of the best marksmen you've got." Wraith hesitated but Raven replied.

"I'll take Kez," she said. "I know his capabilities."

"Then it's almost settled," Wraith concluded. "The team will consist of myself, Luciel, Alaric, Jordan, and Kez. And Raven, of course."

"We still need another Hex and perhaps a couple more fighters," Alaric pointed out. "I'll ask around."

"Only volunteers, remember," Wraith reminded him. "This mission will be dangerous and I don't want to take anyone who doesn't want to come."

Halfway across Europe two children were walking into a danger they had never asked for but they didn't have any choice. Padua was not a large city by the standards of the Federation, and it was nothing in comparison with the sprawling metropolis that was Transcendence. But to Tally and Gift, who had avoided cities throughout their lives, it was alarming. Julietta, the old lady who had given them a lift, seemed perfectly comfortable as the old float-truck weaved its way through the congested roads thronged with skimmers and flitters. Padua was still mostly on one level, although on the west of the city rose about thirty corporate starscrapers, and Julietta gave her husband constant advice in how to navigate the twisting streets to Grego's bar. He gave no sign of listening to her but eventually the float-truck came to a halt in a shady avenue and a man in his thirties came out of an attractively fronted building to greet them.

Julietta started talking the moment she saw him and didn't stop until all four of them were inside the bar and seated at a table with cool drinks in front of them. Somewhere in the flood of talk the old lady had told her son who Gift and Tally were and asked him if they could use one of his computer terminals. Tally, who had been half afraid that Julietta would forget her promise, was relieved when Grego said it would be no problem at all. Gift was obviously elated that things had gone so well but Tally was almost reluctant to approach the terminal, squatting like a primitive god in the next room. She had almost no idea how to use it normally and still less of a concept of how a Hex could interact with it.

"We'll go in a minute," Gift whispered to her. "Don't worry, Tally. Look how well things are going!"

"Yeah," Tally agreed. "Maybe it's a good omen." Now wasn't the time to talk about her secret fears. After a few minutes they finished their drinks and excused themselves to go and find the terminal.

"Good luck contacting your parents," Grego said cheerfully. "If you can't reach them you can wait here until they're in."

"Thank you," Tally said sincerely, but when they were out of earshot she added, "We shouldn't stay though, Gift. Once we've used the terminal we should get moving. It's not safe to stay any-where for long."

"Tally, you're paranoid," Gift said with a smile. "No one even knows we're here."

"I'm not paranoid," she protested. "Just careful." But she stopped speaking as they came face to face with the terminal.

It was on, the screen glowing with a faint light and displaying the words:

> **> enter network id password <**

Tally looked at Gift hopelessly and he shrugged.

"Touch the keypad," he suggested. "Come on, I'll do it too. Touch the keypad, close your eyes and concentrate."

"On what?" Tally asked but she followed his instructions.

"On the network," Gift said quietly. "It's there, just millimeters away. Close enough to reach out and touch."

Obediently Tally concentrated. She could hear Gift breathing softly next to her, the warmth of his hand resting next to hers on the cool terminal. She could hear Julietta's voice rising and falling in a flood of chatter in the next room and the hum of the city outside. And she could feel something else. It hovered just at the edge of her perceptions like a half-heard whisper. It was close enough to touch, a word on the tip of a tongue, an elusive memory. She tried to concentrate on it and it slipped away. Tried again, held it for a second and lost it.

"Damn," she said, instinctively opening her eyes. "I think I almost had it, then."

"Me too," Gift whispered. "Try again. Let it come naturally."

Tally closed her eyes again and tried to block out all distractions, letting her mind drift. She could feel the network but she didn't try to reach for it, allowing it to hang just beyond her reach until it seemed as if it had been there forever. Then slowly, hardly daring to breathe, she concentrated on that sensation and all of a sudden felt herself falling toward it. In her mind she was standing at a gateway and all she had to do was open a door. Reaching out more confidently she touched it and it swung open invitingly.

"Tally!" Gift exclaimed and her eyes snapped open. "Look," he said. "You did it. Look at that!"

The screen had produced a new line of text.

> password accepted—access granted <

"That was incredible," Tally breathed.

"What about you, did you feel it?"

"I think I did," Gift replied. "Try again. Try and enter it properly."

The twins closed their eyes again and Tally reached for the gateway in her mind. It was open now and only just out of her reach, leading into an alien world full of possibilities. Suddenly she wanted to be a part of it more than she had ever wanted anything in her life before. This was her heritage and she reached to claim it. The fall was dizzying, the gateway a black pit beneath her feet and she gasped as she fell through it and found herself flying. It was like being delirious. She had no concept of direction anymore, her mind couldn't translate what it was experiencing into the evidence of her senses. It was so much more than she had been led to believe. The network was alive, and she could feel it. A living breathing entity, not a sterile web of electronic signals and connections. She allowed herself to drift, trying to find a way of assimilating it all into her mind. Then she felt the presence of something close by and reached for it.

> ? < her mind asked, unable to formulate any more coherent thought.

> tally—? < the presence responded and excitedly Tally tried to ask a real question, holding the words in her mind and then directing them at the presence.

> **gift?—is that you/me/us/network/here/this . . . ?** <

The words were jumbled up, her thoughts tangled with each other, but the response was reassuring.

> **tally—difficult to think/be/imagine/dream—where/here are you/me/we?** <

> **somewhere/everywhere—hold on** < Tally responded, certain that if they lost track of each other they wouldn't be able to find each other again. Delicately she moved toward Gift's mind, a presence so similar in feeling to her own that she felt as if she was touching her mirror image. As she reached for him, Gift reached back for her and then they were together; their minds transmitted information to each other too quickly to be considered as words, trying to make sense of the net. They hung there for what seemed like eons until their linked minds were able to make some sense of what surrounded them.

> **a city** < they thought together. > **city of light/sound/movement** <

It surrounded them in all directions and they regarded it with wonder, amazed that they had achieved this much. Then the urge to explore grabbed them simultaneously and their minds shared one single thought.

> **let's fly** <

The first thing Drow did when he connected to the net was to check the mail drop he had left for himself. There was no response to his message and he tried to ignore the disappointment he felt. It had been a crazy idea anyway, he told himself, sending a message to no one. But he had hoped so much, more than he had realized until this moment, that somewhere out there might be a person like himself who could understand what he felt when he was connected.

"It's too early to give up, though," he told himself firmly. "I've hardly looked properly, anyway. Just sent one message." Even as the thought came to him he felt a sudden certainty that there were people like him in the web and he knew he had to find them. Functioning on instinct alone, he let himself be pulled by the currents of the network, drawn one way then another, allowing the dataflow to take him with it. As he drifted it was clear to him that the contagion was spreading. He could feel its tendrils sliding through the network looking for a place to take hold. Whenever he neared one of those blindly grasping tentacles he changed course, not allowing it to take hold of him. He sped along the data pathways, searching for the unusual, knowing with an inexplicable certainty that he would find it.

He had left the city network long ago and as he moved out of England into the European network he could feel the black pestilence receding behind him. Rejoicing in the freedom, he coasted on the dataflow for a few moments longer then lifted above it, flying free through the network. Hurtling through the virtual world he felt something pass him, and ten systems later realized there had been something strange about it. He retraced his direction and couldn't find it. Puzzled now, he engaged the mapping program he had stolen only days ago and asked it where he was. Obediently it displayed the section of the network he found himself in and a schematic of the systems he had passed through to get there. He studied the map for a while then decided it had been in the Italian section of the European net that the strangeness had found nothing. Trying to dismiss it from his mind he let himself fly and passed it again almost immediately. This time though he was prepared and he halted almost instantaneously. The strangeness did the same and they circled each other warily for a few moments before Drow reached out to it and asked:

> **what are you?** <

When the answer came it was a strange mixture of personality and intellect, unmistakably human but unable to visualize itself properly, overwhelmed by the net.

> **we are gift/talent—help us** <

The plea instantly got Drow's attention and he moved closer.

> **help how/why/who?** <

> **help us—gift/talent/hexes/twins—help us** <

> **your thoughts are not clear/understandable/precise** < Drow told them, not even knowing as he thought it exactly what he meant. > **can you focus?** <

There was a pause as they struggled for identity and meaning and Drow realized during that space of time that the twinned minds were very young and even more inexperienced. That they called themselves Hexes frightened him with all the implications it had about his own abilities. But he was too concerned for them to worry about himself. These minds were lost in the net and beginning to panic.

> **help us** < they pleaded. > **you are like us/with us/part of us—help us** <

Realizing that he wasn't going to get any more sense out of them like this, Drow engaged his mapping program again and extended it toward the strangers.

> **where did you come from?** < he asked them, trying to make the question as firm as he could. > **show me** <

For a while there was a silence, then the minds reached back to him, handing him his own map with a location marked on it.

> ***here**** <

Reaching for the minds of the strangers, Drow enfolded them with his own and was overcome by confusion like a blow. They were mixed up in each other and in the net, rapidly losing their sanity in trying to assimilate too much at once. Imagining himself as pulling them behind him, Drow began to travel through the net and slowly they followed. He didn't dare move too fast in case he lost them, and the journey back to the location they had marked seemed to take forever. All the while their minds cried out to him to help them until his own head rang with the plea. Eventually the mapping program signaled to him that he had reached his destination and he released his hold on the minds.

> **leave now** < he told them. > **return/let go/detach** <

> **how?** < they asked him in confusion and he attempted to show them, filling his mind with his own experience of the network, of how he entered and left it. Then abruptly they were gone and Drow found himself alone in a small private system.

> **system identity** < he demanded and the amateur security precautions melted away to inform him where he was.

> **system licensed to gregori vecci—padua—italy europe** <

Drow had no idea what that indicated about the identity of the two children he had rescued but he intended to find out. Reaching toward the only terminal in use on the system he told it what words to display.

> **gift/talent—can you understand me?** <

6
POWER TO SHUT HEAVEN

Gift shook his head to clear it and stared blankly at the computer
terminal in front of him, trying to figure out what had happened.
He had to remember who he was. It seemed as if he had been Gift-
Talent for a hundred years, so long that he couldn't think straight
as an individual, but the wall chronometer informed him that only
five minutes had passed since they had attempted to make contact
with the terminal. Remembering that he was Gift reminded him to
look for Tally. She was lying on the floor beside the terminal and
he bent to shake her lightly.

"Tally, Tally?" he said, checking her pulse. It was beating quickly
but steadily and his sister's eyes blinked open, wide with fright.

"Gift?" she said hesitantly.

"Yes, it's me. And you're Tally," he said with a quick laugh.
"Can you remember that?"

"I can now," Tally said, sitting up carefully. "What happened?"

"I suspect the answer's on the disk," Gift replied. "But it's not difficult to guess. We're not experienced enough with this. But I think we met someone in there who was."

"Yes." Tally stood up too quickly and then swayed with a momentary dizziness. Gift reached to support her and then froze.

"Tally, look!" he said eagerly. The message on the terminal had changed. Now it read:

> **gift/talent—can you understand me?** <

The twins stared at the terminal together and they turned to look at each other with wide grins.

"We found them!" Gift exclaimed. "It actually worked."

"Maybe," Tally was more cautious. "We don't know who this is yet."

"Then let's find out," Gift replied and reached for the terminal, searching for letters on the keypad that would enable him to form a response. Slowly he inputted the words:

> **This is Gift. Who are you?** <

> **my name is drow.** < came the reply instantly. > **are you all right, gift? is talent all right?** <

Tally moved toward the keypad and Gift pointed out the keys to type with. She composed her own message even more slowly, taking time about what she wanted to say. Gift could barely contain his impatience; he was so elated that he was almost dancing on the spot.

> **This is Talent. I am fine. I think we may owe you our lives. Thank you.** <

> **it was my pleasure.** < the stranger reassured them. > **but i don't know how i did it. i'm not much more experienced than you with this. what did you mean when you said you were hexes?** <

Tally glanced at Gift and he frowned, then shrugged, reaching for the terminal to type.

> **This is Gift. Tally and I are both Hexes. Our lives are in danger because of it and we need your help. You must be a Hex too or you couldn't exist in the network this way. Please help us.** <

It took Gift a long time to finish his message but this time the response was not instantaneous. The twins waited anxiously and then gradually the words appeared on the screen.

> **you know much more than i do, i think. i've used computers all my life but i never realized that this ability made me a hex. i could never understand it. i didn't know what being a hex meant. now it makes sense. i want to know more but what you want is more important, right now. how are you in danger? how can i help?** <

Tally breathed a huge sigh of relief and clung to Gift.

"Thank God!" she said. "He'll help us." But then her natural wariness returned and she said with a troubled look, "How *can* he help us? What should we ask for?"

"This was *your* idea," Gift reminded her.

"I never thought it would work though," she replied. "I never imagined—"

"Well, let's tell him about our problem then," Gift interrupted her. "Maybe he'll have an idea of what to do." Reaching for the keypad he replied:

> **We are in Italy in a city called Padua. We are being hunted by**

the Security Services and Federation troops. We are trying to contact a group of Hexes in England. A Hex escaped from Federation custody there. We thought that person could help us. Is that you? <

> no, it's not. i'm sorry. <

The answer came back slowly and Gift felt sure that the person they were speaking to was thinking hard about what they were saying.

> but perhaps i can help you find them. first tell me though how urgently you need help. are you safe where you are? <

> For the time being. < Gift replied. > But we can't stay where we are for long. <

There was a long pause and then a long answer began to reel itself on to the screen and Gift and Tally leaned forward so as not to miss any of it.

> even a small city has crime. padua must have some gangers somewhere. find them. gangers mean fixers and fixers will do anything for creds. find a fixer and give them this call-code: eu/lonnode/bethnel/chr#34850. say i will pay money for them to find a safe place to hide you. ask for a room with a terminal and then call me again from there. don't say anything to the fixer about being hexes. don't say anything about the seccies or the feds. just ask for a room and offer the money. look confident enough and they will agree. do you understand? <

> Yes. Thank you. < Tally responded. > How much will it cost you? I am sorry to cause you trouble. <

> don't worry. < Drow replied. > i'm a hacker. i can find the creds. i will do my best to help you. go now and find a safe place. write down the call-code. don't lose it. <

> **We won't. Thank you.** < Tally replied while Gift fumbled in
their bag for something to write on. As he scribbled down the code
Tally keyed in one last message.

> **We owe you everything.** <

Drow stared at his terminal screen but nothing more was added.
He had dropped back through the net after making the connection with the Italian system and had watched with fascination as
the strangers he met in the net explained their problem to him.
Stunned by the revelation that he was a Hex he had hardly been
able to think straight but he had suggested the only idea that
occurred to him and hoped desperately he had told them the right
thing to do. Now their last words hung on the screen.

> **We owe you everything.** <

He had no idea what to do now. Talent and Gift had been
searching the net for a savior and had found him. Now he would
have to take on their search himself. He needed to find a Hex and
he had no idea how to do it. With a sigh he turned off the terminal
and went to find his father. Maybe he would have an idea. Drow
had no doubt that his family would accept the knowledge that he
was a Hex with equanimity. They cared nothing for Federation
laws and restrictions, and the injunction against mutants was no
more than a Federation law. He hurried down the stairs into the
main room and came face to face with the net.

It hung on the vidscreen in the room. The same vision of the
net that he saw from his terminal. The vision he had never been
able to describe to anyone.

"That's it!" he exclaimed. "That's what I see."

Electra and Innuru were sitting in front of the vidscreen and they both turned around at his words, their expressions alarmed.

"Drow—" Electra began but her words were cut off abruptly as the images on the screen changed and Drow took a step backward instinctively.

In his worst nightmares he could never have imagined a horror like this. The city of light that had hung tantalizingly on the screen was replaced with a room that seemed a bizarre cross between a high-tech laboratory and a medieval torture chamber. A small childish figure lay enclosed in instruments, writhing in silent agony as a group of white-coated scientists stood around making notes. A list of statistics scrolled past on the screen. Details of experiments that made Drow's throat contract with nausea and finally a death date. It hung on the screen for a second, superimposed over the face of the mutilated child. Then the image was replaced by another scene, almost identical except that this child was younger still. Incongruously, music was playing in the background. A haunting twisted guitar sound that burned into his brain like a wire.

"Turn it off," he gasped, reaching for the control. But Innuru got there first and the vidscreen faded into blackness. Even with it off the images still played in Drow's mind and he stared at the blank screen transfixed.

It wasn't until Innuru shook him hard that Drow realized his sister and her husband had moved and were standing on either side of him, looking into his eyes with anxious expressions.

"Drow, are you all right?" Electra was shaking.

"I think so," he said shakily. "What was that?"

"The end of Populix as a news channel," Innuru said grimly. "That stuff's going to get them taken off the air for sure."

Drow looked at him blankly and Electra explained further.

"It was a program about the new release from Avalon. The rock singer who went underground? A collection of music was released on the net claiming to be by her and Populix is the only channel playing it. The city images were also released by the terrorists Avalon's supposed to have joined but the torture stuff comes off the news feeds. Four years back that stuff was released about experiments on Hex kids. But the government denied it all."

"Looks like some people didn't believe them," Innuru pointed out and Electra nodded.

"Do you believe them?" Drow asked. "Did that . . . were those images real kids, or not?"

Innuru and Electra looked at each other and then Innuru took charge.

"Sit down, Drow," he ordered, leading him to the battered sofa. "I want to ask a question first. When you said that the city was what you saw, did you mean what I think?"

"You mean am I a Hex, don't you?" Drow said slowly. He studied Innuru's face but could find no clue to what his brother-in-law was thinking. For the first time he wondered if it was wise to reveal his secret. But Electra and Innuru were family, and suddenly remembering Tally and Gift and how desperately they needed help, he knew he couldn't wait to be certain. If he couldn't trust Innuru, who could he trust?

"That's what I'm asking," Innuru agreed, waiting for his answer and Drow bowed his head.

"Yes," he said quietly. "I think I am."

"That's what I thought," Innuru replied and turned to Electra. "Get the rest of the family," he said. "Your father and your sisters."

Without a word Electra left the room and Innuru turned back to Drow. Drow looked back at him with wide scared eyes, uncertain of what to say, and when Innuru smiled, his relief was enormous.

"No Chrome should be ashamed to be a Hex," the older ganger told him. "Hexes have a genetic gift for the skills the rest of us have to teach ourselves." He touched Drow's shoulder lightly. "Don't worry, Drow. The family has talked about this before. You're not the first Chrome this has happened to."

"And not the last either," a strong voice came from behind them and Drow turned around to see his father. "Don't you start getting scared of the Seccies or the other Federation lap-dogs now. There's no one in this family who wouldn't hide you from them, and if we can't do it, there are others even better at it."

"Do you mean the terrorists?" Drow asked, his mind working quickly. "The ones Electra said Avalon's with. The ones who released the music?"

His father came across to sit beside him and his sisters gathered around the sofa to hear his explanation. But it was Innuru who spoke first.

"First thing you gotta know is that we don't talk about it," he said. "Not ever."

"That is important," Drow's father agreed. "Half the city's

looking for the people who blew up half the Federation Consulate to rescue one of their own and if the Seccies found them—"

"The people who blew up the Consulate?" Drow interrupted suddenly. "They must be the ones I'm looking for!"

"Looking for them?" His father frowned. "Why? Surely you know you're safe here?"

"Yes, of course." A rush of relief flooded through Drow as he properly understood that for the first time. His family was as trustworthy as he had always thought they would be. But the realization made it all the more urgent to help Gift and Tally. They had no one to rely on except for him.

"It's not for me, I'm looking for them," Drow began to explain. "It's for someone else, two kids in Italy."

"In Italy?" Electra asked, puzzled, and Drow continued quickly.

"They contacted me through the net," he said. "At least we met each other there. It was kind of an accident that they found me. But they were looking for other Hexes. Their names are Gift and Talent and they're very young but they're on the run from the Federation. It sounds like everyone's hunting them and they badly need help. I promised I'd try and find Hexes in England for them. There's supposed to be a group that can help and it must be these terrorists. I'm certain of it."

Tally clutched the precious call-code, scribbled on a piece of sandwich wrapper, tightly in her hand all the time while Gift talked to Julietta. He admired the fluid way her brother lied to the old lady, assuring her that they had contacted their parents and were on the way to meet them. He thanked her and Grego politely for their help as if he had nothing to worry about. No one could possibly have guessed from his behavior that he had been trapped inside the computer network less than ten minutes earlier. At that thought Tally had to repress her hysteria. Of course no one could guess that, she thought. It's insanity.

She attempted to smile her own good-byes as Gift took her hand and led her out of the bar but she was still shaking inside and her brother knew it. As soon as they were outside he set a brisk pace down the street, talking to her confidently

"It's all right, Tally, really," he said. "We're both OK and Drow's going to help us. He already has. All we need to do is find the kind of people that Seccies think of as criminals." He squeezed her hand tightly as he added, "Now, don't worry about that either. I know what you're like. But just because the Seccies think gangers are criminals doesn't mean that they're people we wouldn't want to meet. And it won't be difficult to find them, either. Look at us." He gestured down at their tattered and dirty clothes. "We'll fit right in, just look for people like us."

"People like us," Tally replied dazedly. But the soothing flow of Gift's words *was* relaxing her. She didn't feel as worried when he was so confident that Drow's advice would help them. Tally didn't know whether to be thrilled that they had actually succeeded in contacting someone or despairing that they had not found the people they were looking for. But she was beginning to recover from the shock of being trapped in the data network and Gift's words were slowly penetrating her mind.

"Yes, like us," Gift replied, continuing to speak soothingly. "I'm sure it won't be difficult—"

"Beggars," Tally said abruptly and he frowned, turning to face her. "What was that?" he asked.

"Beggars," she said again, her mind slowly beginning to work again. "That's what we look like."

"And beggars are street people who might know where we can find a fixer," Gift replied. "Or at least know someone who knows." He grinned. "Tally, you're brilliant. Even when you look as vacant as a blank wall you still come up with the goods." He hugged her impulsively and Tally hugged him back, smiling.

"We should find the city center," she pointed out. "Beggars approach tourists and there are always more tourists in the center of town."

"Good idea," Gift agreed and they looked around for signs. Tally was the first to spot what they wanted.

"Look!" she said, pointing to a sign which read *Centro Historico*. "That looks promising."

"Come on then," Gift said, heading for it. "What are we waiting for?"

It took Drow a while to convince his family how urgently Gift and Tally needed help. But, once he had told his story a second time, answering their questions as best he could, Innuru and his father got a look of determination.

"All right then," his father said. "We'll have to make contact with the Hexes here and tell them that two of their own need their help. But someone will have to stay ready in case any Italian fixer calls that code and asks for money. Electra, that's something you can do." He looked around at the others, considering for a moment. "Selver, you watch the news feeds while we're gone. Keep up with what's happening. I have a feeling that this story of Populix's is going to stir things up. And, Arachne, you go and find us transportation. We've got a trip to make."

"A trip where?" Drow asked. "To see these Hexes?"

"Unfortunately not," his father replied. "All we have is one contact. A fixer who they trust. But if we can persuade her it's urgent enough she may tell us how to find them."

Drow waited impatiently while Arachne went to borrow a flitter from another gang member and Innuru carefully checked through his weaponry. Unusually he collected a snub-nosed blaster and handed it to Drow.

"Best to have some protection," he said.

Drow glanced at his father, but when he made no objection, he hoisted the weapon carefully, feeling its weight.

"Thanks, Innuru," he said gratefully. Despite the fact that he had wandered the city without weapons many times, he was starting to feel an irrational fear that this time the Seccies would pick him up and know him for a Hex.

"Be careful with it," his brother-in-law warned him. "Don't use it unless you have to."

It was then that Arachne returned with the news that a flitter was waiting outside and Drow hastily got to his feet.

It was early evening outside, the streets still filled with hawkers and visitors coming into Chrome territory to do business with the legitimate traders. But, with the approach of night, more gangers were out on the streets too, ready to do a different kind of business. A Chrome patrol loitered in the plaza nearby, watching passersby with a studied casualness. The little light that filtered down from the upper levels of the city during the middle of the day had been extinguished and across the ganglands the artificial lighting had been intensified so that Drow felt as if he was walking in a black and white landscape: the brilliant pools of light intensifying the shadows around them. He shuddered as he remembered the images he had seen on the vidscreen. Horrors could live in the light as easily as trust could lie in the shadows, he reminded himself. As he climbed into the back of the little flitter that stood waiting, he found himself thinking of the levels controlled by the Ghosts. The throng of people moving through Chrome territory now was a vivid contrast to the eerie emptiness of the Ghost levels, brightly lit even when no one walked their streets. For the first time he wondered if that was deliberate. So little was known about the Ghosts that anyone who passed through their territory would have to guess as to their intentions. All those lights and surveillance equipment were impressive but they were made all the more intimidating because a passerby had no face to put them to. Here the Chromes made a show of force but the Ghosts kept their force hidden and were respected for it.

Drow realized that the elusive gang had been more intelligent in their use of the areas they controlled than he had realized and he felt a sudden curiosity about what so much secrecy was designed to conceal. If the revelation hadn't come just as he was thinking about the Hexes he might not have made a connection. But, as it was, a sudden certainty hit him and he almost spoke it aloud. Then he stopped himself. It was possible that the Ghosts hid the Hexes within their midst but there was no reason to assume that made it true. For now he would hold on to his suspicions until he had met this contact of his father's. Hopefully that would shed more light on the situation and perhaps prove or disprove his ideas.

It had taken Cloud some time to find Raven. After the discussion of the attack on Transcendence she had disappeared and his enquiries had discovered no trace of her. Although the others at the meeting were divided between anger and hurt at her announcement, not one of them had attempted to confront her. Ali had told him outright that she wouldn't dare and Luciel and Kez appeared to feel the same way. Avalon had obviously decided it wasn't really her business to speak to Raven and had turned her attention to trying to talk to Wraith, who was more than usually silent. Cloud didn't envy her that task. The white-haired ganger was someone that *he* found intimidating and he hadn't tried to broach the subject of Raven with him. Alaric was likewise absorbed in trying to calm down Geraint, who saw Raven's behavior as an outright betrayal. Lots of ruffled feathers was Cloud's own verdict on the situation. But although the group's behavior made an interesting social study it didn't help him in tracking down the person who had started it all off.

Ironically, it wasn't until he had abandoned the search that he found her. The larger of the Ghost enclaves contained an old vidplex building: a series of large vidscreens which had once been open to the public. Now it was mostly disused, although the group had held some of their larger meetings there. However, the screens were still connected and Cloud had wandered inside with the vague intention of trying to pick up a news feed on one of them. When he reached the building he realized that it wasn't completely deserted. The long hallways echoed with the sound of his footsteps, but in the distance he could hear the sound of music, and following it, he came to the hall which held the largest of the five screens. The double doors slid open as he approached and for a moment he was blinded by the light from the screen, filling the darkened room. He recognized the vid playing instantly—he had designed most of it, a sequence to accompany Masque's last release. It had been called "Transformations" and its images of dark passages filled with shadows had been Raven's first clue that Avalon was a Hex.

Cloud walked down the ranks of seating to where a figure sat at dead center of the first row. Raven didn't look at him, her black eyes focused on the screen, but as he sat down she asked:

"How long have you been looking for me?"

"A few hours," Cloud replied. "But now I've given up, I have a feeling you don't want to be found."

"Maybe I just don't want the search to be easy," Raven said, glancing sideways at him with a half smile. "Why were you looking for me?"

"Curiosity perhaps," Cloud told her. "Why did you tell the others you wouldn't stay with them unless they faced the Federation?"

"Why do you think I did?" Raven asked him and he studied her carefully before answering.

"I wondered if you did have any intention of leaving," he said. "You knew that their reaction would be to agree with you. They hadn't any other choice. So, did you really intend to leave?"

For a few moments Raven was silent, watching the darkness unfold on the screen in front of her. Then she said softly, "I always mean what I say."

"So if they'd called your bluff you'd have left?" Cloud asked her.

"It wasn't a bluff," Raven said sharply. She swung around in her seat to regard him seriously. "But there doesn't always have to be a plan. If I leave, I can find my own future." She laughed briefly. "Sometimes, the way they rely on me here, I wonder if it makes much difference with or without them."

"Would you go up against the Federation on your own?" Cloud asked quickly. "Without the support of the Ghosts?"

Raven smiled secretively, moving her head slightly so that her long curtain of hair swung forward, obscuring his view of her.

"Cloud," she said quietly. "Every breath I take on this Earth is a strike against the Federation. My entire life is a terrorist action. The only way for me to stop fighting them would be to stop living. Does it matter very much how or where I do it?"

"Yes," said Cloud. "To quote your brother: yes, it does."

"Why?"

"Because danger isn't consistent," he said with an edge in his voice. "Hasn't Avalon increased her danger by joining this group, despite the fact that she was always a Hex?"

"She's put herself less at risk by learning how to use her abilities," Raven pointed out.

"Point taken," Cloud granted. "But tell me honestly, how much would the danger to you increase when you move against the heart of Federation power?"

"Exponentially," Raven replied. "As it does every day."

"How?"

"Because," Raven said slowly, "somewhere, not so very far away, a group of bureaucrats sit in a room being berated by a government official who can't believe that after four years they are still no closer to catching me and wiping the rest of the Hexes off the face of the Earth."

"How do you know?" Cloud asked.

"Because that's the way the world works," Raven replied. "Until we change it."

7

THE KEYS OF HELL

Arachne piloted the little flitter skillfully through the city. The weaving course she took was as much to avoid rival gangs as the Seccies or other law enforcement agencies. The flitter was unmarked but all four of them were wearing Chrome colors and the silver metal threaded into their braids would have identified them even without that. Drow looked around curiously at the course Arachne took. His practiced eyes could tell that she was being extra careful. She didn't pass through any territories controlled by gangs with which the Chromes had even minor disputes, keeping to friendly or neutral ganglands despite the erratic path it meant she had to fly. But he was surprised when she finally brought the flitter to the ground in the center of Snake territory.

The Snakes were a gang with which the Chromes had almost no contact at all. They were a minor, if respected, clan. Although they were loyal to each other as a group they had diverse interests and were often found hiring themselves out to other gangs as mercenaries. But, despite their lack of unity, Drow had never heard anyone disparage the Snakes' firepower, and he felt nervous as a large man dressed in battered combats appeared from the side of a building to block the end of a narrow spur of walkway ahead of them. The walkway was the only route to a section of building with metal-shielded windows all the way up to the next level. The unknown ganger didn't move out of the way as they approached. Instead he leveled a heavy assault rifle at them and said slowly:

"That's close enough."

"We don't want trouble," Innuru said, speaking for all of them. "We just want to see your fixer."

The man looked Innuru up and down, then turned his attention to the rest of them.

"Chromes, aren't you?" he said. "Don't you have any fixers of your own back in hacker town?"

"They don't have the information we need," Drow's father said, meeting the big man's eyes. "The Countess does."

"The Countess doesn't take on much work nowadays," the man told him. "What makes you think she'll want to see you?"

"She's seen Chromes before," Drow's father continued. "And it is important."

The man considered them for a while longer; then eventually he nodded.

"Reckon it must be," he said. "You're not the usual types we get around here." He stepped back a little to let them past. "You can go in," he continued. "But walk softly or you'll get more than you bargain for."

The four of them trooped across the narrow spur of walkway to the entrance to the building. The main door stood open and they stepped through into a wide hall. Inside, two gangers in Snake colors, their hair dyed a distinctive dark blue, loitered near an impressively high-tech flitter. Another three people stood on the other side of the hall, guarding the only door which was not blocked up with rubble. The Snake gangers ignored them as Drow and his family crossed the hall to approach the door guards. They were only a few meters away when one of the guards, a blonde woman, gestured toward a gleaming vidcom unit to her right.

"State your names and business into the vidcom," she said. "The Countess herself will decide if she wishes to see you."

As his father moved toward the unit, Drow looked around thoughtfully. The building was undecorated and the doors blocked up with rubble gave the impression of dilapidation. But the flitter looked custom-designed, built for speed and power, and the vidcom unit was a recent model from a specialty computer hardware company. He wondered how much of the apparent disrepair of this building was intentional.

"My name is Mohan," his father was saying. "With me are my son-in-law Innuru and my children: Arachne and Drow. We believe we have information of interest to some contacts of yours." He glanced at the guards. "Contacts who guard their privacy seriously."

They waited for a few moments in silence until a dry voice spoke out of the vidcom unit.

"All my associates guard their privacy seriously," it said. "Or else I would not do business with them. I hope that you will show a similar discretion. Leave your weapons and approach the stairway."

The guards looked at them expectantly and Drow's father stepped forward to divest himself of his blaster and two knives. Innuru and Arachne followed suit and Drow handed over his blaster after them. However, the guards did not move away from the door and when Innuru attempted to pass them the blonde woman raised a hand in warning.

"*All* your weapons," she said. "Including those stealth pistols."

Innuru and Drow's father exchanged looks. Then they each reached down to produce a slim lightweight pistol from their boots. Drow blinked in surprise. The pistols had an iridescent sheen, showing that they had been coated in a material intended to baffle scanning devices. But despite this protection the Countess's guards had still spotted them, and he wondered what kind of security system this fixer had that would make that possible.

Once the pistols had been surrendered the guards moved away from the door and it slid open to allow their group to enter. They found themselves standing at the bottom of a wide sweeping staircase and were almost immediately confronted with multiple images of themselves. Every surface in all directions was made of reflective shielding, strong enough to withstand a bomb blast as far as Drow could tell. He was certain that there was enough equipment behind the walls to scan every inch of their bodies and probably tell the Countess what they had eaten for breakfast if she wanted to know. It made him nervous to head up those stairs, conscious that he was under invisible observation. Traveling through the Ghost territory had been unnerving enough but at least then he had seen the surveillance equipment. Here he knew it existed but there was no sign to confirm his suspicions.

"Hell of a setup," Innuru muttered to himself, and Arachne smiled.

"Come on, Inni," she pointed out. "At least it lets us know we're dealing with talent, yeh?"

"Talent and quality," Drow's father agreed. "And, since the lady is almost certainly listening, she may as well know she has all our admiration."

That silenced them for a while and they climbed the rest of the stairs quickly. At the summit they found themselves standing on a narrow landing and facing a plain mirrored wall. Drow glanced at the others quizzically and Innuru shrugged. As he did so the wall slid out of the way and they saw a room full of screens and terminals behind it. All of them relaxed imperceptibly at the sight. Up until now the fixer's base had been alien territory but this room was much like any building controlled by Chromes. It was unmistakably the property of a computer fanatic. The cases and crates of equipment stacked against the walls were the latest in tech and the plainly dressed woman standing at the center of the room had the typical casual arrogance of a hacker. She had short shaved dark hair and wore black coveralls. Her only other adornment were the multiple bands that circled her arms, covered with controls and miniscreens.

The fixer didn't bother with greetings but launched straight into the matter of their business.

"You say you have information for my contacts," she said sharply. "But I doubt you bring it as a gift."

Drow's father opened his mouth to speak but Drow interrupted him. It was he who was the cause of their contacting this woman and he didn't want to hide behind his family when the responsibility should be his.

"It's strange you should say that," he said. "For it's a gift and a talent that we bring you."

Innuru looked at him sharply but didn't stop him from speaking and his father rested his hand on Drow's shoulder in silent support.

"A gift and a talent," the fixer mused, then smiled suddenly. "I like you, boy," she said. "You have a way with words. But speak to me openly. Which of my contacts is it that you truly seek?"

"We're looking for Hexes," Drow said boldly. "And my father gave me to understand you have a connection with them."

"It's known to certain of our gang," his father explained. "In the past when children have been at risk from the CPS you were a contact between us and those who were able to hide them. I come to you on behalf of my son, who may need the help of these people. But his concern is for friends of his who need it even more."

"Such altruism," the Countess said. "But it seems that your kind are increasingly supporting each other, boy. So my connections may help you. Though I make no promises."

"Then you do know the Hexes?" Drow asked eagerly. "Will you put us in touch with them? That's all I ask."

"I shall endeavor to," the Countess replied.

"We will of course pay a finder's fee," Drow's father added but the Countess shook her head.

"It's not necessary in this case," she replied. "Those who you seek are generous with their resources, especially when I can pass them news of their own. One moment and we shall see if they will meet with you."

She walked over to one of the many terminals that lined the walls and spoke to it, the unit responding perfectly to her voice commands.

"Dragon's Nest," she told it and the screen sprang to life, revealing a young girl with brown hair and a serious expression.

"Dragon's Nest," she said immediately. *"What can I do for you, Countess?"*

"It's a question of what I may do for you," the Countess replied. Then she turned to Drow and beckoned him toward her. "I have one of your people here, anxious for help," she said.

The girl on the screen looked at Drow and her blue-green eyes flickered for a second in what looked like surprise. But her voice was level as she asked, *"How may I help you then?"*

"My name is Drow," he said hesitantly. "I'm a hacker and, I think, a Hex as well. I'd like to meet you, to learn more about you. But first I urgently need your help. I have friends, two kids, who are in danger from the Federation. They're Hexes although they don't know much about how to use the net and they told me that Hexes in England might be able to save them. If you can help—"

"Naturally we will help as much as we can," the girl said and smiled quickly. *"But I don't have the authority to say how. You'll have to speak to my superiors. Probably with Raven herself."*

"The Raven?" Drow asked, looking up at the Countess for clarification.

"Raven brought down the CPS laboratory that performed experiments on your kind," the fixer explained. "She escaped EF custody and it's her skills that have helped the Hexes become ghosts on the net."

"Ghosts!" Drow exclaimed. "Are you the Ghosts?" He looked eagerly at the girl on the screen. "I was almost certain of it," he confessed. "Will you let me come to you and explain?"

The girl hesitated for a moment then said, *"One minute, while I confirm."*

The screen went black and Drow turned to his father with a smile.

"They *will* help," he said with relief. "I'm sure they can."

His father nodded but had no time to say anything else as the screen brightened again and the girl's face reappeared.

"You may meet with us," she said. *"Countess, are Finn and Jeeva still with you?"*

"Downstairs," the fixer confirmed. "Shall I send this boy with them?"

"If you would," the girl nodded.

Innuru looked doubtful and frowned at the Countess.

"Drow shouldn't go alone," he said. "Ask if his family may come with him."

"Innuru." Drow turned his face to his brother-in-law. "There's no need. This is my trouble and my concern. I trust these people. To help me and to help Gift and Tally. I don't mind going alone."

"Then we'll expect you shortly," the girl on the screen said and her image blanked out abruptly.

"Don't be concerned," the Countess said seriously. "Drow has nothing to fear."

Innuru still looked uncertain but Drow's father nodded and hugged his son quickly.

"You will be safe with these people," he said. "We've trusted our children to them before and what news we have reports them safe and well. That these Hexes can offer such security when they are being hunted as the Federation has never hunted anyone before shows that they are trustworthy."

"Take care of yourself, Drow," Arachne said quietly.

"And contact us as soon as you can," Innuru added.

Drow nodded, almost too excited to speak. But he looked at all of them, soaking in the sight in case he didn't see them again for a long time.

The twins waited anxiously outside the crumbling warehouse. It had taken all Gift's powers of persuasion to convince the Italian kids they had found begging from tourists to tell them where they might find gangers and when they had reached this unprepossessing building a surly young boy had told them only to wait while he went inside.

"Look at it this way," Gift said positively. "We have got this far. It looks like our luck might have started to change."

Tally nodded but didn't say anything. Now that she had recovered from the shock of her experience in the net her mind was racing. Gift was right to say they had done well to achieve as much as they had but she was trying to concentrate on the steps ahead. Her musings were interrupted by the reappearance of the boy who had told them to wait.

"You're to go inside," he said in thickly accented Italian, jerking his thumb at the warehouse. "Rosso will meet with you."

The twins got to their feet slowly, hoisting their battered pack between them, and headed toward the door. The boy watched them expressionlessly as they entered the darkened building. Inside, the warehouse had been divided into low-rent accommodation. Flimsy-looking partition walls had been put up around the sides of the warehouse space and a rusty metal stairway led up to a second floor which was similarly divided. A group of people were clustered around a kind of seating area near the bottom of the metal steps. Torn sofas and chairs had been pulled into a rough semicircle facing an antique vidscreen. As Gift and Tally approached, squinting in the poor light, a teenager with reddish hair signaled to them to come closer. They did so reluctantly. There were about nine young people watching the screen and all of them looked confident and relaxed despite the shoddy surroundings. Gift was the first to speak as they reached the seating area.

"Are you Rosso?" he asked in careful Italian.

"I am," the redheaded boy said with a penetrating stare. "And who are you?"

"I'm Gift and this is my sister, Tally," Gift explained. "We need somewhere to stay for a couple of days. We can pay."

"Just as well," Rosso said with a short laugh. "Otherwise we wouldn't be talking. How much cred you got?"

"Nothing with us," Gift admitted. "But we have a friend who can send you the creds by data transfer and we can pay extra for the inconvenience."

"Maybe." Rosso looked thoughtful. "What have kids like you got to be hiding from anyway?"

"We have a couple of convictions for theft," Gift lied smoothly. "And if the Seccies catch us we'll end up being made wards of the state. We're orphans and they'll put us in a blockhouse if we're caught."

"Yeah?" Rosso didn't look entirely convinced but something on the vidscreen had caught his attention: a sports match was beginning and the other teenagers were turning up the sound on the ancient unit. "All right then," he said quickly. "Give me your friend's call-code and take room sixteen for now. That suit you?"

"That's great," Gift said thankfully. "Thank you."

"No problem," Rosso replied, already turning away to look at the screen.

Room sixteen turned out to be a small windowless room on the second floor. Through the flimsy partition walls they could hear the sounds of the vidscreen even from this distance and sounds of conversations and arguments coming from nearby rooms. There were three stained mattresses lying on the floor and a heap of equally dirty blankets piled up in the corner of the room.

"Doesn't seem like much of a palazzo, does it?" Gift said with a half smile.

"I'm more concerned that the door doesn't lock," Tally replied and her brother looked frustrated.

"What are you worrying about now?" he asked. "That lot downstairs couldn't care less about us. And Drow's plan worked fine."

"I suppose so." Tally said. She sat down on the edge of one of the mattresses, uncertainly. "But if they knew who we were we'd be in real trouble. I just don't feel safe here, that's all."

"You never feel safe anywhere, Tally," Gift pointed out. "Come on, I've got a deck of cards somewhere in my pack. Let's play a game or something. It'll take your mind off it."

"All right," Tally agreed. "I suppose there's not much else to do."

Outside the door to room sixteen an Italian teenager leaned on the rail that overlooked the next level with a thoughtful expression. Rosso hadn't cared that the two kids were telling an obvious lie but he'd gone upstairs after them to fetch a crate of alcohol from his own room and overheard Tally's remark. Now the crate lay forgotten beside him as he considered what to do. His gang was about as low as they came in Padua's hierarchy and right now they could barely afford to eat, let alone buy alcohol or repair the increasingly unreliable vidscreen. If by chance the two kids were important to someone there might be a chance for him to make money from it. Slowly he picked up the crate of beer and carried it downstairs, dumping it by the rotting sofas.

"I've got to go and make a call," he told his friends. "I'll be back in a moment."

None of them paid him much attention, although one started to hand out drinks. Shrugging, Rosso wandered toward the door of the warehouse. He didn't own a vidcom and would have to use a public one in town. But, before he called the kids' friend to arrange money, he'd contact a friend he hadn't seen for a while. Nikki wasn't much of a friend, never using his position in the local Seccie force to help Rosso, but he did sometimes pay for information and these kids might be worth something to him.

Raven and Cloud wandered out of the vidplex slowly with no particular plan of where to go next. Raven had spoken vaguely of checking up on Charis, the Hex they'd recently rescued, to give her an initial evaluation. But they had only reached the end of the street when a figure rushed out of a nearby building and raced up to them. It was Maggie, one of the Anglecynn members, and Raven and Cloud paused to wait for her.

"Raven!" she said breathlessly, as she reached them. "People have been looking for you. An emergency meeting's been called at the Fortress and they want you to be there."

"Who does?" Raven asked sharply. "And who called this meeting?"

"I've no idea," Maggie said blankly. "I thought you might know what it was about. But I think Alaric and Jordan are there."

"What kind of emergency is it?" Cloud asked. "The kind where everyone has to assume battle stations and prepare for serious trouble or the kind that's called because people have nothing better to do with their time?"

"How should I know?" Maggie said again, then she gave Cloud a suspicious look. "But speaking of having nothing to do, why doesn't anyone ever see *you* working?"

"Perhaps because my work is too important for you to know about," Cloud replied mischievously.

Raven shook her head at him. "We don't have time for this," she said. "Cloud, pull in your claws and find me a flitter so we can find out how urgent this emergency is."

It took them half an hour to reach the Fortress and Raven was distracted most of the time, concentrating her attention on piloting the flitter. She didn't travel as fast as she could, to Cloud's relief, obviously trusting that whatever the problem was it wasn't important enough for the other members of the group to make a serious attempt at finding her. But she made good time through the nighttime traffic, avoiding Seccie and EF troop patrols with the ease born of long practice.

There was no obvious sign of trouble when they touched down outside the Fortress. Two of the older Hex children, both girls, were standing guard by the door and they saluted as Raven exited the flitter. The movement gave her pause for thought and she stopped, regarding them.

"Apparently a meeting is going on," she said. "Do you know what it's about?"

"Finn and Jeeva, the Snake gangers, brought in a boy about

an hour ago," the older of the two told her. "After that Alaric and Wraith arrived, so perhaps the meeting is to debrief a new Hex," she suggested.

Raven looked at the girl for a while. She looked about fourteen and, like Raven, she had dark hair and dark eyes.

"You're observant," she commented. "It's Cara, isn't it?"

"Yes." The girl smiled, pleased to have been recognized.

"I remember you from your training," Raven told her. "You were one of the fastest to learn. Are you as good with that gun?" She gestured at the laser pistol the girl was holding firmly.

"I'm better," Cara said, grinning. "But it's not as hard to learn weapons."

Raven raised an eyebrow.

"The net *is* a weapon," she said dryly. "It just has a different sort of trigger."

Both children looked at her with wide eyes but Raven was already turning away, heading inside. Cloud had to take a few fast paces to catch her up.

"What were you trying to teach them?" he asked when he reached her.

"To think," she replied. "Those kids may find their lives changing very soon."

"We all might," Cloud said under his breath as he watched her head up the stairs. Then he turned back to where the door guards kept their posts. He doubted he would be welcome at whatever meeting was being held. In the circumstances he might as well see if Raven had succeeded in encouraging thought.

• • •

The door to one of the smaller meeting rooms was open, and when Raven paused in the doorway, she saw Alaric, Wraith, Ali, and a stranger. Not precisely a stranger though. As Raven stood, unobserved for the moment, her eidetic memory recalled where she had seen this boy before. He was the intruder who had triggered a low-level security alert a few days ago. When Jordan had shown her the surveillance footage Raven had felt a tremble of recognition and had wondered if he might be a Hex. Now, before she had even had time to check up on him, he had appeared.

"Is this our emergency?" she asked and all four people turned around to look at her.

"Not exactly," Wraith replied, unfazed by her sudden appearance. "But Drow has brought us interesting information that I think you should hear."

Raven came into the room and swung herself up to sit on the edge of the meeting table and waited expectantly. It didn't take the others long to fill her in—Drow had described Gift and Tally's situation to them as best he understood it and then they had questioned him about his meeting with them in the net. It was that aspect that most interested Raven and her dark eyes remained fixed on the boy as he stammered his own description of the encounter.

"Interesting," she said eventually and Alaric smiled at her.

"We thought you'd think so," he said.

"We've contacted Drow's family and apparently a gang member called Rosso called in about twenty minutes ago and requested payment for helping Gift and Tally," Ali added. "It appears for the time being they're safe."

"It was well thought of," Wraith said, looking approvingly at the boy. "It was brave of you to try so hard to help them despite the danger to yourself."

"I didn't think it was all that dangerous," Drow confessed, tearing his eyes away from Raven, who had held him transfixed since she had first entered the room. "I only found out I was a Hex today. But my family, they've suspected for ages and not said anything. They helped immediately when I asked them to. Tally and Gift only had me."

"And now they have us," Wraith assured him. "Don't you agree, Raven?"

"Hmm?" Raven blinked and looked at him blankly for a moment before nodding. "Yes," she said quickly. "It shouldn't prove too problematic to help them, despite the distances involved but—"

"But what?" Drow asked, alarmed, and Raven fixed him with an unreadable onyx stare.

"There's something strange about this," she mused. "If Drow met them during their first foray into the net, how did they know they were Hexes? More than that, how did they come to bear those names?"

The others glanced at each other and shrugged. Alaric was the first to speak.

"Why does it matter?" he asked.

"Because there's a mystery here," Raven replied with a flash of annoyance. "And mysteries require discovery."

"But you will help them," Drow said pleadingly and Raven smiled for the first time as his silver eyes met her black gaze.

"Yes," she said. "I promise."

The others relaxed slightly and Alaric said thoughtfully, "We had better consider how best to approach the matter. Perhaps we could combine this rescue with the trip to Transcendence."

"Which might have to happen sooner than we'd planned," Wraith agreed, rising to his feet. He glanced at Drow. "You should go with Ali," he told the boy. "She can tell you more about us and explain a little of our history. Then you'll need to repeat your story to some more of our group, if you don't mind."

"Not at all," Drow said politely, rising to follow Ali out of the room. But at the door he paused and turned back. "Raven?" he said hesitantly.

"Yes?" She turned to face him and he swallowed nervously, still obviously in awe of her.

"Do you know anything about the darkness?" he said.

"The darkness?" Raven's eyes widened and her pupils dilated slightly. Wraith, turning in surprise at the question, was alarmed to see that the color had drained out of her skin, leaving her paler than ever, like the ghost she claimed to be. "What darkness?" she whispered.

"The darkness in the net," Drow replied, looking at her with concern. "I don't know how long it's been there. But it's spreading all the time and everything it touches turns dark."

8

THE SUN
BECAME BLACK

Raven launched herself into the net as if leaping from a cliff.
She hadn't waited to explain, even though Wraith and the others
had stared after her in confusion when she ran from the room.
Darkness, the word rang in her mind like a curse. Only once before
had the net been dark to her. It had been when Dr. Kalden, the
scientist whose experimentation was responsible for the death and
torture of thousands, had begun to shred her mind. Absorbed in
her own pain, all she had been conscious of was darkness, until
she had escaped into the net and found the strength to strike back
against her torturers.

With the preparations for the attack on Transcendence and
the media manipulations required in releasing Avalon's music,
Raven had been separated from the network that was her lifeblood
too much recently. Now, as her fingertips rested lightly on the

keypad, her mind hurled itself out of the shielded system of the Fortress and along the flow of data. Separating herself, she sent her awareness in a hundred different directions down the data pathways, each line of thought dividing itself over and over again as she quested through the net. Information flooded through her. A million different commands and requests a second were channeled past her consciousness and each one was considered, evaluated, and rejected. What she was searching for was the absence of movement: a place where the chattering of the net ceased. She spread herself further and thinner. She was the web now, thousands of different strands drawing in around the object of her search. She drew the net tighter and tighter until, with a shock, she hit a wall.

The message sped through her brain, informing each tendril of the search that something unusual had been found. The different parts of Raven ceased their own progress through the dataflow and reached toward the point of contact. Gradually her mind coagulated until she was standing at the edge of the blackness. It rolled over the light and movement of the net, extinguishing everything in its path for an instant as its darkness fogged the datastreams. Raven watched its approach. It quested blindly, snail-like in its progress, but huge and inexorable. As it came nearer Raven blurred her own presence, hiding within a shield she had constructed of misleading access routines and bounced commands. Now that she was invisible to almost every presence in the network and cloaked in a blur of light she moved closer still and reached out to brush the edge of the cloud.

> **dark—death—black** < it whispered and she pulled back.

She felt numbed by even that slight contact but it wasn't enough. She needed more information. Doubling her shield, she steeled herself to enter the cloud of contagion. Then, taking a deep breath, she leapt forward and fell into the well of darkness.

It overwhelmed her. Fragments of thought echoed forward and backward inside the darkness. The only mind it had was this roiling fog of words.

> **dark down in the darkness of death . . . roving searching questing . . . question? question? . . . black/attack/turned on the rack . . . darkness here darkness here darkness** <

Reaching out delicately Raven inserted a single word into the fog.

> **light?** <

The response was like a thunderstorm, flashing of thoughts coursing through the darkness, giving it motion and speed with the violence of its reactions.

> **light blight spite . . . here the darkness here the darkness here the darkness here . . . flowing/moving/enfolding/dimming . . . stopping the quick/light/color . . . stilling the city that sings . . . clipping the wings . . . darkness brings . . .** <

The ominous words rolled on, forward and backward, as the cloud continued its passage, leaving the net dark behind it for microseconds until the data currents recovered and flashed back into active life. Raven could measure a perceptible time lag caused by the cloud. It wasn't yet long enough to seriously interfere with the operation of the net, measurable only in the microseconds of data transfer. But the period was increasing. The cloud was grow-ing, and the larger it became, the longer its effects lasted. Raven could imagine that this thing was capable of dimming the entire net if its growth rate continued. But what was it?

A horrible suspicion was growing in her mind and she moved out of the cloud to consider it, allowing it to creep on without her. She stood in the wasteland it left behind, waiting as the lights around her reappeared. Then, slowly, she circled around to the front of the darkness. Reaching for the strands of the web, she pulled them to her, filling her presence with the flow of data cur-rents. Cloaked in light she stood before it and presented an inter-rogation like the point of a sword.

> who/what/why are you? <

The question fell into the pit of the cloud and echoed back to her.

> why ... what ... who ... you? <

Raven reached further into the net and drew more of it toward her. A thousand minor access routines were diverted to flow about her position so that she stood in a cloud of light facing the dark-ness. Flourishing her sword once more she announced:

> i am raven—i rule here—identify yourself <

With a roar the cloud engulfed her and all the lights went out. The sword she had created splintered and shattered, its fragments melting like ice into nothingness. Around her the darkness beat against her cloak and shield until they also were shredded and fell away, leaving her defenseless before a rage that was like a force of nature.

> RAVEN ... <

Her own name beat against her brain over and over again. The cloud buffeted her about with the power of its fury, throwing images of darkness, death and pain at her until she screamed with the sensory overload. She flew for the edge of the blackness, but, as in a storm, she was dragged back into the whirling eye of the hurricane. It was trying to break her and the moment she realized that she let go.

Her fingers lifted from the keypad and her connection to the net, a constant humming presence in the back of her mind, locked shut. She had closed out the horror that dwelt within the network by shutting out everything. Now she stood, completely alone, staring at the computer screen. Something inside the net hated her and it would stop at nothing to destroy her. Even if that meant destroying the net in the process.

The Minister for Internal Affairs was a busy man. His children were at an age where the cost of their education seemed to double in price every year. His position had led his friends and family to expect lavish hospitality from him and he had married a trophy wife who had found spending his money a major attraction. In order to avoid running even further into debt he had embezzled money from several different sectors of the government and accepted bribes from people who even the corrupt EF elite considered dubious. The continued strain on his nerves from his tangled personal affairs had led him into an expensive drug habit, which in turn had allowed him to be blackmailed.

But these were the problems that came with high office, and the Minister understood that it was necessary to make sacrifices. What was annoying him right now was that he was expected to deal with another department's work as well as his own. Charles Alverstead, the governor of the CPS, had angered the President of the Federation with his continued excuses for his failure to locate the rogue Hexes. President Sanatos was not a man it was healthy to annoy. He had put the entire cabinet on notice that he expected this Hex named Raven to be found and would brook no further incompetence. So all across Europe criminals and agitators were openly criticizing the Federation, and the Minister for Internal Affairs could do nothing about it while his entire staff were occupied in the quest. Every minute another ten false leads and foolish suggestions came to rest on his desk. Now a functionary was bringing in yet another.

"What is it now?" he barked. "A suggestion that we search for this Raven in London Zoo aviary? Or perhaps a report from a Seccie in Australia that he saw a girl with black hair and dark eyes two years ago but he can't remember where?"

The functionary quailed, hugging the datapad he carried closely to his thin chest.

"Uh, no, Minister . . . ," he stammered. "Not exactly. It's not really to do with this Raven character."

"Then why are you bothering me with it?" the Minister roared.

"Don't you know I have a meeting with the President in"—he paused to check the ornate chronometer hanging on the wall of his office—"ten minutes?" He slammed his fist down on his desk. "Are you perhaps not aware that I am not permitted by His Excellency to work on any subject other than the apprehension of this mutant? Well, man? What have you got to say for yourself?"

"It's the other Hexes, Sir," the functionary gasped.

"It's the other Hexes?" The Minister drew his brows together in a massive frown.

"The Freedom ones," the functionary told him. "Possible descendants of Theo Freedom? The Minister of Propaganda passed on a list of possible candidates on his arrest list?"

"What of them?" The Minister for Internal Affairs had stopped shouting. Instead he was almost standing, leaning forward across his desk, his eyes intent on the datapad the functionary carried.

"Well, we've found two of them," the functionary said simply, presenting the pad. "It's not much of a lead, I know. But it's the only one we have so far and I thought you might want to—"

"Give me that!" The Minister snatched the pad out of his subordinate's hands and read through the data quickly. "Goddammit," he breathed. "This might actually be worth something. Get me Alverstead on the vidcom. No, wait! Get me the Head of the Security Services. Let's bring these two in for questioning first. Once they're secure we can worry about whether they're the right ones."

Wraith knocked softly on the door to Raven's room. There was no answer but he didn't allow that to stop him. When she had departed so abruptly he'd questioned Drow about the thing he'd seen in the net and the very idea of it alarmed him. Raven's reaction had been even more violent than his and the closest terminal was the one in her room. He knocked again, louder, then paused to call:

"Raven, open the door."

It had been a long time since he had tried to tell his wild sister what to do and he was doubtful if he'd get any response at all. But after a few moments he heard footsteps approaching and the door slid open. Raven was standing in the doorway but from her expression Wraith could tell her mind was miles away. She looked like a statue, staring through him at some unimaginable distance.

"What is it?" he asked quietly and her eyes tracked to meet his.

"Death," she said softly. "Death and darkness, that's all it knows."

"Is it dangerous?"

"More than you can possibly imagine." A bitter smile suddenly appeared on Raven's face and she laughed mockingly. The laughter seemed to pull her out of whatever trance she'd been in and she looked at him directly as she said, "We've talked about shutting down the net in the past to combat the EF. What would happen if we tried and succeeded?"

"Communications would be disrupted?" Wraith replied. "A lot of information would be lost." He frowned. "What are you getting at?"

"The end of the world," she told him. "If the net goes dark that's a catastrophe. It's not just that the speed of information retrieval is slowed, or that some data is lost, it's everything. Economies are solely electronic—it's the net that keeps track of creds, without the net we lose that. Food as well, all production and distribution is controlled by the network, without it we have stacks of food rotting on one side of the country and famine on the other. What else?" She shook her head at the enormity of it. "All public services shut down, all vidcoms, all terminals, every media outlet in the world. Even those areas that the EF doesn't control use the same net. Without it, there's chaos."

"And you think that might be about to happen?" Wraith took Raven's shoulders and pulled her around so that he could look straight into those obsidian eyes. "This darkness is going to engineer a net crash?"

"If it can," she confirmed. "If it hates enough." The twisted smile reappeared and her eyes glazed over. "And it does," she whispered.

"How can it hate?" Wraith asked in confusion. "What does it hate? Raven, what *is* it?"

The Hex held herself perfectly still as she answered, the words painfully dragged out of her in an admission that she would have given almost anything not to make.

"It's Kalden," she said. "What's left of him. He's back. And how can you kill someone who's already dead?"

Gift sometimes wondered if Tally had always been like this. Had there ever been a time, when they were babies maybe, when her automatic response to everything hadn't been to worry? Sometimes he doubted it. As long as he could remember he had been traveling with Tally's anxiety. Sometimes it seemed as if it had more of a personality than she did. Now, when everything was going well at last, when they were safe and about to strike back against the Federation for the first time in their lives, she was still incapable of doing anything but fretting.

With a sigh he threw down his cards and took Tally's out of her hand. She blinked and looked at him in surprise.

"Have we finished?" she asked.

"No," he told her. "We haven't finished. But it's actually impossible to play a game with a person who stares into space all the time and keeps biting her nails and picking at the mattress. What's the matter with you?"

"I'm sorry," Tally sighed. "I don't mean to be annoying, really I don't. But I keep thinking of what's going to happen next and . . ." She shrugged. "Here we're just waiting, we have no way of contacting anyone and no idea what's going on." Suddenly she stood up. "I think we should find a public vidcom and call Drow," she said.

"For God's sake, Tally!" Gift exclaimed, slamming his fist on the floor in anger. "Haven't we discussed this already? Didn't we agree that we weren't safe on the streets where any Seccie patrol could pick us up? Would you please at least wait until it's daylight and we can hide in the crowds. Or maybe try to get some sleep?" His tone became sarcastic. "That's a radical suggestion, I know, but it's past midnight in London as well as here. Drow will be asleep just as you should be. One thing's for certain. He's not insisting that someone stays up and plays a card game with him, which he can't even be bothered to concentrate on for more than half a damned second!"

"He's also not carrying the most important piece of data any Hex could imagine," Tally hissed in a fierce whisper. "And I don't care how nasty you get, Gift. Something's not right here, I'm certain of it. Every second that passes just makes me more and more certain that somewhere something's gone wrong." She whirled around and began packing their few possessions into the pack, glaring at him through her tangle of auburn hair. "I'm going to make a call to Drow," she told him. "And you can't stop me."

Gift closed his eyes and counted to ten silently. She was right that he couldn't stop her. It was obviously futile to argue. He could try to overpower her but he didn't like the idea of using force on his own sister, and Tally was strong enough to escape him unless he tied her down or knocked her out. In the circumstances he only had one option, and crossing to sit beside her, he began to help her pack.

"Listen to me carefully," he said as he did so. "Whether you're right or wrong, I'm getting tired of this emotional blackmail. I'm warning you, Tally, this constant worrying of yours is making you hell to be with. If you could stop fearing ghosts and shadows for a while you'd be a lot less insane."

"Maybe I am insane," Tally said quietly, buckling the worn straps of the pack. "But when the EF's after you it doesn't hurt to be paranoid."

The warehouse was dark as they made their way down the

rusty staircase and toward the massive double doors. Gift unbarred them and pushed them open enough for them both to slip through, then pushed them closed behind him. Hefting their pack on his shoulders he began to retrace a route back into the center of town, where he had seen vidcoms. Tally followed close behind him but she didn't try to initiate a conversation. Just as well, he thought, or I might have to strangle her. He trudged along grimly, thinking angry thoughts about sisters who made you wander around town in the middle of the night because they had funny feelings. But as they approached the town center something caught his attention and he stopped walking. Immediately Tally walked into him from behind and gasped.

"Shhh," he warned her. "Look at that."

The sky was unusually bright, as if from the glare of many streetlights, and ahead of them, he could hear indistinct voices.

"Something's going on," Tally said, stating the obvious, and Gift rolled his eyes.

"No kidding," he replied. "Keep quiet and let's go find out what."

Walking on a little further they came to the edge of a small square and Gift looked cautiously around the edge of a building. Immediately he pulled back and turned to look at Tally with wide surprised eyes.

"There are three Seccie skimmers around that corner," he told her. "And about nine Seccies just standing about."

"Can you hear what they're saying?" Tally whispered and Gift shrugged.

"I'll try," he told her. "Keep well out of sight and I'll try to get closer."

Tally tried to grab his arm and stop him but Gift was already away, moving under the cover of shadow around the side of the building. Clutching their pack and shrinking into the corner, she waited for him. After about ten minutes he returned, slipping silently around the corner like a shadow.

"Not good news," he said softly. "Come on, follow me." He turned away from the square and Tally hastened after him as he worked his way through the narrower streets until they were well out of earshot. Only then did he tell her what he had overheard. "A whole load of EF troops have arrived in town and the Seccies have been told to keep out of the way. The troops are closing down the borders in a hunt for some dangerous criminals." He looked grim. "I think we can probably guess who they mean."

"How did they find us?" Tally asked, horrified.

"Ask your paranoia," Gift replied. "I have no idea. But we'd better get out of this rattrap as quickly as we can."

"We can go cross-country to Verona," Tally suggested. "It'll take a long time but we'll do better to keep off the roads."

"We'll have to get past the troops here first," Gift reminded her. "But at least we've had warning. Your funny feelings might just have saved our lives."

Drow was still getting over the shock of realizing how many Hexes there were and how organized the group was. He'd had a vague idea that the Ghosts were a large gang—they controlled too much territory to be anything else—but the sheer amount of people and technology they possessed staggered the imagination. Ali, the blonde girl in white who had interested him what seemed like years ago, had tried to explain the organization to him, but before she had finished, a mass meeting had been called and he'd been unable to retain much of the information.

Now, seated at the front of a large meeting hall filled with people, he tried to work out what was going on. It was clear that the Ghosts were divided into two main factions. One faction was terrorists, Anglecynn they called themselves, who were mostly adults without Hex abilities but with impressive weaponry and the skills to use them. The other faction was the Hexes themselves: kids for the most part and the people who seemed to be the leaders of the group. Those leaders confused him the most. Alaric and Geraint, the Anglecynn leaders, were like every gang-boss he'd encountered, taking their strength from the confidence of their followers. But the leaders of the Hex faction seemed to be considered with an almost mystical awe by the younger Hexes. He supposed that made sense if every last one of those children owed their lives to the skill of the people now standing on the platform in front of him, but he found the group strange. There was Wraith: a ganger in appearance but he seemed as honest as a priest. Ali and Luciel were corp-kids, the kind of people he'd have thought couldn't last five minutes on the streets, but they talked like generals in a war; and Kez, a streetrat, who seemed completely at ease with them. Then there was Avalon, the rock star, who was in some way the inspiration of the group, and Cloud, her friend, who appeared to have almost no role whatsoever. Finally there was Raven.

Drow still didn't know what he thought about Raven. The group seemed unable to move without her. Every word she spoke was treated as some kind of sacred pronouncement, and Ali's description of the Ghosts had been punctuated with constant repetitions of "Raven says." But they all did that. On the platform Wraith was saying it now.

"Raven believes that the danger in the net is unlikely to become a serious problem before the mission to Transcendence and that controlling the orbital satellite network might well give us a better idea of how to combat the menace. Therefore, we've decided to go ahead. The longer we delay the more danger there is that the EF will locate us. According to Raven the search for us has been stepped up across Europe. . . ."

Drow tuned out again. He was frankly amazed that a group of Hexes this large had been able to survive for as long as they had. Whatever this mission to Transcendence was, he hoped for their sake it would succeed. His own concern was for Gift and Tally and it was that which had convinced Wraith to allow him to go with them.

"You're very inexperienced," he had said with regret. "But Raven says you must be a strong Hex to have achieved as much as you have, and, of all of us, you're the only one to have had contact with Gift and Talent. They trust you and they don't know us. As for the real purpose of the mission, we'll have to explain that on the way. We're out of time now."

The clock was certainly ticking. Ali had whispered to him as they entered the meeting that this was more to prepare for the results of their mission than to discuss its wisdom. Apparently Raven had said or done something that meant that the journey to Transcendence was certain to happen, and through hacking the net, the group had obtained seats on a plane that would leave that very evening.

Drow blinked as he realized that Wraith had finished speaking and that Raven had taken his place at the front of the platform. One thing he agreed with the Ghost on was that Raven was everything he had imagined a Hex to be. She looked competent and dangerous and there was something about her that didn't seem entirely sane. She stood in silence until the murmurs of the crowd had died down, then began to speak in a very different manner from the others.

"To most of you here the name of Doctor Kalden doesn't mean much. The stuff of nightmares perhaps but a danger that no longer concerns us. But apparently when I killed him I didn't do it thoroughly enough. He died in the course of conducting a dangerous experiment, the results of which were unpredictable and intended to satisfy torturers and politicians rather than scientific enquiry. The subject of this experiment . . ." Raven blinked for a second, a hesitation that would be almost imperceptible to anyone unfamiliar with her normal measured speech, then continued. "The subject was linked to a machine intended to affect and control the bioelectrical energies of the mind. But the subject took control of the machine and created a link to the net, something unanticipated. At the moment of his death, some fragments of his consciousness took advantage of that connection and were preserved inside the net.

"There's not much of him left now, barely even what could be called a consciousness. Yet, in a way, it is conscious, although all it knows is hate. The reason I'm telling you this is that from now on the net isn't safe for any of us. Kalden's mind is now the focus of a dark cloud, eating its way through the network. So far the damage it has caused is barely noticeable but that will change. No group, agency, or government exists that can stop it. But we can. Once we hold the orbital satellite network we will move to eradicate it. But for now, stay clear of the darkness."

Jordan had stayed on duty throughout the meeting. It was procedure that a small team monitor communications and news nets at all times. In the past that had proved important. But this time Jordan wondered if they'd have been better off not knowing this piece of news. The Ghosts had come out of the meeting in a positive mood. Most of them seemed confident that Raven's team would succeed at taking control of the net and wiping out this new menace with no difficulty whatsoever. This latest news was bound to bring down that mood.

But Jordan had no choice. As the Ghosts streamed out of the meeting she made her way inside to where the mission team were clustered around the platform. Alaric looked up and smiled as she arrived, then his face clouded over.

"Looks like you have bad news," he said.

"I do," Jordan replied reluctantly, looking at Drow. "News

came in from some underground contacts in Europe that the EF have congregated some forces in an unlikely area." She swallowed and then added, not looking at any of them, "They've sent a troop detachment to the city of Padua. It looks as if Tally and Gift have been found."

9

I STAND AT
THE DOOR

In the year 2300, to commemorate the founding of the European Federation, the government had decided to build a European city that would stand as an example of their wealth and might. Transcendence, the culmination of that dream, had been created in the south of France. Seventy years later it had swelled to become the largest of the European megaplexes and, in actuality, the largest city in the world. Like an iceberg, much of its colossal size was underground. But the inhabitants didn't care about being cut off from the sun. Transcendence was dedicated to technology. No windows allowed the crude light of day to penetrate where artificial lighting could be endlessly adjusted to the precise requirements of the citizens. Equally, the grassy slopes of the French countryside didn't interest a population who increasingly sought the pleasures of virtual realities created for them in holoparks underneath the ground.

It was a playground for the rich. Only the most successful companies were allowed to own business space there, only individuals with an impeccable security record were permitted to work there and throughout the city the Seccies kept watch with a diligence not seen in any other megaplex. No inch of Transcendence was left unwatched or unguarded—hidden in the walls of the arcology were surveillance devices constantly monitoring the well-being of their citizens. The government of the EF boasted that no crime ever committed in Transcendence had been unpunished for more than twenty-four hours.

It was to this city, owned and controlled by the EF like a willing slave, that Raven and her companions came. For Wraith their arrival brought back old memories of the time he and Raven had first come to London. Sitting next to Raven as the stratojet began its descent, he touched her arm lightly.

"It's as if we're beginning again," he said under his breath, and she glanced sideways at him.

"Or finishing what we started," she replied and turned to look over her shoulder, at the seats behind them. Alaric and Jordan sat together, dressed like an affluent young professional couple. Neither of them had extensive Seccie files, and the fake IDs Raven had constructed for them should be enough to fool even the most thorough of investigations. Wraith was glad they were there. They were both skilled with several different kinds of weaponry and their experience as terrorists made them versatile companions for this kind of mission. Behind them sat Luciel and Kez. It had been harder to construct believable fake identities for them since their youth made them unlikely corporates. It had been Ali who'd come up with the ideal disguise. Among its many celebrated institutions Transcendence contained one of the most renowned European universities: the Academy of Progressive Thought. It had been the work of moments for Raven to enter the boys' identities on the academic roll. They were dressed as young students whose wealthy families had been able to afford the exorbitant fees the university charged and the IDs claimed that they were physics students, a masquerade which their recent devotion to education would enable them to perform creditably. Wraith smiled to himself as he watched them, thinking how much they had changed.

Luciel, idly watching the stratojet's in-flight entertainment screens, was a very different person from the tortured experimental subject they had rescued, addicted against his will to dangerous and life-threatening drugs. Kez, beside him, his bronze hair shining in the low lights of the jet, had changed the most. No one would recognize in this sober and self-assured young student the streetrat whom Wraith had picked up on a whim.

Wraith looked further back and his smile faded. Drow sat on his own, behind Luciel and Kez, staring blankly into space. Back in London, Jordan was monitoring the call-code he had given Gift and Tally, hoping against hope that they had escaped the siege in Padua. It was for that reason that Drow had been included on the mission, although Wraith doubted if there was much chance of rescuing the two young Hexes about whom he knew little more than their names. Drow had similar doubts and Wraith recognized the mixture of guilt and shame that the boy had displayed when he heard about the EF's action to surround Padua. He had felt the same way himself when he had failed to return Rachel, his youngest sister, to sanity after Kalden's experiments. Drow seemed barely conscious of their presence. He had not even objected to having his long black hair cut short and the silver circuitry removed from his braids in the interests of concealing his identity. His fake ID had been the most difficult of all to invent. Finally, Raven had fallen back on an old ruse and identified Drow as a hopeful young actor, journeying to Transcendence to play a minor role in one of the vids produced there by a successful media company.

Wraith sighed ruefully and looked at himself in the reflective window of the stratojet. He also had submitted to having his hair cut, shaved so close to his head that its unusual white color was barely noticeable. But, if Drow's identity had been the hardest to construct, his and Raven's were the most dangerous. They both wore the black uniforms of EF soldiers, their rank tags identifying them as Force Commanders in the Intelligence Division. Raven had risked the impersonation because it had seemed the safest way to avoid any detailed checks into their background. Intelligence Officers were feared even by Seccies for their ability to interrogate anyone under any circumstances and the fact they were answerable only to their own superiors and the EF President.

A dull roaring noise came from the engines of the jet and Wraith glanced at Raven.

"Landing in five minutes," she told him. Her fingertips rested on the vidscreen on the stand in front of her seat. To any observer she would have appeared to be adjusting the controls of the entertainment unit but in fact both she and Luciel were linked into the stratojet's computer systems, keeping track of its movements and its connection to the network of Transcendence itself. Throughout the mission the Hexes would endeavor to keep in constant touch with the network. If their impersonations were discovered it might give them enough warning to escape with their lives.

"Anything unusual?" Wraith asked and Raven shook her head.

"No, but several things we should be aware of," she replied. "For instance, security has recently been increased in all important EF installations and cities in order to combat the threat from the rogue Hex, Raven."

"I see." Wraith smiled wryly. "How do the activities of this dangerous criminal affect us in particular?"

"A Seccie squad is stationed on permanent duty at the arrivals terminal," Raven informed him. "As senior officers they may offer us escort."

"How should we refuse it?" Wraith asked, lowering his voice.

"Refuse it?" Raven arched an eyebrow at him quizzically. "We are senior Intelligence Officers, our intention is to tour the Space Operations Center to assess its vulnerability to terrorist attack. How better to do so than with a Seccie squad in attendance?"

Ali rubbed her eyes, trying to make sense of the datapad in front of her. But the information kept blurring out of focus. Irritably she threw it down on the table in front of her and was startled as a soft voice commented dryly:

"There's nothing wrong with the screen, you're just too tired to make sense of it. Why don't you try and get some rest?"

"Perhaps because I'm trying to do five people's jobs at once?" Ali replied. "And prepare for God knows what if Raven's team fails."

"It must be difficult to prepare for an unpredictable situation," Cloud said sympathetically.

"Yes, it—" Ali broke off and then smiled ruefully. "It's impossible, isn't it?"

"I think your time could be put to better use," Cloud admitted. "Such as getting some rest maybe?"

"I've only been awake for five hours," Ali pointed out. "I don't need rest."

"You've been working solidly for all that time," Cloud reminded her. "At least go and find something to eat and take your brain off the hook for a while." He glanced around the control room. "Is anything drastically important likely to occur in the next hour?"

"No," Ali admitted.

"Would your assistants be capable of summoning you if it did?" he continued, gesturing at Avalon and the three Hex children who were manning the control room.

"Yes."

"In that case, go and rest. Watch the vid or something," he told her. "Unless you're worried I'll take advantage of your absence to call the Seccies and tell them where you are?"

Ali blinked at him in surprise and he laughed out loud.

"That was a joke," he added.

"I know," Ali replied and sighed. "OK, you win, I'll go and rest—"

"If anything happens we'll call you," Cloud replied.

Stretching, Ali climbed out of the chair she'd been sitting in. She felt as if her muscles had been turned to jelly. All morning she'd been reading reports and contingency plans until they had stopped making any sense. Cloud was probably right, she admitted to herself, she did need to rest. Wandering into the living area of the Fortress, she dialed a cup of coffee from the Nutromac and slumped in one of the large armchairs. The moment control to the vidscreen was lying beside her and she considered it for a while. Recently she hadn't felt like watching any of the channels. The media was locked down by EF law and she was getting tired of watching news that never criticized the government or reported the activities of those who did. However, one of the entertainment channels might be amusing for a while, she thought. Touching the control, she keyed the vidscreen on.

The logo of Populix appeared on the screen and Ali hesitated. She hadn't meant to watch the channel her father owned or to watch the news at all. But whoever had last been using the screen had obviously left it at that setting and Ali left it there as she tried to decide what to watch. In a few seconds her decision had been made for her. Instead of the familiar face of one of the announcers the screen displayed a single line of text:

This channel has ceased transmissions by order of the Security Services for broadcasts not in accordance with EF regulations.

Ali stared at it for a while, her mind at first unable to assimilate the meaning of the words. Then finally she slumped back in the chair. The control fell from her hands and she didn't bother to pick it up or change the channel. She heard the hiss of the door slide open behind her but her eyes didn't leave the screen.

"Ali," Avalon's voice asked. "What's happened?"

"Populix has been shut down," Ali replied, turning to face her. "Probably because of their broadcasts of your songs."

Avalon's eyes dropped and she said quietly, "I'm sorry."

"No, don't be." Ali stood up and forced a half smile. "You didn't do anything wrong."

"Isn't Populix one of the channels your father owns?" Avalon asked. "Could this affect him?"

"Maybe." Ali shrugged awkwardly. "I don't know."

"Do you want us to find out?" Avalon asked. "There'll be news somewhere on the network."

"No, Raven said we shouldn't use the net," Ali replied. "Besides, I'm not sure I want to know." She was silent for a moment and then she continued. "When the CPS took me away I was angry at my father for not trying to stop them. But recently, when we rescued Charis—and now that he might be in danger himself—I don't think about it the same way. There really wasn't anything he *could* do. That's what it means to live in a tyranny." She laughed suddenly. "Isn't that strange? I've been working against the government for four years now but it's only recently that I realized we were right."

"That's what Wraith believes," Avalon replied. "We just tend to forget it when we're fighting to save our own lives. Maybe we should remember we're fighting for right more often."

"Except Raven," Ali said without bitterness, as a statement of fact. "She's fighting for herself."

"I suppose that makes sense," Avalon replied. "Raven's unique after all. If she doesn't support her own cause who will?"

"We will," Ali replied. "That's the point. Even when it's useless. A tyranny only succeeds when people stay silent while injustice goes on, the way my father stayed silent when I was taken for extermination. But yesterday Populix made the opposite decision. They tried to fight and they've been crushed." She looked back at the screen. "But at least they tried," she said softly.

"And so will we," Avalon replied.

"Yeah." Ali hunched her shoulders resolutely. "Come on," she said. "Let's get back to work. Somehow I don't feel like resting right now."

Tally and Gift made their way through the street quickly, checking constantly to see if they were being watched. When a tourist so much as glanced in their direction they hurried away, keeping their heads down and trying to make themselves look as small as possible. The trek to Verona had not been pleasant. On the edge of Padua they had reached the transport terminus just in time to see the last lev-train preparing to depart. EF troops were closing down the facility but were having difficulty finding staff to shut down all the machinery. The lev-trains were automated and stopped only briefly at the station before whizzing off into the night. Softly as shadows, Tally and Gift had climbed up into one of the freight cars and hid, expecting to be discovered any minute. But the terminus manager with the key to shut down the trains had been late and as he arrived, panting and wheezing, the elevated train finished its automatic unloading and sped off with the twins on board.

The lev-train continued on through the night, humming quietly and almost soothing the children to sleep. But sometime before dawn they worked out that the train would turn soon and head north through the mountains to Switzerland without passing through another Italian city. That could last for days and Tally knew that with every moment that passed the chances of their discovery increased. So the twins waited for a smooth stretch of countryside and jumped from the train, turning in the direction of Verona.

They had stumbled on throughout the night, keeping off the roads, worried all the time that they would hear the EF troops behind them. Gift had ditched the pack with their possessions to make better speed, and half dead with fatigue, they had staggered on. Now all they carried was a few creds, the precious data disk, and the scrap of paper with Drow's call-code.

"Look, Tally," Gift said in a whisper, despite the bustling crowds around them. "Vidcom booths."

Tally looked up wearily and saw the row of shiny booths ahead of them.

"Thank God," she said. "At last."

They had to wait for one of the booths to be empty and they leaned against the outside of one of them, trying to stay upright. The first one to be vacated had been being used by a large Italian woman and as she squeezed herself out of the booth she looked at them with disgust. Tally quailed beneath her disdainful stare but Gift looked the woman back straight in the eye and she stalked off with a huff. He knew they weren't much to look at, dirty and bedraggled as they were, but he wasn't ashamed to be stared at. He was too relieved to be alive to care what a stranger thought of his appearance.

The twins crowded into the small booth and Tally dragged out the scrap of paper while Gift punched in the code.

> **eu/lon-node/bethnel/chr#4856** <

It seemed to take an age to connect but when it finally did it wasn't Drow who looked back at them. Although they didn't know what their friend looked like he couldn't be the person who was staring back at them from the vidcom screen. This was a girl: her ash-blonde hair brushed back neatly from her face but dark shadows under her eyes making her look almost as tired as they were.

"Gift and Talent?" she said when she saw them and abruptly her face broke into a smile. "Thank God, we were hoping you would call. Are you all right?"

"Just about," Gift replied suspiciously. "But who are you?"

"I'm Ali," the girl said. "Drow contacted my people and they went to look for you but we were afraid you'd been captured."

"Your people?" Tally asked eagerly. "Are you the Hexes we were looking for?"

"Yes," the girl said. "I think so, at least. We've been working against the Federation for some time but there isn't time to explain that to you now. This is a safe signal but you must be in danger. Where are you?"

"In Verona," Gift explained. "We had to leave Padua quickly. Someone must have recognized us."

Ali frowned, considering.

"Our team is in Transcendence right now," she said. "Is there a safe place near you where you can wait for them to get to you?"

"I think we've had enough of safe places," Gift replied.

"We'd rather keep moving," Tally agreed. "But . . ." She glanced down at herself and made a face.

"Yeah," Gift said. "We look pretty scruffy and we can't afford to buy anything better."

"All right," Ali said thoughtfully. "Does the vidcom you're using have a credstick slot?"

"Yes, it does," Gift told her. "But we don't have a credstick."

"Do you have enough money to buy one?"

"I think so," Tally said, checking through their meager funds. "Yes, we do."

"In that case go and get one and call me again when you've succeeded," Ali told them. "I'll book you tickets on the next flight out of there and wire you enough creds to get better clothes." She smiled reassuringly. "We'll get you out of there, I promise."

Avalon was relieved when Ali relayed the news that the kids were safe, at least for the time being. But when she saw the young Hex preparing to enter the net she became anxious.

"You said yourself Raven had forbidden it," she warned. "That thing is still in there somewhere."

"Raven didn't *forbid* it, she advised against it," Ali pointed out.

"And she went into the net herself to create new IDs for the team. Besides," she said, shrugging, "what choice have I got?"

"There must be other ways to help the twins," Avalon said but Ali shook her head.

"They want to leave Verona as soon as possible and they won't be safe until they meet up with Raven's team," Ali replied. "That means booking them onto a fast jet out and without IDs they can't do that themselves. But through the net I can hack into the transport system and arrange tickets, which they can pick up at the airport." She looked around the room. "Does anyone have a better idea?"

Cloud raised his eyebrows but didn't say anything and the three Hex children on duty murmured their apologies.

"In that case, I'm going in," Ali told them and deliberately reached out to the terminal in front of her.

It was never as easy for Ali to achieve the almost psychic bond Raven had with computers. The dark-haired Hex could interface with the net in an instant. But it took Ali a few minutes of sustained meditation before she could feel the network opening itself to her, and it was difficult for her to see the metaphor of the city of light the other Hexes described. Slowly she felt her way into the net and reached out toward Italy. Ali wasn't much of a hacker but Raven had taught them that a Hex didn't need to be. Manipulating the net from inside was very different from the way a normal hacker attempted to influence strange computer systems. Ali's progress toward the systems that controlled European transportation was slow and ponderous but she got there eventually and slid past the security protocols easily. Once she was in the system it was the work of moments to cancel the bookings for two people leaving on the next stratojet for Transcendence and substitute fake names with Gift and Talent's descriptions.

She didn't have Raven's experience in creating fake IDs but it was easier to invent false identities for children than for adults. She informed the transportation system computer that the twins were Edward and Elsie Anderson, traveling from the residence of one of their parents to that of the other. Then, backing out of the transportation system node, she inserted fake identities for their parents into the network's public access database. One parent she made an art dealer in Verona and the other a corporate business-man working in Transcendence. Deciding that was sufficient to keep Gift and Talent safe, she stopped there and headed in the direction of the Transcendence network to inform Raven that the twins had been found.

Sergeant Dwayne Crispian of the Security Services was not having a good day. He'd been on active duty for the past month and there seemed no prospect of getting leave any time soon. Just like every other Seccie team across Europe his squad was occupied in check-ing the IDs of every civilian they encountered in case one of them turned out to be fake. It was tedious, time-consuming work and the monotony was beginning to get to him. Therefore, when a routine check of the passenger list of the stratojet currently arriving at ter-minal 35 of Transcendence's airport revealed that two senior Intel-ligence Officers were flying in, he ordered his squad to meet them.

"That type always appreciates a little deference," he told his men. "And if we offer our services as an escort we'll at least get a break from this drone work."

Accordingly, Crispian's squad were standing at attention when the two officers arrived in the terminal. The Sergeant recognized them at once. Even if he hadn't been in uniform, the tall man with close-cropped white hair had an authority that would have identified him, and his female companion had that look of casual menace that seemed to characterize the Intelligence Division of the EF standing army. Snapping a brisk salute Sergeant Crispian stepped forward to greet them.

"Good afternoon, Sir, Madam," he said politely. "Sergeant Crispian, Security Services, reporting. I hope you had a pleasant flight."

"As much as can be expected," the white-haired officer replied, returning his salute. "I'm Force Commander Rhys Barrow and this is Force Commander Rachel Wing."

The dark-haired woman in the black greatcoat nodded briefly to Sergeant Crispian and he swallowed nervously, meeting that black-eyed stare. She looked young for her rank but he found himself not doubting her competence. She held herself with a casual arrogance that spoke highly of her abilities and Crispian didn't like to speculate on what had earned her her position. Intelligence Officers were involved in the least pleasant of Federation work and many of them had a reputation for cruelty and sadism in carrying out their main work in extracting information from captured dissidents.

"Pleased to meet you, Officers," he continued. "If I or my squad can assist you in any way I place us entirely at your disposal."

"Thank you, Sergeant," Commander Wing said curtly. "Your willingness is most appreciated." There was an ironic edge to her voice which made Crispian wonder if she was aware of his ulterior motives in offering his services but she continued smoothly: "Commander Barrow and I require an escort to the Space Operations Center. Can you have another team relieve you of your duties here?"

"Certainly, Madam," Crispian replied with another salute. "Although, there's no real need. My squad was simply checking the IDs of the passengers arriving here. Routine work since all of them will have been thoroughly vetted before being able to purchase passage to Transcendence. We can accompany you now, if you'd like."

"Shouldn't you wait for your relief?" Commander Barrow asked but his companion shook her head.

"I prefer not to wait," she told him. "If the Sergeant's duties are as routine as he describes them it won't matter if this one group of passengers isn't rechecked. None of them appear to be dangerous terrorists."

Commander Barrow laughed and Sergeant Crispian joined in quickly. Behind him his men allowed themselves discreet smiles. The Force Commander was right, Crispian thought as he fell into step behind the two officers. At a glance he could tell that this group of passengers was perfectly innocuous. Two young students had followed the Intelligence Officers off the stratojet and were chatting eagerly about their university course. He had better things to do with his time than interrogate boys about their vacation. Assisting these officers would be real work, even if they were somewhat alarming.

"Do you have any luggage, Sirs?" he asked. "We can collect it for you if you wish."

"That won't be necessary, Sergeant," Commander Barrow informed him. "This is a brief visit. We only need this." He tapped the portable terminal case he carried as if assuring himself it was still there and the Sergeant nodded.

"In that case, Commander, I'll arrange immediate transportation," he said. "We have a staff flitter on permanent duty here. I'll have it summoned immediately."

Luciel and Kez marched briskly out of the terminal. Raven and Wraith seemed not only to have gained themselves an impressive escort but managed to prevent the rest of the team from undergoing ID checks. Kez had found it hard to keep from grinning as he overheard the Seccie sergeant's words to Raven but Luciel's constant flow of chatter about their totally fictitious career as students gave him a good excuse for his amusement.

As they left the terminal they could see Raven and Wraith ahead of them climbing into a sleek black military flitter that would presumably take them to the Space Operations Center. Luciel and Kez would be making their own way there under the guise of tourists visiting the center's museum. The plan called for Alaric and Jordan to collect a hired skimmer at the airport and for them to take a public flitter from the taxi rank. Behind them Drow would take a similar route, hopefully resulting in them all arriving at roughly the same time.

"Things seem to be going well," Luciel remarked quietly and Kez nodded.

"Things look chill for R and W," Kez replied. It had been discussed earlier that no one would use the word "Raven" while they were in Transcendence. It was possible that the surveillance devices had been calibrated to automatically alert any use of that name.

"Most impressive," Luciel agreed. "A very smooth . . ." His voice abruptly trailed off and both boys came to a halt. They had left the environs of the airport and suddenly Transcendence lay before them and they both caught their breath at the sight.

When Kez had thought of the city he had imagined it as either a larger version of London's starscrapers or as a maze of corridors that felt like being constantly indoors. The reality was very different. The space that stretched out before them was a work of art. As far as the eye could see lay a succession of spiraling staircases and gently curving walkways, each one ornamented with animated sculptures and lit with shifting patterns of subtly shaded light. Even the skimmer routes and grav-tubes that hummed through the huge fretwork of carefully constructed beauty were designed with an eye to their aesthetic appeal. The boys gazed at it speechlessly, their eyes trying to make sense of the loops and swirls of architecture through which the crowds and people and vehicles rushed.

"It's amazing," Luciel breathed and Kez nodded slowly.

"Like a dream or something," he agreed.

"Incredible that the EF could have produced anything this

beautiful," Luciel added and the thought brought back the recollection of their mission.

"We'd better get going," Kez said, reluctantly tearing his eyes away from the fantasy before them. "Maybe when all this is over we can look at it properly."

"Maybe," Luciel echoed but neither of them really believed it. Transcendence was stunning but it didn't seem quite real. There was too much EF power here for them to be entirely comfortable with the city's vision of mingled science and beauty. They had seen into the heart of the darkness that Transcendence's glory attempted to conceal and to them the city was a facade hiding the ugly truth of the Federation's might.

10

THE TIME IS AT HAND

Raven leaned back into the capacious seat of the military flitter. The chauffeur drove carefully, as befitting someone conducting VIPs to their destination. On either side of the aerial vehicle a Seccie flitter kept pace with them. Raven smiled to herself as she opened the black case containing the portable terminal and allowed her hands to rest on the keypad.

So far everything was going well. Cruising gently into the Transcendence central node, Raven could see that the local Seccies were completely unaware that anything was wrong. Allowing her perceptions to link with the Transcendence surveillance network, Raven located the other members of their group with ease. Luciel and Kez were sitting in a public flitter not far behind her own, chatting innocuously about science. Alaric and Jordan had collected the rented skimmer she had arranged for them and were piloting it in accordance with all the speed regulations in the direction of the Space Center. Drow was still waiting at the airport for the public flitter but there was enough leeway in their plan to compensate for his delay. None of their conversations had been flagged as subversive by the Transcendence security system and none of their fake IDs had triggered any alerts. Satisfied, Raven began one last circuit of the local network before returning to her body and paused as something nudged the edge of her perceptions. She frowned, unable to place the feeling she had experienced, and concentrated. Something about the data current had struck her as familiar as she passed it. Curiously she returned, retracing her path through the net, and scanned the area. Whatever it was had disappeared. But her instincts had been roused and she began a more methodical search. Her consciousness spread outward through the net until with a start she ran into a pattern that was more familiar.

> **ali** < she exclaimed. > **why are you here/in the net/transcendence** <

> **urgent/important/essential work** < Ali explained. > **relieved/grateful you found me—i have news** <

> **?** < Raven asked wordlessly.

> **gift/talent found!!!** < Ali informed her joyfully. > **location verona—i have arranged transport to you/transcendence/city—will arrive 1800—?can you meet them?** <

> **believe/hope/think so** < Raven replied. > **inform/advise/communicate with gift/talent that drow (insert picture) hex will meet them—return now** <

She detached herself from Ali as the other Hex sped down the data current back toward England but, without Ali's knowledge, followed her pathway. Ali had obviously negotiated the net safely but Raven wasn't certain if her student was capable of evading the remains of Kalden's mind, should she encounter it. She watched from a distance as Ali returned to the Ghost computer system and vanished inside its security. Then she turned to leave.

A black tendril snaked past her. Raven pulled herself hurriedly out of its way. It moved like a snake, questing sinuously through the net, darkening for a microsecond everything it touched. The darkness was obviously spreading itself thinner. Raven wondered if Kalden had enough mind left to realize that this strategy would be more efficient in finding her. She wasn't sure if he was consciously looking or even aware of the effect his twisted mind was having on the network. But, regardless of his intentions, this dispersal of the dark cloud was unwelcome news. Carefully staying out of its way she moved back into the dataflow and allowed it to carry her toward Transcendence.

Drow leaned against the softly glowing balustrade, his eyes blind to the appeal of the city. His mind was full of Gift and Tally. He feared that it was his advice that had led them into danger and he dreaded to think what would become of them in EF hands. One of the first things he had asked Ali about in London was the images of mutilated children that Populix had broadcast to accompany the Hexes' music. Now he wished he hadn't. Ali had turned pale as she recounted the story of her short stay in the experimental lab and explained a little of what had occurred there. It was easy to believe that the man whose mind had become the blackness he had encountered in the network was evil. The cloud of contagion had been terrifying enough to be a demon. The thought that such a person had actually been permitted to conduct experiments on children was appalling. Now he feared that Gift and Tally had fallen victim to a similar fate.

He clenched his fists, trying not to think about it, trying not to think about anything, and then started as a voice said his name. He looked about wildly but there was no one near him. He frowned in confusion, then suddenly remembered the small transceiver that the Hexes had surgically implanted in his ear. Subvocalizing, barely moving his lips, he replied:

"Hello?"

"At last," an acerbic voice remarked. *"Were you deliberately ignoring me or just wool-gathering?"*

"I—" Drow began uncomfortably but Raven's voice cut him off.

"Forget it," she said. *"I have information for you. The situation has changed."*

"Changed how?" Drow murmured. "Is something wrong?"

"Precisely the opposite," Raven replied. *"Gift and Talent have been located, free and unharmed."*

Drow was unable to prevent a gasp of relief from escaping his lips and he began to grin.

"Stay chill," Raven warned him. *"We're not out of the woods yet."*

"What did you want me to do?" Drow asked her.

"Proceed as planned to the rendezvous at the Space Operations Center," Raven told him. *"Gift and Tally will be arriving early this*

evening on a stratojet which gets in at 1800 hours. Assuming we succeed as planned, we'll arrange for you to return to the airport and escort them to the prearranged meeting place. Do you understand?"

"Yes," Drow assured her. "And . . . ?"

"Yes?"

"Thank you. I owe you."

"Don't consider it a debt," the Hex said. *"This is what gives me a buzz."*

And with that she was gone. Drow was unable to stop himself smiling. Not only was he relieved that Tally and Gift were safe, Raven's words had relieved his mind of another burden. The Hexes had told him something of their situation and the reason for this assault on the center of Federation power and it had seemed as if the outlook for them would be grim if this mission failed. But if Raven, heading into danger and uncertainty, could still find life exciting maybe things weren't as bad as they seemed. For the first time he wondered what the world would be like if the Hex cause succeeded.

Sergeant Crispian sat in the front of the flitter, watching the city flow past the windows as one of his men piloted the craft. Ahead of them the Space Operations Center was becoming visible. It was an impressive building, like all the buildings in Transcendence, reaching up in a slender point toward the sky. Crispian wondered why the two Intelligence Officers thought it might be vulnerable to terrorists. He couldn't imagine why terrorists would be interested in it. Space exploration was one of the lowest priorities of the European Federation. Scientific progress had been confined to the Earth for hundreds of years. Like genetic mutation, space exploration was an alarming and unpopular subject for science to explore. The current government, like all of its predecessors, wanted the human race to remain exactly what it was and where it was.

As the flitters approached the spire of the Space Operations Center, Crispian wondered to himself how such an unpopular field of research had gained a prized position in the most impressive city on Earth. Although he'd lived in Transcendence for almost six years he had never visited the center, even though sections of it were open to the public. He hoped that the Intelligence Officers wouldn't expect him to know the details of its operation. But they seemed unconcerned as the Seccie team formed itself into an escort around them.

"The main entrance is that way," the female Force Commander said authoritatively and her companion nodded.

"Shall we observe the museum first?" he asked.

"We may as well. Our brief is to study the facility in detail," she replied and Sergeant Crispian's squad fell into step behind them as they headed toward the arch of the entrance.

It didn't take long for the staff of the Space Center to realize they had important visitors. Professor Moore, the senior scientist in charge of the space project, hurried down to meet them as the two Commanders looked idly around the main foyer. Objects from the first European ventures into space had been displayed in glass cases around the room and the Intelligence Officers studied them with apparent interest as Moore told them how pleased he was to meet them.

"I had almost come to believe that the government didn't attach much importance to my work," he confessed. "I can't tell you how glad I am that you've come to inspect the Center. I only wish I'd had more time to prepare."

"Would you have time to prepare for a terrorist attack, Professor?" the woman asked sharply, her black eyes studying him assessingly.

"No, Commander, I suppose not," Moore admitted.

"That is why you were not informed of our inspection," the white-haired man explained. "Now, to explain our wishes."

"Certainly, certainly," Moore said eagerly. "But first, may I offer you refreshment, anything—"

"Thank you, no," the man said firmly. "We will begin immediately, starting with the parts of the Center that are open to the public—the museum and the viewing gallery. We will then require an explanation of the operation of the private parts of the Center, its security system and its computer database. Finally, we will inspect the specialized security system which controls the orbital satellite network. Is that possible?"

"Of course, Commander," Moore replied. "We will put ourselves entirely at your disposal." He glanced over at the squad of Seccies. "Will your men wait here?" he asked. "Would *they* like any refreshment?"

Sergeant Crispian doubted whether senior officers were likely to be at all concerned about his comfort but it seemed he had misjudged them. The female commander gave the squad a long look and then smiled.

"I believe they would, Professor," she said. "Perhaps one of your staff could conduct them to a private room to await us?"

"Anything you wish, Madam," the scientist said, clearly relieved to be able to offer someone something, and signaled to one of his assistants. As a polite young lady led Crispian and his men away, the Sergeant grinned at his squad. This was much more preferable to inspecting the IDs of an endess flow of tourists. He still had no idea why the officers could be bothered to inspect so unimportant a facility, but with a much-needed rest awaiting him, he couldn't bring himself to care.

Wraith was conscious of a genuine fascination as the senior scientist began his tour. The man was trying hard to be pleasant, despite a slight nervousness in the presence of the important guests he imagined they were, and his description of the history of spaceflight was more interesting than Wraith had imagined.

The ganger had never really thought much about the exploration of space. Like most people, he knew that it had been a prominent issue about three hundred years ago and that it had been more or less abandoned since. It had never occurred to him to wonder why. Now, as he studied the carefully preserved objects of a history of reaching into the unknown it occurred to him for the first time that space exploration had an important significance. To many of the citizens of the EF, trapped in misery or poverty, the simple idea of there being other worlds and other possibilities might have relieved some of the hopelessness of their situation. He had lived all his life with people who genuinely believed that the world would never change. But space exploration was a field of science full of potential new discoveries. Every word the Professor said confirmed that.

"Of course we have only a limited budget," he was explaining. "Cuts in funding over the past few years have meant that we've had to scale down several of our projects. But the museum brings in extra revenue, and I assure you, Commanders, we keep the public carefully isolated from the most sensitive areas." He paused as a group of tourists entered the museum and, lowering his voice, asked, "Would you like these people removed while you make your inspection? We can easily close the public parts of the building for a short while."

"There's no need," Wraith told him. "We prefer to observe the building as it is normally used."

Raven said nothing, but her eyes flickered briefly across to the tourists and she smiled to herself. Alaric and Jordan were doing an excellent job of examining the exhibits with a slightly bored expression and Luciel and Kez had equipped themselves with datapads and were making a more careful inspection and taking notes as they did so. Drow looked somewhat out of place, but although he ignored some exhibits entirely and studied others with an obvious interest, Raven didn't think his behavior was out of character for a tourist.

As Professor Moore moved on, lovingly describing the exhibits and how they came to be there, Raven found herself regretting what would become of this building. But, she thought to herself, it was fitting for this collection of dusty memorabilia to disappear from view forever. Although the Professor cared deeply for the objects in his custody, the EF had entombed the study of space in this building. The friendly scientist had refused to accept it but the government had no interest in aiding his research.

Sergei Sanatos stared glumly out of the window of his splendid apartments in the Palace of Versailles. At a meeting that morning his officials had informed him that the quest for the rogue Hex could not continue much longer. All over Europe, Security Service operatives had been pulled from their jobs in order to aid the CPS with the quest. Every department in the massive EF bureaucracy was helping with the search. The elderly Minister of Propaganda had given up every last drop of information he recalled about the previous Hex threat and the Minister of Internal Affairs had locked down the entire city of Padua on the basis of a thread of information about two of Theo Freedom's possible descendants. Nothing had done any good. The Hex was still at large and the President was running out of time and options.

Angrily Sanatos drummed his fingers on the windowsill. He found it a source of immense frustration that his enemies were using the net against him. His ancestors had been fools and traitors to introduce the Hex mutation into the populace. He knew the secret that had been hidden from the citizens of the Federation for hundreds of years. The Hex gene was a true virus. It had seeded itself in the genetic code of people throughout the world. In only a few was it truly active but there were hundreds of thousands, maybe even millions, of people who had the potential to become Hexes. Now, it seemed, all it required was for a Hex to rediscover the information Theo Freedom had learned, the secrets of how to unlock a Hex's potential, and then there would be anarchy. A nation of Hexes would be a nation of data thieves, privacy would disappear, politicians could be held truly accountable for their actions. Sanatos's hand clenched into a fist and he slammed it down with a crash. The Hex must be caught at all costs.

Striding across the room he tapped a familiar key combination into his personal vidcom and waited impatiently for the face of Joseph Levi, Minister of Technology, to appear on the screen. When it appeared, Joseph looked surprised but he smiled affably at the President.

"How may I help you, Your Excellency?" he asked.

"I want a net search," Sergei barked. "I want you to devote all available computing resources to finding this Hex. I want you to scan the entire net for her identity. We have pictures of her, we have her DNA code, her precise genetic map. I want every security system in Europe scanning for her. No matter what it takes."

The Minister of Technology blanched.

"Sir," he said uneasily. "To initiate a network search of that magnitude would require all the computing power at our disposal. We would be able to carry out very few other tasks while it was in progress. The EF will be crippled while we look for this Hex."

"Were you not listening to me?" Sergei demanded. "Are you deaf? Have you suddenly become terminally stupid? Did you not hear me say that I didn't care what was necessary? I want the Hex, do you understand?"

"Yes, Sir." The Minister bowed his head. "I understand."

"Then do as I say," Sergei thundered and snapped the connection shut.

At the other end of the vidcom line, Joseph Levi let his breath out in a great gust. He had never seen the President in such a towering rage. Joseph had grave misgivings about devoting so many system resources of the net to the search for the Hex but he had no choice. Ponderously he reached for the keypad of his vidcom unit to issue the orders the President had given him.

Inside the computer network small subroutines fired up and passed their commands to insignificant applications, those applications passed on their information to larger programs, and those programs began to construct huge, wide-ranging search parameters. Gradually the flow of data through the net slowed as more and more resources committed themselves. Terminals across Europe suddenly began to run at half the speed as the net began its quest for Raven.

But as the dataflow slowed something gathered strength. With every encumbered connection, every delayed access request, the cloud of darkness grew larger. Tendrils of blackness began to snake their way across the net. The city of light still caused it pain but in the depths of its dim consciousness it was becoming aware that the light was telling it something important, was searching for something that the darkness craved.

> **RAVEN? RAVEN?** < it asked, over and over and over again. It was a name the darkness knew, a name that gave its hate form. Gradually it gathered itself, and wherever the light searched for the thing named Raven, the darkness followed it. And with every microsecond that passed the cloud grew in size and strength.

Professor Moore was coming to the end of his tour. The two Intelligence Officers had politely listened to his explanations with an attentiveness that gave him hope that maybe this time the government would change its mind. Every year he feared that the Center would be closed but perhaps his fears had been in vain. Certainly he had nothing to be ashamed of in his work for the Center. Every piece of equipment had been treasured and lovingly cared for. The security system was constantly manned, the computer network protected from hackers by its separation from the EF computer network and his staff dedicated and loyal. He assured the Commander with the cropped albino hair of this as his companion inspected the computer system.

"I'm sure you have done your duty, Professor," the Commander said politely. But it was clear that most of his attention was taken up by his colleague whose fingers flew across the keypad as she investigated every last scrap of data in the computer system.

"I assure you, everything is in order," the Professor said with concern as the woman finally turned away from the terminal and rose from her seat.

"As you say, Professor," she said with a slight smile. "Everything is in order." She glanced at the other officer. "It only remains for us to inspect the system which controls the orbital satellite network. Then our duties here are complete."

"Very well," Professor Moore nodded amicably. "If you would be so kind as to follow me?"

Raven's fingertips tingled in anticipation as the scientist led them to a separate control room. She could feel the system already, calling to her with promises of power and control. From within that system the net would be hers. She would take it and own it and no force the EF possessed could wrest it from her. Downstairs the other members of the Ghost team were already placing the explosive devices that would bury these computer terminals with the rest of the Space Center under tons of rubble. By the time the twisted blackened hulls of the computers that now awaited her so enticingly had been unearthed from the wreckage it would be too late for the EF to reclaim the satellites. They, and the net, would obey only her commands.

As they entered the satellite control room Raven glanced at Wraith and raised an eyebrow. He nodded imperceptibly and turned to the scientist.

"Thank you, Professor," he said smoothly. "You've been most helpful and I'm certain this system will prove in as admirable condition as the last."

"I certainly hope so," Professor Moore replied, looking anxiously at Raven. "We realize how important the satellites are to the information network although we have many other projects that are of greater significance to the space program—"

"Indeed," Wraith replied with a smile. "In fact, while my colleague inspects the system, perhaps you would like to tell me about some of them in greater detail. I think that the refreshment you offered earlier might now be appropriate."

"Oh, of course." Professor Moore beamed at him. "I'd be delighted." He turned to Raven with an anxious expression. "I hope you don't mind us leaving you, Commander Wing? I can arrange for one of my assistants to attend you, if you wish?"

"There's no need, Professor," Raven replied, seating herself in front of the terminals. "This shouldn't take me long. I'll join you shortly."

"Very well then," Professor Moore bowed in acquiescence and turned back to Wraith. "If you'll be so good as to come with me, Commander?"

They left the room together and Raven could hear the Professor expounding on his pet projects as they headed down the corridor. She grinned fiendishly. Before her lay the brain of the orbital satellite network, exposed and unguarded. The mission had proceeded even more smoothly than they had hoped. Laying her hands on the keypad of the terminal, Raven plunged into the system.

The password protocols of the satellite network had been safely constructed to foil attempts by hackers or spies to subvert them. For microseconds Raven hung at the edge of the system, observing the security subroutines clustering like a pack of wolves around the edge of the system, keeping her from the chained gates that led inside. Then, carefully, she moved forward. One of the subroutines saw her and rushed forward to meet her.

> **who you?** < it demanded, sniffing her suspiciously.

Raven reached down to touch it, sending a sequence of commands that would soothe its suspicions.

> **a friend** < she told it. > **be calm** <

Another one noticed her and began to clamor for more information.

> **password! password! password!** < it demanded, its yelps attracting the rest of the pack.

She reached out to it and examined its design, using its behavior as a clue to what the password might be. She remained touching it for a few more microseconds until her mind located in its programming the unique phrase which would render it dormant.

> **through adversity to the stars** < she informed it and the subroutine lay down at her feet, satisfied.

The rest of the pack of subroutines was approaching now, yapping more inquiries.

> **identity!** < they demanded. > **system user protocol!—purpose of interface!—security code!** <

Raven could have worked out the answers to their questions but instead she adopted a simpler method. Reaching down to the two subroutines she had already reassured, she pointed them toward their fellows.

> **reassure them** < she ordered.

The subroutines hastened back to the pack and rubbed themselves against their fellows, touching tails and noses sociably.

> **no trouble here** < they barked. > **relax—relax—return to posts** <

Following them, Raven moved through the pack to the entrance of the system. As she passed she touched other pack members lightly, and tamed by her now familiar scent, they clustered about her slavishly. Programmed to recognize the pack's satisfaction, the great gates swung open and Raven passed within.

The system was ancient, designed long ago and never upgraded to keep it in tune with developments in the net. But Professor Moore had cared for it rigorously and every data file was as perfectly formatted as the day it had been introduced into the system. Streams of commands flowed through it, informing the five hundred and twenty-three satellites currently in orbit of what their duties were. For the most part these commands were simple, dictating the patterns of their journeys around the world, but within the stream of code was one significant section. It informed the satellites who they belonged to and who had authority to change their orders.

> **display full security parameters** < Raven ordered the system and examined the code. It was complex, allowing for any number of specialized circumstances in which the EF government could use the satellites to control the flow of data through the net.

> **erase parameters** < Raven ordered and the stream of code vanished. Now the satellites were free agents, passing data across the net without priority or prejudice.

> **save new parameters** < Raven told the system and listed

the names of its new masters. > **raven—ali—luciel—avalon— wraith—kez—alaric—geraint—jordan—cloud. require authorization from named users for future changes** < Deciding that was sufficient, she turned her attention to a new file.

> **display restrictions on access** < she commanded and an immense stream of code fell into her hands.

The EF had made the network their tool and the orbital satellite system was the whip they used to control it. The satellites had been ordered to hold back all transmissions that contained key phrases the Federation had flagged as seditious, all transmissions emanating from locations the EF believed to be controlled by dissidents, and all information that could possibly be used against them. Raven smiled as she ordered the satellites to erase those restrictions and inserted her own.

> **refuse transmissions from all security services agents+operatives past/present/future** < she began. > **refuse transmissions from all cps agents+operatives past/present/ future—refuse transmissions of arrest warrants/censorship/government directives—refuse all ef orders relating to the capture of criminals/subversives/mutants** <

> **request authorization?** < the system asked, obedient to her previous commands, and Raven smiled to herself.

> **authorization *raven*** < she confirmed and the system hastened to obey her.

11
LOOSE THE
SEVEN SEALS

The terminal screen went dark. The Minister for Technology, Joseph Levi, tapped the key combination to bring it to life. Nothing happened. Irritated now, he keyed in another combination intended to be used in the event of a system crash. Again nothing happened. He frowned and turned to the vidcom unit, intending to summon a subordinate to address the problem, and tapped in a call-code. The vidcom unit failed to respond.

Levi got up from his desk and went to the door of his study. It slid open to reveal his outer office, normally filled with assistants quietly performing the tasks he had set them. Now it was a scene of chaos. All over the room the screens had blacked out and men and women frantically tapped in a series of combinations onto their unresponsive keypads. It took a few minutes for one of his assistants to notice him standing there. Finally one of them turned and saw him.

"Minister!" she exclaimed, and the other occupants of the room turned to regard him.

"What's going on?" Levi demanded. "Is there a problem with the system?"

"I think it might be a problem with the network, Sir," the woman who had first observed him responded. "Nothing seems to be working. I've tried everything I can think of."

"So have I," a young man added, not looking up from the terminal into which he continued to key useless codes. "I've used all the security passwords for my clearance level. Nothing seems to work."

"Perhaps your clearance, Minister?" the woman asked hopefully and Levi nodded curtly.

Crossing to the nearest terminal, he ordered his subordinates to look away as he typed in the highest security clearance passwords, known only to him and the President. The screen stayed dark. He sat back from the screen and thought for a while. Then, turning back to his assistants, he ordered:

"Close down our connection to the network and restart the terminals."

Everyone in the office held their breath as the young man manually adjusted the setting of the main server connection. Then they heaved a communal sigh of relief as the terminal screens brightened again.

"Don't relax yet," Levi warned. "This only means our computer system is still working. We still don't have net access." He looked quickly around the room and gestured to his assistants one by one.

"You, go and get a report from the technicians at the Versailles Computer Complex; you'll have to take a flitter since the vidcoms aren't working. You, visit every office and department in this building, find out how many of them, if any, still have net access and inform the others to close their net connections until the problem has been isolated. You, go and take a message to the office of the President and inform His Excellency of what has occurred here. You, summon two additional detachments of troops to guard this building; this may be the initial strike of a terrorist attack."

He paused for breath as his subordinates scuttled to do his bidding. He was sweating and breathing heavily and he felt nauseous.

"What can be the meaning of this?" he asked quietly to himself.

"Minister?" One of his assistants interrupted his musings.

"Yes?" he replied sharply, annoyed at the interruption.

"Minister, just before the crash, my terminal had reported a result on that search you requested," the man said diffidently. "I don't know if it's relevant but—"

"Search." Levi frowned to himself then his eyes brightened. "The search for the Hex?" He hurried over to the terminal in question and stared at it. "Show me the result!"

Fumbling with the keypad the assistant produced the last screen of information he had seen before the crash. Words formed on the screen and then an image was produced beneath them.

> security vidcam (no.#2356346567) in transcendence, unity district, captured image (rendered on screen) at 1600 hours today. correlation with subject "raven," probability 97% <

The Minister and his assistant gazed at the image. It was a

young woman. She was dressed in a heavy black greatcoat, which swung open slightly to reveal a military uniform. She had black hair, braided in accordance with military regulations into a long plait, and her eyes were dark and secretive.

Levi stared at it, transfixed. He wondered if it was actually possible that the President's last-ditch attempt to locate the renegade Hex had actually succeeded. Then suddenly he stiffened.

"What uniform is that?" he demanded.

The assistant whose terminal it was shrugged and looked embarrassed.

"Not sure, Sir," he admitted. "I'm not aware of all the grades and you can't see very much—"

"No excuses," Levi snarled. He looked wildly across the room. "You!" He beckoned urgently. "What uniform is that?"

Lieutenant Armitage, the Seccie assigned to him as a personal bodyguard, hurried across the room and came to look at the screen. Unhesitatingly he answered.

"Military Intelligence, Sir," he said quickly. "And the tags are those of a Force Commander."

"A Force Commander?" the Minister's voice rose to a yell. "There's a Hex in Transcendence wearing a Force Commander's uniform? How is that even possible?"

Everyone turned to look at him, the horror on their faces a mirror of his.

"Get in touch with Transcendence Military Command!" Levi shouted. "Now! I don't care how you do it. Give them that picture and tell them to capture that woman at all costs."

"Yes, Sir," the Seccie guard replied, snapping to attention. Then he raced out of the room as if the fires of hell were at his back.

"Then get me Alverstead," Levi continued, still trembling with emotion. "The head of the CPS. I want him to identify this woman. He's the only one who's met this Hex. Maybe it isn't her."

Another assistant left to find the CPS Governor and the Minister sank into the nearest chair. He hoped against hope that the computer system's probability estimate was incorrect. But he doubted it would be. Somehow, against all possibility, a Hex had managed to infiltrate one of the most powerful strongholds of the Federation. By now she could be wreaking untold havoc with her stolen military authority. Levi shook his head silently as he catalogued the powers an Intelligence Division Force Commander had. She could order almost anything in that uniform. Only a tactical nuclear strike required a higher clearance.

Levi felt the rule of the EF crumbling around him. They had lost control of the net. The rogue Hex was working against them in a city she should not have been able to come within a hundred miles of. Somewhere other Hexes concealed a disk that would unlock their true potential. The President of the Federation was a man obsessed. He had ordered Raven's capture at any cost while the Federation rocked on its foundations. Levi suspected that the troops stationed in Transcendence were about to fight the last battle of a war that had already been lost.

Sergeant Crispian sipped his second cup of coffee, slowly savoring the bitter taste. His men were wolfing down the plates of delicacies the Space Center's staff had provided, but, for now, Crispian was content just to get the weight off his feet. He was amused by the eagerness with which the Center staff were serving his squad. Perhaps he should have visited this facility before, he wondered. The people here had been neglected by the important powers of the Federation for so long that they were prepared to go to any lengths to impress the Intelligence Officers. That including hosting Crispian's squad in luxurious comfort.

Crispian stretched out his legs and leaned back in the comfortable chair, wondering if it would be inappropriate to have a brief nap while he was waiting for the officers to return. He lifted the cup of coffee to his lips once more and then, with a start, spilled the remaining hot liquid across his legs. He jumped to his feet with a curse. A loud alarm was going off, almost deafening him with its siren blaring.

"What the hell is that?" he demanded.

"Evacuation alarm," the pretty young girl who'd been serving them drinks said fearfully. "We must leave the building at once."

"Why?" Crispian asked anxiously. "What would trigger the alarm?"

"I've never heard it before," the girl told him. "But it's supposed to go off in the event of a fire or if the security system detects an explosive device."

"An explosive device?" Crispian signaled to his men and they headed for the door, the girl running to keep up with them. "There are two Intelligence Officers assessing your facility for vulnerability to terrorists. I hope for your sake they don't end up being blown up in the middle of their inspection."

• • •

Jordan waited impatiently in the pilot's seat of the skimmer. Kez and Luciel sat in the back, surreptitiously clutching their guns. The weapons had been coated with a material to render them invisible to the scanning devices of Transcendence but Raven had warned them to keep them out of sight of the vidcams. Alaric was standing at the skimmer door, holding his own gun in one of the deep pockets of his coat, watching for any sign of Raven, Wraith, or the Seccie squad.

"I hope we set the timers right," Jordan fretted. "If Raven's injured I'll never forgive myself."

"She'll be chill," Kez said with an exaggerated confidence. "She always is."

"And the timers were fine," Drow said, speaking confidently despite his unfamiliarity with the other Ghosts. "That tech was elite."

"There they are!" Luciel exclaimed and Jordan whirled back to look at the entrance of the Space Center.

A group of people were racing out of the building. Among the scientists and Seccie guards Raven was instantly recognizable, her flag of long black hair flying loose and her long coat flapping like wings behind her. Wraith was keeping pace with her and the two of them were outdistancing the Seccie squad who hadn't yet realized that the "officers" were heading in a slightly different direction from them.

"Over here," Alaric called, waving wildly with his free hand, and the leader of the Seccie squad glanced over at him. The man's mouth dropped open in amazement as he saw that the two Force Commanders, whose orders he had been unquestioningly following, were racing for the skimmer.

As Raven and Wraith threw themselves inside the vehicle Jordan heard a dull thunder noise. Alaric fell in after them and slammed the door shut as there was a second thundering boom and the Space Operations Center began to cave in on itself. The Seccie squad leader was still staring, openmouthed, as Jordan gunned the engine of the skimmer and sped away from the collapsing building as fast as she could.

As the skimmer raced through the city toward the rendezvous point Jordan didn't need to ask if Raven had been successful. The city was in uproar. Seccie flitters were everywhere, racing past the elegant pinnacles and minarets of Transcendence's sculpted buildings with their sirens wailing. Crowds of people milled about in the street, still not entirely aware of what had occurred. Jordan doubted that the collapse of the Space Operations Center would even be noticed in the hubbub.

"This is unprecedented," Alaric said, looking at the city as they skimmed through the crowded streets. "It looks like a broken ant's nest."

"Isn't it one?" Raven said with a faint laugh from where she lay back, regarding the confusion passively from the window of the skimmer.

"It worked then," Luciel asked needlessly. "Everything went as planned?"

"Even better than planned," Wraith assured him.

"We still have to get out of this mess," Jordan pointed out, wrenching the controls to avoid a Seccie skimmer abandoned for some reason in the middle of the roadway. "Think your uniforms will buy us passage?"

"I wouldn't rely on it," Raven informed her. "Too risky."

"Let's just get to the rendezvous point and lie low for a while," Alaric recommended. "Then we'll see if Force Commanders Barrow and Wing have had their identities compromised."

"First we have to let Drow off," Jordan pointed out. "To collect Gift and Tally."

"I'm not certain he should go alone," Wraith said seriously but Drow shook his head.

"No," he contradicted. "I can do this. The rest of you could be recognized by the Seccies, they have your descriptions on file. Gift and Tally are my responsibility first. Trust me not to fail them."

Alaric nodded to himself and Kez grinned at Drow.

"Good luck then," Wraith said, accepting the inevitable, but Raven raised an eyebrow.

"Luck?" she asked. "This isn't luck. Destiny is on our side now."

There was in fact only one Force Commander in Transcendence. His name was Sieben Winter and he commanded five divisions of Federation Troops. He fitted almost exactly Sergeant Crispian's idea of a Military Intelligence Officer. For thirty years he had worked for the Federation and during that time he had followed orders scrupulously, even when those orders involved the torture and murder of rebels working against the interests of the government. He remembered the names of every last one of those victims of EF justice. A man with no illusions as to who or what he was, Commander Winter was nevertheless respected by the men under his command. Now his aide stood beside him with lowered eyes waiting for the Force Commander's decision.

"The order came through unconventional channels," Winter mused.

"Yes, Force Commander," the aide replied.

"You were unable to authenticate it because of the network's failure to respond to our passwords."

"Yes, Commander."

"In which case it is possible our orders are not genuine," the Force Commander mused and his aide nodded. Winter remained silent for a while. When he spoke again it was in a strange tone of voice.

"I would have your opinion, Craddock," he told his aide.

"Yessir."

"We know that the net has been disrupted by a force unknown," the Commander began. "Possibly as a prelude to a devastating system crash. Our only source of information are the media broadcasts. However, I have had to order my men not to watch these because of the almost certainly illegal and seditious information they are broadcasting."

"Yessir."

"These reports from the media indicate the following," the Force Commander continued. "That the city of London is in a state of chaos. That President Sanatos has fled the palace Versailles with a fortune in gold bullion and his whereabouts are currently unknown. That all over the Federation riots are breaking out, triggered most probably by rumors that the Security Services have been crippled by the loss of the net. These riots are likely to lead to revolution since almost all the Federation troops are similarly crippled." He looked levelly at the aide. "In short we are facing the complete breakdown of our civilization."

"So it would appear, Sir," Craddock replied. An exemplary soldier, he didn't break his position although a twitch at the corner of his mouth betrayed his anxiety.

"With this in mind, Craddock," Commander Winter went on. "And think carefully, bearing in mind that we are honor-bound to obey any legitimate order we receive. Does it seem likely to you that the Military Command would order what are possibly the last five active and operational troop divisions in Europe to search the city for a young female Hex and have her eliminated?"

The aide's face was studiedly blank. Craddock had served Commander Winter for twenty years. Throughout that time they had both followed every order they had received, believing unquestioningly in the rule of law. Now they had received what would possibly be their last order ever. That is, if it was genuine.

"Well, Craddock?" Commander Winter asked. "Does it seem likely to you that Military Command would give such an order?"

"Yes, Sir," the aide replied. "It does."

The Commander nodded.

"I agree with your assessment," he replied. "It is unquestioningly the most ludicrous and futile order I have ever received.

It will almost certainly prove impossible to carry out and, if we should succeed, will not do one iota of good in limiting the chaos that is now upon us."

"Yessir."

"Nevertheless," Commander Winter concluded. "It is an order. Have the troops begin the search."

The crew of the stratojet hurried to fasten all the compartments and check that all the passengers were fastened into their seats. The pilot's voice was projected across the plane.

"Ladies and Gentlemen," it said, pretending to an unlikely confidence. *"A situation of possible emergency exists. We are experiencing some difficulties making contact with Transcendence air control. We are also experiencing some difficulties with our connection to the information network. Therefore, could all passengers please prepare for a possible crash landing. I repeat, a situation of possible emergency exists, could all passengers brace themselves for a crash landing."*

The auburn-haired boy in seat 16B, whose name on the passenger list was given as Edward Anderson, turned to the person in the next seat and whispered:

"Is this something to do with us?"

"How should I know?" the girl replied equally quietly. Her name was officially Elsie Anderson and her similarity of features to the boy beside her identified her as his sister. "But I think it might be genuine. If we'd been identified they'd have stopped us during a routine check at the terminal, not faked a stratojet crash." She paled as she realized what she had just said. "Which means the jet *is* about to crash."

"Fasten your seat belt, Tally," her brother warned. "And brace yourself."

"What if we do crash?" she asked with a frightened look.

"Then the second they open the doors we slip out and find Drow. And if we can't find him we hide until we can." Gift looked grim. "Strange things are happening, Tally," he said softly. "I'm sure of it."

"Me too," his sister whispered and then she closed her eyes, burying her head in her arms as she prepared for a crash landing.

Similar events were occurring all over the Federation. The combination of the EF's commitment of all their system resources to finding Raven, the Federation's loss of the orbital satellite network, and the increase in strength of the darkness of the net that had once been Kalden's mind had resulted in accidents and emergencies all across Europe. In England, the media channel Populix had resumed broadcasting to inform the people of London of what was going on. The other media channels across the Federation followed suit, providing the EF's citizens with their only information about a world becoming gradually insane.

But, despite the riots and revolutions beginning in many of the European cities, civilization had not completely broken down. In many places volunteers had stepped forward to rescue the victims of accidents caused by the failure of the net. In others citizens had disarmed the local Seccies and were taking the law into their own hands to protect and serve the population. In London, Geraint and Ali had organized the Ghosts into bands and were policing the streets. Their presence alone was controlling the rival gangs while the Seccies fled en masse from the area.

However, the decay of the information network continued. Too much had been asked of it in too short a time. It struggled sluggishly to continue the flow of data but was opposed by a dark and heavy force.

The remains of Kalden's mind exulted. Everywhere the city of light was fading and dying. The chattering data channels were slowing and stopping, a flood becoming a narrow stream and finally a pathetic trickle. In the space the net had occupied the cloud of darkness flowed unimpeded. Coiling over and over itself it stretched its multiple tentacles through the remains of the network. A mighty kraken in an ocean of thought, it lurked in the dark depths and waited for its prey. At whatever point the object of its hate entered the net, the darkness would be waiting to consume it.

Drow scanned the rushing crowds desperately. The chaos had begun gradually in the airport as the terminals had darkened. But, once it had begun, the panic spread rapidly. Now people ran wildly hither and thither, some carrying heavy luggage, others abandoning their possessions in their urgency to get to safety. Three incoming stratojets were reported to have crashed on arrival but Drow couldn't get any sense out of the staff who were frantically attempting to get their useless computers back on line. Something had gone badly wrong, the young hacker realized—

Raven's takeover of the satellite network had not been intended to have these effects. He had an ominous feeling about the confusion and misery that surrounded him now and shuddered.

He walked on, trying not to let the passersby jostle him too much in their flight. Somewhere in this terminal were Gift and Talent. He had let them down once before, giving them advice that might have led to their deaths; he was determined not to do so again. If they were here, he would find them. He continued to scan the crowds, uselessly. There were children of all ages everywhere, some crying pathetically, separated from their parents. None of them looked like the ones he was looking for. Drow's heart was racing and he could feel his own fear like a physical pain, tight and sharp in his chest. He willed himself to calm down and wondered what one of the Ghosts would do in his place. Even without the net to help her, someone like Raven would have thought of something.

Suddenly he remembered something Ali had told him back in the Ghost enclave in London.

"Raven recognized Avalon," she had said. "She knew the first time she saw her that she was a Hex. She knew when she met me for the first time as well. There's something about us she can recognize."

It was an ability Ali had admitted she herself did not possess but nonetheless it was possible. Drow had touched Tally's and Gift's minds. More than that, he had virtually touched their souls. He knew that when he saw them he would recognize them immediately. Of that he was certain. The only problem was finding them.

He stopped stock-still and closed his eyes. People slammed

into him and swore as he got in their way. He ignored them, concentrating. Somewhere in all this confusion Tally and Gift were looking for him. Without him they had no one to protect them and nowhere to go. With every fiber of his mind he strained toward them. Filling his mind with all his hope and desperation he reached out. And connected.

Drow's eyes snapped open. There they were. Two small figures standing about thirty meters away by a graceful fluting pillar. They were looking around, holding each other's hands so as not to get separated. As he looked at them they turned, almost as one person, and their eyes met his. He felt a sudden grin break out on his face and in unison the twins smiled back. Together they crossed the terminal to meet each other and within minutes came face-to-face.

"I found you," Drow said. "Despite everything."

"I was sure you would," Gift replied, grinning back.

"I wasn't," Tally admitted. "But I'm glad you did."

"We'd better get out of here," Drow told them. "Everything's on the fritz. The net seems to have gone down."

"Where to?" Gift asked. "What's the plan?"

"There's a rendezvous point," Drow explained. "The others are waiting for us there."

"Then let's go," Tally said quickly and they headed for the exit.

"We should hurry," Gift said as they forced their way through the crowds. "There's something we didn't tell you before."

"What's that?"

"We have a disk," Tally explained. "It's the only copy that exists. But the information on it is incredibly important to our kind of people." She looked around her at the frantic crowds. "Whatever's going on," she said, "maybe the information we have can stop it."

Raven was the first to realize that something was wrong. The others, elated by their success, were chattering eagerly as Jordan expertly navigated the skimmer through the city. But Raven, watching the movement of the crowds and activities of the Seccie flitters, remained silent. At the back of her mind there was a nagging doubt. The darkness in the net had been growing slowly. In her assessment the rate of its development had not been fast enough for it to have become a serious threat. And yet the chaos in the streets was increasing. Transcendence was a bastion of EF power. It should have been one of the last places to be affected by her appropriation of the satellite network. But the city was falling apart before her eyes and she wondered if she had made a tactical error. It was possible that recent events had changed the growth rate of Kalden's shattered mentality. If that was the case they might be in serious trouble.

Raven reached forward and touched Jordan's arm to get her attention. The girl glanced back at her with a quick smile.

"What is it, Raven?" she asked easily. "Something up?"

"Something's wrong," Raven said softly and the others fell silent. "Speed up," she continued. "I should get to a terminal as soon as possible. I think we might be in trouble."

The humming of the skimmer's engines changed note and became a low whine as Jordan coaxed every last atom of power from the vehicle. No one said a word as they swept on through the city. Raven's words had disturbed their mood of euphoria and now each of them felt the tension in the air. No one countered her assertion that something was wrong.

It seemed half a hundred years until Jordan stopped the skimmer with a skid in the forecourt of a huge hotel. There was no one on duty at the desk as they entered but that didn't stop them. They took the elevator, miraculously still working, to the rooms they had booked the night before. When they got there Kez produced a set of tools from his coat and efficiently picked the lock. Alaric and Jordan stood guard duty in case they were disturbed. Raven waited in silence and Luciel and Wraith watched her. Her face was expressionless but her pupils were dilated, a response that in anyone else they would have identified as fear.

The door opened and they entered the suite. Raven spotted the terminal immediately and crossed the room toward it even as Kez was carefully shutting the door behind them. Without a word she rested her hands on the keypad and immediately gave a soft gasp. Then she was still, a statue carved in ivory and obsidian, as her eyes glazed over in communion with the network.

12

ALPHA
AND OMEGA

It had seemed to Raven that the net had been with her all her life.
In the asylum blockhouse where she had grown up it had been her
only real sanctuary, whispering secrets to her from another world.
For years she had only really felt alive when her fingers touched the
keypad of a terminal and her mind melded with the net to become
her true self. Inside the network she became the legend others
saw her as. Even when Kalden had experimented on her she had
been able to reach out to the pathways of the net and draw them
to herself. Never had she been unable to reach the infinite city of
light.

Now she fell into darkness. It seemed unimaginably far.
She fell as if in a dream and could not stop herself. Nowhere
around her could she find the network. The last time she had
faced this darkness she had been armed in light. Now there

was no light to find. Instead the darkness spoke to her.

> **raven** < it said. > **i begin to remember** <

Force Commander Sieben Winter watched the rioters in the streets from the armored military flitter. His aide, Craddock, was piloting, keeping the vehicle well above the raging crowds.

"It is anarchy," Commander Winter said. His voice was calm but his eyes were angry. Craddock didn't answer him. In all the years he had served with the Force Commander he had known him for a dangerous man. He had killed ruthlessly and tortured without mercy. But unlike other military officers, especially those in the Intelligence Division, he had never shown any pleasure in his actions. He had seemed more like a robot than a man, dedicated to performing his duties with every fraction of his being. Craddock feared his Commander's anger but trusted his judgment implicitly. There were few soldiers, even among the officers, that the aide admired. But Commander Winter could be relied upon and there was nothing more likely to gain Craddock's respect.

The Commander's com unit chimed, not needing a link to the network to perform its functions, and he answered it.

"Winter, here," he said precisely, and waited.

Craddock couldn't hear what was said on the other end of the signal but he saw the Force Commander's eyes change. He looked almost regretful but when he answered he sounded as efficient as ever.

"Surround the building," he said. "I will be there directly."

Closing the connection, he turned to his aide.

"A Seccie squad has reported," he said. "While fleeing the devastation of the city they observed a group of people, two in uniforms of Force Commanders, entering a hotel in the Serendipity district. One of the uniformed officers was female and had long black hair."

"That is the description we received of the Hex, Sir."

"Correct," the Commander replied. "Accordingly we will proceed to this hotel, the Gardenia, in the Serendipity district. Then we will enter the building and eliminate the Hex in accordance with our orders."

"Yessir," Craddock said and touched the controls of the flitter directing it toward the district of the city the Commander had named. He glanced sideways at his superior officer and coughed to attract his attention. "Sir?" he asked.

"Yes, Craddock?" The Commander looked surprised to hear his aide speak, as well he might seeing as his orders had been easy to understand.

"May I ask a question, Sir?" Craddock asked.

"You may."

"What about after we've apprehended the Hex, Sir?" the aide asked apologetically. "What do we do then?"

The Force Commander thought for a while before speaking. Finally he answered.

"Well, Craddock," he said. "Seeing as the world we know is ending, in the circumstances I believe it would be appropriate for you to take some leave."

"Yessir, thank you, Sir," Craddock replied. "If I may ask another question, Sir?"

"Yes?"

"What will you be doing, Commander?"

Commander Winter looked surprised.

"I shall stand duty and await orders, of course," he said.

In London three children were also standing duty. Cara and Lucy were veterans of the Hex cause and had lived among the Ghosts ever since being rescued from extermination or worse. Charis was a newcomer who barely understood the controls of the laser pistol she was holding. But all three were loyal to their charge. They stood outside a building in the Ghost enclave waiting for Ali to join them. Since the decision to attack, it had been agreed that none of the senior Ghosts should travel anywhere without an escort.

"But I'm still not sure why I was assigned," Charis was saying. "I don't know anything about weapons or fighting."

"You'll learn," Lucy assured her. "We all did."

"If she has the time," Cara pointed out. "I mean, I don't want to sound weird but it looks as if everything's happening right now."

"You're right," Lucy agreed. "Charis, we should probably try to teach you a little more now."

"Don't look so worried," Cara added. "I know why you're here even if you don't. Ali must want to keep an eye on you. I heard Raven telling her you had a lot of potential and she should know. She's the best there is."

"Really?" Charis's expression was doubtful. She was dubious of the wild-looking Hex who had appeared so alarmingly in her parent's apartment. "Ali impressed me more."

653

"You're skitzo!" Cara exclaimed. "I mean, Ali's a good leader, but Raven is . . ." She shook her head, at a loss of words.

"Ignore her," Lucy advised the new recruit. "It's getting to be like the cult of Raven around here. It's about time someone introduced some perspective."

Cara opened her mouth to object but she never said the words she had planned. Instead her eyes widened as she stared up through the levels.

"My God," she breathed quietly. "Look at that!"

The other two girls looked up automatically and stared, equally transfixed. Across the city lights were flashing, whole city blocks were darkening while in other areas lights flashed on and off too quickly to see other than as a blur.

"Something strange is happening," Lucy said, stating the obvious. "We should go get Ali."

"Tell her it looks like the net is crashing," Cara added.

"It is?" Charis's rapt gaze switched to the young Hex in alarm. "How?"

"I don't know." Cara looked back with a troubled expression. "But I've listened to stuff the older Ghosts have said about net crashes. It looks to me as if this is it."

"But . . ." Lucy paused at the doorway, looking back at her friend. "What are we going to do?"

"Hey," Cara said suddenly, snapping back to reality. "Stop looking like the sky is falling. Even if it is that's no reason to fall apart. We've trained for this, you know we have. This is why we were taught to use weapons, this is why we were taught to be

Hexes. This is the moment we've been waiting for. It's no use being scared of it. We're supposed to be fighting a war, remember? Now go and tell our Commander the battle has begun."

Drow ran into the hotel, Gift and Tally following only paces behind him. The chaos in the streets was growing. They had had to avoid groups of rioters, smashing into buildings to look at what lay inside, more than once as they headed for the rendezvous. Drow had stolen a flitter, believing they would be safer in the air than on the ground. Tally and Gift had sat in the front with him, crammed into the forward passenger seat, and watched out for Seccies. They had seen a few but they hadn't been stopped by them. Drow was more worried about the Federation troops he saw everywhere. They moved purposefully through the city, carrying heavy blasters, but they made no attempt to stop the rioters or impose any other kind of order.

Flinging himself into the elevator, Drow waited as Tally and Gift joined him then touched the keypad to take them to the seventh floor.

"Something's very wrong," Tally muttered to herself and Gift looked angry.

"It always is, Tally. Isn't it?" he said sharply and Drow glanced at him quickly. "She's always predicting doom and gloom," Gift said quickly, looking slightly embarrassed.

"Let's hope she's wrong," Drow replied, pacing in the small elevator space like a caged animal. "But I have a feeling . . ."

The elevator stopped and Drow looked out into the corridor. It was empty.

"Come on," he said, and they headed out of the elevator, Drow reading the suite numbers until he came to the correct one. He knocked on the door, three quick raps, and it opened immediately to reveal Alaric standing there holding a gun.

"Drow!" he exclaimed in relief. "Quick, come in, all of you."

As the twins followed Drow into the hotel suite, all the Ghosts except Kez turned to regard them. Wraith was the first to speak.

"Gift. Talent," he said. "I am immeasurably relieved to see you here. You've braved greater dangers than you should ever have had to face and done credit to your names."

Tally stared, wide-eyed, at the white-haired man in the military uniform, unable to speak. But Gift felt something inside him resonate at the stranger's words.

"Thank you, Sir," he said simply. "But I think you've put yourselves in even greater danger to help us."

"One of us has," a girl spoke and the twins looked at her. She didn't look much older than they were and she clung to the arm of the young man who had opened the door to them. "There's something wrong with Raven," she said.

"Raven?" Tally asked in a whisper. The name called out to her as the white-haired man's words had called to Gift.

"Raven," said a thin boy who stood nearby. "She's our hacker. The leader of us Hexes. She went into the net an hour ago and she hasn't come out. She hasn't even moved." He stepped aside so they could see and the twins drew in their breath sharply.

Across the room, before a computer terminal, were two figures. The boy sat on the floor. He was crying, soundlessly, but his eyes didn't blink or waver from the girl sitting as still as a statue in front of the terminal. She was barely breathing. Her black eyes stared blankly in front of her. Her thin pale hands rested on the keypad in front of her. The terminal screen was blank.

The thin boy who had spoken before and stepped aside so they could see their leader spoke again.

"I'm the only other Hex here," he said. "I tried to go in after her. But I couldn't. There's nothing there. I couldn't find her. I couldn't find anything."

The twins looked at each other. Then Gift reached into an inside pocket and pulled out the data disk. He extended it to Wraith.

"Sir," he said carefully. "We have this. Our grandfather was a Hex and a scientist. He studied the Hex abilities and recorded everything he learned on this disk. The EF killed him and my father to get it. My mother died to protect it." He stopped for a moment to take a deep breath. "Tally and I don't even know what's on it," he said. "But maybe it can help Raven."

Wraith reached out to take the disk and opened his mouth to speak. But before he could say anything there was a loud booming noise, the sound of an announcing device being turned on. Then, outside the hotel, a voice thundered:

"*Hexes,*" it said. "*This building is surrounded. There is no escape. Deliver the criminal named Raven to us for execution and the rest of you may live.*"

Craddock watched the building anxiously. There was no immediate response to Commander Winter's announcement. He wondered if the

Hexes inside understood that the Commander was speaking the truth. The troops had moved into position soundlessly, ringing the hotel in black-uniformed soldiers. Now they stood ready. In no direction was there any escape. The aide wondered if the Hexes would give themselves up. In the circumstances it would be suicide not to.

"It seems they are reluctant," Commander Winter said. He lifted the announcer a second time and spoke into it.

"*Hexes,*" he said. "*We have enough firepower to destroy the building. But my orders only require the elimination of the Hex named Raven. Deliver her and you have my word you will live.*"

There was another delay and Craddock watched the building carefully. Just when he thought the Commander's words would go unrecognized, a figure appeared on one of the elegant balconies of the upper floors of the hotel. It was holding a piece of white fabric, apparently a sheet or blanket, and the wind whipped it into a flag.

"It would appear they wish to parley, Sir," he said.

"So it would seem," the Force Commander returned. "It is pointless in the circumstances. But we have some leeway as to time." He raised the announcer again.

"*If you are prepared to negotiate, approach the edge of the balcony and wait to be collected,*" Commander Winter announced and the figure followed his instructions. It had closed the door through which it had emerged and stood waiting.

The Force Commander signaled to one of his men and the soldier hastened to the nearby military flitter and climbed into the pilot's seat. In moments he was guiding the craft up to the balcony where the figure waited.

"Are we not to storm the building then, Sir?" Craddock asked deferentially.

"We almost certainly will, Craddock," the Commander replied. "But I am curious to see what this rebel has to say for himself. I would like to know his rationale for bringing about Armageddon."

Commander and aide waited as the flitter returned and touched down. The soldier who had been piloting it exited, saluted, and opened the door for the rebel to exit. It was a man with short-cropped white hair. He wore a Force Commander's uniform and he regarded Commander Winter levelly.

"I am prepared to negotiate," he said. "In private."

"Then negotiate," the Commander replied. "Your request for privacy has been evaluated and denied."

"Very well." The man seemed untroubled. "You may call me Wraith."

"I am Force Commander Sieben Winter," the Commander replied. "At present I hold the highest authority in this city, which is under martial law. I demand that you deliver the Hex named Raven to me for execution. Then you may depart with such companions as you possess."

"Are you aware, Force Commander," the man named Wraith began, "that the information network is about to experience a permanent systems crash?"

"I would estimate the likelihood of such an occurrence as high," the Commander agreed.

"Are you also aware of the result of such a crash?"

"I am," the Commander replied. "Moreover, I have been

informed that you and your companions were responsible for this situation."

"You have been informed incorrectly," Wraith told him. "The instigator of the crash is one of your own operatives, a Federation scientist named Kalden."

"I fail to see how one scientist could engineer a disaster of such epic proportions," the Force Commander replied.

"The scientist in question has been believed dead for two years," Wraith returned. "The Hex you referred to earlier, my sister, Raven, thought that she had ended his life. However, this event occurred while he was conducting certain experiments on her. The experimental equipment preserved what remained of Kalden's mind in the network. He is insane."

"That would explain a great deal," the Force Commander replied. "I had wondered why a Hex would destroy the network. You have relieved my mind of its curiosity. Accordingly, will you deliver the Hex so that I may proceed in carrying out my duty?"

"The Hex Raven," the man called Wraith said, "is currently engaged in attempting to prevent the systems crash we spoke of earlier. In the circumstances, will you withdraw your request that we surrender her?"

"I fear I will be unable to do that," Commander Winter replied. "My orders clearly state that I am to apprehend and execute the Hex."

"Carrying out your orders won't improve the situation we find ourselves in," Wraith stated baldly. "Perhaps you should consider other options?"

"I would be willing to," the Force Commander told him. "Regrettably, there are none."

Raven hung suspended in the darkness. As yet there was no pain. But she knew that would come later as her mind became increasingly divorced from sensation. She had no idea how long she had hung there, entrapped and enfolded in the dark cloud of Kalden's mind.

> **you thought you could escape me** < the darkness told her, its words echoing through her mind. > **you were incorrect. now you will suffer as i have suffered. i am not what i was but there is enough of me to assure you of that. you will suffer an eternity for every second i have suffered.** <

Raven was silent and the darkness clenched tighter around her.

> **why do you not speak?** < it demanded. > **do you fear to?** <

> **what is there to fear?** < Raven replied, speaking directly into the heart of the darkness. > **you are nothing.** <

> **i am PAIN!** < the darkness roared, thrashing around her, its voice an agony beating into her brain. > **i am TORMENT. i am DARKNESS. DEATH. THE HORRORS OF THE VOID. I AM YOUR NIGHTMARE. FEAR ME** <

> **you are nothing.** < Raven replied simply. > **you have no life in you. even if you kill me you will still be dead. i have nightmares to give you life.** <

"Perhaps there is an option," Wraith said. "Are you prepared to hear it?"

"I am prepared to listen," Force Commander Winter agreed.

"Orders may be suspended when your superiors change their minds," Wraith pointed out. "Isn't that correct?"

"They have been in the past," the Commander acknowledged. "However, in this instance that possibility is unlikely since my superiors have no way to contact me and no prospect of doing so in the future."

"It is my belief that your superiors no longer hold any form of authority," Wraith informed him. "The President has fled. The rule of the EF is over. Your government has fallen."

"You may be correct," the Force Commander replied. "It makes no difference. I have my orders."

"I have every expectation that a new government is about to be put in place," Wraith said. "A coup has been mounted. Power now rests with the Hexes since they alone control the net. The European Federation is being effectively held to ransom. It has the option of committing suicide and condemning its citizens to the chaos of a network crash. Or it may surrender."

He looked about the plaza at the troops, then back at the Force Commander.

"I am a representative of the new government of the Federation," he said. "I am accordingly your new superior officer. You and your men may surrender to me."

Drow carried the disk to the terminal. Outside, everything seemed quiet. Whatever Wraith was doing it had bought them some time.

"Will she know it's there?" Tally asked anxiously.

"I don't know," Alaric answered her. "But I don't have any better ideas."

"Raven," Drow said quietly. "I hope this works." Then, with a quiet click, he slid the disk into the terminal slot.

The Force Commander regarded the man before him. He was serious. Outnumbered by over a hundred to one, he was genuinely requesting that they surrender to him. The Commander approved.

"I will require proof of your authority before I can take your orders," he told the man. "Do you have such proof?"

"Will demonstrating that the information network is completely in our power suffice?" Wraith asked.

"It would," the Force Commander agreed. "Do you have such proof?"

"The Hex Raven is currently preventing a complete systems crash of the network," Wraith said, as if he was only informing the Commander of this for the first time. "If you are prepared to wait for her to succeed I can then provide you with proof of our authority."

"If she fails I will have to take it that your authority is illegitimate," the Force Commander told him.

"In which case I will deliver my sister to you for execution," Wraith replied.

His heart ached as he said the words but he knew that he was making the right bargain. If Raven failed it meant she was trapped in the network forever, effectively dead anyway. Furthermore, if she failed, civilization would crumble. They would all die anyway.

Everything depended on Raven now. But then, he thought to himself, it always had.

"That would be satisfactory," the Commander told him. "We will wait."

They stood together and waited for the end or the beginning of the world. Around them the lights were still going out. The city of artifice was failing as it lost its power. All over Europe the lights were going out and citizens of the Federation waited in darkness to discover what would become of them.

Something flickered at the edge of Raven's consciousness. A whisper of a memory of a thought. The darkness was still ranting and raving, ordering her to quail about it. Raven ignored it. It wanted her fear. Just as it had when it was Kalden, it wanted her to run screaming from it. But Raven had lived with fear all her life. She might be alone in the darkness but she had been alone and in the dark for most of her life. Ever since the death of her parents she had been alone. Only in the net was she alive. Being alone and in pain had become a part of her nature. She had refused to surrender to the darkness every day of her life. She would not surrender to fear now.

> **FEAR ME** < the darkness roared.

> **no** < she informed it.

It howled with rage, whirling around and about in the heart of itself. Everywhere was pain. Every thought in her mind was an agony. She ignored it.

The flicker came again and this time Raven reached for it. Any thought right now would distract her from the torment the darkness was holding her in. She reached for it and it burst into her brain, a torrent of information, a stream of words and thoughts. Every phrase glowed with light.

> **The Freedom Files** <

The darkness hesitated. Then it flinched, light was pouring out of Raven and into the net. From the very heart of the black cloud she was emanating a flood of data, rebuilding the net out of her own essence with the flow of thought as her guide.

Deliberately she spoke the words that had been kept secret for twenty-five years, the truth that had waited to be heard ever since the Hex gene had first been discovered. These were the words that had explained to Raven the mystery of her own existence, clarifying everything she knew in one burst of illuminating freedom.

> **The HEX gene is a discovery unparalleled in the history of human evolution. The melding of mind and machine is a development that has awaited the human race since its creation. To the HEX no space is a void. The universe can be traveled in an instant. The HEX is a mind ready to transcend the narrow boundaries of the body and become thought without flesh. It takes no trauma to unlock the potential of the HEX. It requires only a mind open to possibilities. Recognize that there are no boundaries and there will be none.** <

All over Europe the lights were coming on. Darkened screens burst back into life and filled with data which flowed on and on. Raven's mind weaved itself into the net and the darkness screamed as it

665

dissolved. In the plaza in front of the hotel, Winter the Force Commander and Wraith the Ghost watched as the lights returned to the buildings surrounding them.

In the hotel suite on the seventh floor Kez gasped and the others turned to look at Raven. Her figure was glowing with a strange light. As they watched it brightened until, in the space of moments, it was too blinding to look at. Closing his eyes, Kez reached for her hand and caught it. It felt insubstantial to touch and he clung to it desperately. He could feel the light like an electric current burning through him. It was becoming physically painful to touch Raven. He clung on. But like a building charge the light continued to grow. Even behind his eyelids he could see it and then he could hold on no longer. Colors flashed behind his closed eyes. He could hear a sound building inside his ears: a single note that seemed to come from an infinite distance and yet grew louder all the time. There was no way of describing the sensation although later Ali, who had felt it even in London, described it as like a leap from a high place.

Then abruptly it vanished and he opened his eyes to see that Raven was gone. No trace of her remained. But on the gently glowing screen four words stood out clearly.

> **Let there be light.** <

EPILOGUE

The world was remade. But not everything changed at once. The dismantling of the old regime took time. Some of the Seccies and the EF troops fought. Others attempted to regain control of the net. Many fled to other countries where Hexes were still illegal and tried to win support for a counter-coup. All of them failed.

However, there were others, like Force Commander Winter, who acknowledged the legitimacy of the new government. It took time to gain their loyalty and many were not accepted as supporters of the Hex government because of crimes they had committed in the past. The new European Communality had to win the faith of its citizens, and many who had been labeled criminals under the old government rose to positions of authority in the new political climate. Even after elections, it took the other world countries more than ten years to recognize the new state. But in the end they caved in.

The European Communality had control of the network and without its support the rest of the world was lagging behind in the race to progress. The achievements of the Hex government were more than political, they were scientific and technological as well. Professor Moore, surviving the devastation of the Space Operations Center, lived for another twenty years, assisted by a young scientist named Luciel, to see his dream come true. The much-neglected space exploration program experienced the first major change of the new government. The first President of the European Communality announced in her inaugural speech that the people of Earth would spread out to colonize the stars.

"In space our future awaits us," she said. "It has been waiting for a long time."

The first spaceships built by the Communality were captained by Hexes. Later their names would also become legends: Gift, Talent, and Drow.

In the early years after the revolution there were many who were surprised that the new government was not led by a more prominent figure. The names of the Hexes who had won freedom for their kind and for the rest of Europe, and later the world, had become legends to the citizens of the Communality. There was a romantic attraction in the idea of Wraith, the ganger who had risen to high political office. There were others who were fascinated by Avalon, the only Hex who had lived in the public eye and preserved her secret, and could not understand why she declined political responsibility in favor of continuing her career as a musician. The first Communality President came as a surprise to almost everyone, including herself. But electing Allison Marie Tarrell was the wisest choice they could have made. Under her careful governance the new state flourished and expanded.

Her first action as President was to place a monument in the Serendipity district of the city of Transcendence. Later it became legendary itself. Carved from black obsidian, the Raven spread its stone wings for flight, exultation in every feather of its being.

On the first anniversary of the revolution two figures stood by the monument as the celebrations expanded in the city around them.

"I never thought it would end this way," Kez said quietly. "That we'd lose Raven to gain the world."

"Don't think of her as lost," Cloud replied. "She wouldn't have seen it that way."

"How would she have seen it?" Kez asked, as the first stroke of midnight fell and celebrations reached their peak.

"As being the first of us to find her wings," Cloud said, and above them the sky exploded with light.

RHIANNON LASSITER is an author of science fiction, fantasy, contemporary, magical realism, psychological horror, and thrill novels for teenagers. Her favorite authors include Ursula K. Le Guin, Margaret Mahy, and Octavia E. Butler. Her own novels explore themes of identity, change, and becoming. Rhiannon lives and works in Oxford, United Kingdom. Her ambition is to be the first writer in residence on the Moon. Find out more at rhiannonlassiter.com.

TURN THE PAGE TO ENTER

In this futuristic world,
nothing is as it seems. . . .

THE GAME

I could feel its heat on my face and I could see a glow through my closed eyelids. I knew what hypnosis was like, of course. It had been one of the many adjustment techniques used in school. I remembered the weightless sensation, as if my body had been floating in a black velvet space.

Funny. It wasn't like that now. The chair pressed hard against my spine. The light beat relentlessly against my closed eyelids. I felt very much awake. It isn't going to work, I thought. I remembered old techniques, let my hands drop to my sides and tried consciously to relax.

My fingertips curled and felt something gritty. That was ridiculous. The chair on which I was reclining was covered in soft gray cloth. I flattened my hand against the surface and flexed my fingers. They closed on a handful of sand. Hot, dry sand. I sat up, opened my eyes, and cried out, "Oh, look!"

Around me, the others stirred and sat up. We seemed to be in the middle of a desert. Brown sand stretched to a horizon of blue in every direction, except to our left, where the emptiness was interrupted by a high flat-topped rock rising abruptly, like a reddish cylinder, from the sand. Overhead a couple of large birds flapped and soared lazily in a current of warm air. Apart from the birds and the eight of us, no living thing stirred.

How quiet it was. Had I gone deaf? I swallowed and the silence pressed against my ears like hot cloth. How empty. A space so uncrowded that one could strain one's ears for five minutes and not hear a thing, could stretch one's eyes to the horizon and not see a single dwelling, a solitary person.

"It can't be real!" I gasped.

"Of course not. It's a typical hypnotic scenario." Trent was definite.

"So what happens next?"

"I suppose we wait and see what happens."

We basked in the sunshine. Overhead the birds circled lazily. The sand stretched emptily to the horizon. The silence was unbroken.

"Well, nothing's going to happen unless we make it." Brad sprang to his feet at last and brushed the sand off his hands. "And if we're to find clues we'd better start looking."

"But where?" I asked. "How will we know a clue when we see one?"

"Something that sticks out, something out of the ordinary."

Karen laughed. "There's only one thing sticking out." She pointed at the mesa. "I wonder if it's climbable? You'd get a spectacular view from the top."

We set off, four walking around the rock to the left, four to the right, looking for ledges, crevices, anything that might be a useful toehold. Almost halfway around, our team found a rounded channel, like an exposed volcanic vent, which meandered up the side of the rock. We couldn't see if it went clear to the top, but it looked possible.

We called to the others and, when they had joined us,

we worked out a plan of action. It wasn't going to be easy climbing without ropes. We had been exposed to adventure experiences at school, so we'd done some mountaineering, but this volcanic plug was totally different from the grass-topped crags we were accustomed to.

Katie, Trent, and Brad were the best climbers. I was nimble, but I was small and didn't have the reach of the others. We set out with Katie in the lead, followed by Paul, Trent, Scylla, Alden, Brad, me, and Karen.

The sun glanced across the fissure we were to climb, so that every toe- and fingerhold was etched in shadow. This was a plus. On the negative side, at times the sun shone full in our faces, almost blinding us.

We spoke very little as we climbed, just a terse word to indicate a toehold. There was a nasty moment when I tried to get a grip on a narrow ridge just beyond my reach. My fingers slipped and pain shot up my arm as the skin tore on the razor-sharp edge of the rock. My left foot slipped and I screamed.

"It's all right. I've got you." I could feel Karen's hand firmly pushing my foot back onto the narrow ledge.

I reached up again, straining for a fingerhold, but my fingertips were slippery with fresh blood. "I can't . . ."

Brad caught my wrist and he and Karen boosted me up to the next ledge. From then on the climb was straightforward, a set of nearly parallel ledges like an eccentric staircase.

One by one, we rolled over the top and lay panting in the clean dry air. There was a thin layer of soil covered with short dry grass and a creeping herb, which gave off a delightfully pungent smell when crushed. Katie said she'd never seen anything like it before. She tugged at its tough stem and managed to break off a specimen to stow safely in one of the pockets of her coverall.

I licked the blood off my fingertips. They were only oozing now, though very painful. I wondered how I would manage the climb down.

"Are you all right, Lisse?" Scylla examined my hand. "We need old Rich in the group to look after wounds like this."

"Even if Rich were here, he wouldn't be able to do anything. We should have a first-aid kit, I suppose." I licked my fingers again. "It's all right anyway."

"Just look at this view!" Katie interrupted, and we turned.

It was spectacular, with nothing between us and the far horizon in any direction. I felt we were getting the same view that the birds must have—the eagle's view.

During the time it had taken us to climb the mesa, the sun had moved from almost directly overhead into the southwest. Scylla found a sharp stone and, on a patch of dirt too thin for even the coarse mountain grass to grow, she scratched a long-tailed cross and marked the points of the compass on it.

"All right, everyone, what do you see?"

"A shining lake, due south."

"How far away?"

"Hard to say. Maybe six miles. Maybe more. This air is so clear, it's hard to judge."

"I can see a hollow, shadowed, a kind of ellipse. It's a

bit west of the lake and about the same distance away."

"All right. What else?"

"Due north it's all misty. That must mean more moisture. Maybe vegetation. But too far away to tell."

"There's a faint greenish color over there, to the northwest." I pointed. "A long way off. I couldn't even guess how far."

"Is that it?"

We all agreed that it was.

"Hmm. No rivers. Not even a stream. Nothing to eat either. We can manage without food for a while, but in this heat we really need water."

"There's the lake."

"Yes, that had better be our first objective. Although we've got nothing to store water in."

"Next time we come we'll be better prepared. Ropes. Waterbags. A first-aid kit."

"Let's get moving, then! We've got to get down off this thing first, and then there's a six-mile walk. Paul, before we leave, have you memorized the map?"

"Got it."

Paul's photographic memory was definitely going to give us an edge in The Game, I thought. If I don't cancel it with my clumsiness.

Going down was far more difficult than climbing up. We couldn't look up and plan our next move, but had to count on feeling with our feet, hoping that the toehold we picked was the right one. The sun was low in the west before Paul, who led the way this time, reached the bottom.

My right hand was throbbing. Hanging on was incredibly painful, and yet my fingertips, because of the damage to the nerve endings, were no longer sensitive to the delicate choice of whether a ledge was firm or flaking, whether or not it would be deep enough to support my hanging weight. Even in the cool shadow through which we climbed, I could feel the sweat running down my face and breasts.

I'd almost reached the bottom when my fingers finally let me down and I swung outward. I had time to scream a warning, so that those below me could get out of the way, and to think: I'm going to land on my back on the rocks and my spine will be broken. What a stupid waste!

There was no pain. Only a whirling sensation and blackness.

SiMONTeeN

Simon & Schuster's **Simon Teen**
e-newsletter delivers current updates on
the hottest titles, exciting sweepstakes, and
exclusive content from your favorite authors.

Visit **TEEN.SimonandSchuster.com** to
sign up, post your thoughts, and find out what
every avid reader is talking about!

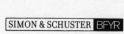

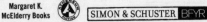

Pulse It

Did you love this book?

Want to get access to the hottest books for free?

Log on to simonandschuster.com/pulseit
to find out how to join,
get access to cool sweepstakes,
and hear about your favorite authors!

Become part of Pulse IT and tell us what you think!